DAMAGED PRINCESS

LAYLAH ROBERTS

Laylah Roberts.

Damaged Princess.

Laylah.roberts@gmail.com

laylahroberts.com

Cover Design by: Allycat's Creations.

Photographer: Wander Aguiar.

Model: Dina.

Editing: Eve Arroyo.

Created with Vellum

LET'S KEEP IN TOUCH!

Don't miss a new release, sign up to my newsletter for sneak peeks, deleted scenes and giveaways: https://landing.mailerlite.com/webforms/landing/p7l6g0

You can also join my Facebook readers group here: https://www.facebook.com/groups/386830425069911/

BOOKS BY LAYLAH ROBERTS

Doms of Decadence

Just for You, Sir

Forever Yours, Sir

For the Love of Sir

Sinfully Yours, Sir

Make me, Sir

A Taste of Sir

To Save Sir

Sir's Redemption

Reveal Me, Sir

Montana Daddies

Daddy Bear

Daddy's Little Darling

Daddy's Naughty Darling Novella

Daddy's Sweet Girl

Daddy's Lost Love

A Montana Daddies Christmas

Daring Daddy

Warrior Daddy

Daddy's Angel

Heal Me, Daddy

Daddy in Cowboy Boots

A Little Christmas Cheer

Sheriff Daddy

Her Daddies' Saving Grace

MC Daddies

Motorcycle Daddy

Hero Daddy

Protector Daddy

Untamed Daddy

Her Daddy's Jewel

Fierce Daddy

Harem of Daddies

Ruled by her Daddies

Claimed by her Daddies

Stolen by her Daddies (coming 2022)

Haven, Texas Series

Lila's Loves

Laken's Surrender

Saving Savannah

Molly's Man

Saxon's Soul

Mastered by Malone

How West was Won

Cole's Mistake

Jardin's Gamble

Romanced by the Malones

Twice the Malone

Men of Orion

Worlds Apart

Cavan Gang

Rectify

Redemption

Redemption Valley

Audra's Awakening

Old-Fashioned Series

An Old-Fashioned Man

Two Old-Fashioned Men

Her Old-Fashioned Husband

Her Old-Fashioned Boss

His Old-Fashioned Love

An Old-Fashioned Christmas

Bad Boys of Wildeside

Wilde

Sinclair

Luke

TRIGGER WARNING

Our heroine has had trauma in her past. She suffers with issues around self-harm and anxiety.

Please read with care.

1

Liam Carmichael was sex on two legs.

And kind of a jerk.

But it didn't stop Lottie from admiring how gorgeous he was. White-blond hair. High cheekbones. Firm jaw. And though he wasn't looking her way, she knew his eyes were icy blue.

Face of an angel — soul of the devil.

Dressed in a suit that fitted him to perfection, as usual. She doubted he even owned casual wear; he probably slept in his suits. They had to be made especially for his tank-like body. He turned from talking to Regent to look at the man next to him. His husband Nicolas.

Not a jerk.

Nico was just as gorgeous, but in a different way. He had that whole bad-boy look down pat. His hair was longer, messy in a way that didn't look contrived. Slimmer and shorter than Liam, but still muscular. Tanned skin. Tattoos down his arms, up his neck. He wore dark jeans and a tight, faded T-shirt that showed off his thick biceps.

Regent walked off down the hallway, leaving the two men

alone in the foyer. She was sitting on the steps, dressed in a long nightgown and robe.

She couldn't sleep, so she'd come down to see if Regent was still awake. He didn't sleep much either. Often, she'd curl up on the sofa in his office and read a book while he worked. Sometimes she'd have to put on noise-canceling headphones when he was making sensitive calls.

She assumed sensitive meant he was talking about things that were less than legal, and she wasn't privy to that information. She wasn't privy to much when it came to any of her brothers' lives.

Had to protect the princess.

She stifled a sigh. That wasn't fair. It wasn't like she did anything to disprove their belief that they had to protect her. In fact, with the way she acted, it was no wonder they were all overprotective.

The princess who couldn't leave her tower because she was too fucking scared.

She was so sick of it.

All you are is a burden.

Shut up. Shut. Up.

She clenched her hands into fists, resisting the urge to bang them against her thighs.

Today had been a particularly bad day. She didn't know why. Some days were just worse than others. Some days, the anxiety had a firmer grip on her, digging its claws in deep and whispering things to her she knew weren't true.

Didn't mean she didn't sometimes believe them.

It was a school holiday, and Thea had dropped her brothers off earlier this morning while she went to work. Thea worked for Lottie's brother Jardin whom she was also in a relationship with. Along with Jardin's best friend, Carrick.

Lottie wondered what it would be like to be with two men. Her cousins, Beau and Maddox, shared their woman too. Poor Scarlett.

Lottie figured one Malone man was enough. And they were Texan Malones, which made them almost completely wild.

She missed her cousins. They were fun and insane. Free.

While she was a prisoner of her own mind. Her anxiety.

Stop it.

Enough with the negative thoughts. If she kept going, she'd do something she'd regret. Thea's little brothers, Keir, who'd just turned ten and Ace, who was seven, had distracted her for most of the day. They'd worn her out too. Which is what she'd been hoping for.

She wished she could sleep without nightmares plaguing her. Tonight's nightmare had been a weird one. Liam had been there, telling her that she was safe. That nothing would happen to her because he would protect her.

She didn't know why she sometimes dreamed that Liam had been there.

So here she was, sitting on the stairs, waiting for her oldest brother's visitors to leave so she could creep down into his office and have him keep the nightmares at bay for a while.

But instead of leaving, Liam and Nico hung around in the foyer. Obviously waiting on Regent for something. She wished he'd hurry up.

Then Liam turned and looked straight up at her. Those icy blue eyes pierced her. Froze her on the spot.

Oh shit.

He knew she was there? Had he known from when she first sat down, or had he just seen her?

He arched an eyebrow as he ran his gaze over her. "Shouldn't you be in bed, little girl?"

Rude.

She was twenty-seven, not a little girl, she didn't have a bedtime.

Nico turned to look up at her. His smile grew wide. "Lottie-bo-bottie."

She rolled her eyes at his foolishness, but a smile twitched at the corners of her mouth. Nico always made her feel better.

"Lottie-bo-bottie? Really?" Liam drawled.

She didn't get what Nico saw in him. Well, all right, she kind of did. He was insanely *handsome.*

But were his good looks worth putting up with his giant ego and dickish personality?

Maybe he had other redeeming qualities. What they were, she had no idea. Regent had known Liam for years, but they seemed to grow closer after her kidnapping.

"You just called her a little girl and told her it was past her bedtime," Nico pointed out.

"Well, she's sitting up there, spying on us like a naughty child who doesn't want to go to bed."

Jerk.

Nico turned to look at Liam. She couldn't see the look on his face, but Liam sighed. Nico smiled up at her again.

"What are you doing up there, pretty girl? Liam could have worded it better, but he's right, it's late. You should be getting your sleep. Of course, some of us need more beauty sleep than others. Some of us get cranky when they don't get enough sleep."

He blatantly pointed at Liam as he said that. Liam just shook his head. As far as she could tell, he didn't need any beauty sleep. If he grew any more gorgeous, she might not survive.

"Nothing to say?" Nico asked.

"She won't talk in front of me. She never talks when I'm around."

Wait. That wasn't true. Was it? Did she never speak when Liam was near? That was . . . ridiculous. Of course, she did.

"I talk when you're around," she said.

Liam tilted his head. "You know, I'm mistaken."

Damn right, he was mistaken. Although she was shocked he'd admitted it. He didn't seem the type of person to admit when he was wrong. "You've said, maybe, a dozen words to me in the three years we've known each other."

That couldn't be right.

She'd first met them when she was dating Liam's brother, Michael. That relationship only lasted three months before he dumped her and basically disappeared.

Ass.

But Liam was friends with Regent so she'd seen him and Nico quite often over the last few years. Liam owned a few gyms in New Orleans.

They must have spoken, right?

"You're exaggerating."

"Am I?"

Nico was silent, watching them. She wished he'd say something. Rescue her from the big, bad beast.

Perhaps you should learn to rescue yourself.

If only she knew how. She knew she was no match for Liam. Not physically or mentally. Definitely not emotionally. Unless he was a basket case as well.

She took a deep breath in, letting it out slowly in an effort to calm herself.

For some reason, Liam and Nico stirred all this emotion in her. Not just admiration for their good looks. She could get past that. Yeah, they were lovely to look at. But so was a beautiful vase or a bunch of flowers. You could admire them, then move on.

There was something about the two of them that messed her up. It wasn't like she wanted them. She never intended to date again.

Besides Liam being a jerk, there was also the fact that they were gay.

Maybe that's why she stared at them so much when they were around.

They were safe.

"You can't, can you?" he said smugly.

Oh, how she'd like to wipe that look off his face.

But then her brother reappeared. "Sorry about that. Urgent call. I know you were meant to be flying back to New York tonight, but are you able to stay a few more days?"

Liam and Nico shared a look.

"I can call the hotel we stayed at last night and see if they have some availability," Liam said.

Regent frowned and nodded. "Don't worry about the hotel. Stay here."

Don't say yes. Don't say yes.

Liam looked straight up at her. "Sure, we'd love to stay."

Regent moved his gaze up, likely wanting to see what Liam was looking at. His eyes widened as he saw her sitting there. Then his gaze narrowed. "Lottie? You okay, darling? What's wrong?"

She cleared her throat. "Nothing's wrong. Just waiting for you, and I didn't want to interrupt."

"You couldn't sleep?"

It wasn't something she wanted to talk about in front of Liam and Nico. Regent seemed to understand this quickly and he turned to the guys. "Take any of the guest rooms on the third floor. I'll see you in the morning. Come here, Lottie."

Lottie rose and moved slowly down the stairs. Last thing she needed was to trip and make an idiot of herself. When she reached the bottom of the stairs, she realized that she was going to have to walk past the two of them to get to her brother.

She only felt safe when one of her other brothers was around. But it was especially true with Regent. They had a different bond than she had with the others. Regent had always been there for her.

Steady. A rock.

Still, she had to take a moment to steel her nerves before moving past them toward Regent.

Liam frowned. "You should go to bed, Lottie."

She paused and shot him a look. He stared down at her, his face stern.

Lottie turned to her brother, waiting for his reply. Regent gave her a thoughtful look then turned to Liam, his voice decidedly cooler as he spoke. "Lottie sometimes has trouble sleeping. We'll say goodnight now."

Regent held out an arm to her and she slipped her hand into the crook of his elbow. He was often old-fashioned in his manners. But she took refuge in them. In an uncertain, scary world, Regent could be relied upon to always be courteous and protective. Calm and steady.

She let the blanket of his protection fall around her shoulders and it steadied her.

As he walked her into his office, though, she could feel two sets of eyes burning into her back.

She just knew that things were going to change.

And maybe not for the better.

2

"It makes me fucking furious."

Liam raised his eyebrows at his husband's words as he followed him into the third-floor guest bedroom. Like all the rooms in this mansion, it was huge and richly appointed. He set down the luggage they'd retrieved from their rental car. They'd only planned on staying last night in New Orleans but thankfully, they always packed extra clothing.

Nico was a coiled spring of energy as he paced back and forth, stripping as he moved. Liam leaned against the wall, watching him.

"Did you see her? Aren't they taking care of her? She looks worse than the last time we saw her!" Nico raged. By now, he was naked and still pacing.

Fuck. He was beautiful.

Liam knew he didn't deserve Nico. But damned if he would ever let him go.

Nico was his..

"She's pale. Too thin. Obviously not sleeping. She needs help.

And they're not giving it to her. I know what you're going to say, Liam!" Nico held up his hand to him.

Liam very much doubted that.

"That she's not for us. That we can't have a third. And especially not someone as delicate as Lottie. But I can't keep walking away from her. I can't do it, Liam. We can take care of her. She needs us."

Liam frowned. He wasn't sure he knew how to be what she needed. Nico, yes. He'd coddle and look after her. Coax her into eating and sleeping.

Liam didn't have it in him to coax and coddle. He was more of a bark and order sort of guy. But he knew he could keep her safe.

"And don't feed me any bullshit about not being interested in her, I know you are. She should be ours, Liam!"

"I agree," he said quietly.

"I know you don't agree," Nico stated, obviously not listening to him. "I know you think that you're too rough for her. Too cold. Too dark. But that's just stupid!"

"Stupid, huh?"

"Yes, stupid! You're a good man, Liam. Sure, you've done some questionable things in the past, but she's hardly going to shy away at that. Not with who her brothers are. She's perfect for us. And before you argue that she's not—"

"I'm not arguing that at all."

"You saw the way she looked at both of us. She was eating us up with her eyes. Yeah, she's got issues, but that just means we'll have to go slow and gently. I want her, Liam."

Nico faced him, arms over his chest. He was trying to hide his nerves, but Liam could see it in the tense way he held himself.

"Well? I know you want her too. I've seen the way you watch her."

He decided to tease Nico a little. It was his punishment for not listening. "Maybe I just think she's fuckable."

Nico narrowed his gaze. "That's not it. Beautiful women throw themselves at you and you don't even notice them. You want her. I know you do."

"I do."

"And I think we should . . . wait, what? You do?"

"I do."

"But you think we should still keep our distance because she's so fragile?" Nico asked, looking confused.

"No. I don't think we should do that anymore."

Nico's mouth opened and shut. "You always said that she wasn't for us."

Liam frowned. "I didn't think she was. But you're right. Every time I'm around her, all I see is her. I figured my attraction to her would wane over time, but it's only gotten stronger. I didn't want the complication of her in my life, yet I think about her constantly. I'd hoped she would get better with time. But she's not."

"So, we're going to step in?" Nico asked, staring at him in amazement. He started moving toward him.

"Yes."

"Fuck, I love you." Nico dropped to his knees in front of him, and opened up his pants, tugging them down.

He took Liam's dick in his mouth.

Fuck. So good.

"If I'd known that would get me a blow job, I'd have agreed earlier."

Nico drew back. "Shut up. You know you can get a blow job anytime you want."

His husband loved giving head. Liam ran his fingers through Nico's hair, his mind drifting to Lottie.

Somehow, she'd dug her way in under his shields. Reaching him in places only Nico had ever managed to get to. He hadn't wanted it. Had fought it. Had known that nothing about her would be easy.

But then, nothing worth having was easy.

She was meant to be their third. He could feel it.

If only he wasn't fucking terrified of breaking her.

Nico took his dick deep. He'd thought that her brothers would take care of her. But every time he saw her, she looked worse.

Exhausted. Pale. Too thin.

"Shall we take her tonight?"

Nico slid his cock out of his mouth with a frown. Someone else might think he was a jerk for not paying attention to the blow job he was getting. But Nico wouldn't take offense. He loved sucking Liam off when he was busy doing something else.

"What? Fuck, no. We can't just take her."

"Why not?"

"She's not ready. We'd terrify her. Then her brothers would cut our dicks off. And I'm rather fond of your dick."

Nico cupped Liam's balls, playing with them lightly. But Liam could tell he was thinking more about the puzzle that was Charlotte Malone than his husband's balls.

She would be theirs.

The center of their fucking universe.

"They're letting her fade away."

Nico raised his eyebrows at his words. "Fanciful talk for you."

Because Liam was a practical guy. He saw a problem, he fixed it. If he couldn't fix it, then he made it disappear.

Simple.

Nothing about Lottie Malone was simple.

Nico licked around the head of his dick. Even in a serious conversation, Nico couldn't keep his mouth off Liam's cock.

Liam hoped he never changed.

Fuck, Nico knew how to give head.

Of course, he got plenty of practice. Nico drew away and walked over to where his jeans were, pulling a small packet of lube out of his pocket. Liam rolled his eyes. Nico bought the damn things in bulk, carrying them around. Just as well their housekeeper was in the lifestyle, or she might not be so understanding about clearing his pockets of lube packets before doing the laundry.

Not that you had to be a Dom or sub to use lube.

But there was also the playroom in the apartment. And they often left their toys around the place. They used to go to a club, but that had lost appeal and a few years ago, he'd put the playroom in.

Before Nico, he'd only played with subs that were strangers. Or near enough. He hadn't even known how to care about someone else.

He'd nearly lost Nico because he'd had no clue about how to cope with his feelings toward the other man. Luckily, Nico was patient. And caring.

And stubborn as fuck.

All necessary attributes to have when dealing with him. Nico knelt before him again and squirted some lube on his fingers.

"I still think I should've killed Michael. He touched her." Bastard. How had his brother found her first?

Nico scowled. "Yeah. You should do it."

"What?" Liam stared down at him in shock. This was a first.

"Put concrete shoes on the bastard. And chop off his hands. And his tongue. Anywhere he touched her. Actually, maybe do that but let him live. That will be more punishing, right?"

"Fuck. I didn't think I could get any harder."

"You're a sicko, you know that, right?" Nico grinned up at him.

"You love this sicko."

"Yeah, I fucking do. Which is why I'm gonna have to be the voice of reason. We can't kidnap Lottie. And we can't kill Michael. We don't even know where he is, anyway." As he spoke, Nico reached between Liam's legs and slid a finger between his ass cheeks.

Liam let out a low breath, pleasure flooding him as Nico drove his finger deep.

"Fuck," he groaned.

"Yeah, that feels good, doesn't it?" With his other hand, Nico drew his dick up so he could lick Liam's balls.

Fuck. Fuck.

"I'm close."

Nico murmured happily as he took Liam's balls into his mouth.

Shit. Christ. Liam ran his fingers through Nico's hair, tugging at it. Nico added another finger to his ass.

Fuck. Yes.

"Take my dick back into your mouth," he commanded.

"No please? Your manners are deplorable."

"Nico," he growled. "Do you need me to tie you up and punish your ass?"

The grin Nico gave him told him he wasn't scared. Christ.

What did I ever do to deserve him?

He had no fucking clue.

Nico drew his dick down and licked at the head. He was such a fucking tease. He just couldn't help pushing, even when he knew that Liam was at the edge of his control. That he needed some relief. He drew Liam's cock back into his mouth, down his throat. Those fingers drove in and out of his ass, then they found his prostate, massaging it.

Liam groaned as he released into Nico's mouth. The other man hummed as he swallowed him down. The pleasure in Nico's face floored him.

Fuck, he loved this man.

"Come here," he murmured as Nico drew back, licking at his cock.

His husband stood, and Liam drew him in for a kiss, not caring that he'd just given him a blow job.

He was toned and colorful, and so fucking gorgeous that it took Liam's breath away.

"Fucking love you, Nico."

He didn't say it often. Likely, not often enough given the way that Nico's eyes widened then filled with pleasure. But he hoped he showed it every day.

He didn't deserve this man. His warmth. His kindness. His undying loyalty. There was no one else he trusted like he trusted Nico.

Wrapping one hand around the back of Nico's neck, he drew him close to kiss him again as he used his other hand to jack him off. Nico grunted, then Liam felt him come all over his hand and he pulled back. They were both breathing heavily. Liam kissed his forehead. He didn't do tender well. But sometimes, he managed it.

Nico leaned his forehead against his shoulder and Liam ran his other hand up and down his husband's back.

"Come on. Shower."

Nico nodded.

"Better pick up that empty packet of lube. We don't know that the Malone housekeeper is as kinky as ours."

"Mitzy would think something was wrong with our relationship if she didn't find an empty packet of lube somewhere at least once a day," Nico teased.

Liam turned him toward the bathroom, slapping his ass playfully. Nico glared back at him. "Ass."

Twenty minutes later, they were both clean and in bed. Liam was exhausted but his mind was still going over everything. They both lay on their backs, staring up at the ceiling.

Nico rolled over, tucking his arm under his head. "We have to make a move."

"Yep."

"We can't just take her. Her mental health . . ."

"She's struggling." He'd seen it every time he was near her.

Sometimes she didn't even know he was watching. Which was surprising, considering how aware of her surroundings she was. But Liam knew how to blend into the background when he needed to. And there were times she was just so tired that it seemed to override all of her other senses.

He ran his hand over his face. Fuck.

"We'll help her."

"It's not that easy, Liam. You can't just wave a magic wand and make it better. It doesn't work that way and you know it."

He wished it fucking did. He wished he could throw money at the problem and make it go away. He'd kill whomever he had to in order to wipe that haunted look off her face. To ease the pain and fear.

To make it so she could leave the goddamn house without panicking. He knew she barely left the property.

"She's not sleeping," he stated. "Did you see the dark circles under her eyes? And she's lost weight. It's like she's become a prisoner of her own fears and insecurities. She's a shadow of her former self."

Had he waited too long? He'd thought she needed time. Had he been wrong? Time didn't seem to be helping.

"Remember the first time we met her?" Nico asked. "At that god-awful dinner the step-monster held. Michael had been dating her a couple of months. I thought she was the most gorgeous thing I'd ever seen."

Liam nodded. He hadn't wanted to go to that dinner. He'd never met Lottie before, but Regent had been an acquaintance, so he thought they had better go to the dinner and check that his brother was treating her right.

It had been the usual disaster. Anything that involved the step-monster usually was. He'd come up with that nickname when he was ten and his father had married her, and it had stuck.

Sometimes, he wondered if he'd have ended up this way, cold

and with emotional attachment issues if his mother hadn't died. He could still remember her laugh, the way she'd sing all the time. Her hugs.

Yeah, maybe he wouldn't be such an asshole. But he couldn't blame it entirely on the step-monster. His father could have stepped in to protect him. Spineless bastard.

He could still remember the first time he saw Lottie. She had a timeless beauty. Classic. Elegant. But that wasn't what drew him in. He'd met plenty of beautiful women. But there was something about Lottie.

She'd been sweet and charming. Sneaky and witty. Far too delicate for his peace of mind, but back then, her personality had made her seem so much stronger. The center of the world with everything revolving around her, just hoping that she might bestow a smile on them.

She'd been raised to believe she was special, precious. Which is exactly what she was.

A jewel.

A princess.

"If I'm not allowed to take her, then we need another plan. We'll show her that she needs us."

"Yeah? You think we can do that?"

"Of course, we can. We'll have to move slowly, though." Which wasn't going to be easy when they lived in New York and Lottie never left this house.

"I knew you'd have a plan. This is why we work well together. You're the planner, the strategist, and I'm the fun one who keeps you from turning into a stodgy old potato."

"Stodgy old potato?" he repeated. "Is that a dig at my Irish heritage?"

"Yes. Wasn't it obvious? I was trying to be obvious. FYI, it was also a dig at your age, old man."

Liam shot out his hand and wrapped it around Nico's throat.

Immediately, the other man relaxed. Pleasure shot through his face and Liam smiled. They were fucking made for each other. Liam could be rough, and Nico enjoyed that side of him. It wasn't a part of him that he could let loose around Lottie, though. He was well aware she couldn't handle that. But she didn't have to.

"Old man? I can run rings around you. You gonna be a smartass to me now?"

"I'm a smartass to everyone," Nico countered.

He wasn't wrong. But right here, right now, he was in charge.

Sometimes Nico was the only thing that kept him sane. That stopped him from falling completely into the darkness. He knew he didn't deserve him. Didn't deserve love. The things he'd done in his life had turned his soul permanently black. But maybe there was some redemption in his love for this man.

And for the precious girl they had yet to claim.

He'd told himself to forget her. She needed someone far better than him.

He'd used all his excuses. She was too broken. She needed time.

But that wasn't about Lottie. It was him. His needs. His fears.

And look at her. She was slowly fading away. Suddenly, his excuses were bullshit. What he needed to do was man the fuck up. To find the gentle side of himself. To make himself into the man she deserved.

Somehow.

He'd do it, because the alternative was unthinkable. They had to have her. The missing link. The piece that would complete them.

"What are you thinking?" Nico asked.

"About all the things I could do to your body," he purred, tightening his hold on the other man's throat just a touch.

"Yeah?" Pleasure lit Nico's warm, whiskey-colored eyes.

"Yeah." He leaned in so his lips were just an inch from his. The man who held his heart. "But I came up with a new way to punish you."

Caution entered Nico's gaze. "What?"

Liam moved his hand from Nico's throat, down his stomach, to his dick. Just as he thought, he was hard.

"Someone likes a hand around their neck," he muttered. He already knew that, of course. But he also knew that talking about it would drive Nico's arousal higher.

The other man moaned as Liam squeezed his cock. "Fuck, you've got a gorgeous dick. Thick. Smooth and hard." He ran his hand up and down the shaft. "I bet you'd like to come, wouldn't you?"

"Yes," Nico gritted out, reaching for him.

"No," Liam told him firmly. "No touching."

Nico groaned. "Fuck."

"Hands up and keep them there."

Nico's breath came in hard pants as Liam moved his hand faster. He threw the covers off, so he could see the other man's fucking magnificent cock. Liam loved Nico's body. Muscular but not too much. Nico was grace. Speed. And sexy as fuck.

Liam let go of his cock.

"No! What the fuck are you doing?" Nico snapped.

Liam bit Nico's nipple and the other man groaned. "You're being punished, remember? For that mouth."

"Liam, no, you can't."

Liam didn't give a shit whether Nico called him Sir or Master or by his name, they both knew who was in charge.

"It was a joke," Nico claimed.

"Can't have been that funny since I didn't laugh."

"But you have no sense of humor," Nico pointed out.

"Roll over, get onto your knees."

Fire lit up Nico's face again as he rolled and slid up onto his knees, wriggling his ass in the air. Liam slapped it. Fuck. That felt good.

"Yeah, baby," Nico crooned.

Liam shook his head at the ridiculous endearment. Nico knew Liam hated when he called him by cutesy names. Getting off the bed, he grabbed Nico's jeans off the floor, knowing he had to have more lube stashed in there. Finding another packet, he tore it, coating his dick in it.

"Save the cute names for Lottie," Liam told him as he knelt behind the other man, then spread his cheeks. He dabbed the last of the lube on Nico's hole.

Slowly, he pushed his dick into the other man's ass.

"Fuck, Liam. Yes. God."

Liam reached around once he was fully seated and squeezed Nico's dick. "Remember, you're not coming."

"I might not be able to stop myself."

"You come and I'll make you regret it."

"Baby, now you're really turning me on," Nico crooned.

Jesus. How did he ever end up with this smartass? He challenged him, annoyed him, fucked with him.

Loved him.

He was fucking lucky that Nico loved him. Nobody else did. Not that he gave a fuck. There were two things he wanted. The man under him, pushing his ass back to take more of his dick.

And Lottie.

Christ. Nico clenched down on his dick, nearly sending him spinning over the edge. But he wasn't coming that quickly. Drawing back, he drove forward.

"I don't know what to call her," Nico said. "Baby girl? Sweetie? Angel? So many fucking possibilities. Fuck, Liam!"

Damn. He might have just had a blow job, but already his balls were tight and the need to come was riding him hard.

"You feel so fucking good." Liam thrust deep, and that was it. He couldn't hold on any longer. A low groan left him as he came.

Panting, he leaned over Nico, trying to catch his breath and slow his heartbeat. Then he slid out of the other man and lay down on his back beside him, an arm over his eyes.

"You're trying to kill me."

"Me kill you?" Nico said. "You're the one who won't let me come. You should feel how hard I am. I'm going to strain something."

"It's to teach you a lesson."

"Is the lesson that my sweetie's mean? Because if so, lesson learned."

Jesus. Ridiculous asshole.

"And now I need another shower," Nico complained.

"You'll live," Liam told him. He removed his arm and turned to look at his husband. "I know what I'm going to call her."

"You're going to give her some cute nickname? You?" Nico gave him a shocked look.

"I am." He smiled as satisfaction filled him. "I'm going to call her mine."

Nico grinned. "Ours."

Lottie Malone was going to be theirs.

No matter what.

3

W*here is she?*

Nico tapped his fingers against the table. He'd been sitting at the dining table for close to an hour now. Liam had left earlier with Regent. They'd agreed to split and conquer.

It was better that Nico approached her first, anyway. Most people found Liam terrifying, and Liam never cared to dispel their fear. But he was going to have to with Lottie. Because scaring her wasn't part of the plan.

So, Nico would pave the way.

Liam wasn't all bad like he thought he was. Could he love Nico like he did if he was? Doubtful.

Yeah, he hadn't always lived on the right side of the law. He'd done things that most people would find unforgivable.

But Nico wasn't one of those people.

He wondered if she was ever going to come down for breakfast. How was he supposed to commence his campaign to win her over if she wasn't even going to appear?

Darn girl needed to eat. Liam was right about her losing weight. It worried Nico. Most things about their girl did, though.

He worried that he wasn't gentle enough to ease Liam's rougher edges. That together they'd be overwhelming. Frightening.

Don't go borrowing trouble. This is what you want. She's what you want.

He'd waited a long time to make his move on her. It had been an ache in his heart, not having her with him. As though he was missing a piece of himself. Lottie would complete them.

Nico didn't know what she'd seen in that worm Michael. That had been a moment of bad taste. He guessed everyone was allowed to fuck up at least once.

Nico had always wanted her. Liam had been more reticent. Nico got it. Change was hard for Liam. He'd known it would take him time to convince him that adding a third wouldn't destroy their relationship. But it had taken him even longer than he could have foreseen.

Because she'd been kidnapped. Terrorized.

After that, even Nico had been concerned about what to do. He'd tried to push her from his mind.

It hadn't happened.

His phone buzzed. Liam.

Great. He should have known he wouldn't keep his nose out of things. For someone who had written off any idea of a relationship with Lottie, he suddenly wanted to move at warp speed.

"Hello, sweetie-pie," he answered with a grin, making his voice sound light and high-pitched. "Do you miss me? Were you thinking about what we did last night in bed? About my mouth around your cock?"

There, take that, you asshole.

Okay, so he might still be smarting from not being allowed to come last night.

"You're in fucking trouble now," Liam growled in response, making him shiver at the deliciously dark tone. "Thought you'd curb that tongue in the hopes that you'd get to come tonight."

Fuck. Had he pushed it too far?

"That's okay, I took care of that problem once you left," he lied.

"I know you're lying, Nico."

"How do you know that?" he queried.

"I can always tell. Also, if you had jacked off you know damn well I'd put you in a cock cage."

Hmm. But maybe he wanted that.

Actually, no, he didn't.

What he wouldn't mind, though, was feeling some soft, warm lips around his dick. Watching as Lottie took him deep.

Fuck yeah. He wouldn't mind that at all.

Damn it, though. Now he was sporting a problem that he couldn't take care of.

Liam wouldn't really know if he solved the issue, would he? Nico enjoyed pushing the boundaries. But that was generally to get Liam to bite back.

Nico liked Liam's bite.

Reaching down, he adjusted himself. He was alone in the dining room, the food on the sideboard likely going cold as he waited for Lottie to make an appearance. With a sigh, he got up and grabbed a plate. He was a growing boy who had to eat.

"So?" Liam snapped.

"So, what?"

"How's it going?"

"Since you told me I can't go jack off in the bathroom, not so good."

A gasp sounded behind him and for a moment he thought it was his girl. But when he spun around, one of the maids was standing there. She'd probably come to clean up the breakfast stuff and heard him talking about jacking off.

Oh, well, she'd get over it.

"I'll just be a moment."

She was still gaping at him. Strange little thing, wasn't she? Then she turned and walked out. He shook his head.

"What's going on?" Liam asked sharply.

"Just corrupting the maid. Nothing new."

Liam sighed. "Don't go causing Regent's staff to quit. You know how pissy he'll get, and we need to stay there to have access to Lottie."

"I know the plan. It's not my fault she took offense to listening to me talk about a natural bodily function. Maybe if she did it more often she wouldn't be so shocked."

"Nicolas," Liam said in a warning tone that made Nico smile in pleasure.

Maybe he was crazy. He didn't give a shit. He was how he was.

"Liam," he said back.

"You'd try the patience of a fucking saint."

"Hey, boyo, don't know what pill ye took, but you're no feckin' saint."

"That was a terrible Irish accent, and I don't even have an accent."

Liam had Irish blood on his mother's side, but he was born and bred in New York city.

"If you could get your mind off your dick and stop terrorizing the maids, I'd appreciate getting back on topic. Where's Lottie?" Liam asked.

"Not here."

"I gathered that much. At least I fucking hope you weren't talking about jacking off in front of her."

"Why wouldn't I? If she's going to be ours, that's something she should get used to."

"What? You speaking about inappropriate topics at the breakfast table?"

"See now, that's just the way you were raised. This is the step-monster's fault. She taught you that only certain topics were acceptable while eating. But the opposite is true, you should be free to talk about anything you like."

"So, you often talk about cranking one out in front of your parents and siblings?"

"Fuck, no, my mother would chop my hand off."

"That's what I thought. Where is Lottie, Nico?"

"I don't know," he said with a sigh. "God, scrambled eggs taste like crap when they're cold."

"I don't give a shit what you're eating. I care what she's eating."

"Jeez, you give a man your innocence, take his hand in marriage, and suddenly, he doesn't care about you anymore."

"You didn't give me your innocence. Hasn't she eaten breakfast?" Liam asked in a low voice, sounding concerned.

Why Liam thought himself unredeemable, Nico had no fucking idea. But he guessed it was his job to make Liam see sense. Someone who was all bad wouldn't worry over anyone else.

"Not unless she got up early and ate before I got downstairs. I've been here close to two hours. It's more like snack time now. Do you suppose they serve beignets around here?"

"It's not a restaurant," Liam reminded him. "And I doubt she was up that early, she was awake late last night."

"But does she really sleep?" Nico had his doubts because of how pale and exhausted she looked.

"Go find her."

"I was planning on it," he replied calmly. "But then you called me."

"Make her eat something."

Lord, oh Lord, help him.

"Liam I can't force her to eat."

"Of course, you can. Sit her down, put food in front of her and tell her she's not getting up until the food is all gone."

"Liam, seriously, are you listening to yourself?"

"What?" Liam replied in a surly voice.

"She's not a child. I can't sit her down and tell her she's not moving."

Liam grumbled. "If she was ours . . ."

"If she was ours, we'd be encouraging her to eat. We wouldn't be going all Captain Caveman on her ass."

"Why not?"

"Because this takes some finesse." Something Liam lacked. Nico admitted he wasn't great with it himself. But he was better than the big bruiser he'd married. "Because she needs to trust us and gift us her submission. Because maybe she has an issue with food and trampling all over what's going on with her will make it fucking worse."

"Fuck, I didn't even about think that. Do you think she does?"

"I dunno. I'm going to see what I can find out."

"My informant hasn't said anything."

"I can't believe you have a spy in the household." He looked around as he whispered that part.

"You disapprove?"

"Fuck no. Just can't believe you got someone to agree to spy on Regent Malone without threatening bodily harm."

"What makes you think I didn't?" Liam said in a low, silken voice.

Right. Christ, he needed to end this call before his balls fucking burst.

"Go find her. Make sure she's eating. And don't jack off."

"Sir, yes, Sir."

"I'd say stop being a smart ass, but I know that's impossible for you."

"Pretty sure it's in my DNA."

NICO FOUND her in the sun room. She was wearing a long metallic gold skirt that had pleats in it. A long-sleeved, oversized black shirt was tucked into the skirt.

Fuck, she was tiny.

They looked like designer pieces, expensive, but he'd expect nothing less for the beloved sister of Regent Malone.

Still, they were odd clothes to wear while painting. She had an easel in front of her and was so focused on her work that she didn't even see him approaching.

That wasn't good.

Or usual.

If anything, he would say that Lottie had always seemed overly aware of her surroundings.

This was tricky. How did he make her aware that he was here without scaring the bejeezus out of her?

He cleared his throat and deliberately bumped into one of the chairs. She still startled, her hand going to the base of her throat as she gasped and spun toward him.

"Morning, Lottie-the-hottie." She went bright red. Hmm, maybe that one was a bit far. Perhaps it was time to go from friendly teasing to speaking to her how someone who wanted to spend the rest of his life with his head between her legs might.

Hmm how would that sound?

Muffled.

That wasn't the only thing he wanted, of course. But it was something he was somewhat obsessed over. Having both of his loves at his disposal for whenever he got the urge to go down on them. Now that sounded like fucking heaven.

However, he also needed to take her into his arms. To promise her that the shadows haunting her would disappear forever because he was going to fucking destroy them.

But, he couldn't do that quite yet.

"G-good morning. Sorry, I didn't hear you come in."

She looked pale and she swayed slightly. Fuck, he'd really startled her. Or maybe she hadn't had enough sleep or food. He bit back his need to demand that she take care of herself.

Chill, man.

It wasn't very often that he felt the need to take control. But that could be because she was the only one who roused those needs in him.

"Please, don't apologize. I hope I didn't frighten you. Liam said I'm light on my feet. But that's just in comparison to him. He's got elephant feet," he whispered.

She gave him a tiny smile.

And didn't that make him feel like a fucking God.

Jesus.

"Don't tell him I said that. But really, I can hear him coming from miles away. Gives me time to hide."

Her smile faded, her face filling with worry.

"You have to hide from him? Why? Does he hurt you?"

"What, no, pretty girl, that's not what I meant. Liam would never hurt me. It was a joke."

"Oh." She didn't look convinced.

Fuck. He'd messed that up. He was supposed to be convincing her to trust them.

"You're not scared of Liam, are you?" He took another step forward, watching with sorrow as she tensed. Did they need to give her more time? He acted like he knew what the fuck he was doing, but he didn't. He didn't have a fucking clue whether he was doing the right thing. Or making it worse.

And that was terrifying.

Usually, when something scared him, he didn't think about it too much. It just became counter productive, and there was no point in worrying about shit.

But this was fucking important. He couldn't mess this up, then walk away.

"Of course not," she replied.

He could tell she was lying. Well, fuck.

He guessed it wasn't anything he shouldn't have expected.

"Liam's not a bad guy." Yeah, most people would see him that way after the things he'd done in his past. But he would never harm her or Nico.

Maybe he was considered a monster, but he could be her monster.

He was big enough, mean enough to keep her nightmares away. To keep her safe.

It was Nico's job to ensure she figured that out. Oh, and that she needed him too. They were a package deal. But of course she'd want him; he was fucking amazing.

"I didn't mean to imply that he was. Please don't take offense." Her fingers were so tight around the paintbrush he was worried she was hurting herself.

"It takes a lot to cause me offense, promise. There's no reason for you to be scared of Liam. He'd never hurt you."

"I know that." She managed a smile, and he breathed out a relieved breath. Okay, maybe she wasn't as afraid of Liam as he'd first thought. "My brothers would kill him if he touched me."

Ouch. All right, back to square one. She only felt confident that Liam wouldn't hurt her because her brothers would protect her.

"Let me tell you a story about Liam. Before I met him, I was in a toxic relationship. It was with the lead singer of this band. I really wanted to make it as a musician, and he said he'd help me. But, basically, he was grooming me to become his sexual plaything."

"Oh, Nico."

"I was young and stupid. When he dumped me . . . well, I thought my world would end. You won't believe how he broke up with me. Kicked me off the tour bus in the middle of bum-fuck nowhere."

"What did you do?"

"Walked. Had a backpack, my guitar, and thirty dollars to my name. Despite the fact that I'd worked like a slave for those assholes, they never paid me."

"Nico, that's terrible."

"There I was, plodding down the road, broken-hearted, when the skies opened up and it started pouring rain. A few vehicles drove past, but no one stopped. I gave up putting my thumb out. And then this expensive-fucking car races past me, straight through a puddle, splashing me. Then to my shock, the car pulled over. Guess who walked out?"

"Your fairy godmother?"

He laughed. "Close. I'd love to see Liam in a dress and wings."

"What did he do?"

"Ran his gaze over me then walked around to the passenger side, opened the door, and told me to fucking get inside."

"You told him no?"

"Hell no. You've seen him. Back then, he was still fighting, and was even bigger and nastier-looking than he is now. I was a good little boy and got the fuck in his car. Then I apologized for getting his car all wet. He told me to shut the fuck up."

"You must have been scared."

"Terrified. But I also appreciated his bluntness. My ex had spent the whole time we were together lying. Just to keep me with them, doing all the jobs they didn't want to pay someone to do. Liam drove me to the nearest town. I told him to drop me off at this flea-ridden motel, which was all I could afford. He just told me to shut up again, then took me to his hotel room. He let me have the first shower, gave me some dry clothes. When I got out of the shower, I asked him if he wanted to fuck me or a blow job."

She gasped.

"He just stared at me and asked me what happened. After I told him, he nodded and asked if I was any good on my guitar. I played a bit for him. He told me that it was obvious why my ex treated me like shit. Because he was jealous of how good I was. That was when I started to fall in love with him. Liam's a good guy. Gruff on the outside, marshmallow on the inside."

"Marshmallow, really?"

He grinned. "He'd chop off his own hand before hurting you, Lottie-ho-hottie."

Oh, seriously.

Did I just said that? I really have issues.

"Ho-hottie?" To his shock, her lips twitched. "I'm almost thinking I was just insulted."

Huh? Oh.

"Not that kind of ho," he said hastily. "You know, the Santa clause sort of ho, the laughter with the bowl full of jelly, not . . ."

"The prostitute kind?" she asked. Her free hand came up to cover her mouth, and he scowled at her.

"Are you laughing at me?"

"What? Me? Never. I wouldn't be so rude." But a small giggle erupted. "The Santa Claus kind of ho?"

"I've lost all cred with you, haven't I?"

"If you hadn't, you would have after using the word cred," she told him seriously. But that twinkle didn't leave her hazel eyes.

"You." He pointed at her. "You're trouble."

"I don't know what you're talking about."

"Sure you don't."

"Hey, I'm not the one who just called me a ho."

"Lord. My mama would twist my ears if she knew I spoke to you like that."

"She would?" She gave him a startled look.

"Don't worry, she'd love you. She'd fill you up on dolmas and baklava."

"Yum. You're close?"

He shrugged, not really wanting to answer that. "I'm the black sheep of the family."

"You?"

"Might have caused a bit of trouble in my misspent youth."

"That I believe."

He put his hand on his chest. "I'm wounded."

"Were you born in Greece?"

"No, I was born here in the states. My parents immigrated about five years before I was born when my brothers and sisters were young. We're huge, we're loud, and we love ouzo."

"Really?"

"Nah, can't stand it, to be honest. But you can't tell anyone. Especially my mother; she'd disown me."

She studied him. "I can't tell when you're joking or serious."

"You'll just have to get to know me better then, won't you?"

A nervous look filled her face. "How long are you staying?"

"A while," he said vaguely.

She set down her paintbrush.

"What are you painting?" he asked when she didn't say anything more.

"Oh, it's nothing. I'm not very good." Reaching down, she grabbed an old sheet, throwing it over the easel.

Curious.

"I've heard that artists can be superstitious about letting someone see their work before it's finished."

"Yes, I guess so. But then, I never let anyone see them once they're finished either." She sent him a smile that he thought was meant to be reassuring.

Instead, it just seemed fucking sad. He wondered why she didn't let anyone see them. And what she did with them once they were finished. Hell, he didn't care if she just painted shapes. He still wanted to see them.

"Well, if you ever want to show someone who knows nothing about art, then I am your man."

"You know nothing about art, huh?" She rubbed at her hand that had been holding the paintbrush as though it was hurting her.

He frowned, wanting to offer to massage it. Damn, he was getting turned-on by the idea of massaging her hand.

You sick bastard.

"Your tattoos look like works of art to me."

He smiled wide, putting his hands in his front pockets and rocking back on his heels. "That they are. But I didn't do them, so I can't lay claim to that talent."

"But you did choose them, right?"

"I did."

"So, you have some sort of an artistic eye."

"Huh, guess so. Or I'm just really good at picking out pretty things." He winked at her, delight filling him as a light blush filled her cheeks. "You must have been early to breakfast this morning since I missed you. Of course, I was rather late. One of the maids was giving me an evil look."

"Really?" she asked. "That's terrible. What maid? I'll have Regent speak to her."

Interesting that she wouldn't talk to the maid directly.

"She didn't really," he reassured her. "She actually caught me talking about something inappropriate with Liam on the phone."

"What was it?"

His eyebrows rose, surprised by her question. Then she blushed bright red and started stammering.

"Um, s-sorry, shoot, I shouldn't have, um, asked that."

"That's okay. You can ask me anything."

"I'm sure there are some things you don't want me to ask you."

"Nope. There's nothing. I'm an open book."

She stared at him for a long moment, as though trying to work out if he was being honest.

"Would you come sit with me? I'm a bit bored with Liam away."

And she looked like she was about to keel over, he wanted to get her off her feet.

"You are? Why didn't you go with him?"

"I didn't feel like going along just to hang off his arm and play the part of trophy husband."

"You have to play the part of a trophy husband?"

"No, I was joking." He grinned at her, hoping to get a smile in return.

The smile she gave him was limp at best. "Sorry, you must think I'm an idiot."

He frowned. He didn't like her talking about herself like that. "I don't think any such thing. Why would you say something like that about yourself?"

She shrugged. "Because I can't tell when you're making a joke."

"And that makes you an idiot? Hell, no. If anyone is an idiot, it's me, for not being funny enough that you can tell."

This time, her smile was small but real.

"Come on, come sit with me. Unless you want to go get some breakfast? Did you eat?"

"Um, oh, no. I guess I didn't. I woke up and came to paint. What time is it?"

"It's nearly ten thirty."

Before she could say anything more, yells came from the front of the house. He moved toward her, prepared to stand between her and whoever that was. It took him a moment to realize that the screams were one of excitement not murderous rampage.

"Are you all right?" she asked, probably wondering why he'd jumped in front of her like that.

Seems he was feeling a bit jumpy. Probably the combination of being in a strange place and having sole responsibility for Lottie. Liam would kill him if he let anything happen to her. Not that he would.

She moved around to his side. "It's just the boys. Did they give you a fright? They are loud."

"Boys? What boys?"

"My nephews," she said fondly.

A boy raced into the room and headed straight toward Lottie. Nico moved quickly to intercept him. He might be young, but he was built solidly, and he had no doubt he'd bowl Lottie to the floor if he hit her at that speed. The kid slammed against him, then staggered back. Nico grabbed hold of his shoulders to steady him.

"Whoa, buddy, not so fast."

"Hey, let go of me!" the kid yelled then kicked him in the shin.

"Holy fuck!" Fuck! The kid could kick.

"Ace! What are you doing?" Lottie cried. "No kicking! And Nico, you cannot swear in front of children."

"Shit. He kicked me."

"You grabbed me," Ace countered.

"Because you were about to fall over."

"Because you stepped in front of me. You got in my way!"

"You were going to barrel Lottie over."

Why am I arguing with a child?

This was a new low. Kids usually loved him. Not this kid. He was glaring up at him like he wouldn't mind kicking him again. Nico fought the urge to step back.

"Don't you touch me! Who the fuck are you?" the kid demanded.

And Lottie had told him off for swearing. Seemed this kid had a worse potty mouth than he did.

"Ace!" Lottie said, aghast. "Language."

The boy looked at Lottie then back at him but didn't back down.

Good for him.

"You get away from my Lottie," Ace demanded, moving in front of her. "I'm not gonna let you touch her, you asshole."

"Ace!" another woman said from the doorway. This had to be Thea, Jardin's girlfriend. "Watch your language. Where do you hear this stuff? And what are you doing?"

Another boy stood with Thea, watching everything with a calmness that surprised Nico. Then a sneer appeared on his face as he appeared to find Nico wanting.

Amusement filled him. One kid was threatening him with bodily harm, while the other one was looking down on him like he was the back end of a cow.

"He got in my way when I was trying to get to Lottie." Ace pointed at him. "Then he grabbed me."

Everyone turned to look at him. Thea eyed him warily.

He offered her a smile. "Hello, I'm Nico."

"Oh, I'm sorry, where are my manners?" Lottie said, sounding flustered. "Nico is a friend of Regent's. He's staying here with his husband, Liam. Nico, this is Thea, Ace, and Keir."

"I'm afraid I did grab your little brother, but only because he was going to fall over," Nico explained to Thea.

"You stepped in front of me," Ace exclaimed again.

"You were running full speed at Lottie. I didn't want you to knock her over," Nico told him in a low, stern voice.

He wasn't letting a kid get the best of him.

Thea placed her hands on her hips and gave her brother a stern look. "Is that so? What did I tell you about running in the house?"

"But we always run in the house. Lottie doesn't care."

"I care. There's a lot of expensive stuff in this house that I can't afford to replace."

"But Reggie got rid of all the expensive stuff," Ace told her.

Reggie? His lips twitched. Why hadn't he thought of calling the very stiff and proper Regent, Reggie?

"That's not the point. What did I tell you after you pushed Lottie over yesterday?" Thea said sternly.

Nico ran his gaze over Lottie, but she wasn't looking at him. Christ, a stiff wind would blow her over. Was she hurt anywhere?

That kid was solid. He had a good kick on him too.

"That I wasn't to race at her to hug her. That I have to be gentle 'cause she's a girl."

"Poor Lottie probably has bruises on her bottom from that fall yesterday," Thea scolded.

The boy's face went from suitably chastised to interested. "Really?"

"I'm all right," Lottie said hastily, looking embarrassed.

"Do you really have bruises on your butt, Lottie?" Ace asked.

"Um."

"Can I see them?"

"Ace," Thea groaned, putting her hands over her face. "Give me strength."

"What?" Ace asked. "I just wanted to see them. I've never seen butt bruises."

Keir sighed. "You can't ask to see a girl's butt."

The smaller boy frowned at this, clearly thinking. "So, if you ever get butt bruises, can I see them?"

"No," Keir replied.

"Why not?"

"Because you'll push me over to make sure I get butt bruises!" Keir replied.

Smart kid.

"Ace," Thea said sharply. "You won't push your brother over just to give him butt bruises. Understand?"

The smaller boy looked sad.

Lottie put her hand on Ace's shoulder. "Why don't you go into the kitchen and get a cookie with Keir? I bet that Gerald made some especially for you two."

The boy's face lit up and he smiled.

"What do you say to Lottie and Nico first?" Thea asked.

Ace sighed. "Sorry, for bumping into you even though you stepped in my way."

Thea started muttering something he could only guess was another prayer for patience.

"That's quite all right," Nico replied.

"And?" Thea prompted.

"And I'm sorry for asking to see your butt bruises, Lottie." The boy hugged her around the middle, sending her staggering back.

"Ace!" Thea said sharply. But she was too far away to help. Nico quickly jumped over to put his hand at the small of her back to steady her.

The kid turned his head and scowled at him before mouthing a word at him.

What the hell? That kid had just mouthed the word mine at him.

Kid had guts.

Nico admired that.

"Come on, Ace," Keir told him. "Before you squeeze her to death."

"Is that possible?" Ace asked as he moved over to his brother. "Can you squeeze someone to death?"

"Yeah, probably. If they're like old or something," his brother replied nonchalantly.

"Cool!" the little punk replied. "I wanna see that."

They both left the room, but he could still hear them as they walked away.

Thea shook her head. "They're gonna be the death of me. Seriously. Ace asked me to cook him up some dinner that he'd found in the garden last night."

"Okay," Lottie said, looking as confused as he felt.

"They were grubs he'd found under a log." Thea shuddered. She sent a curious look toward him, then Lottie. That was when he realized that he still had his hand on the small of her back.

And she hadn't moved away from him.

Hope surged inside him. This was definitely a sign. If she was scared of him, she wouldn't have stayed close. There had to be some part of her that maybe trusted him . . . just a little.

As though she'd just figured out the same thing, Lottie took a step away. She sent him an embarrassed smile.

"Are you sure you're okay to look after them today, Lottie?" Thea asked. "I know they're a lot, and you had them all day yesterday."

"We'll be fine," Lottie reassured her. "You know I love having them."

"And they love being here with you. They're just so full of energy at the moment. I don't want to tire you out."

Nico frowned as Lottie's shoulders curved and she kind of hunched in on herself. It was like she'd received a blow.

While he got Thea's concern, it was almost like she didn't have faith in her. As though she didn't trust Lottie to know her limits.

If her family didn't have faith in her how could she have faith in herself?

"I'm going to be around today." He gave Thea a reassuring smile. "I'll help Lottie."

"You will?" Thea appeared a bit startled.

Maybe it was the tattoos. They didn't make him look that trustworthy. Or it could be that he was a stranger.

"I have lots of experience with kids. Big family."

"Oh, do you have children?" Thea asked.

"No, but I have several nephews and nieces." Sure, he hadn't spent much time with them, but looking after children couldn't be that hard. It wasn't like they were babies.

"It will be good practice for when I have kids."

"You want to have children?" Lottie asked.

"Yep. Well, I'd need to find someone who'd want to have them with me, of course." And convince Liam that it was a good idea. He'd have to ease him into that idea.

"Oh, like a surrogate?" Lottie had a funny look on her face that he couldn't quite decipher.

"Something like that."

"All right, if you're both sure. Remember, if they're too much of a problem, then call me. Otherwise, Carrick will be by at around five to get them. Thanks so much." Thea was gone before they could even say goodbye.

"She left quick."

"She's running late for work. Jardin has a big case coming up," Lottie explained.

"Well, what shall we do with the boys first?" At first, he'd been annoyed when they'd turned up, thinking they would cut into his Lottie time. But this might just work in his favor. Give him an excuse to spend time with her.

"You really don't have to hang out with us," Lottie told him. "You must have better things to do with your time."

"I really don't."

She gave him a skeptical look.

You're losing her.

"Truth is, I would love a distraction."

"Is something wrong?"

"I'm just feeling a bit lonely. Liam won't be back for hours, and I was going to be stuck here doing nothing. You'd be doing me a favor."

"Well, all right, if you're sure."

"It's a nice day, what do you think about making up a picnic and go have lunch outside?"

. . .

Outside?

A picnic? She turned to look out the window. The boys would love to go outside to play, and it would help them burn off some of their excess energy. Truth was, she did find it exhausting looking after them. She loved them, but they were a lot of work. However, she hadn't wanted to admit that to Thea.

Lottie was getting tired of everyone treating her like she was fragile. As though she wasn't as capable as everyone else.

As though she was helpless.

Don't trust Lottie with anything. She can't handle it.

She took a deep breath in and let it out slowly as she dug her fingernails into the palms of her hand. The small bite of pain cleared the thoughts away, giving her a rush of energy.

"Lottie?" Nico asked. "Are you all right?"

"What? Yes, of course."

Act normal, Lottie.

It was just so hard around Nico. Because he flustered her. Distracted her. Anyone would be distracted by his delicious muscle and those tattoos. Today he wore a dark-blue T-shirt and yet another pair of jeans that fit him perfectly.

"We don't have to go outside if you don't want to. Is there something else you had planned?"

Planned? She never had anything planned. What was wrong with her? She was suddenly questioning if this was really what she wanted to do with the rest of her life. Live in this huge house, where she was practically a ghost, haunting the hallways.

"Lottie?" Nico was now looking really concerned. "Why don't you come sit down? I'm going to get you some water. Maybe a snack. You look pale."

"What? Oh, no, I'm fine. I just . . . I didn't have anything planned." But going outside was a big step. She couldn't remember the last time she'd left the house. She never left the grounds. Ever.

But surely, a picnic just in the garden would be okay. Where she could get inside the house quickly if she needed to.

She knew that Regent had the whole grounds under surveillance. There were guards outside. Nobody could get through the walls to her. And Nico would be with her. It was probably foolish to trust him, she didn't know him that well.

But what she did know, she liked. He was always so happy. So confident. She wished she could be more like that.

"I'll ask Gerald to pack up a picnic lunch," she told him.

His smile was filled with warmth. "Come on then, let's go have a cookie."

"You're dreaming if you think the boys left you any cookies."

4

You can do this.

Just step out into the courtyard.

"Are you all right, Lottie?" Nico asked. "We can stay inside if you like."

"I'm fine," she said hastily.

Liar.

He didn't call her a liar, but his face told her that he didn't believe her.

"What if we open up the double doors?" he asked suddenly. "We could put the blanket out on the floor and eat here while those two burn off energy racing around."

She wanted to nod, but that wasn't helping herself. That wouldn't show everyone, herself included, she was stronger than they thought.

"No. I want to have it outside. But maybe we could put it just there." She pointed to a few feet away. The grass out here was lush. Regent had a full-time gardener who took care of the grounds.

"All right," he replied. "But if you start to feel ill or panicky, I want you to tell me right away, understand?"

The words weren't stern exactly, but they were said in a firm voice. A voice that told her he expected to be obeyed. Funny, Nico had never struck her as particularly dominant.

"You don't need to worry about me." She didn't need someone else thinking she was weak and needed to be sheltered.

"Funny, that's all I seem to do," he muttered.

She frowned. She couldn't have heard him right.

He stepped through the doors and went to set up the picnic. Ace and Keir were already outside. She hoped they weren't doing anything too reckless. What she'd learned from being around them was that little boys didn't have a good sense of safety. If it was messy, dangerous, or crazy, then they were completely into it.

Lottie stared down at the steps that would lead her outside. Just three steps down. Then two more to where the blanket now lay on the ground. Nico was setting out plates and glasses from the wicker basket that Gerald had prepared for them. He'd even offered to make more cookies; the boys had demolished the first batch.

Just take a step, Lottie. You can do it.

But all her earlier bravery seemed to have fled. The idea of stepping over the threshold had her feeling nauseous. She gulped in breath after breath.

Ridiculous. You're being ridiculous.

She could do this. She'd promised the boys a picnic and they wouldn't understand why she suddenly changed her mind. She didn't want to explain to them that she was a nutcase who couldn't take a few steps out of her house because of some irrational fear that someone might hurt her.

If she really believed that she wouldn't let the boys go out there on their own. She'd insist on them staying inside.

So, the danger wasn't real. It was just all in her head. And she needed to get it out.

Stop acting like a crazy person.

"Lottie? Hey, pretty girl. What's the matter? Breathe for me. That's it. Just breathe. Good girl."

The tone, more than the words, penetrated first. She felt her hands being taken in a pair of calloused warm ones.

"Look at me. Lottie, look at me."

She raised her gaze up to his dark eyes.

"That's it. Nice slow breaths. Good girl."

One breath. Then another. As her anxiety faded another feeling took residence. Attraction. Interest.

What would it be like to wake up each morning and see those eyes, to be able to kiss those lips, to feel his arms around her?

A fantasy that will never happen. Even if she was capable of being in a relationship with someone, she couldn't forget that Nico was taken.

He wasn't interested in her like that, he was simply being kind.

"That's it. Feel better now?"

"Sorry," she muttered.

"No need to be sorry. I'll move the blanket inside."

"No." She shook her head. "I can go outside. I'm just . . . usually . . ."

"Tell me," he urged.

A laugh, barren of amusement escaped her lips. "Usually, I have someone with me. Someone that I . . ."

"That you trust," he finished. Something filled his face. Something that looked like disappointment. "And you don't trust me. How can you trust me when you don't know me? We haven't exactly talked much. Just that awkward dinner when you were dating the worm and sometimes when we've been here to see Regent."

She licked her lips, grateful he understood. Then a smile curved her lips. "The worm? That's what you call Michael?"

"Apt, don't you think?"

She placed her hand over her mouth to try to smother her giggle. "I shouldn't laugh, but . . ."

"But he's totally a worm?"

Yeah, he was a worm. He'd broken up with her the same day she'd been kidnapped. And she hadn't heard from him since.

He was worse than a worm.

"Maybe that's a bit harsh," Nico pondered. "On the worms."

A burst of laughter shot out of her, shocking her.

"Who said worm? Do you want worms, Lottie?" Ace called out, appearing out of the trees. His hands were coated in dirt and there were streaks across his face.

Oh, Lord.

"Um, no," she said. "I don't want any worms."

"Oh." His little face fell. "What about grubs? I can get you those."

How did she tell him no without disappointing him?

"Why don't we leave them in the ground where they're safe?" Nico suggested.

"That's no fun," Ace muttered. "Aren't you coming out, Lottie? Keir said that maybe we could build a tree house. You could come sit in it when it's ready."

"A tree house? Perhaps we should get someone to go and get some stuff. Or can you buy them premade? Maybe I could call and buy one. I'm sure they'd deliver it today, but I'm not sure how you get it up in the tree."

Ace and Nico stared at her.

"Did I say something wrong?"

"You don't buy a tree house," Ace told her. "You build it, and we don't need no adults to help us."

"You don't? That doesn't sound all that safe. Where are you building it?"

"I dunno. Out in some tree. Come see." Ace grabbed her hand, tugging.

"Oh, I um—" Ace was surprisingly strong, and she stumbled forward as he pulled at her.

"Whoa, easy there, Ace," Nico said, wrapping an arm around her waist.

A shiver raced through her. One of arousal and need, not fear. It was bizarre. If anyone other than her brothers touched her, she would freeze. But with Nico, all she felt was warmth. But she didn't understand why she felt that way with him.

Maybe it's because you can't have him.

Yeah, maybe that was it.

Ace frowned up at Nico. "Let Lottie go. I wanna show her."

"She doesn't want to go right now," Nico said firmly.

"Ace, what you doing?" Keir called out.

"I wanted Lottie to come see where we're building the tree house, but this guy won't let go of her."

Keir frowned and ran over. His too-knowing gaze took everything in.

"We'll show her later. Once we've got it all done. It will be better then."

Ace sighed. Loudly. But he let Lottie go. Keir drew him close and whispered something to him. Ace looked up at Lottie and nodded.

"Oh, yeah, I forgot," he said to his brother.

Embarrassment flooded her.

"Sorry, Lottie. I didn't hurt you, did I?" Ace asked, looking worried.

"Course not," she replied. "I'm tougher than I look."

Ace scowled, looking at where Nico stood. "You can let go of her now."

Lottie cleared her throat and stepped away from Nico. Ace gave a nod of satisfaction then turned to run off.

Keir studied Lottie for a moment. "You okay, Lottie? I'm sorry about Ace."

"Nothing to be sorry about," she told him. "But I think maybe you should have some help building the tree house. It doesn't sound safe."

"It'll be fine. We built one at home."

"You did?"

"Uh-huh. Better go, though. Ace'll mess it up if I leave him." He raced off before she could say anything more.

"Let's set up the picnic inside, okay?"

She nodded. That was a big fail. "I'm sorry I'm so difficult."

"Hey." Reaching out, he took grasped hold of her chin. "You're not difficult at all. Understand me?"

She gaped at him, not quite knowing what to say.

Maybe it was because he'd already seen her starting to panic and hadn't made her feel bad or awkward, but she felt more at ease now. A wave of tiredness hit her after they set the picnic up just inside the doors.

"Sit down," he said with concern. "You look pale. Here, drink this." He poured her some sparkling orange juice and handed it to her once she was sitting on the blanket.

"Thank you."

"Will you be all right if I go check on what they're up to?"

"Yes, thank you."

As he strode away, she couldn't help but stare at his ass.

What was she doing?

~

After checking on the two boys, Nico hurried back to Lottie. He didn't like how pale and breathless she'd gotten before. She was clearly exhausted. He wondered if he could get her to nap. Although how he'd do that when he couldn't even get her outside with him, he had no idea.

She said she could go out with someone she trusted. So, all he needed to do was build up her trust in him.

Easier said than done, however.

Impatience bit at him and he forced it down. He'd waited this long; a few extra weeks or months wouldn't matter. Right?

The problem was that they couldn't stay here with her until she learned to trust them. And coming back and forth might not work. It would take him longer to earn her trust.

One step at a time.

First, the picnic. Getting to know her better. Building a relationship. And trying to put Liam in a good light.

Not the easiest of tasks that was for sure.

Nico put a big smile on his face when he saw her worried expression. "They're fine."

"Are you sure?"

"Yeah, Ace wanted to build the hut up high in this huge tree, but Keir had already told him that wouldn't work. Got a sensible head on his shoulders."

"Good. So, they're doing it on the ground?"

"Wouldn't be much of a tree house on the ground," Nico pointed out, sitting down on the blanket, just inside the open double doors. "But Keir has chosen a tree with a good spot that's only a few feet up."

"Oh, good. I'm still not sure this is a good idea, though. What are they using for building materials?"

"Just what they can find. You never built a tree house as a kid?"

"Me? No."

"Your brothers?"

"No, not that I can remember, anyway. Regent was always with my father, even from an early age. Jardin was more into his studies. Victor loved sports. And Maxim, well, he was usually getting into some mischief, but I don't remember a tree house. Did you?"

"I tried. But I did a pretty poor job of it. I did have fun throwing water balloons from it at anyone who walked past, though. Our neighbors were not happy with me."

"I bet."

"I'm shocked it lasted as long as it did. It wasn't exactly high construction. I think some of it was held together with masking tape."

"That doesn't sound safe." She glanced off toward where the boys were. They couldn't see them from here, but occasionally, they could hear them call out to each other.

"They'll be fine," he reassured her.

"Sorry. I guess I worry too much."

"I get it. They're not yours. You want to return them in one-piece."

"Preferably," she joked. "It's some weird rule Thea has. They must come back with all their limbs."

"Sheesh, that's tough. I hope you get a bonus when you return them each day safe and sound."

"Hazard pay, maybe."

"Definitely hazard pay. It's good of you to look after them for her." He poured her some more of the fizzy orange juice, noting with satisfaction that she'd drunk it all. It might not be as good as actually eating something, but it was something.

"You do for family," she murmured. "Besides, it's not like I've got anything better to do."

He frowned at the self-deprecation in her voice.

"You have your painting," he pointed out.

She let out a delicate snort, a noise he'd never imagined would come from her. "That's not important. Thea is helping Jardin with his work, that has far more importance than spreading paint on a canvas."

"Hey, that's not true." Reaching out slowly, he placed his hand on hers. She jolted but didn't pull away. Satisfaction filled him. Maybe she needed touch. He wondered if anyone hugged her when she was down or upset, or if her brothers offered comfort when she was scared or unsure.

"If it's something special to you, then it has importance."

"Jardin is a lawyer. You can't compare the two things."

"People need lawyers. But people also need art. What do you think the world would be like without music? Could you imagine it? When I'm feeling down, I pick up my guitar and play, it instantly makes me feel better."

She tilted her head to the side and studied him. He kept his hand on hers. Yeah, getting her used to his touch was definitely one of his main goals.

Touch and trust.

"I can't imagine you feeling down."

"Everyone feels down at some stage, Lottie."

"I suppose that's true."

"And there are people who need art to lift them up. To make them smile. What you do has importance. Just in a different way from your brother."

"But I don't share my art."

"Perhaps you should." He rubbed his thumb over hers. Felt her shudder. But still, she didn't push him away.

Fuck. He was good at this wooing shit.

"Maybe it's crap."

"Could be," he agreed. "But then, so is half the stuff I've seen in art galleries."

Her lips twitched. "You go to art galleries?"

"Hey, are you implying I'm not cultured?"

"Of course not. My apologies."

"Accepted. At least I have better taste than the step-monster. Do you remember that ugly ass painting she has of herself in the living room?"

"Oh, man, I forgot about that." Lottie grinned. "It was awful. It made her seem like she was looking down on all of us."

"That was the point."

"Wait, you call her a step-monster?"

"You met her. You don't think it's appropriate?"

"She was, um, a little difficult."

He snorted. "Difficult? That's a very diplomatic way to put it. She's a complete bitch."

"Nico!"

"She is. She made Liam's life hell when he was a kid. Part of the reason he decided to use his mom's maiden name. He couldn't even stand sharing a last name with her."

"That's terrible."

"Yeah, she's always hated him. She dotes on her precious Michael and acts like Liam is a dirty secret."

"That's terrible. Poor Liam."

Wow. He really was good. He already had her feeling sorry for Liam. Of course, Liam would kick his ass if he found out Nico was telling her this stuff.

"What do you paint?" he asked her. He lay back on his side but kept his hand on hers. His T-shirt rode up as he moved, revealing his abs. He watched as her gaze moved down his stomach.

Oh, yeah, she was interested.

"Lottie!" The scream came from the trees, and she startled. Her hand slid out from his and he immediately missed her touch.

Damn it.

Children had terrible timing.

"What is it?" she asked, getting to her feet as Ace appeared, running. "What's wrong? Is it Keir? Has something happened? I'll go get Gerald."

"We're hungry!" he yelled. "Can we take some food out there so we can eat while we're building?"

"Oh, thank goodness." She put her hand to her chest. "Yes, I suppose. I'll pack some in the basket."

"Thanks." Then Ace frowned at him. "You wanna come eat with us, Lottie?"

"Thank you, honey. But I'm fine here."

"Sure?" Ace leaned in closer to her as she started spooning some food out onto two plates that he guessed was for the two of them. She left the rest in the containers and put them in the basket for the boys. "'Cause if this guy is bothering you, I can take care of him."

The little boy's chest puffed out.

Oh, thought he could take him, did he? Yeah, this kid had gumption. Kind of reminded him of himself when he was a kid.

"Ace, that's not very nice. Here you are." As she stretched out her arm with the basket of food, Ace tripped and grabbed hold of her arm just below her elbow to steady himself.

Lottie winced, and Nico frowned. What was that about?

But then Ace righted himself and grabbed the basket, racing off with a shouted thanks.

She shook her head. "All the food is going to be a mess by the time he gets it there."

"Boys don't care about that. What's wrong with your arm?"

"What?" She turned to him, looking startled.

"You flinched when he grabbed you. Why?"

"Oh, nothing." She turned away, picking some of the cutlery she'd laid out.

Nico frowned. He wanted to insist that she tell him. Show him. He hated that there were things about her that he didn't know. But more than that was the fact that she was hurting. Maybe Ace had just grabbed hold too hard. He was a solid kid.

Or was there something wrong with her arm?

Fuck.

He needed to find out without scaring her off. She'd already turned away and was moving around nervously when just before she'd been relaxed and smiling.

Patience.

Liam could be far more patient than Nico was, however, he wouldn't like her keeping things from them either. But they couldn't expect her to just divulge her secrets to them, particularly when she had no idea what they wanted from her.

He wanted to tell her. The words burned on his tongue, but he held them back.

Instead, he stretched. Her gaze once again traveled to his bared stomach.

Sitting, he took the plate she offered, noting that hers barely held any food.

Shit.

This was going to be more complicated than he'd first envisioned. That wouldn't stop him, though. He wasn't looking for easy.

Lottie was it for both of them. He just had to work on getting her to open up.

"Is Liam going to be gone all day?"

"I think he's coming back later this afternoon."

"Oh, right."

Was she almost disappointed by that? He couldn't quite tell.

"You don't have to be nervous around him," he told her quietly. "What I told you earlier is true, he'd never harm you."

She gave him a false smile. "I know."

"No, you think he won't hurt you because of your brothers," he countered.

Her eyes widened. She seemed surprised at his words and that he was arguing with her. Did no one ever challenge her? Argue with her? Push her?

That could be his job.

He wanted to fix her. To help, to guide. But he also knew that what she really needed was someone to support her while she found her own way.

Something Liam would struggle with. When they'd first gotten together, Liam had expected Nico to come to him with every issue he had and let him fix them. But Nico didn't need that. He just wanted someone to listen. Not to take over. His submissiveness was tied in with pleasure and play. Not everyday life.

He wondered about Lottie. He had a feeling she'd need more from them, at least in the beginning. But once she got that confidence back, well, they'd see. Because he didn't intend to go anywhere.

Lottie was biting her lip, obviously thinking about what he'd said.

"Is it just Liam you fear hurting you? Or all men?"

She paled, and he worried he'd pushed too hard.

Idiot.

He should be sticking to lighter conversation. Making her smile. Not pushing her about her fears.

"I don't think all men are going to hurt me. I know there are good men out there."

That answer was both good and bad.

"So just Liam?"

She sucked in a breath. "No, not Liam."

"You trust him not to hurt you?"

She grasped her necklace. It was a gold locket that looked old.

When she didn't say anything more, he decided to press a bit further.

"Liam has a bad reputation, but then so do Regent and Victor. That doesn't mean any of them would ever hurt a woman."

She sucked in a breath. "No, I know."

"Then why do you look so frightened when you're near him? Has he said something, done something to upset you? I mean, it is Liam. I love him, but the guy has some real social issues. He says what he thinks."

"Sometimes honesty is a good thing," she murmured.

"And sometimes it's just rude."

She gave him a tiny smile. Better than nothing, he supposed.

"I don't know why I feel nervous around him."

"What about me? Do I make you nervous?"

"A little bit," she confessed. "Sorry."

"Don't be sorry. But you're safe with me, pretty girl. With Liam and me. We'd kill anyone who tried to hurt you."

She sucked in a breath, looking shocked.

Too far, idiot.

Before he could say anything, there was a scream from the wooded area. Fuck, he'd forgotten about the kids.

Only there was something different about this scream. It sounded like the person was in pain. Afraid. Jumping up, he moved to the door then paused, looking to Lottie.

"Stay here. Don't move."

~

LOTTIE STOOD AT THE DOORWAY. She stared out at the trees. Peter, one of the guards, had rushed over there, behind Nico.

Who screamed? Ace? Keir? Had someone gotten them?

Even now, they could be hurting them. And here she was, fighting demons that didn't exist.

Move, Lottie. Be stronger than this.

She managed one step. Then another. She felt like she was trudging through mud. But she was doing it. There was no one here. No one to hurt her. She was safe. She moved toward the trees as Nico burst out with Ace in his arms. He was crying. Keir walked beside Peter, talking animatedly.

Relief slumped through her. They were okay, but was Ace crying.

"What happened?"

Nico gave her a surprised look then his gaze narrowed as he studied her sternly. "I said to stay inside."

She was taken aback by the scolding. Nico was always so gentle when he spoke to her. This was another side of him. One she hadn't realized existed.

"I'll go get the car," Peter said.

"What's going on?" she asked as Nico walked inside with Ace, setting him down on the sofa. The boy was sobbing, holding his arm.

"Ace fell from the high tree," Keir said. "I told him not to climb it. But he wasn't listening. And then he slipped and fell."

"Oh no, Ace." She knelt beside the small boy. "Where does it hurt?"

"My a-arm."

"I think it might be broken," Nico said, drawing out his phone. "He'll have to go to the emergency room."

"Gerald!" she called out, running over to open the door. "Gerald! Where are you? Gerald!"

Gerald rushed down the passage. "What is it?"

"It's Ace. Ace is hurt. He needs to go to the emergency room. We suspect he's broken his arm. Peter has gone to get the car."

"Right. Do you have your phone on you?" Gerald asked as he moved into the solarium.

She patted her thighs, only then realizing she had a skirt on. "No, I don't know where it is."

Nico turned to give her a frowning look. "You don't know where your phone is?"

"I . . . no. I can go find it." Why couldn't she think of what to do? Poor Ace. "I need to . . . to . . ." Why couldn't she think?

"Miss Lottie," Gerald said in a cool, calm voice. "We need to take Ace to the emergency room. I need you to call Thea and get her to meet us. Peter will drive. I'll get Andrew to follow us."

"I'm going too," Keir said. "I'm not leaving Ace."

"All right," Gerald replied. "I'll also call in Trent to stay with you, Miss Lottie."

"Okay. All right." Trent and Andrew were both guards employed by Regent.

"I'll be here with her," Nico said.

"No!" Ace cried. "I want Lottie to take me."

Pain slashed through her.

"Ace, I'm going," Keir said. He sent Lottie a worried look. Poor Keir. He knew she was a wimp. A failure.

"Ace, I . . ."

"Please, Lottie. Please."

She couldn't even go into the trees where the boys had been because she couldn't stand not being able to see the house. The few times she'd gone off the property, she'd always had Regent with her.

Could she go to the hospital?

No. Absolutely not.

But Ace needed her. She had to go with him.

"I—"

"What if I come instead?" Nico suggested. "Thea will meet us there. Lottie needs to stay here and call her. Let her know what happened."

It made no sense since she could easily call Thea as they drove to the emergency room. But she knew he was doing it to try to help her. Although she didn't think Ace would be overly enthused about Nico coming along with him.

"No, Lottie! I want Lottie."

"I'm sorry, Master Ace," Gerald said in that overly stuffy way of his. "But Miss Lottie has to stay here."

"I'll go."

Everyone gave her surprised looks. Even Keir.

"I'm coming. Let's go. He's in pain."

"I . . ." Gerald looked utterly flummoxed. "That's not a good idea, Miss Lottie."

"I'm going." She gave Gerald a firm look. "Nico, can you carry Ace? I'll get, um. What will I need?"

"Your handbag," Nico told her. "Phone."

Right. The panic was already starting to overwhelm her.

Just breathe, Lottie. You can do this. He's a child. He needs you.

She raced upstairs, feeling breathless and ill by the time she got to her room. There was her phone. She didn't know where her wallet was. She never went anywhere.

No time. No time.

She dashed back downstairs, then saw Nico carrying Ace toward the front door. She stilled as she reached the door.

She flushed hot then cold, her stomach turning over.

Can't do this. Can't do this.

Nico turned, studied her.

"Lottie, you should stay here."

God, she wanted to. So much. The thought of going somewhere with a bunch of strangers . . . she had to swallow down a mouthful of bile. What if she had a panic attack? Fainted? Threw up?

"Lottie," Ace cried out.

But she had to do this for him. It was her fault that he'd hurt himself. She was supposed to be taking care of him but look what had happened.

"Lottie," Nico said in a low voice. "Come to me."

His words were filled with steel, and she found herself moving to him without thought.

"Why is Lottie breathing funny?" Ace asked. "Is she hurt too?"

"Lottie is fine. She just needs to keep her eyes on me. I'm going to help her. And she'll be fine. Nothing is going to happen to her."

Nico's words slowly penetrated the panic threatening to send her spiraling.

"Deep breath in, nice and slow. That's it. Take hold of my arm."

There was that commanding tone again. It filled her with strength. She didn't know how or why.

"Don't let go unless I give you permission."

Permission? Seriously? She should probably object to that wording. She didn't need his permission for anything. But she still clung to his arm as they walked outside toward the waiting town car.

"Eyes on me, Lottie. Don't you look away," Nico commanded.

She couldn't do this.

"It hurts," Ace cried.

She had to do this.

5

Liam climbed into the back of the car beside Regent.

He blew out a breath as he sat back, and the car started moving forward. The partition was up between them and the front seat where two of Regent's guys sat. There were two more in a car behind him. More security than either of them usually traveled with. But Regent had wanted a show of force for this meeting. With good reason.

"What did you think?" Regent asked, without looking at him.

To look at him, you'd think he was unaffected by anything that had just happened. But Liam had known him for a while now. He knew from the tight way he held his jaw to the forced casualness of his pose that Regent was concerned.

"There's something off with him," Liam said.

Regent let out a slight breath then nodded with a frown. "That's what I thought."

"Doesn't mean he has anything to do with your problems, though."

"No, but he could be willing to take advantage."

Yeah, that could definitely be it. Patrick held control of a smaller part of New Orleans than Regent did. So if he wanted a bigger share, he could be waiting for Regent to fuck up then make his move.

"I've got a rat in the ranks," Regent muttered.

They'd been friends for years, and Liam had nothing to do with Regent's business dealings. Which is likely why the other man felt safe discussing this with him. "Nobody should have come close to intercepting the last shipment from Mexico and I can't work out how they came so close unless I have a rat."

Made sense.

"Victor is down there now, smoothing things over?"

"If by smoothing things over, you mean he's busting heads and intimidating people, then yeah."

Regent's phone rang. He looked at who was calling and frowned, answering the call.

"Gerald? What is it? What? Why is she at the hospital? Fuck. Is it broken?"

Liam glared at Regent. Who was at the hospital? Lottie?

He tapped out a message to Nico.

LIAM: *Where are you? What's going on?*

NO REPLY. Fuck.

"We're on our way. No, stay there with them. Is she all right? Fuck. Yes. Fifteen."

Regent ended the call with a grunt.

"What is it?" Liam asked, staring down at his phone. He was going to kill Nico. Liam preferred to move around without guards. Yeah, his wealth and connections could make him a target but he stuck to the shadows and there wasn't much he wasn't capable of doing himself.

But Nico was his weak spot.

Nico and now Lottie. Which meant that he might have to review how he operated. Because Lottie would need protection.

And if Nico wasn't going to do what he fucking told him to and stay in touch, stay put, then he might find himself with a guard too.

"You haven't heard from Nico?" Regent asked.

"No. What is it?"

Regent raised an eyebrow but didn't say anything about his tense tone.

"Ace fell from a tree. He's had to go to the hospital. Looks like he's broken his arm."

"Ace? Jardin's woman's brother?"

"Yes."

"Doesn't sound good. He was at your house?"

"Lottie takes care of them sometimes during school vacations while Thea works. But usually, I'm around to help. She gets overwhelmed and tired easily."

"I'm sure she's capable of taking care of two boys."

Regent shook his head. "Yeah? Look what just happened."

"Accidents happen. He fell from a tree. Kids like to do reckless things. You can't blame Lottie."

"I don't blame her." Regent glared at him.

Liam raised his eyebrows. Regent didn't usually show much emotion. The only time he could remember him losing it was when Lottie was kidnapped. When he'd called Liam for his help, he'd been furious. Cold. Lashing out at everyone.

"Then why are you—"

"She went with them."

"To the hospital?" Okay, now Liam understood. As far as he knew, Lottie never went out.

"She never goes anywhere without me. And then, only if it's because I can't organize for it to happen at home."

"So, you bring everything she needs to her?"

"Yes, of course. She can't even walk through the gardens alone. She has to be able to see the house. To know that someone is close by. So, I bring what I can to her. The only time she's ever gone out of the house is when she's needed to go somewhere with specialist equipment that can't be moved. The last time was when we were worried she'd broken a bone in her foot, and she needed to have it X-rayed. But then I arranged for a private clinic and had it emptied out of everyone but the few key personnel. She should have stayed at home."

"You don't think you should try and encourage her to go out of the house?"

"This isn't her being difficult, Liam. She has panic attacks. After that bastard kidnapped her, it changed something inside her."

"I get that. But there must be something that can be done. That's no way to live."

Regent gave him a curious look with just a tinge of suspicion. "She's my sister. How about I worry about her, and you stick to worrying about your husband?"

Liam straightened. Was that a threat? They'd been friends a long time, but he was well aware that they weren't family. And Regent always put family first.

They pulled up outside the emergency entrance of a small hospital. A private one, he was guessing. Regent wouldn't allow his family to go to a public one with no way of managing their security.

When they walked into the hospital, Regent moved forward as though he knew exactly where he was going. Maybe he had a private room here. Fuck, even a wing. Who knew?

Nobody stopped them as they strode down a passage and into a room at the back. One of Regent's guys stood outside of the room, standing guard. He stepped aside so that Regent and Liam could walk in. The guard who'd trailed them in here, stayed outside. There, sitting close to Nico, who had his hand on hers and was speaking quietly to her, was Lottie.

Her face was pale. Her hair was slightly messy, as though she'd been running her fingers through it. But she was all right. Both of them were.

Relief flooded him.

He was still going to take this out on Nico's ass for not calling him and telling him he was leaving the house.

Regent strode forward. Lottie looked up at the sight of her brother. Her eyes were wide, slightly wild. Liam looked to Nico, who tried to grin back at him.

Yeah, he knew he was in trouble.

"Darling, what are you doing here?" Regent asked, crouching in front of Lottie.

Liam moved over as well. "Are you hurt? Either of you?"

Lottie jumped slightly and he realized his tone had been a touch too harsh. Fuck. He didn't mean it to be. Concern had him speaking before he thought.

"We're fine," Nico told him. "Ace was the only one hurt. Broken arm. They've X-rayed it and he's in getting a cast. Thea, Jardin, Carrick, and Keir are back with him. It was already too many people, so we decided to wait out here. Gerald and Peter are with them."

Reaching out, Regent took hold of her free hand, before glaring at Nico in an attempt to get him to let go of her other hand.

"Do you mind?" Regent said stiffly.

Nico gave him a huge, toothy smile. "Nope, don't mind at all."

"Let go of my sister."

Liam scowled. He didn't like that. Nobody forced his husband to do anything he didn't want to. He moved closer to them, prepared to tell Regent to get fucked when Nico widened his eyes at him, giving him a quick shake of his head.

Liam wasn't happy. He crossed his arms over his chest, prepared to still do it when Nico gestured at Lottie who was nodding at something Regent was whispering to her.

Fine. Fuck.

Liam turned his gaze from Nico to take in their girl. A fine tremble shook her. He looked to Nico in concern.

"Lottie, what are you doing here?" Regent asked. Her gaze settled on her brother.

Fuck. He hated that she looked to him for guidance and strength.

Instead of Liam.

"Why didn't you stay at home and let Gerald handle all of this?" Regent asked in a gentle voice. Liam had only ever heard him use that voice with his sister.

"Ace wanted me to come. I couldn't let him down. It was my fault he got hurt."

Her fault? Why? Because she'd been watching him?

"It wasn't your fault, Lottie," Nico told her firmly. "We were both watching him. We told him not to climb the high tree."

"Of course, it's not your fault," Regent soothed. "You shouldn't have been looking after them without me there. I'll make it clear to Jardin that's not to happen again."

Lottie's shoulders slumped and Liam clenched his hands into fists. Didn't he see what he'd just done to her? Shouldn't Regent be praising her? Be lifting her up, rather than telling her that she wasn't capable?

"Yes, of course," she whispered.

"Let's go. We need to get you home. You're exhausted. I'm going to carry you."

Carry her?

Liam waited for her to tell her brother she was fine. To stop being so overbearing. But she seemed almost out of it. Like she'd sunk inside herself.

Liam shot a look at Nico, but he was staring at Lottie worriedly.

"Lottie?" Nico asked. "Do you want to go home, or do you want to wait and see how Ace is?"

"You need to butt out, this has nothing to do with you," Regent shot at Nico.

"And you need to watch your tone," Liam said in a low, warning voice.

"She's my sister. I know what she needs. And right now, she needs to go home. The two of you need to step back."

"My husband has been with her the entire day. He's been taking care of her. You owe him a debt."

"Liam," Nico said warningly.

Liam ignored him as he glared at Regent. The other man gave him a cold stare back.

"This is a family matter. Neither one of you is family."

Liam got it. And if it had been anyone other than the two people in this world he truly cared about, he wouldn't say a word against Regent. He'd agree with him.

But this was his girl and his husband.

"Nico was merely asking Lottie what she wants to do. Something, as her brother, I'm sure you're concerned about. Shouldn't you be asking the same question instead of just telling her you know best?"

"You both need to stop. Now." The power in Nico's voice surprised Liam and he turned to look at the other man. He was staring at them both furiously. And his arm was around Lottie, who had curled her legs up to her chest. Liam frowned, not liking her defensive posture.

Fuck. He was doing the same thing Regent was. Thinking of himself. Not her.

"Shut up, both of you. Think of someone else other than your egos for once, huh?"

He deserved those words, even as they made him grind his teeth, wanting to snap back.

That wouldn't solve anything.

"Shit," Regent said in a low voice. "Lottie? Darling, look at me."

She raised her face slowly, looking at Regent. Then to Liam's shock, she turned her gaze to his. Those hazel eyes were filled with such pain that it made him flinch.

Fuck. Be gentler.

"There's no need to be scared," he reassured her. "No one here would harm you."

"Remember. Marshmallow," Nico said to her.

Marshmallow?

But for whatever reason, that seemed to work. She lowered her legs.

"What do you want to do?" Regent asked her, putting a hand back on her knee.

She was silent for a long moment, taking slow breaths in.

"I want to go home."

"Then that's what we'll do."

"Wait, though," she said, grabbing Regent's arm. "I can't leave without knowing how Ace is."

"Thea is here, isn't she?" Regent asked.

"I'm sure we can find out," Liam said in a firm tone. "Can't we, Regent?"

Regent glared up at him. "I'll find out."

Lottie gave him a shaky smile. "Thanks."

He moved to the door and opened it, speaking quietly to the guard.

"You're in trouble," Liam said to Nico instead of doing what he really wanted to do, which was sit next to Lottie and draw her into his lap.

"Sorry," Nico said in a casual voice.

"Why is he in trouble?" she asked, looking confused. "It wasn't Nico's fault."

"I'm not talking about what happened with the kid," Liam replied. "I'm talking about the fact that he left the house without calling me."

"Oh." She looked from him to Nico. "He wasn't supposed to?"

"No, he wasn't supposed to. He was supposed to stay in the house with you. Where he would be safe."

"You're in danger?" she asked Nico.

Nico winked at her. "Only danger I'm in is Liam lecturing me to death."

A lecture? Is that what he thought he had coming? Liam didn't think so. But Nico shot him another look. Right. He didn't think Lottie could handle the truth? Had anyone bothered asking Lottie what she could handle?

"That was my fault, though. If you're going to blame someone, blame me."

"And how would it be your fault, Lottie?" Liam asked curiously. He turned to look at Regent, wondering what was taking him so long. But he had his phone to his ear.

"It was my fault Ace was hurt and we had to rush out the door. Nico was trying to carry Ace and keep me from panicking. I had a panic attack when I got here, and he helped me. So, you see, it's my fault."

"Is this the way it's going to go then?" Liam said with some amusement. "The two of you ganging up against me?"

"Well, together we don't even have a chance of making your body weight, so . . . " Nico teased.

"Watch it," Liam warned. But he'd toned down his voice for Lottie's sake. She was staring between them both with wide eyes.

"Gang up on you? Why would I . . . I'd never," she told him, sounding anxious.

"Marshmallow," Nico said.

Her nervousness seemed to fade.

"Is that some sort of code word or something?" He liked that they were so close. It would help their effort to win her over. But a part of him acknowledged that he couldn't let Nico do all the work. At some stage, Liam had to figure out a way to get close to her without running her off.

It was going to be tough for a man who didn't usually care who the fuck he alienated.

"I've just talked to Jardin," Regent said as he returned, putting his phone in his pocket. "They're going to be taking Ace home soon. He's fine. They gave him something that's made him sleepy. Got a cast on his arm that Jardin says he wants everyone to sign. Jardin said he'll bring him around in a few days to see you, okay?"

"Good," Lottie said with relief. "I just didn't want to leave until I knew."

"Then it's time to go home. You don't need to be here." Regent held out his hand to her and she reached up, taking it.

Regent nodded to them coolly. Lottie tugged on Regent's arm, and he bent down while she whispered something to him. Liam turned to Nico, who looked so disappointed that it hurt him.

"I need to apologize for the way I just behaved. Lottie just told me how much you helped her, took care of her and Ace," Regent said stiffly to Nico. "I owe you a debt of gratitude. There's another car here waiting to take you both back to our place. Let's go. Darling, you want me to carry you?"

Lottie shot a look at Nico then shook her head. "Just guide me. I don't want people looking at me."

Regent wrapped his arm around her, pulling her in.

Well, at least they weren't being kicked to the curb.

6

Nico paced up and down the bedroom.

"Are you going to come to bed or wear a hole in the carpet? It's ugly as shit anyway. What's with the red carpet?" Liam asked as he lay back on the bed.

"Something's wrong," Nico told him.

"Yeah, you're over there and I'm here. Come here. We still need to chat about today."

Nico shook his head. "Not now, Liam."

What the fuck?

Liam felt a surge of worry followed by anger. He breathed through it. He'd been cold for so long. Any emotions other than anger or resentment had been long frozen. Until Nico. He was the only one who could truly get to him. Well, him and Lottie.

"Excuse me?" he asked.

Nico turned to face him, letting out a deep breath. "I didn't . . . I don't mean it like that. I'm not dismissing or rejecting you. But you didn't see what I did today."

"What do you mean? What did you see?"

"With Lottie. There's something . . . " He ran a hand over his face, looking drained.

"You're exhausted. You need sleep." Liam found this part harder. Trying to care for someone else. He could only go by how Nico acted with him and from what caring he could remember having from his mother before her death. But he'd been young, and those memories were hard to access. "Come to bed."

"I can't. Liam, she needs us."

"Lottie? She'll be asleep by now."

"And if she's not? You didn't see her today. There's more going on than we know."

"What do you mean?" Liam sat up, staring at his husband. "More what?"

"She's so much braver than they give her credit for. She struggles, Liam. Every day. Today, when Ace and Keir were screaming, she tried to follow me. To help."

Liam frowned at that. "Maybe it's good for her to push herself."

"Not under those circumstances. The stress can't be good for her. Always worrying and fearful."

Liam grunted. "I wonder if she's still talking to a therapist."

"I don't know. But there's more. She paints, but she doesn't let anyone see it."

"Aren't a lot of artists like that?"

"She thinks they're meaningless. That she's worthless."

"What?" Liam barked. "Why the fuck would she think that?"

"Because she doesn't think she does anything of value. She has no purpose, Liam. She's drifting."

He nodded. He kind of understood that. His brother was similar. Only he was a complete bastard, and Lottie was . . . sweetness and light.

"She needs something to do," Liam said.

"I think she needs to learn that she can do whatever she wants to. She's not helpless. Those boys adore her. That Ace, shit, if he were a few years older, I'd be worried he'd be giving us a run for our money with her."

"So, we help her build up her self-confidence. Teach her that she has value. Make sure that she's talking to someone that knows their shit. Because I sure don't. I'm likely to make things worse."

"There's more," Nico told him.

"What?"

"I'm not sure exactly. When Ace grabbed her arm today, she flinched like it hurt."

Liam frowned. "So, the kid obviously grabbed her too hard. Jardin needs to talk to him about that."

"I don't think that's it."

"Maybe she hurt it. Is that really what has you pacing?"

"She didn't come to dinner."

"I know. But she was exhausted. You heard what Regent said. I'm sure today was a lot for her."

"It was. She had a panic when we attempted to have a picnic outside, then another as we left the house to go to the hospital. And another at the hospital."

"See. It's no wonder she's exhausted."

"I just . . . I need to make sure she's all right."

"You want to go see her?" Liam asked. "If Regent catches us . . ."

"I know. But I have to know."

Liam looked thoughtful. "Oh, what the hell? What's the worst he can do? Not like I'm scared of Regent Malone."

Nico let out a deep breath. "Thank you."

"You're going to owe me, though." He climbed off the bed and strode toward Nico. Lightly grabbing the other man around the neck, he walked him until his back hit the wall. Then he pushed him against the wall, leaning into him. Nico's eyes filled with heat. He licked his lips. It might have looked like a nervous gesture on someone else, but there was hunger and need in his face.

"Owe you, huh?"

"Yep. And let's not forget that you were disobedient today. That's coming out of your hide."

"What are you planning on doing?"

"I don't have my kit here."

"Aw, that's too bad. Oh well, nothing to be done then, huh?"

Liam grinned. "I wouldn't say that." He reached down and cupped Nico's balls through his jeans, squeezing lightly. "Were you a good boy today? You didn't come?"

"No, you bastard, I didn't come." Nico groaned. "Fuck."

"Good. Because you don't get to come without my permission, do you?"

"Christ," he muttered as Liam grabbed his firm dick, running his hand up and down it. Then he undid the top few buttons of his jeans, sliding his hand in to grab Nico's cock, pumping it.

"Liam," he moaned.

"You *are* hard, aren't you? Was it hard to behave yourself today? Especially being around our girl."

"She smells so fucking good."

"I'm hurt," Liam told him, nipping at his lower lip. "You never say I smell good."

"You smell good," Nico said with a moan as he continued to jack him off. "But she smells amazing."

"And that made your dick hard? Smelling her all day? Having her close without being able to touch her. Or did you?"

"A few times."

"Yeah?"

"Her skin is like fucking silk. It's like nothing I've felt before."

"You tell me I'm going to need to start a skincare regime and I'll have to hurt you."

"You like hurting me," Nico pointed out.

Liam grinned. "Sometimes. And you like it when I hurt you."

"Sometimes."

Liam barked out a laugh then slid his hand out of Nico's jeans. "Do them up. Time's wasting."

Nico groaned. "You're such a bastard. All the fucking blood is in my cock. How am I supposed to even walk?"

Liam headed to the door. "You'll figure it out." He opened it and Nico walked past with a grumble, hastily doing up his jeans.

Liam smacked his ass and Nico jumped, turning with a glare. "You're a real ass sometimes."

"Watch it," Liam warned. "You're being given a reprieve. But at some stage, there will be a reckoning. At the rate you're going, you won't sit for a week."

"Promises. Promises."

He'd never met someone more perfect for him than Nico. He knew he couldn't be as rough with Lottie. She needed a far more delicate touch.

There was nothing delicate about Nico.

As though he sensed where his thoughts had gone, Nico turned back and wrapped his hand around the back of Liam's neck, pulling him down for a kiss. It wasn't often he took the more dominant role like this. But every so often, his dominant side pushed through.

"I love you, Liam. We've got this. Okay? She needs us. And we need her. It's going to be the three of us. Forever."

"Forever," Liam agreed.

"You know which bedroom is hers?" Nico asked as they quietly moved down the stairs.

Liam just shot him a look over his shoulder. Of course, he did. This was Liam. He didn't leave much up to chance.

Liam held a finger up to his lips as they moved silently down the hallways. That sense of urgency in Nico's gut grew.

Suddenly, Liam stopped, and Nico nearly plowed into him. Turning, Liam sent him a scowling look. Yeah, he hadn't been paying attention to his surroundings. He got it.

Bad Nico.

Thankfully, Liam was always hyper-aware. Liam pointed to a door. That had to be her room. Then he raised an eyebrow as though asking Nico what he wanted to do.

If they knocked, then they ran the risk of Regent hearing them. Turning, he looked around. He didn't know where her oldest brother slept. At least Victor wasn't here. And Maxim and Jardin no longer lived here.

Liam pointed at a door two down then mouthed a word.

Regent.

Okay, knocking was out. They could walk in, but what if they gave her a fright and she screamed?

Fuck. Too bad he hadn't thought this out. He didn't even have her phone number to send her a text, which would have been the sensible thing.

But he needed to see her.

Taking a deep breath, hoping this wasn't a fucking mistake, Nico stepped up to her door.

Liam didn't say a word, just turned, keeping an eye out as Nico gently opened the door. If she was asleep, he didn't want to wake her. He knew that she didn't get enough rest.

If she was sleeping, he'd just get a look at her and leave.

The door slid open, and he peered in.

"Lottie?" he whispered. The bed was made. No one was sleeping in it. He glanced around but didn't see her. Had she gone downstairs?

Obviously, his instincts were off. She didn't need him. But then a sound from behind a door caught his attention. He turned to Liam and nodded his head to indicate that he should follow him in.

Liam silently moved in behind him, shutting the door. Nico wondered if they should lock it. Glancing down, he frowned when he saw there was no lock. The door handle was different than all the others in the house. Either someone had broken this one or taken away the lock deliberately.

Liam gave it a glance too, and Nico could see he was thinking hard. Not much got past Liam.

He heard another noise, a sob. Then the sound of rattling and something being flung. Fuck. What was going on? He moved swiftly over to the door that he assumed led to an en suite bathroom. Like all the bedrooms in this house, this one was enormous. There was a huge bed centered against the opposite wall. It had a white wrought-iron frame with a soft, lavender-colored bedspread. The curtains were cream and light. The whole room was soft and feminine, down to the vases of fresh flowers on the bedside. It suited Lottie.

He and Liam looked completely out of place. Especially Liam, who glanced around the room assessing. He motioned to the door.

Right. Fuck.

Nico had to be the one to go in. Liam took the lead in a lot of things, but he couldn't with Lottie. Because Nico needed to forge a bridge between the two of them.

Not wanting to second guess himself, Nico walked over and knocked on the door.

There was silence in there.

"Y-yes?"

He heard some noise. Drawers shutting? What was she doing?

"Go in. Now," Liam commanded.

She might be naked or in the shower. Not that he wouldn't mind seeing her naked. Nope, he wouldn't mind at all. But he didn't want to completely terrify her. Or unravel all his progress with her.

Liam didn't give him a chance to make up his mind, though. Instead, he opened the door and barreled in.

She wasn't in the shower or undressed.

Damn it.

Instead, she was sitting on the floor amid a pile of stuff that she was trying to hastily pack away in the cupboard under the sink. Dressed in some sort of billowy nightgown, her hair lay down in soft, gentle waves. She looked almost ethereal.

The bathroom was all white tile except for the wall behind the bathroom counter, which had a pale lavender subway tile. Nico spotted a first aid kit next to her. Then he frowned as he glanced down at the tile. There was something red on the floor next to her. Was that . . .

"Where are you bleeding?" Liam demanded.

Trust Liam to notice first. He stepped forward, making her cower back.

Fuck, Nico hated seeing that. Hated her fear. Liam came to a stop and froze. Nico knew the other man could look terrifying with his cold eyes and huge build.

Nico came closer and crouched down, hoping to reassure her. To his surprise, Liam followed his lead and bent down as well. That wasn't usual.

"Pretty girl," he murmured. "What happened? Where are you hurt? What were you looking for?"

Her wide eyes moved from him to Liam, whose gaze was taking in everything before narrowing down on her hands.

Which she had hidden in the skirt of her nightgown.

Bingo.

Liam sat back on his ass. Slowly. She still watched him like a deer watching a hunter. Terrified that at any moment he might pounce. But Liam kept his hands where she could see them, his gaze steady. No quick movements.

"Lottie," Nico pressed.

But her gaze remained on Liam. The biggest, baddest threat in the room. Nico didn't blame her. But he wouldn't get anything out of her like this.

Nico opened his mouth to suggest that maybe Liam should wait in the bedroom. He didn't like to do it, but she was barely responsive. The last thing he wanted was to push her into a panic attack. Or to have her start screaming and alert the rest of the house.

Before he could say anything, though, Liam spoke up.

"Charlotte, look at me."

Her gaze snapped up to Liam's. Her eyes widened. Her breath coming in sharper pants.

"Liam," he warned.

"Where are you hurt?" Liam asked her. His voice was quiet. But there was a definite stern tone to it. He wasn't going to be denied.

She shook her head. Damn, she'd just denied Liam. He did it all the time, but most people didn't.

"Hmm. You're going to go with no, huh? You sure?"

With eyes filled with trepidation, she nodded.

"I don't think so," Liam replied in that still soft voice. "Show me your hands. Right. Now."

Her mouth parted slightly, her eyes so wide they seemed to take up most of her face. He was concerned they were stressing her out too much. It wasn't healthy.

"Liam," he warned.

"There's a time to go soft and a time to go hard. We both know our roles. And I'm telling you right now, it's my time."

Fuck. Okay, he had to trust Liam knew what he was doing.

Her gaze dropped.

"No. No looking away," Liam told her. "Look at me." Reaching out slowly, he took hold of her chin and raised her face.

Nico could see how fast her chest was rising and falling. If she had another panic attack, he was taking her to the hospital. Fuck it. This wasn't healthy.

"You know me. You might think you're scared of me. But you're not."

Her gaze narrowed.

"You want to know how I know that? Because you would have yelled for your brother as soon as I walked in if you were."

Nico had been wondering if they should go get Regent, but Liam was right. She hadn't screamed, and despite looking panicked and unsure, she was actually standing up to Liam.

"I'm not going to ask again," Liam warned.

Her eyes narrowed, but then she turned just her gaze to Nico since Liam still had hold of her chin.

"Marshmallow," he told her.

Her lips twitched.

"I'm going to need to know what that means at some stage," Liam told them both.

"Nah, you don't need to know, does he, Lottie-toe-tottie?"

Both of them shot him looks.

"I know, I know," he said dramatically. "It's hard to be this gorgeous and funny. But you know, someone has to do it."

Another lip twitch.

Hey, if he had to act like a clown to get her to smile then he was here for that. All day long.

Whatever she needed, he'd provide.

Liam dropped his hand from her chin. Relief filled her face. Oh, dear. She was in for such a rude awakening if she thought he was giving up.

He placed his hands palm up on her lap. She stared down at them.

"We can wait all night. I've got nowhere else to be."

"You don't want him to be up all night, Lottie," Nico told her. "He's a bear if he hasn't had enough sleep."

She let out a small sigh, then to his surprise, she drew out her hands. The knuckles on her right hand were red and swollen, and one had a cut on it.

What the hell?

She placed her hands on Liam's. He raised them up, staring at them, then her again.

"Who?"

Nico heard her suck in a breath, knew she was surprised by the question.

Liam leaned in. "Who?"

"N-no one."

"You hit someone. Why? What did they do? Who was it? Tell me." Liam shot out the questions like bullets from a semi-automatic. Hard. Relentless.

Her breathing grew rapid again.

Nico moved in closer. "You're not in trouble. No one is going to harm you. Liam just wants to know so he can protect you. Who was it?"

"Nobody."

"Don't lie to us," Liam warned in a dark voice. "Don't you fucking dare."

"Liam, shit." He was going to completely terrify her.

"No," Liam said to him. "No lies. That's something we won't have between us. Ever. She needs to know that."

"Why?" she asked. Confused, she glanced between them both. "Why do you care if I hit someone? If they tried to hurt me? What is it to do with either of you?"

Nico shot Liam a look. Should they tell her that they wanted her?

"You just need to know that we're not going to let anyone harm you."

She shook her head. "This is . . . this doesn't make any sense. I'm no one to you. Is this because I dated your brother? But I thought the two of you didn't get along and that was . . . that was years ago. I haven't spoken to him since."

Good.

"It has nothing to do with that jerk," Liam reassured her. "This is about you. Tell me."

Her gaze dropped, shoulders slumping.

With what? Fear? No, that didn't seem right.

Shame.

She's ashamed of what happened.

"There was no one," she whispered.

"Then why do your knuckles look like that?" Liam asked in his low, raspy voice. "What did you hit?"

"The wall."

Why would she hit the wall?

"And this mess in here?" Liam's voice was calm. Collected. But if she raised her gaze and looked into his eyes, she might see the wildness that Nico could see.

He was close to the edge. Nico knew he didn't like not knowing what was going on. Liam didn't like secrets when it came to those close to him. He'd had enough bullshit and subterfuge growing up with his bitch of a stepmother.

"Were you searching for something to clean them with?" Nico asked her gently, picking up the first aid kit. They weren't that bad. Painful, but not bleeding a lot.

"No," she told them.

"Then what were you looking for? Pills?" Liam asked sharply. "Were you looking for drugs?"

She shook her head. "No. I just . . . the pain . . . it helps. It makes me feel better."

Oh. Fuck.

This was it. The last part of the puzzle they were missing.

. . .

Lottie couldn't believe she'd just admitted that.

To Liam and Nico. Two of the most gorgeous, sexy, together men she'd ever met. She didn't know what they were doing here. Wasn't sure why they'd sought her out.

Maybe Nico had insisted on coming to see her. He'd been worried about her today. Even though he'd tried to keep things light, she'd still seen the way he watched her closely.

Funny, she'd have thought he would be glad to be rid of her. To have the burden of her care lifted from his shoulders. She knew it was no fun dragging around her dead weight.

Stop it, Lottie.

She couldn't keep doing this. If Regent saw her hands, he would be so upset. So disappointed in her. That was worse than him being angry. But then, Regent rarely got angry. And never at her.

But she didn't want him to worry over her. She didn't want to be under watch again. To have all of them follow her with their eyes, wondering when she would break.

Thing was, she was already broken. It was putting herself back together that was the problem.

"You were trying to hurt yourself," Liam said slowly. His gaze had moved so he was no longer looking at her.

Probably because he was disgusted by her. Horrified. Maybe he just wanted to figure out a way to get out of the room without having to say anything else.

She attempted to remove her hands from his, certain it was what he would want. But he tightened his hold on her, not letting her go. She gasped. He was so warm. His hands were calloused and rough, but they didn't hurt. They just held hers in their huge grasp, and all she felt was . . . safety.

Lottie risked a glimpse over at Nico. His face was an open book. He wasn't as good at hiding what he was thinking as Liam.

Few people were as good as Liam. Regent was. But he'd had years of practice. She thought it might be the same for Liam.

Nico looked so sad, so devastated that she instantly wanted to make things better for him.

"I'm sorry," she whispered.

Liam's gaze shot to hers. Those blue eyes seemed to shine. They were electrified. "Why are you sorry?"

Wasn't that obvious?

"For upsetting Nico."

"You're sorry because I'm upset?" Nico whispered.

"Yes. And I'm sorry for being like this. For disappointing people. I wasn't supposed to do this anymore."

"This has happened before?" Liam asked sharply.

"Not for a while . . . but after I was kidnapped, it happened a few times."

Liam started swearing and she curved in on herself. She tried to draw her legs up, but he was still holding her hands.

"Liam's not upset with you," Nico soothed, moving so he was sitting next to her. "You're shivering? Are you cold? We should get her off this floor."

Liam nodded and before she even knew what was happening, she was being lifted and cradled in the huge man's arms.

She tensed, waiting for the panic to come over her. Nobody touched her except her family. Oh, and Nico today. But for some reason, she didn't panic when he touched her.

Although panic bubbled in her stomach, it didn't manifest into an attack. The anxiety didn't overtake her. And she wasn't sure why.

Liam Carmichael wasn't a safe guy. He was imminently dangerous. Maybe not to her physical health. But her mental and emotional health couldn't take him. Couldn't stand up to him. She stiffened. Prepared to fight him off.

"Easy, baby," Liam whispered, making her tense for an entirely different reason.

Baby?

He'd called her baby. And it wasn't just the word, it was the way he'd said it. In a soft croon that filled her body with warmth. Suddenly, she wasn't cold or afraid.

Liam carried her out to the bedroom, where Nico sat on the bed. He patted his lap. "Give her to me."

They were treating her like a doll. Precious and easily breakable. She didn't want to be like that. But right then, she felt very, very fragile. And their care was like a bandage on her wounds.

She was placed in Nico's lap. Then Liam picked up the blanket at the end of her bed and gently tucked it around her.

Lottie couldn't help but stare at him in amazement.

"Told you," Nico murmured as Liam turned away and walked into the bathroom. "Marshmallow."

"Why are you both here?" she asked as Liam returned with a wet cloth and the first aid kit.

"We wanted to check in on you after today," Nico told her. "You weren't at dinner. We were worried."

Liam was silent as he crouched in front of them. He grabbed her sore hand and gently started washing it with the cloth. She hissed as he touched a particularly sore spot, reflexively trying to draw her hand back. But he kept hold.

"Easy, baby. I've got you."

He was being so gentle, it brought tears to her eyes.

"Sh, pretty girl," Nico whispered in her ear. "Everything is going to be all right."

Liam had moved to cleaning the other hand. She shook her head.

All right? How can anything ever be all right?

"Because Liam and I won't allow you to be anything else," Nico told her firmly.

"I said that out loud?" she asked. Now, she was really losing it. She didn't even know what she was thinking and what she was saying.

Liam didn't look up from his task. Didn't say anything. He just took care of her silently, but with such attentiveness that she could feel tears filling her eyes.

Lottie was loved. She knew that. Her brothers adored and protected her ferociously. And if they didn't, her cousins would. She'd always been loved. Always.

But there was something about having this big man, a man who'd obviously lived a hard life crouching in front of her, taking care of her. While his sweet, loving husband held her like she was precious.

Like he never wanted to let her go.

It was something else. She wasn't a beloved sister or cousin.

She felt like a woman.

She couldn't remember when she last felt like that. Delicate, not because her mind was fragile, but because these two men dwarfed her. Yet they wouldn't use their strength against her, but for her.

"You can't make me better," she told them.

"No," Liam said as he wrapped her knuckles with gauze then a bandage, going a bit overboard. They were just swollen with a small scratch. "Only you can fix you."

She sucked in a breath. Yeah. He was right. Only problem was she had no idea how to fix herself. And sometimes, she thought she was scared to try.

"But you don't have to do it alone. There are people who will help you," Nico told her. "People you can lean on. You're not supposed to do this sort of thing on your own."

"I have my family," she pointed out. "I'm hardly alone."

"Aren't you?" Liam said. "If you're not on your own, then why haven't you asked them to help you? Why isn't one of them here, taking care of you?"

His words were bitten off, as though he found them almost bitter.

"It's not fair on them for me to be a burden all the time."

Nico tightened his arms around her, while Liam's gaze spat blue fire. "A burden? That's what they think of you? They told you that you were a burden? I'll fucking kill them."

"No, wait! They didn't say it to me," she said hastily as he stood.

Liam froze, staring down at her. His hands were clenched into fists. The last thing she wanted was for him to go off and tell Regent about this.

"But they made you feel it," Nico said while Liam stood there. She got the feeling he was barely holding onto his control. Tension coiled inside him, ready to explode.

And that wasn't going to be a good thing.

"No," she said urgently. "Never. They'd never make me feel that way. I know they love me the same as I love them. They've done nothing but support and take care of me."

"They let you hurt yourself." Liam's voice was a harsh whisper

"It . . . they . . . " She sucked in a deep breath. "They didn't let me hurt myself. When I first started doing it, they insisted that I talk to someone. I was having problems. Nightmares. I couldn't leave the house. I was paralyzed by fear. If I hurt myself, then for a while some of those feelings were muted. I felt more in control."

"How did we not know about this?" Liam said in a harsh whisper.

"How could you know? Only my brothers know."

"What happened when they found out?" Nico asked her.

"Regent got me a therapist. She would come to the house twice a week. I finally found other ways to manage my emotions and need for control without hurting myself."

"Until now?" Nico asked. "Or have you been hurting yourself before tonight?"

"I . . . I . . . " He couldn't know. No one knew.

"Show us your arm, pretty girl," he told her.

Shit. Shit.

Liam just stared down at her. And she felt him willing her to do it.

"I don't want to."

"Why not?" Nico asked her.

Wasn't it obvious?

"I'm ashamed."

Liam crouched once more and reached for her chin, turning her face to his. "There's no shame between us. Only truth. Show us."

She didn't know what it was about him that made her want to be better, do better, to make him proud. She felt that way with her brothers, but not like this.

She drew back the arm of her nightgown. It had elastic at the wrists so it couldn't accidentally ride up. Chosen on purpose.

When she drew it back, she heard Liam let out a hiss while Nico tensed against her.

"Nico," Liam said in a voice that sounded almost pained.

"I know," Nico replied.

"This is completely fucking unacceptable!"

She jumped, startled at this reaction.

"Liam," Nico replied sharply. "Calm down."

"Why? Look at her arm." It was almost a wail. "Look what they let her do."

"I don't understand. Who let me do this? If you're talking about my brothers, then they didn't let me do this. They don't know." She didn't like the implied criticism. They were her brothers. She was loyal to them. Always.

Whether they were in the right or not.

But this time, there was no reason for anyone to be upset with them.

"This is all on me. It has nothing to do with my brothers."

"They should have been taking care of you," Liam countered.

"Liam," Nico warned. "You need to quieten down. Do you want to alert someone that we're in here?"

"I don't care," Liam said with a snarl. "Fuck it. We're taking her with us. Pack up anything with sentimental attachment and get her dressed. I'll call for a car and get the plane prepped. We're going."

He headed toward the door.

"Shit," Nico muttered.

"Has he lost his mind? I'm not going anywhere."

"I'm not certain he ever had his mind to begin with. Liam, we can't just take her with us." Nico put her gently down and jumped up, striding toward Liam.

"We can. We will." Liam had reached the door. "Why is there no lock on this?" He turned back to her.

She drew her legs up, putting her arms around them. "So, I couldn't lock myself in here."

Shame flooded her. She didn't care what they said. This wasn't normal. She wasn't normal.

Nico said something in Greek, then he came back to her, sitting and drawing her back into his lap. "Liam, calm down and think because we can't just take her."

"I don't understand what's going on. Take me where? Why would you want to? Why do you even care what I do?"

Liam had his hands resting on the door, his head was bent. He wasn't wearing a jacket, and his shirt stretched across his back. Any more pressure and she worried it might rip. Then he might burst out of it like the Hulk.

Actually, she could totally see that happening.

"She needs support, Liam. Not for you to lose it at her brothers," Nico told him.

"Why is he so mad?" she asked. "I really don't understand."

"You don't understand because I was fucking stupid," Liam said.

Nico turned her on his lap, so she was sideways, facing Liam who still had his back to them. He gently pressed on her legs, getting her to let them go so they hung over the edge of his lap. No one had held her like this in years. She shouldn't like it as much as she did. These guys weren't hers. They never would be.

Except they were acting rather protective for men who had no attachment to her.

"We should have known, Nico. Why didn't we know?" Liam asked, pain in his voice.

"I know," Nico replied.

"My fault. I kept you away. Told you we needed to keep our distance from her."

"You didn't know, Liam," Nico told him.

She felt like an intruder in their private conversation.

"Should have. Fucking should have. Look at her knuckles. Her arm. She can't leave the property without a fucking panic attack, and she has to control her emotions by harming herself."

She flinched.

"Liam," Nico warned. "Stop."

Liam turned so suddenly that she gasped and leaned into Nico.

"He's only this upset because you're hurt and he blames himself," Nico explained to her.

That made no sense. Why would he blame himself?

Suddenly, Liam was kneeling in front of them again. He gently grabbed hold of her hand, running a finger lightly over her knuckles. He was silent for a long while, so long she didn't think he was going to say anything again.

"Why did you hurt yourself today, baby?" he finally asked.

She couldn't tell him. This was something she didn't speak to anyone about. Well, except her therapist but they'd gotten rid of her. She'd started to pay more attention to Regent than Lottie.

"It was my fault that Ace got hurt."

Nico made a noise, but Liam glanced at him, and he didn't say anything.

"So, you blamed yourself?" Liam asked.

"Of course."

"What if he'd done that while Regent was watching him? Would you expect Regent to punish himself?" Liam asked.

"I wasn't punishing myself."

Weren't you?

"I didn't really mean to hurt myself, though. I just got so angry, and I needed a way to relieve the pressure. So, I punched the wall."

"So, you felt out of control?" Liam asked.

"I guess," she whispered.

"I don't want you doing this anymore," Liam told her calmly.

It wasn't like she wanted to do it. She hated that she had to do this.

"The bruises?" he asked.

"I just . . . I don't know."

"Yes, you do."

"I couldn't go to my cousin's wedding," she blurted out. "I really wanted to, but I couldn't bear the idea of leaving the grounds, let alone traveling to Texas. I let him down."

"Lottie," Nico said on a pained groan.

"Did he tell you that?" Liam asked.

"Of course not. West would never tell me that."

"Did anyone make you feel like you'd let him down?" Liam queried.

"No, but I feel like that. A failure."

"You're not a failure, Lottie. You're just dealing with shit the only way you know how. In a way that, I'm guessing, gives you a temporary reprieve, am I right?" Liam asked.

"Yes. It doesn't last. It's a short-term fix."

"And you know what the long-term fix is," Liam prodded.

Of course, she did. But sometimes it was hard to see that far ahead. All she could see was what was right in front of her.

"It's not something you have to do on your own," Nico told her.

"What we can't do is let this continue on," Liam agreed.

"I don't understand why. Why do you care?" She felt like she'd said it so many times and they weren't answering her. "Why are you reacting like this? I'm no one to you."

Liam gave her an intense look. "I disagree."

7

Liam knew this wasn't the time to tell her this.

It was probably the worst time. When she was already upset and completely overwhelmed. Nico was staring at him wide-eyed, obviously thinking the same thing. But the words had burst out of him without real thought.

He had to tell her that she was theirs.

Guilt swirled in his gut. He'd live with this guilt for the rest of his life. The knowledge that her pain was so deep that she harmed herself to get it out. That she bled because of it.

His informant had either kept this information from him or her family had covered it up so well that he hadn't known.

How could they do that?

"I don't understand what you're saying."

Fuck. He stared at Nico, begging for his help. Yep, he'd dug the hole. And normally, Liam was the problem solver. Only, he tended to solve problems with his fists.

Obviously, this wasn't that sort of situation.

Nico sighed. "Lottie, do you remember the first time we met you?"

She frowned. "At that awful dinner Michael's mother organized?"

"Yeah. It was terrible, right?" Nico said.

"She invited that other woman who flirted with Michael all night. It was obvious that she didn't want Michael with me. She wanted that other woman to lure him away from me."

Liam snorted. He'd moved to lean against the wall. He thought some distance might be a good idea. Give her some space to breathe. Also, if he got too close to her, he was worried he'd just throw her over his shoulder and storm away with her.

Still so fucking tempting.

"Stupid cow," Nico said. "You had more smarts, beauty and breeding than that other girl."

"Michael and his mother didn't seem to think so," she said. "But yeah, I totally do."

Liam raised an eyebrow at that show of self-confidence. That was the Lottie he remembered from that night. She'd known who she was. A fucking princess.

His step-mother was a dumb bitch. She hadn't even looked into Lottie. If she had, she'd have discovered that Lottie came from a lot of money and a well-known family. But she'd decided that because Lottie wasn't from New York, she didn't count as anyone she'd want her precious Michael to touch.

And that fucking idiot, Michael had ignored Lottie all night to flirt back with that other girl, whom Liam couldn't even picture. She'd been nothing next to Lottie.

"I told them I needed the bathroom," Lottie said. "I was thinking about leaving and you came up to me and said you had a better idea." She smiled up at Nico. "We snuck into the kitchen, and you found every tub of ice cream they had, and we had an ice cream party."

"Best one I've ever had. Whipped cream, maraschino cherries, and the most beautiful girl I've ever seen in my life."

She blushed at Nico's words. "Then Liam came in. I thought he was going to tell us off."

"Tell you off? Why would I do that?" he asked.

"For leaving you alone in the viper's nest?" she asked.

"True. That was naughty of you both. Do that again, and I'll have to punish you both."

"Punish us?" Her eyes were wide. *Fear?* He couldn't have that.

"Hmm, I think a fair punishment would have been for me to have all the maraschino cherries."

"Hey!" she protested. "Hands off my cherries."

Fuck.

That sounded so dirty.

He needed help. Here she was, hurt and in need of care and all he could think of was getting her naked and sucking on her nipples. What would they look like? What noises would she make?

Nico cleared his throat and Liam turned to the other man, then Nico flicked his gaze down to Liam's crotch.

Not the right time to get a hard-on.

He should probably feel a little bad for sending Nico down here with an erection.

Should. But he didn't.

"That night, I thought you were the most beautiful girl I'd ever seen," Nico told her. "My stomach was tied up in knots. I could barely talk to you."

"But why?"

"You didn't feel anything like that toward me?" Nico asked, pushing her hair back behind her ear.

"Well . . . I mean, the two of you . . . Nico, you're married," she hissed, giving Liam a nervous look.

He found himself holding in a grin. He didn't want to make her uncomfortable. But her nervousness was cute. Did she really think Nico would tell her this without Liam's knowledge, while he was standing right there?

"Hmm. True, I am. Well, Liam?" Nico challenged.

Liam narrowed his gaze at his husband. He definitely needed a session. He was getting a bit crabby because he'd been forbidden from coming.

When Liam turned to Lottie, he saw her staring up at him worriedly. Was she concerned that he'd be mad?

"When I first saw you, Lottie, do you want to know what I thought?" Liam asked.

"I don't know. You kind of looked annoyed. Grouchy. You barely said anything to me."

"That's just his resting bitch face," Nico said.

Liam glared at him. "I was grouchy but not at you."

"Then whom?"

"I was grouchy because I was attracted to you, and I didn't want to be."

"But I thought the two of you . . . you're gay, right?"

"We're both bi, sweetie," Nico explained gently. "And while we love each other, it's always felt like something was missing."

"And the piece that is missing is you," Liam added.

Her mouth dropped open then she looked from Liam to Nico before reaching down to pinch her thigh.

"What the hell are you doing?" Liam yelled.

"Liam, fuck, shut up!" Nico hissed at him, looking nervously at the door.

Fuck.

He wanted to say that he didn't give a shit whether her brother stormed inside, but this conversation was too important for interruptions.

They were all still, silent, waiting.

When nothing happened after a few moments, Liam stepped forward and knelt in front of them.

"Baby, what did you just do?"

"I just pinched myself. I thought I'd better check that this was actually happening."

"You hurt yourself. Again. Right in front of our fucking eyes." Liam glared up at her.

"I didn't pinch hard."

"Show me."

"I . . . I . . ."

"Liam," Nico said quietly. "You can't push her too hard."

"Her health is the priority right now, Nico. If she keeps hurting herself . . . even small pinches to check that she's not dreaming aren't acceptable. Not now."

"I can't show you."

"Please." The word was difficult to say. Wasn't one he said often, and he sensed rather than saw Nico's surprise.

Lottie took in a sharp breath. But she started to slowly raise her nightgown. She kept her other leg hidden. But he'd always known she'd be modest. Even if she hadn't been kidnapped and hurt. This was the type of woman she was.

And he loved that.

His beautiful girl.

He ran a finger over the red spot a few inches above her knee. "Don't do this anymore, Lottie."

"It's not . . . I wasn't trying to hurt myself."

He smoothed down her nightgown. "Don't hurt yourself in any way, for any reason."

"I don't think it's that easy."

He raised his gaze. "We'll get you whatever help you need. We'll support you all the way. But you have to help yourself. Do you want to help yourself?"

"Yes," she said quietly. Her gaze was down. Not good enough.

"Look at me when you say that. Not your knees."

"Jesus, Liam," Nico muttered.

Liam gave him a sharp look and Nico sighed, nodding. He'd trust him.

Her gaze raised to his.

"Good girl. Do you want our help, Lottie? Do you want to help yourself?"

"Yes."

"Yes, Liam," he pressed.

"Yes, Liam." Her eyes were wide. He took hold of her hands, being gentle with her knuckles. He placed his finger over her pulse. Fast.

She'd been through so much today. He wished that he could have put this conversation off until tomorrow at least. But going slow just wasn't possible.

"You're really stressed, aren't you, baby?" he murmured.

"I'm all right."

"Don't, pretty girl," Nico admonished. "Don't brush your feelings and needs away because you think we can't handle them or don't want them. We do."

She licked her lips nervously. "I don't . . . I'm finding it hard to believe this is actually happening."

"Believe it," Liam said firmly.

"You wanted me? Back then? Both of you?"

"Yep," Nico confirmed.

"It was a physical attraction. Or so I told myself. But that changed over time. We want you to be ours," Liam told her.

"How can you?"

Liam scowled, not liking the way she said that.

"I think it should be how could we not want you," Nico said firmly. This time, he was the one to grasp hold of her chin, turning her face up. "Why wouldn't we want you, Lottie? You're smart and kind. Gorgeous and sexy. Loyal and sweet."

"And completely fucking messed up."

"Lottie," they both scolded at the same time.

"You are not messed up," Nico told her firmly. "And talking about yourself like that isn't permitted."

She was gaping up at Nico in shock.

"As well as being bi, Nico is also a switch," Liam told her helpfully. "Wasn't sure until I saw him with you today whether he was going to want to dominate you as well. But I can see that he will. At least in some situations."

"Way to hit her with a whole lot of information at once, sweetie-bum," Nico said.

"Sweetie-bum?" she asked, staring at Nico.

"Liam loves cutesy nicknames," Nico told her.

"Nico obviously loves being denied pleasure," Liam muttered back.

"So, you're saying that both of you are . . . " She closed her eyes for a moment, rubbing at her head.

"Headache?" Nico asked.

"This is a lot," she admitted. "You guys telling me that you wanted me that first night you met me. That you still want me now, for some reason."

"Lottie," Liam growled. "Enough."

Her eyes shot open, her gaze going to his.

"So you're a Dom, right?" she asked.

"Yeah. Nico is my sub."

"I'm not a sub," she stated.

"How do you know?" Liam asked.

She licked her lips. "I couldn't go to a club or do a scene or have someone h-hurt me."

"Nobody is going to hurt you," Liam told her firmly.

"Everything we do is consensual, Lottie," Nico reassured her. "Nothing would happen that you didn't agree to. And being a sub isn't all about pain or going to clubs. There doesn't have to be any of that. In fact, we don't go to clubs anymore. We don't necessarily like to follow all the rules."

"I don't think I'd want you at a club anyway," Liam said. "Too many eyes on what belongs to me. It's bad enough when everyone starts sniffing around Nico, I know he could handle himself. But we'd spend all night just keeping people away from you."

"I don't belong to you," she said quietly. "Either of you. All of this . . . it's too much."

"You don't want us?" Liam asked. His gaze shot to Nico's, who looked worried.

"Don't want you? How could anyone not want the two of you? I know it's terrible to admit because I was with Michael at the time, but I felt that attraction too. The pull. I thought it was just because you were both so gorgeous. I mean, I couldn't have you. You were with each other. You were gay. I figured it was a safe fantasy."

"It's not wrong when your boyfriend was all over another woman," Nico told her. "Besides, I was flirting my ass off with you."

"I just thought that maybe you were like that with everyone."

"If he were, he'd never sit again," Liam said dryly.

Her eyes widened. "Do you mean that you'd . . . "

"Redden his ass, yep."

"And you agree with that?" she asked Nico.

"Oh, I'd make him work for it," Nico drawled. "I don't like to make things too easy for the lord and master."

"You like it? Him hurting you?"

Liam shared a look with Nico. They'd need to tread carefully. Lottie had known pain and force. While she hadn't been raped, that asshole who'd taken her had touched her, terrified her.

Liam didn't ever want her to look at him as though she thought he might harm her.

"I like to be dominated, Lottie."

"Do you ever swap roles?" she asked.

"No," Liam told her. "I'm not a switch."

"Liam is my Dom. He's also my husband, and I love him. Everything that happens between us is something I want. He knows that I like a bit of pain with my pleasure. That I enjoy when he takes charge. I make him work for it because that turns us both on. I like to push and know that he can control me. I can't do any of that without an emotional connection."

She blushed red. "I don't think I could ever do that. The thought of being tied up, of being hurt, it doesn't make me feel good."

"You make the rules here, baby," Liam told her. "I don't know exactly how much you know about BDSM . . . "

"A little. I overheard Jardin and Maddox talking once a while ago. Maddox is my cousin. I got curious and read some books. I like reading about it, and maybe before I was kidnapped, I might have enjoyed it. But not now."

"We get it," Nico told her. "And nobody will force you into anything, but you shouldn't let fear rob you of something you want."

"But I don't know if I would like it."

"And you won't know unless you try," Liam said. "There's no time frame, no pressure."

"For any of this," Nico added.

Liam frowned. Part of him wanted to demand that she be with them now. But he got that wasn't what was best for her.

But once he'd realized she was fucking lost and needed him and Nico to show her the way, then his patience was gone.

"And if I couldn't do any of that?"

"Then you wouldn't have to," Liam told her firmly. "If you're not interested in BDSM, then you don't have to be our sub."

But he was certain that she would like it. Would come to crave it. That she was a sub. But they would never force her. Ever.

She sucked in a breath. "And you both want me?"

"Yes," Nico told her. "We both want you."

She looked to Liam for reassurance.

"We do."

"It's not weird that I dated your brother?"

"For three months," Nico scoffed.

"We all know he didn't deserve you. He left you with us while he flirted with that woman. And I no longer call him family. My family is the man holding you on his lap. And you."

"You can't claim me as family. We barely know each other. If you'd really wanted me . . ."

Liam swore under his breath. Fuck. He should have known she wouldn't believe them. Because how could they have stayed away if they claimed to want her as much as they did.

"We were giving you time to heal," Nico explained.

Liam clenched his jaw. "I didn't think you'd want me. I'm rough, harsh, I have a lot of darkness inside me."

Nico and Lottie gaped at him.

Standing, he started to pace. "You were hurt. You were terrorized. It takes time to get over shit like that. Thought I was all wrong for you. Told myself I'd give you time. Ended up giving you too much time and messing it all up. Now you're hurting yourself. You still have panic attacks. Probably nightmares too. Staying away didn't make things better, if anything it made things worse because you doubt it when we tell you we want you. That we want you no matter what. No matter if you can't be our sub. No matter if you have issues. Issues that are not a fucking joking matter. So, this is what is going to happen."

"Oh, hell," Nico muttered.

"You disagree with me?" he barked at Nico.

Nico looked at him then down to Lottie. "Not the sentiment, but maybe the delivery."

"Suck it up. This is how it's got to be." He stared down at Lottie. "We want you, Lottie. You're ours. The only thing that's going to stop us from claiming you is if you say you don't want us. If you don't feel attracted to us, then tell us now and we walk away."

"And if I don't tell you that. Then what?"

"Then we stay. Then we prove to you that this can work. I'm likely too rough and dark for you. Maybe you'd be better off with just Nico. But I'm not giving either of you up, so yeah, you've got to suck it up too."

"She's not hesitating because she only wants me," Nico said.

Liam turned to her. Needing to hear it from her.

She was staring at him, her mouth slightly open.

"Doms have insecure moments too," Nico said to her. "Liam thinks you just want me because how could you want a beast like him?"

"Seriously?"

"Uh-huh," Nico replied.

"That's so stupid," she muttered.

"Yep. Doms have their stupid moments."

"Do you?"

"Me? No, never. I'm perfect." Nico winked at her.

"If you've both finished, I'd like an answer."

"Was there a question in there somewhere?" Lottie asked. "Because it seemed to me like you were demanding that I want you both, even though you seem think that you're not good enough for me. Not sure where you'd get that idea."

"You don't know everything about me. There are things I've done that aren't good. In fact, for most of my life, I've lived in the shadows. The only good thing I've ever done in my life is love Nico."

"Bullshit," Nico coughed into his fist.

"Got something to say, my husband?" Liam drawled.

He saw Lottie stiffen slightly.

"Marshmallow," Nico said, making Lottie relax and smile.

It was irritating not to know the joke, but if it helped ease her tension around him, then he could deal until he got it out of Nico.

"Liam, you're forgetting who my family is," Lottie said. "Do I love my brothers less because of the things they do? No."

"They've sheltered you," Liam pointed out. "They never let that stuff touch you."

"And you would?" she asked, sounding curious.

"Absolutely not," he said adamantly. He looked down at his fists, saw the blood dripping off them even though logically he knew it wasn't there. "I'm not good enough to touch you."

"Liam," she said softly, climbing from Nico's lap and moving toward him. "I'm not hesitant because I don't think you're good enough for me. Or that I don't feel an attraction toward you. Both of you." She placed her hands over his fists.

Liam's heart stopped at her words then her soft touch left him, and he felt the loss deep inside. She stepped back, her arms going around herself defensively as she stared from him to Nico. Her gaze was hungry. And he knew what she was going to say before the words came from her mouth.

"I'd like you both to leave now. And I think it would be better if you didn't return."

8

Nico sucked in a breath. He opened his mouth to tell her that they weren't going anywhere when Liam spoke.

"Why do you want us to leave? Are we scaring you?" he asked in the softest tone Nico had ever heard from him.

"Scaring me?" She shook her head. Then she paused, thinking it over. "Not because I worry you might hurt me physically."

"But you're scared of being emotionally hurt."

She nodded.

"All relationships are like that," Nico said to her. "There's always an element of risk, of needing to trust."

"And you think I should instantly trust you both?"

"We're not asking for that," Liam told her. "We're asking for time. For you to give us a chance."

And Nico knew how badly they'd both react if she couldn't give them that.

"I don't think I can do it."

Nico's stomach dropped. He felt like he was going to be ill. He'd known it wouldn't be easy to convince her of their feelings for her. But he thought they could bring her around.

"I don't think this is about trust, is it?" Liam queried. "Being vulnerable is hard. But if you got to know us, you'd realize that Nico and I are completely serious about you. I don't care for people, Charlotte. I have emotional attachment issues. I have some friends, like your brother. However, I could walk away from him today and not be concerned about it. The only reason I would care was because it would affect you. I only became friends with him because of you."

"But . . . but no, you knew him before you knew me."

"Did you meet me before? Did I come here? Did my name ever get mentioned much?"

"Well, no," she whispered. "But . . . "

"Before I met you, he was an acquaintance. After I met you, I built our connection. I wanted to be sure you lived in an environment I approved of. Especially after you were taken."

She sucked in a breath.

"I struggle to make connections. I struggle to give a fuck. You know who I do care about? Who I most definitely give a fuck about?"

"Nico."

"Of course. And you."

"This is crazy. Insane."

"Most people would say two men and a woman loving each other is insane," Nico pointed out.

"Do you have a problem with that?" Liam asked.

"You know I don't. I know that can work. Jardin has Carrick and Thea. My cousins share a woman. Where my cousins live, there are a lot of different sorts of relationships. There's one I know of with three men and one woman."

That sounded like a place they might want to visit.

"People are accepting of different sorts of relationships there," she explained.

"Do you have a problem with us being bi?" Nico asked.

"No. This just . . . you're failing to see the issue!"

"What is it, baby?" Liam asked in a low, silky croon. "What is the issue?"

"Me!"

"Because you were attacked?" Nico asked gently. "Because you struggle with leaving the house?"

"With hurting yourself?" Liam asked darkly.

"Because I have problems with it all! I'm a mess! I don't even know if I could have you kiss me, let alone have sex with you. Now, will you please just get out before I have to call the guards." She moved to her dresser and picked up her phone. "I'll do it. Please, go."

Nico sucked in a breath. Would she do that? Maybe she would if she thought she was doing it for them. To help them.

Fuck.

He waited for Liam to explode. Or to go all caveman on her. But instead, he simply watched her, his arms crossed over his chest.

"It's better this way," she cried when they didn't move. "Go find someone normal. Someone who can give you both what you need. Someone who isn't me."

"We've told you how we feel," Liam told her. "Those feelings don't just change simply because you say they should. Our feelings aren't so shallow that we can just turn them off. I'll never turn them off."

"Me either."

"Please."

Liam watched her worriedly.

"Liam, we can't just leave her," Nico whispered as he grew closer to the other man. Not only because he didn't want to, but if she was stressed and upset . . . he worried about what she might do to cope.

"We're upsetting her further by being here," Liam replied quietly.

"But she might hurt herself more."

"Fuck," Liam muttered. "Baby, we both know you're not calling security so put the phone down."

"I'll do it." Her knuckles were tight around her phone, and it nearly broke Nico's heart to see her like this.

"You won't," Liam told her. "Just like you're not going to hurt yourself any further."

"I don't want to."

"I know, baby. I know. It's a lot. And we haven't helped matters by piling all of this on you. It wasn't what we intended but we needed you to know that we care about you. Want you."

"We hate hearing you talk about yourself like that," Nico added. "You're not baggage or a burden."

"You're our everything. You're going to be our fucking queen," Liam told her.

"I can't."

"You can," Liam said with quiet assurance. "You just can't see it yet. But we can be patient. We can show you. We can be confident enough for us and you."

"I'm not special."

"You are," Nico told her. "We'll make you see that."

"You need to go." But there was no conviction in her voice, and she slumped on the bed.

"We're not going," Liam told her. "We're not leaving you."

"Tonight?"

"Ever."

"What if I opened myself up and said yes to all this. What happens when you decide you've had enough of me?"

"What if the reverse happens?" Liam asked. "What if I open myself up to you, and then you decide I'm too much for you?"

"That wouldn't happen."

"It might. But I can tell you now, I wouldn't let you walk away. I keep what's mine. And you're mine, Charlotte Malone. Just like Nico is. The two of you are fucking mine."

She sucked in a deep breath, then let it out slowly. Putting her phone down, she rubbed at her temples.

"Let us take care of you, Lottie? Please?" Nico asked. "I get this is overwhelming and way too much after the day you had. But please, just give us this small moment to show you how we feel."

She looked so exhausted and lost as she sat there, staring at them. "I want to be alone."

"Do you?" Liam asked. "Or have you been alone for too long?"

"I have my brothers."

"Who you haven't confided in. They don't know about this, do they? About the fact that you've started hurting yourself again."

"It was just twice," she whispered.

"Don't lie to us or yourself," Liam said sternly. "If we hadn't arrived when we did, what would you have done? Cut yourself?"

This was killing him. Thank fuck he'd listened to his gut. The thought of her harming herself made him want to puke.

"We can't leave her," Nico said.

"You don't trust me. See? There's no hope."

"Trust is something that has to be earned on both sides," Liam said. "Give us a chance to show you that you can trust us."

"How?"

"By spending time with us. That's the way trust is built, isn't it?"

"I suppose so."

"Here's what's going to happen. Nico is going to put our numbers into your phone. The minute you think about harming yourself, you're going to call one of us. I don't care what else is going on, you're going to call us."

"And if I don't?"

"Then there's going to be consequences," he said sternly.

"You'd hurt me?"

"Fuck, you best figure out quickly that I would never hurt you because it kills me a bit inside that you think that's a possibility."

She closed her eyes, looking like she was in pain.

"Never, baby girl. Understand me?" Liam pressed.

"But you hurt Nico, with his permission," she added hastily.

"Yes, because it's what he likes. What he enjoys. I don't want an unwilling partner. That's abuse. The minute he tells me he no longer wants that, then it's off the table."

"Just like that?"

"Yes."

Nico raised an eyebrow. Liam turned to look at him, including them both in his stare. "Nothing means more to me than the two of you, got it?"

"Sometimes, I push Liam into taking charge because it helps me let go for a while. I tend to hide things that upset me behind jokes and laughter. Liam gives me a space where I don't have to think. I trust him. And if something went too far, then he'll always listen to my safeword."

"I still don't know."

"It's not all bondage and pain. Of course, if you want to mix in some spanking and role play, then Liam won't say no. His favorite is where he's the uptight, grouchy boss and I'm the naughty employee who comes to work late."

"Nico," Liam groaned.

Lottie looked shocked, then she actually smiled. "You're joking."

"He is," Liam told her.

"I'm not."

"Personally, I've always wanted to try the butler and the maid, but I don't have the legs to pull off a maid's uniform."

"Dear Lord," Liam moaned. "He's making this shit up, baby."

Nico shook his head, eyes wide. "Just think of the possibilities.

He could be a builder. Just imagine him, bending over, showing you his builder's crack—"

Liam slammed his hand over Nico's mouth. "I'll be doing something to your crack soon."

Lottie just watched them and for a moment, he thought they might have gone too far. He didn't want her scared of Liam. But her eyes started to twinkle. "You know, I've always thought that Liam would make a better farmer."

"Yeah, I can see that. Him out, milking the cows," Nico said after he'd pulled Liam's hand away from his mouth.

"Tending the crops."

"Oh, he'd be aces at that. Potato growing is in his blood."

"You're both in trouble." Liam pointed a finger at them both while happiness swum through Nico's veins.

He'd always known she'd fit in. She wouldn't let Liam take himself too seriously. Wouldn't let Nico get too carried away.

Nico handed over her phone. "Our numbers are in there."

She nodded, looking a bit sad. Because she wanted them to stay?

"Lottie, if you hurt yourself again, then I'm going to have to tell Regent," Liam warned.

Her eyes widened. "You wouldn't."

He wouldn't. He couldn't. Nico stared over at Liam. That would break any sort of trust between them.

"Baby, you can't keep doing this. It has to stop. And I'll do whatever it takes to help you. Even if it means you hate me."

Fuck.

Damn bastard was right. They would sacrifice their own happiness for her. To keep her healthy. Safe.

"I don't want you to say anything," she told them.

"Then you know what to do."

"You're blackmailing me." She shot Liam an angry look.

"I'm keeping you safe. You think I can go back to my room and sleep, wondering if you're down here and all right? I can't. I need you to do this."

She nodded tiredly. "Okay."

"Your promise."

"I promise," she whispered.

"Good girl." He turned to Nico. "It's late and Lottie needs some sleep. Let's clean up the bathroom."

"You don't need to do that," she said.

"We do," Liam said firmly.

Nico knew he likely had two reasons for insisting on helping. To get it cleaned up so she didn't waste time doing it when she should be sleeping. And to ensure there was nothing in there that she could use to hurt herself.

He hated that they had to do that.

Without listening to her protests, they got to work tidying up the bathroom. There was nothing that he could see her using to hurt herself, but it wasn't like she couldn't go searching in another bathroom or the kitchen anyway.

Either she was watched all the time, or she was trusted to keep her word.

By the time they'd cleaned up, she was swaying on her feet clearly exhausted.

"Time for you to go to bed." Liam moved to her and held out his hand.

Nico sucked in a breath. Liam could be affectionate. But generally, only in private and pretty rarely. He didn't hug a lot or kiss all that often.

Please don't reject him.

Lottie reached out and slipped her hand into Liam's. Nico let out a breath as he walked out of the bathroom towards the bed.

"I still don't think it will work, Liam," she whispered.

"It will work, pretty girl," Nico told her as he drew back the blankets. They were soft. And they smelled like her. Sweet and light.

Shit. Wrong time for his dick to get hard.

"We're going to stay with you until you fall sleep," Liam told her.

Nico tensed, wondering if that would freak her out. But she simply nodded. Probably too tired to argue. And maybe she trusted them more than she thought she did.

"Is your head still hurting?" Nico asked her.

"A bit."

"Would it help if I rubbed it?"

She stared at him, and he prepared himself for her to say no.

"Okay," she whispered.

He moved to the other side of the bed and sat before gently massaging her scalp.

A small noise of pleasure escaped her, making his dick harden.

Fuck.

Liam gave him a knowing look. But this was partially that bastard's fault.

"Will you be leaving tomorrow?" she suddenly asked.

"No, baby. I told you. We're not going anywhere."

"But if Regent doesn't want you here . . ."

"You let me worry about that," Liam told her. "You need it, I'll take over worrying about everything. All you have to do is tell me."

"Don't need you to take over my life," she murmured. "I need to find a way to take control. To find a purpose."

"We can help with that too," Nico reassured her. "That's what a relationship is, leaning on one another, supporting each other. I was lost for a long time too. I get what it feels like."

"Seems like everyone else has it together and I'm just floundering."

"Then let us help," Liam told her. "You're not supposed to do everything alone, Lottie. We're here. And we're not going anywhere."

"Until you get sick of me . . . can't let any man . . . touch . . . me . . ."

Nico's gaze hit Liam's, but the other man just shook his head. Nico started singing to her as he massaged and soon, she was asleep.

Liam stepped back, gesturing to Nico. He climbed off the bed. He was slightly surprised that she'd gone to sleep so easily when she had issues sleeping. But he was grateful she had. She desperately needed sleep.

"I don't think we should leave her, Liam," he said.

Liam ran a hand over his face. "We have to show her that we trust her."

"It's not about trust . . . "

Liam shot him a look. Okay, that was exactly what it was about. But how could he sleep while worrying about her?

"We have to do this. If we don't, we start off with mistrust. It won't work."

"Fuck. Fuck. I hate this. Maybe you had the right idea. We should just take her. I can't stand the idea of her . . ." he trailed off, holding in a sob. "She was hurting, and we didn't fucking know."

Liam wrapped a hand around the back of his neck, holding onto him with a firm grip, helping him to pull himself together. When he felt he was unraveling, Liam always knew how to bring him back.

Liam drew him forward. Nico wasn't much shorter than Liam, but people tended to think Liam was much taller because of his bulk.

"Listen to me. I'm not going to let anything happen to her. I promise."

"Liam, you can't promise that."

"I fucking can."

They both stilled as she rolled over. Liam nodded toward the door. Nico didn't want to go. But he knew if he stayed, they might wake her.

Liam opened the door and they slid out into the hall. Nico wondered if Regent was downstairs. Considering how loud Liam had been, he was guessing that was the case. They managed to make it to their room where he slumped back on the bed. Liam straddled him, looking down at him. "What is it?"

"What if she hurts herself?" he asked. "Then you'll tell Regent and she'll push us away."

"I'm not going to tell him."

Nico stared up at Liam who gave him an "are you insane" look.

"You said you would."

"Of course, I did. Because it's obvious she doesn't want him to know. You think I wanted to leave her? I'm thinking about ways I can sneak fucking cameras into her bedroom and bathroom."

"Liam, you can't. If she ever found out, she'd never forgive you."

Liam grunted. "I find out she's hurt herself again and that's what'll happen. But I guess I'll give her a chance."

He didn't look happy about that.

"So, you wouldn't tell Regent?"

"That fucker had his chance to take care of her. To help her. No more chances for him. You've got a problem with me not telling him?"

"Fuck, no. I don't want her taken away from us. She's ours."

"Which means we do whatever we need to in order to help her."

"Including lie?" He felt uneasy about it. That wasn't usually Liam's way.

Liam sighed and lay back on the bed next to him, his arm over his face. "It's not a lie."

"But you just said . . . "

"I'd tell him if I needed to. If it came down to her mental health or having her, I'd choose her health every time. I just don't think it's the best move."

"He'll fucking kill us if he ever finds out."

Liam snorted. "I'm not worried about Regent Malone. Besides, if we play this right then he won't find out. Or by the time he does, she'll be ours. I'm certain that once Lottie gives herself to someone, she'll be all in. Her brother won't have a chance to attempt to come between us."

Nico hoped that was true. "So, what now?"

"Now, we show her that we are meant to be with her. That all those stupid statements she made about herself were ridiculous and not true. We show her that she's ours. And we make sure she never wants to be without us."

"And how do we do that?"

Liam's face turned thoughtful. "We might have to get strict with her."

Nico gave him a doubtful look. "Are you sure that's wise? I mean you . . . "

"I what?" Liam raised an eyebrow.

"You can be intimidating. You might scare her."

Liam snorted. "Lottie is stronger than she appears to be. How does everyone treat her?"

"Like she's fragile."

"And how is that working out?"

Nico frowned. "That doesn't mean that being hard with her will be any better. That could backfire."

"I'm not going to be harsh. I'm just thinking the sooner we lay down some rules and teach her that there are consequences for breaking them, the better."

"I don't know, Liam. I don't think she's ever going to be our sub."

"Then she's not. But there are rules in any sort of relationship.

Even living here with her brothers, there are rules she has to follow. Just might be our rules for her are slightly different. And so are our punishments."

"I doubt she's ever been punished before."

"Oh, I can guarantee she hasn't," Liam replied. "She's been spoiled and coddled all her life."

"There's something wrong with that?" Nico asked.

"Not at all. And I intend to continue doing that."

"You? Spoil and coddle someone? Do you know how?"

"Do I not spoil and coddle you?" Liam asked, leaning in to nip at Nico's neck.

His heart sped up. "Fuck, no. I'd kick your ass if you did."

"Doesn't mean I can't learn how. With Lottie, I feel different. Not more. Just different."

Nico got Liam's confusion. He wasn't used to caring about people. It had been hard for him to open up with Nico, so letting Lottie in wasn't easy. In his more bitter moments, he'd wondered if Liam made the early call not to pursue any feelings for her because it was easier for him. Not because of her traumatized state.

"Lottie feels out of control. When those feelings get too much, that's when she likely hurts herself. Or thinks about it. She worries about going out into the world because there's so much unknown. We need to help her find some control. We can help her."

There was a gleam of knowledge in Liam's face. Nico knew he was talking from experience.

"My world was out of control when I started boxing. Fighting gave me the rush I was looking for."

"And you nearly killed yourself doing it."

Liam nodded. "But I learned ways of coping over the years. Of honing my control. You helped with that. Showed me how to feel. And that I could be in control without being a complete jerk."

"Yeah, I don't know about that. You're still kind of a jerk."

"You know, I'm sure I could send one of Regent's guys out for an extra-large butt plug and some chili lube."

Nico's eyes widened. "That won't be necessary."

"Hmm. We'll see. I'm going to need to get some things if we're going to be here a while."

"How long can we possibly stay? Regent is going to get suspicious. And what about work?"

Liam owned several gyms, juice bars and restaurants. Everything was now legitimate and he had managers, but there were still things he had to do.

"I can work from here for a while. And I've got a plan for keeping Regent from suspecting anything."

Nico rolled his eyes. He should have known. Liam always had a plan.

"But it might involve me being away, so you're going to have to watch Lottie. And work on convincing her that we really do want her. That this could work."

"What are you going to do?" Nico asked.

"I'm going to find Regent's rat."

"How?"

"I'll try to be seen with Regent. People aren't really used to seeing us together. I'm thinking it will create some rumors. Especially if someone pushes the idea that I'm looking for a business partner."

"But you're completely legit now."

"Doesn't mean that I'm going to stay that way. Many of them do know who my grandfather is."

"Oh, fuck, he'll kill us."

"No, he won't. I'm not going to use his name. But stir the pot and see what floats to the top."

"This is a bad idea."

"You don't trust me," Liam whispered. "Where's the faith?"

His voice had gone dark. He wrapped his hand around the base of Nico's neck.

Oh. Fuck.

He moved his hand to Liam's cock, which was pressing against his black pants. He loved the feel of the other man over him, pushing him against the bed. That threat of his hand against his neck.

A shiver ran through him.

"It could be dangerous."

Liam's gaze narrowed, then he pulled up Nico's T-shirt, baring his chest. Liam twisted one of his nipples, making him groan.

"I can take care of myself," Liam told him, leaning down to lightly lick at the abused nipple. He moved to the other one, biting down.

Nico moaned. Fuck, fuck, fuck.

His dick was so hard, his balls full. He needed to come.

"Liam," he groaned.

"You're going to apologize for doubting me."

"I've never doubted you. Ever."

Satisfaction filled Liam's face. "You're still going to have to pay." Liam moved off him. "Get undressed."

Nico hastily climbed off the bed and stripped while Liam took his time removing his clothes.

When Nico was finished, Liam strode over to him and grabbed his dick. Hard. "And here I was thinking about letting you come tonight."

He moaned at that. "Please let me come."

"Poor boy. These are full, aren't they?" Liam dropped his hand to Nico's balls, playing with them. "Not being allowed to come isn't fun, is it?"

"No." Nico dropped his head back, panting through the agonizing pleasure as Liam massaged his balls then jacked his cock.

"Fuck, please, Liam. I need to come."

Liam leaned in and bit the spot where Nico's neck and shoulder met. "Then you shouldn't have disobeyed me today, right? Or at the very least, you should have called me."

"I'm sorry."

Liam pointed at the floor. "Knees."

Nico dropped to his knees and waited.

"Suck."

Yeah, he could do that. He fucking loved doing that. What he'd really love, though, is if he could touch himself at the same time.

Hmm. Maybe he could. It's not like Liam would notice.

Nico dropped one hand to his cock, running it up and down the shaft.

Oh. Hell. It wouldn't take him much to come. He knew it. Could feel it.

Then Liam took a step back, sliding his cock from Nico's mouth.

No. Not fair.

But when he glanced up to tell Liam he was being a cruel bastard, he noted that the other man had his arms crossed.

Uh-oh.

"Were you given permission to touch yourself?" Liam asked coldly.

Nico glanced down at himself. "Well, now, how did that hand get there?"

"Maybe because you put it there. Without asking first. You're just adding to your punishment." Turning, he pointed at the bed. "Hands and knees."

Fuck. Fuck.

But Nico got up and positioned himself on the bed.

"Take hold of the rungs of the headboard and don't let go," Liam commanded.

What was he doing?

Then Nico heard a swishing noise. Turning his head, he saw Liam pulling his belt from the loops of his pants.

Fuck. Yes.

He could barely stop himself from wiggling his ass and begging to feel the touch of the leather against his bare cheeks. Knowing Liam, that would just spur him on to do the exact opposite of what Nico wanted just to be a jerk.

Fucker was lucky Nico loved him.

"I get the feeling you're eager for this," Liam murmured. "Maybe I should put the belt away. Get one of Regent's guys to grab that plug and lube."

"No, Liam. Please." It wasn't the plug that made him object and Liam knew it. But the idea of sending someone out to get it, that was the issue. And he knew Liam wouldn't actually do it, knowing that Nico would hate it. Liam just liked to torture him a little with the possibility.

He could be a real sadist sometimes.

"Let's see how you feel after a few licks." The belt swung against his ass and Nico moaned as his skin heated.

Felt so damn good. Christ. He couldn't remember how long had it been since Liam had done this.

"Have I neglected you, Nico?"

"Never, Liam."

Another lick of the belt. Warmth erupting across his ass. Fuck. Fuck.

"I'm not so sure."

Two in quick succession. Nico dropped his head, breathing through the sting. It moved through his blood, his dick so firm it hurt.

Then Liam laid three more smacks of the belt across his ass, and he cried out, grateful they were on their own on this floor. The last thing he needed was someone coming to check on the noise.

"You've got the most gorgeous ass, my boy," Liam told him,

running his hand over his heated cheeks. "Firm and hard. And red."

A kiss was pressed to one cheek then the other. "Where's the lube?"

"Suitcase. Front pocket."

Liam returned quickly, kneeling on the bed behind him. "Lean down."

Nico rested his head and arms on the mattress, pressing his butt up into the air.

"That's it," Liam murmured. He parted Nico's cheeks to push two lubed fingers deep into his ass.

Nico bit his lip, his breath coming in harsher pants as Liam thrust back and forth.

"You're going to learn to obey me," Liam told him as he removed his fingers then moved in close behind him. The head of his cock pushed against Nico's back hole.

He let out a deep breath as Liam pushed into his ass. He was breathing heavily as Liam drove this thick dick inside him. His muscles stretched, there was a slight tinge of pain, but it just added to the pleasure rushing through his body.

"You'll watch her while I'm not around. Can you reinforce the rules if you have to?"

Nico always took the submissive role with Liam, but he knew that things were different with Lottie.

"Of course, I can."

"You can be strict with her if she disobeys? If she puts herself down or places herself in trouble?" Liam nibbled at his neck, making it harder for him to think.

"I can. She comes first. I'll protect her. Take care of her."

"Good boy. We'll get our girl, Nico. I promise."

Liam pulled back and drove forward. He slammed into him. Nico loved being taken. But he also needed to come. So badly.

"Liam, please," he begged.

"What do you need?" Liam murmured.

"To come. Please."

"Hmm. I'm not sure you're desperate enough."

"I am. I promise."

Liam reached around to tug at Nico's cock. "So hard. I bet it hurts."

"It does. It really does."

"But I'm not sure you've learned your lesson."

"I have. I have. I'll be good. I promise. Just please."

"Put your hand around your dick," Liam told him. "You're going to jack yourself off while I fuck you. You're not to come until I give permission, though. Can you do that?"

"Yes. Yes."

He'd have likely said anything right in that moment to come and he wasn't ashamed of that fact.

Slowly, he moved his hand up and down the shaft. Last thing he wanted was to come too soon. Then he'd definitely find himself in a world of trouble.

Liam grabbed him around the hips, driving himself in and out of Nico's ass. Fuck. He was going to kill him.

"Move your hand faster," Liam commanded. "You feel so damn good, Nico. Your ass is sucking on me. It's so hot and tight. Shit. Keep moving your hand. You stop and you don't get to come."

Then he suddenly hit that angle just right, and Nico found himself so close to the edge he was hanging on by a nail. It wasn't going to take much to tip him over.

"That's it. Fuck." Liam moaned as he came and Nico found himself pausing, reveling in the feeling of Liam letting go.

He was always so controlled that Nico loved it when he came.

"Don't you stop," Liam commanded, sliding out of his ass. He smacked his hand down on one cheek then the other. "Keep moving that hand on your dick."

His hand landed over and over as Nico ran his hand up and

down his cock. His ass was burning, his balls so tight and full it was painful, yet he couldn't stop, didn't want to stop.

"Come, my Nico. Come nice and hard. Let me hear you."

He couldn't stop the cry that built up inside him, exploding out as he came, ropes of cum landing on the bed and over his hand. He slumped down, not caring about the mess, his breath coming in deep, fast gasps as Liam ran a hand up and down his ass.

"Good boy. That's it. I bet that feels better now, doesn't it?"

"My balls feel better, can't say the same about my ass."

"Every time you try to sit tomorrow, you'll be thinking about me."

"I'm always thinking about you." Except when he thought about her. Lottie. "You really think we can do this?"

"Trust me. I have this."

9

Liam sat down at the breakfast table the following morning at the opposite end from Regent. Nico sat next to him.

Regent looked up briefly. "You both slept well?"

"We did." Liam glanced at his watch. It was eight. If Lottie was still sleeping, he didn't want to wake her up, but he also didn't want her thinking it was okay to keep skipping meals.

This was tricky. Generally, he was used to taking what he wanted, the consequences be damned.

This required finesse. Something he wasn't good at.

The maid quickly took their breakfast orders. No breakfast buffet today.

"Are you both headed home today?"

Liam had to grin. Regent was always so stiff and formal, but he also had no problem letting anyone know exactly what he wanted.

"Actually, I wanted to talk to you about that. After breakfast."

Regent eyed him. "All right."

"Where is Lottie?" Liam asked. "Is she all right after yesterday?"

"She'll be fine," Regent said. "You don't need to worry about her. That's my job."

Liam held back a retort then he pulled out his phone while the maid returned with Regent's food.

Liam: *Breakfast time.*

He sent the text off to Lottie. He thought it was probably best that she knew his expectations for her early on.

Sipping from his coffee, he glanced over at Nico, who looked worried. There was a buzz of a reply.

Lottie: *I'm not hungry. Thank you.*

Not hungry? She was skin and bones. It didn't matter if she was hungry or not, she needed to eat for her health. Liam took a sip of coffee, thinking about his next move.

Liam: *I still want you to eat some breakfast. Come downstairs.*

He probably should have added a please. But he wasn't exactly a please sort of guy.

Lottie: *You realise you're not the boss of me.*

Liam: *Ah, so that's where we're going wrong.*

. . .

There was nothing for a moment. He looked over at Nico and winked. Regent was ignoring them both, but that suited Liam's needs for the moment.

Another buzz in his hand.

Lottie: *Wrong?*

Liam: *There's obviously been a miscommunication.*

Lottie: *Because you think you're the boss of me?*

Liam: *Because I am most definitely the boss of you.*

Lottie: *You're delirious.*

Liam: *You're beautiful. Now get your gorgeous butt downstairs for breakfast.*

He left off the or else. He'd wait for her to ask.

Lottie: *Or what?*

Liam: *Or I come upstairs and carry you down.*

A few minutes of nothing. Okay, seemed he was going to have to make good on his threat. Liam never threatened something without following through.

"Where are you going?" Nico asked.

"Retrieving a package."

"Oh, shit. You're going to get murdered." Nico shot a wary look at Regent.

"You're forgetting who I am."

"Yeah, but we're in his house," Nico whispered just as another text came through.

. . .

Lottie: *You wouldn't dare.*

Liam: *Do you really want to find out?*

Lottie: *Grr. Fine. I'm coming. Do not come get me.*

Liam just smiled. First step taken.

The damn arrogance of the man.

Does he seriously think he gets to order me around?

She didn't want breakfast. She'd only just woken up. Which was actually a miracle in itself. Last night was the best sleep she could remember having in forever. Maybe it was Nico's magical voice. She could remember him crooning to her. The man was so damn sexy.

And then there was Liam. She didn't understand what was going on with him. It was like something had snapped inside him.

His sanity. Whatever bit he'd had had obviously gone. Because there was no way that anything could happen between them. Between her and them.

Perhaps they just wanted her because she was someone they couldn't have. Regent would throw a fit if he found out that Liam and Nico had been in her room last night. She couldn't ever tell him that.

Not if she wanted Liam and Nico to live.

And she did. Because as much as she shouldn't want them, she did.

She couldn't believe they wanted a third. That they thought she could be part of their relationship, it was both ludicrous and . . .

Amazing.

Wonderful.

Insane.

She reached the door to the dining room and took a deep breath. Meals had always been such a formal affair in this house, even when their parents were alive. There was no eating a plate of food while watching TV or . . . or going on a picnic like she'd attempted to do with Nico yesterday.

Before Ace had gotten hurt, she'd been having fun.

What if she could be with them? What if it wasn't such a crazy idea? What if they actually wanted her?

She was so sick of hiding. Of not having a life.

What if she said yes to dating them? What was the worst that could happen?

They could break my heart.

But she couldn't really be worse off than she was. At least she would have tried. And Lottie was so damn sick of dog paddling just to keep her head above the water but never getting any closer to the shore.

Suddenly, the door opened, and she shot forward. Two large hands grabbed her around her upper arms.

"Whoa there, you okay?"

She gasped, glancing up at Liam. He gave her a concerned look.

"Um, yes, thank you."

"Get your hands off her!" Regent demanded, moving up behind Liam.

She winced at the cold tone in his voice.

"Would you rather I let her fall over?" Liam asked.

"Let her go now," Regent demanded.

Liam winked, then slowly let her go. He stepped to her side then leaned in. "Nice timing, baby. I was just coming to get you."

A shiver ran through her as he moved away to take a seat at the table.

"Darling? You okay?" Regent reached out to touch her gently, running his hand lightly over her arm. "He didn't hurt you, did he?"

She gave him a shocked look. "No, of course not. Liam wouldn't hurt me."

"Your lack of trust is wounding."

She glanced over to see Liam had his hand on his chest. Her lips twitched. Nico was always the dramatic one, she hadn't actually realized Liam had much of a sense of humor. Seems she was wrong.

But she wasn't entirely sure it was a good thing he was showing it now. He seemed to be enjoying winding Regent up way too much.

Mind you, it was good for her oldest brother to be challenged. Not many people did.

Regent was now scowling at Liam. "Are you sure you don't need to be leaving now?"

No! She didn't want them to go.

Shit! Just as well she hadn't said that out loud. Imagine trying to explain that to Regent. But from the smile on Nico's face and the arrogant smirk on Liam's, she had a feeling that she'd given herself away.

Schooling her face, she smiled up at Regent, sliding her hand around his arm. If there was something she knew, it was that Regent had a tough time denying her anything. Not that she ever asked for much. But she'd pretty much always gotten whatever she wanted.

Was she spoiled?

Yep, she was.

"I'm sure you didn't mean that the way it sounded, right?" she said to her oldest brother. "Liam has more business to attend to, doesn't he?"

"I've thought of a way to help with your problem, but if you're not interested . . ." Liam flicked some imaginary lint off his shirt.

He was wearing a white shirt with black pants. He looked as put together as always. Where Nico looked delightfully rumpled

"See?" she said. "He and Nico might as well stay here. It's no bother. Kind of nice to have company."

Regent scowled. "You want their company?"

"Nico really helped me yesterday." She knew that Regent would get the subtle reminder. They owed Nico a debt. Letting him and Liam stay would be a way to repay that debt.

"We'll talk about this soon," Regent said to Liam.

Liam nodded, looking unconcerned.

Regent's phone rang and he pulled it out, swearing. "It's Victor."

"It is? Is he coming home?" Her second oldest brother was the quietest of all of them. But he was also a good listener and had a big heart. Something most people didn't realize since he was built like a tank. Similar to Liam. Maybe that's why he didn't scare her as much as he likely should.

"I need to take this, darling. Why don't you go rest?"

She smothered a sigh. Seriously?

"Didn't she come in for breakfast?" Nico asked hastily before Liam could speak.

Liam had his bright blue gaze fixed on Regent. She could just imagine what he'd been about to say.

"You were coming in for breakfast?" Regent asked as his phone stopped ringing. He frowned down at it.

"Uh, yes, I was feeling a bit hungry," she lied.

"Really?" He looked so shocked and happy that her stomach twisted in sorrow. Apparently, her coming to eat was a cause for celebration.

She felt terrible.

His phone started ringing again.

"Go! Say hi to Vicky for me. Give him kisses." She grinned as Regent just gave her the look. As if he wouldn't be lowering himself to such a level where he gave kisses to anyone. She knew that would rile him up.

"Alice can bring you your meal upstairs," he said.

"Regent!" she scolded. "I'm fine eating here with Liam and Nico."

"We don't have cooties," Liam goaded.

Regent opened his mouth, but his phone started ringing again, interrupting him. With a groan, he pointed at Liam.

"I'll talk to you after breakfast." He slammed the door shut and she jumped.

"You okay, pretty girl?" Nico asked gently.

"Um, yes. I think so. I've never seen Regent slam a door before. He's upset with me."

"He's upset with *me*," Liam countered. "Not you."

She bit at her lip. It didn't feel like that. It felt like she was going against his wishes. "Regent has always taken care of me. I don't want to make him mad."

"Hey, look at me." Nico suddenly appeared in front of her, cupping her chin and raising her face. "There is no way you could ever make him mad. He adores and protects you, as any big brother should. But that shouldn't stop you from having a life of your own. You're allowed to be happy."

"I know that." She flushed. "I'm not saying Regent would stop me from being happy."

"If he's smothering you, dictating to you, then he's not giving you a chance to live," Liam told her from where he still sat at the end of the dining table.

"Oh, you mean like you dictated to me when you told me if I didn't come down to breakfast that you'd carry me down?" She turned, Nico's hand falling from her chin as she put her hand on her hip and glared at him.

Liam leaned back in his chair, looking like a King surveying his kingdom. She wished she had an ounce of his confidence. He didn't seem worried at all about Regent, or all the obstacles between them.

Liam simply saw a problem then decided how to tackle it. Yeah, she wished she was more like that.

You could be. You could be brave for once. Just try.

"That's different."

"Why? Because it's you dictating to me rather than Regent?" she challenged.

"Exactly. I like you like this."

"Like what?" she asked carefully.

"Full of sass. Standing up to me. This is how you should be all the time."

"Oh, you like someone who fights with you?"

"It's foreplay to him," Nico told her with a grin. "If you wanted to turn him off, you should have been all meek and agreeable."

"Great. You could have given me this advice earlier," she grumbled.

"Why? I don't want him turned off. I want you with us." Nico wrapped an arm around her waist, laying a kiss on the top of her head. As he did that, the door opened and one of the maids walked in.

She came to a stop as she saw her with Nico, her jaw dropping open. Then her gaze went to Liam and her mouth shut. She grew pale. She was scared of Liam.

He could be rather intimidating. But she realized with surprise that she wasn't scared of him. She didn't think she'd ever been. Just wary.

Alice just stood there, as though waiting for something.

"Are you here to take Lottie's breakfast request?" Nico asked gently.

"What? Oh, yes. Sorry. What will you have, miss?" she asked politely. Although her gaze still moved over the three of them, flitting back and forth.

Lottie frowned. It wasn't that weird, was it? Sure, Nico had his arm around her, but it wasn't like they were having an orgy at the table.

"Just coffee, please."

"Try again," Liam pressed.

She narrowed her gaze at him. Dictator.

"He won't let her leave until you order some food," Nico whispered to her. "And I'd rather she wasn't here, wouldn't you? She stares a lot."

Did she? She'd never noticed it before, but maybe he was right.

"I'll have some fruit and yogurt."

"And a boiled egg and toast," Liam added.

"Is that what you're having, Liam?" she asked sweetly as Alice left with a nod.

"No, I already have my breakfast coming, baby."

"I don't want the egg and toast."

He shrugged then stood and pulled out a chair. "Come. Sit."

Nico put a hand on the small of her back, reassuring her. "It's all right."

Lottie realized her newfound bravery was already cracking, and she straightened her shoulders, walking over to the chair to sit. He pushed her in, then grabbed the napkin, placing it on her lap. Her cheeks blushed at the gesture. It seemed so intimate for some reason. And not something she'd pictured him doing for her.

"How are your knuckles?"

"Much better." She showed them to him. They were only slightly swollen. If Regent asked, she'd just tell him that she bumped them.

"Did you sleep okay, pretty girl?" Nico asked her as he placed some coffee and creamer in front of her. She picked out her favorite hazelnut creamer and poured some in.

"Are you sure you want coffee with that creamer?" Liam asked with a grimace.

"I like it."

He just grunted and she turned to Nico. "I did. Thank you."

"Good. I was worried we'd upset you further. You didn't wake up?"

"No, I slept all the way through." She glanced down at her coffee. "I'm sorry for what happened last night. I'm sorry you had to deal with all my craziness."

"Look at me," Liam said to her firmly.

She let out a soft sigh. What was his obsession with her looking at him? But she raised her gaze. She knew what he was going to say. That they didn't mind. That she wasn't crazy. That she had no need to be sorry.

"Things have changed for you."

Um. What? That wasn't what she'd been expecting him to say.

"What do you mean, things have changed?"

The door opened and Alice walked in with his and Nico's meals. Nico had bacon and eggs, while Liam had muesli and yogurt as well as an omelet. How did they both eat so much?

Neither of them touched their food. Nico was looking slightly worried while Liam just stared at her, his elbow resting on the arm of the chair, his finger rubbing over the slight stubble on his chin. Had she ever seen him with stubble before? She didn't think so.

"You're not dealing with this alone any longer."

She bit her lip before realizing what she was doing. It wouldn't pay to let this man see she was nervous. But then, she doubted he missed anything.

"I don't need your help. I have my brothers."

"Who, we established last night, have no idea what's going on. Unless you're planning on telling Regent about last night."

A flash of panic filled her. She didn't want to tell Regent. Especially as something was going on with him. It wasn't like Victor to leave suddenly, and she hadn't seen Maxim in a while either. She wondered if there was something keeping them all busy.

"He doesn't need to know."

"And what about the bruises," Nico pointed out gently.

"They were from several weeks ago."

"They've been there for weeks?" Liam asked, straightening. "What? That's not normal. It can't be healthy."

Nico shook his head. "Could be something else. Anemia, maybe."

"Explains why she's so pale," Liam muttered. "Doesn't eat enough."

"Yeah, she probably needs to be checked by a doctor."

"Let's figure that in somehow."

"I am still here, you know," she told them. "And I don't need a doctor. I feel fine."

Liar.

Liam arched an eyebrow. "There'll be no lies between us, baby girl. Not even small ones. You tell us everything."

"This isn't going to work, you guys. I can't . . . I can't be what you need."

"Can't? Or are you too scared to try?" Liam challenged her. "Because those are two different things. Are you going to let what happened define you? Are you going to let it rule you? Or are you going to move on, find happiness, be everything you ever wanted to be despite it?"

Nico watched her worriedly. "Liam's right, Lottie. You can let something like that destroy you, or it can make you stronger."

"I'm not destroyed," she protested.

"No. Because you're so fucking brave. You're a fighter." Liam gave her a firm look.

"Now who's lying," she said dryly. "I'm no fighter. I'm a wimp."

"I won't have that." Reaching over, Liam took hold of her hand, squeezing lightly. "That's your first warning."

"Warning?"

"About putting yourself down," Nico told her. "Liam hates when you do that."

"It's a rule," Liam added. "And neither of you are to speak badly about yourself."

"Why would you put yourself down?" she asked Nico in shock. "You're perfect."

Nico snorted. "Hardly. I'm a slacker in a family of over-achievers."

A slacker? She didn't think so.

"Someone doesn't want to sit comfortably tomorrow," Liam drawled.

"I'm not sitting comfortably now." Nico glared back at him.

She had noticed him shifting around a lot on his seat.

"So, you'd think you would be mindful of what you said."

Her mind spun, trying to catch up with what they'd said. "Wait. Are you saying that. . ." She could feel herself growing red as she looked from Nico to Liam. "That, um Liam . . ."

"Spanked his ass?" Liam asked. "I sure did. He deserved some punishment."

"You hurt him?"

"It was consensual," Nico told her quickly. "Like we talked about last night. And that doesn't mean he'd do that with you. It's something I enjoy."

"What about now, though? Afterward . . . I mean, after . . ."

"After the pleasure?" Nico asked, with a return of his playful smile. But that faded quickly. "I like the reminder of what we did. It's also a way of me remembering what he feels for me."

Liam observed her carefully. She wanted to ask more but didn't want to insult either of them.

"You should both eat, it's growing cold," she said instead.

Wimp.

"Don't do that." Liam leaned forward.

"What?"

"Don't try to change the subject. Don't bury your needs. Ask what you wanted to ask."

"I don't want to upset you or make you think that I . . . I don't want to make you mad," she confessed.

"You think I'd get mad at you?" Liam asked.

"I don't know. I just don't want to make either of you mad."

"You know what would upset me?" Liam was back to rubbing at that stubble on his chin. She wondered what it would feel like against her skin. What it would feel like to have his arms around her.

She was certain she'd feel safe. Like nothing could touch her.

"What?"

"If you needed something and didn't ask for it. If you did something to endanger yourself. If something happened to you that I could have prevented. That would upset me. Questions about our relationship, they don't upset me. In fact, I want them."

"You do?"

"I do."

"Nico?" she asked. She didn't want Liam talking for him.

"Me too."

She pondered that as she stared at their food. "Why aren't you eating?"

"We don't eat until you do," Liam told her simply. "Unless you want some of my omelet?" He cut a piece off and then held it out to her. "Open."

"Oh, no, I didn't mean I wanted any," she told him.

"Open. Have some."

"Best just give in to him," Nico advised.

"Does he always get what he wants?" she asked, raising an eyebrow.

"Pretty much. That's why he's so arrogant."

She snorted then covered her mouth at the uncultured noise.

"Maybe he should be challenged a bit more often. We don't want his head getting too big."

"Yeah, it's already pretty large," Nico agreed. "Getting his way all the time isn't good for him."

"No. I agree."

Liam sighed. "If the two of you are finished? Lottie, eat."

She took the forkful of omelet without really thinking. That was pretty good, if a bit cold.

"What did you want to ask, Lottie?" Nico asked her.

"I just . . . well, you obviously trust Liam not to take things too far. How did you develop that trust?"

"Time," Nico told her. "I got to know him. Fell in love with him. And I know he'd cut off his right arm before he'd harm me."

"But we also have safeguards," Liam told her before feeding her another bite of omelet.

The door opened as he finished feeding her the bite, and Alice walked in. She didn't look at them as she served Lottie her breakfast. Maybe she'd decided she'd been rude earlier when she'd gawked.

"Is there anything else?" she asked after setting down Lottie's food.

"No, you can leave us for a while now," Liam told her.

"Thank you," Nico added, rolling his eyes at Lottie, who nearly giggled.

"I constantly have to remind him to use manners."

"And I have to remind you not to be a smart ass," Liam growled back.

Nico just smiled. It was amazing for her to see the way they worked. Liam could snarl, growl, and threaten, but Nico never looked worried. In fact, he often seemed excited.

"What are the safeguards?" she asked, finding it easier to ask questions.

"Another bite first," Liam held out some more omelet.

"I have my breakfast now." But it looked unappetizing.

"Don't you know things taste better off someone else's plate?" Liam chided.

"They do, huh?"

"Yep. Open."

She took the offered bite.

"Now, swallow."

Nico made a strange noise as she chewed and swallowed. "Are you feeling all right, Nico?"

"Yes, Nico," Liam drawled. "Are you feeling all right?"

"Yes. Just remembered something."

"In our case, safeguards like a safeword that Nico can say at any time. Just in case something happens. He gets a cramp, say, and I don't notice."

"Like that would happen," Nico added. "He notices everything, Lottie. Even when you don't want him to."

"You mean like when you're driving too fast and scratch your car against a post?" Liam asked, feeding her another bite. "Or when you attempt to hide another speeding ticket? Oh, or when you destroy your car and try to buy another to replace it without telling me?"

"Nico!" she said, shocked. A bark of laughter leaving her. "You did all those things?"

"I am innocent until proven guilty."

"You're guilty," Liam said. "And you know it."

"What can I say? I like to drive fast. I live wild."

"Not anymore, you don't," Liam said to him sternly. "You used to live wild, now you have rules to keep you safe."

"Rules," Nico sighed, waving his hand in the air. "Liam loves rules and order."

"They keep you safe. I don't want anything to happen to you."

"That's so sweet," she whispered.

"Sweet?" Nico spat out. "Liam?"

"I can be sweet," Liam agreed with her while Nico just stared at him.

"You can?" Nico asked.

Liam ignored him. "It's hard trying to keep Nico safe sometimes. I could use some help."

"Really? What sort of help?" she asked.

"Someone to watch him when I'm not around."

"Hey! I'm not a child," Nico protested. But there was something in his gaze when he looked at Liam.

"He's a daredevil, Lottie, I won't lie. He gave me all the gray hairs I have."

"You don't have any gray hairs," Lottie pointed out.

"But if I did, they'd all be from him."

She had to smile.

"Don't listen to him, Lottie. I'm nothing like that. If anyone worries over anyone, it's me worrying over him."

"You two are such a sweet old married couple," she told them.

"Old?" they both said at the same time, looking shocked.

She started giggling.

"She's a brat," Nico said to Liam.

"Undoubtedly," Liam agreed.

"Good thing we love brats," Nico added.

"Isn't it."

She sobered quickly. "I still don't see how this would work. I can't . . . I'm not sure I could ever let you touch me. Either of you."

"You seem fine with us touching you so far," Liam pointed out.

"That's not the sort of touch I was meaning."

"We'd go as fast or as slow as you needed, Lottie," Nico reassured her. "You'd be in charge."

"Of that part," she clarified.

"Of that part," Liam agreed. "Safety and health are my areas. And, to be frank, you need some help with those."

She couldn't deny that. She licked her lips. "What about my

brothers? They're not going to want me to get involved with you both."

"Let us take care of them," Liam reassured her.

But that didn't seem fair. They were her brothers. It wasn't like they'd hurt her. But they might do their best to stop her from getting involved with Nico and Liam.

"You don't even live here. If we tell them and Regent kicks you both out . . . I'm not ready to leave the house. I can't . . . I . . . " Panic suffused her. She wanted to be stronger. To be ready for all of this. To confidently walk out that door and not worry that she was going to lose her mind in public. But she just couldn't.

"Breathe, Lottie. Just breathe," Liam's voice was steady. His words penetrated the haze of her panic. He touched her hands with his, and rather than shy away, she latched on.

"That's it, we're here. You're safe," Nico murmured in a softer voice. More cajoling. "Breathe for us, pretty girl."

"One deep breath in then out. In again. Out." Liam's voice was commanding, firm.

She started following his orders without thinking. In. Out. In. Out.

"That's a good girl. There you are." Liam cupped her face between his warm, calloused hands, anchoring her in the present. While Nico practically wrapped himself around her, holding onto her tight, protecting her back.

She'd never felt safer. Even with Regent or one of her other brothers around, she'd never felt like this.

"S-sorry."

"Uh-uh." Liam shook his head. "You don't apologize for this."

"I don't?"

"Nope. I don't want to hear it, understand?"

"Are you sure this is what you both want? Maybe you should think about it. Because . . . because I don't know if I could stand it if you changed your mind further down the road. I just, I think . . . I need some space."

She quickly left.

~

Nico rose, ready to go after her, the urge beating inside him. He didn't want to be apart from her. Ever.

"Wait." Liam grabbed his arm, stilling him.

Nico gave him a worried look. "How are we going to convince her that we're not going to run at the first sign of trouble?"

"It'll take time. And that's what we need to buy ourselves. And look how far we've gotten in a short time."

"What do you mean? She just ran from us."

"She came to breakfast, though. She ate a few bites. And she talked to us, asked us questions about our relationship."

He let out a breath. "Right. She did do those things."

"I'm going to go talk to Regent. Tell him my plan. You go track her down, make sure our girl is all right."

"Okay."

Liam leaned in and kissed him, nipping at his lip. "Good boy."

"Fucking asshole," Nico muttered as the other man laughed. Sometimes, he was a jerk.

He walked with Liam to the study. "What if he says no?"

"This has become a real problem for him. He'll say yes."

Liam didn't seem nervous at all. But Nico felt nervous enough for both of them.

"And when he finds out we have feelings for his sister?"

"Uh, then we might want to make sure he's not armed and there are witnesses." Liam winked at him after saying that.

Definitely a jerk.

10

W*hy do I run when things become too much? Why do I just give up?*

She was so damn annoyed with herself. She flung the paint at the canvas, knowing she was making a mess of things. But this was the only way she knew to safely let her emotions out without . . . without hurting herself.

But she refused to do that anymore.

"Am I going to get to see this one?"

She turned with a gasp, finding Nico standing in the doorway to the solarium, leaning against the doorway.

"No." She should have known they'd come after her. But when they hadn't stopped her from running off, she'd been worried they'd given up on her already.

"One day, you'll show me," he said confidently.

"Don't be so sure."

"You mad at me, Lottie?" He walked in and sat on the sofa across from her. She stared down at him, examining her emotions.

Am I mad at him?

Yeah. She was.

"Yes."

"Why?" he asked, not looking upset, just interested.

"I . . . I don't know. It's stupid. I've got no reason to be mad at you."

He leaned forward, placing his hands on his thighs. "Not stupid if they're your feelings."

She shook her head, closing her eyes for a long moment. "Where's Liam?"

"Securing our stay here."

Her eyes popped open. "What? What do you mean? Don't you have to go home?"

It all felt too hard, too much. Them wanting to be with her. Too many obstacles.

Perhaps she was putting up all these obstacles to stop things before they even started. Looking for the negative instead of thinking about all the good things that could happen.

"I don't know when I became so negative," she whispered. "I never felt this way before. I could always bounce back from anything. Nothing bothered me. Maybe if I had more experience at being angry or upset or disappointed, I wouldn't be struggling so much."

"There's nothing wrong with being resilient and happy," he told her. "Or with being mad and upset. There's nothing wrong with emotions. What is a problem, is when you let them stop you from doing something that you want to do or love to do because you're letting them take over."

"I get what you're saying. But it's one thing to know it and another to do it."

"I get that, pretty girl. Probably more than you know. Come sit with me." He patted the sofa next to him, and she put her paintbrush down then checked that she didn't have wet paint all over her before she sat. He simply held out his hand, waiting for her to decide whether to take it.

Without thinking, she reached over and slipped her hand into his. His warmth filled her with a strength she wished she could always feel.

"I'm the youngest of five."

She nodded, failing to see what his point was but willing to take the change in subject.

"I have two brothers and two sisters, and do you know what they do?"

"No. What?"

"My oldest sister, Zoe, is a defense attorney. She made partner at her firm last year. She's the youngest partner there."

"Wow."

"Yep. Then there's Cy. He's a doctor. Orthopedic surgeon."

Okay, she was starting to see where he was going with this.

"My next brother, Theo, he's basically a genius. Works for some hush-hush think tank. Even we're not allowed to know what exactly he does."

"Wow."

"My next sister, Ana, she's a teacher."

"Well, that's something more normal, right?"

"Professor of physics at Harvard."

"Nico," she said quietly.

"Do you know what I've done with my life, pretty girl? Absolutely nothing. I'm ten years younger than Ana. A surprise baby. My oldest sister was already in college when I was born. I've never fit in with my family. I was unexpected and unwanted."

"I'm sure that's not true."

"I guess not. But it's what I told myself. I acted out. That's what led to me taking off with the jerk and his band of other jerks. I would do these crazy, dangerous things because I told myself that no one cared if I died. Wasn't until I met Liam that I saw how self-destructive I was."

"What sorts of dangerous things?"

"You name it, I've probably done it, pretty girl. Liam helped me. Cleaned me up. Made me see that I had worth."

"Are you telling me this because you think he can help me?"

"I know we both can."

"But you and Liam love each other. Where would I fit in?"

"Right in the middle," he told her. "You're the missing piece of us, Lottie. Neither of us are complete with you. We both love you."

She sucked in a breath. Should she believe him? But why would he lie? There were easier women they could be with. They had each other. They had no need for her.

Unless they really did want her. And the idea of that was both terrifying and exhilarating.

"I'm so lost, Nico. I'm stuck in nothingness. No way forward, no way back, scared to move."

"Do you want to move?" he asked gently.

"I didn't think I did. I thought I was happy where I was. Until I did this." She moved her hand and placed it over her bruised arm. "I was so angry at myself because I wanted to go. I wanted to see my cousin get married. I wanted to not be this mess. Poor Lottie, so traumatized that she can't even leave the house. Poor Lottie, who has to be sheltered and protected and babied."

"Hey. There's nothing wrong with needing to be protected."

"I'm not strong."

"You are strong, Lottie. You survived. You get up each day and you keep going. What happened to you was horrific, but you are here. Fighting."

"I'm not, though, Nico. That's the whole fucking point." She stood up and strode up and down the room. "I'm not fighting. I'm stagnant."

"What do you need to fight?" Liam asked from the doorway.

She gasped, turning.

"That was quick," Nico said. His voice was calm, but she saw a hint of worry on his face. "Did he not go for it?"

She didn't know how Liam would convince her brother that they should stay, but he had to, there was no way this would work if they couldn't. It wasn't like she could go with them.

She sucked in a breath.

Am I really going to do this?

Yeah. She was. She wanted it so badly she could taste it.

"He went for it."

"Went for what?" she asked. "What's going on?"

"I'll tell you in a moment." Liam moved in, shutting the door behind him and locking it. She stared at the door.

"It's only to keep others out," Nico soothed, coming up beside her. "Not to keep you in."

"Any time you need to leave, all you need to do is say so," Liam reassured her. "We would never want to do anything to scare you or make you not trust us. What do you need to help you fight?"

"To move out of that safe bubble?" Nico added.

"I don't know . . . I guess, I need to feel like I'm going to be safe."

"You need a safety net," Liam said with a surety that she wished she felt. "Someone to catch you if you start to fall. To be strong when you can't. But to stand back when you need to do something yourself. You want boundaries because then you'll feel safe. And consequences, because then you'll feel cared for. And freedom so that you can fly."

"And you both want to provide that? What would you get?"

"Besides seeing you happy and settled and not scared and a pale version of yourself?" Nico asked.

"Yes, besides that." Because she knew that Liam didn't do things out of the goodness of his heart.

"You, Lottie," Liam told her. "We get you."

Seduction, promise and threat. All rolled into one. She swayed slightly and Nico wrapped an arm around her waist. "Easy, pretty girl. We have you. We'll always have you. All you have to do is be brave and believe in yourself and us."

"Oh, that's all?" she said dryly.

Liam moved forward, standing in front of her. Maybe it should have felt threatening, but it simply made her body heat. Need flooded her.

"You learn to trust us, Lottie," Liam said, cupping her face. "And we will do all the rest. We'll have your back, always."

"You can't promise that."

"I damned well can. And I don't promise anything I can't deliver. Are you going to try this with us, Lottie?"

"You're not going anywhere? Because I'm not ready to . . . to leave yet."

"We're not going anywhere. Even if Regent made us leave, neither of us would give up," Liam told her.

"Not unless you wanted us to," Nico added.

Liam smiled, it looked slightly cruel but for some reason that didn't scare her. "Not even then."

Oh, Lord. He was such trouble.

"Liam," Nico snapped.

That bright blue, too-sharp gaze moved to Nico. "No. She needs the truth. Not pretty, flowery words. She needs the assurance that we're here, no matter what."

"That doesn't mean she doesn't have a say. We're not like the fucker who abused her."

She opened her mouth to tell them that she knew that. That she could never think of them that way when Liam's gaze grew cold.

"Of course, we're fucking not. But she knows that, don't you, Lottie?"

"Yes," she whispered. "I know that. And I . . . I consent to this."

"To being with us?" Liam clarified. "To following our rules? To bearing the consequences?"

"I want to know what they are."

"That will be part of the negotiations," Nico told her. "You always get a say."

"And what do you want from me?"

"Everything."

She sucked in a breath as Liam laid it out. He wanted everything. Not just one side of her. All of it.

He stepped back then held out his hand. She knew what this was. Her choice. Go to him, trust him, find out what everything entailed.

Or stay safe. Safe and alone and always scared.

Nico would keep them both from going too far. Would surround her in warmth and sweetness.

"If you give him everything, then he'll never leave you. He'd never give up. No matter what is thrown his way, Liam fights. He always fights for what he believes in." Nico moved around from behind her, toward Liam.

Liam would be the one standing between her and the world. And it would be Liam who would drag her out of the hole she was stuck in. He didn't love often, but when he did . . . he never gave up.

And that was precisely what she needed.

Nico added his hand to Liam's, both of them reaching out to her. Darkness and light. Heat and cold.

Stepping forward, she slid her hands into theirs. And a feeling of rightness, of safety stole over her. They drew her in, holding her between them. She still wasn't sure how it would all work, but it felt so right . . . like she really was meant for them.

A heavy hand went around the back of her neck, holding her steady.

"Stop thinking," Liam ordered.

A ridiculous command. You couldn't just stop thinking. Yet, she found herself wanting to obey him.

"I can't stop thinking," she whispered.

"You can," he told her. "All you need do is concentrate on us. On what we want from you. Your submission. Your obedience. Your trust."

"Your sweetness. Your loyalty," Nico added.

"Your love."

That last one shocked her into stillness. Especially as it came from Liam. She glanced up at him, studying him.

"That surprises you? That I believe in love?"

Well, kind of . . .

"Shocked me too," he told her with a wry grin. "I've been loved. My mother loved me. Nico loves me."

Nico gave him a look of such adoration that it made her tummy ache. With need. With hunger.

"You'll give us that, Lottie."

"You're so arrogant," she told him.

He bent then nipped at her lower lip. She moaned.

"It's one of my best qualities."

Nico snorted.

"Oh, you disagree?" Liam drawled. He grasped Nico lightly around his neck. She froze, waiting to see how Nico would react. But he instantly relaxed, giving himself to Liam.

Then Nico looked at her, and worry filled his face. "I don't think she can do this yet, Liam."

That blue gaze hit her, studied her. Did he find her lacking?

"I think she could surprise everyone with what she can take. Does this frighten you, Lottie? Look at Nico. Tell me what you see."

"Liam, you can't push too far too fast."

"And we can't stay at a standstill either," Liam said firmly. "Charlotte?"

She turned her gaze to Nico. She realized he was worried over her reaction.

"He likes it, when you take control," she said.

"He does. But Nico is right. We can't go too fast. Last thing we want is to scare you away."

Disappointment filled her.

Liam grinned. "I love that look on her face. Don't you, Nico? Sad because she doesn't get to see you suck my cock."

"Is that what you'd do? If I wasn't here?"

Shit. She hadn't meant to say that.

Liam nodded. "Yeah. It is."

She licked her lips.

Be brave.

"Could I watch?"

Both of them stared at her in surprise.

"You want to watch me suck him off, pretty girl?" Nico finally asked.

"Fuck." Liam cupped himself. "We can't do that here. Not when someone could walk past the window or hear us."

That was disappointing.

"There's my sitting room," she suggested. "No one will disturb me there. It's on the second floor so no one can see in."

"Fuck," Liam groaned. "Take us."

11

Was she really doing this? Sneaking them into one of her private rooms?

But she had panic buttons in every room of the house as well as on her. She fingered her necklace, knowing all she had to do was open the locket and hit the small button inside. And some part of her had to trust them for her to go this far with them.

"You sure about this, pretty girl?" Nico asked her with concern, eyeing her.

No. But was she stopping? Also, no.

"Yes."

"Then tell us the rules," Liam said as they walked into the room, and she locked the door. They'd all snuck upstairs. She'd thought for sure that at any stage Regent would walk out of his office and see them.

Her heart was racing. She felt more alive than she had in years. And that was down to them. They were pushing her, but they were also supporting her.

But it remained to be seen whether they really would stick around.

"Don't you make the rules?"

That's how she thought it worked. Liam in charge, and the two of them were supposed to obey.

Liam shook his head. "Not right now. And even when I do take charge, the orders I give are in the parameters you set. What are the boundaries?"

"I just want to watch," she told them. "Not participate."

"Does being touched by us scare you?" Liam asked.

She thought about that for a moment and shook her head. "No. When you touch me, I don't feel panicked or afraid. I feel safe."

Both of them nodded.

"Charlotte, go and sit on the sofa and not move from there, understand?"

She nodded again.

"I have to insist that you use words, Lottie," Liam told her. "So there's no misunderstanding."

"All right. I understand." Sitting, she was all too aware of how wet she was between her legs, of the way her clit throbbed. Her nipples were hard, pressing against her bra. She hadn't felt aroused since before she was kidnapped. This was all down to them.

"Pick a safe word," Liam said.

She jolted when she realized he was talking to her. Well, of course he was because Nico must already have one.

"Nico's safe word is beans."

"Beans?"

"Argh, hate the things," Nico told her. "If I'm saying beans something is wrong."

"Why do I need one?"

"In case this gets to be too much and you need us to stop," Liam told her. "Even though you'll be staying where you are, you're still a participant and you need a safeword."

"I don't . . . I guess I could go for oranges. I don't like oranges. So sticky and messy on my fingers."

"Yeah, I know all about sticky and messy things," Nico said with a sigh. "That's just what it's like when I touch—"

"Nico!" Liam snapped.

"What? I was just going to say when I touch a kiwifruit."

"Lord, give me strength," Liam muttered as she giggled, and Nico winked at her.

"I'm surrounded by a pair of smart asses."

"What are you gonna do about it?" Nico challenged.

"Awfully cocky for someone who wasn't able to sit comfortably at breakfast. Maybe I shouldn't have let you come last night. Perhaps then you wouldn't be feeling so smart today. Maybe you need a few more days of being denied an orgasm."

"You wouldn't let him come?" she asked.

They both turned to stare at her, and she flushed red. "Sorry, forget I said anything. I'll just be quiet."

"No," Liam said firmly. "That's not the way this works. If you need to ask a question, if you have something to say then you speak up. I won't be angry at whatever you ask, I'll only ever get upset if you hold back when you need something, understand?"

"Yes," she replied quietly. His answer gave her more confidence than he probably knew.

"And yeah, the big meanie wouldn't let me come the night before last and all day yesterday." Nico gave her a pouty look that shouldn't have been as sexy as it was. "Can you believe how mean he is?"

Liam looked mean. But from what Nico had told her, he had a mushy inside. When it came to Nico anyway.

And maybe her.

What would that be like to have a man who was scary enough to keep the monsters at bay, but who would go all marshmallow for you?

Like heaven.

"Why wouldn't you let him come?" she asked Liam.

"Because he has a smart mouth. And because he needs to know who holds the reins. Sometimes he wants me to pull him back in."

Nico sighed. "Not into pony play."

"Pony play?" she squeaked.

Liam gave her an interested look. "What do you know about it?"

"Just what I've read."

"I've got to see your books," Nico said eagerly.

"Later," Liam told him. "For now, you're going to strip and show our girl how fucking sexy you are."

"Yes, Liam."

"Liam, not Sir?" she asked.

"No, I don't need to be called Sir or Master."

"Our lord and master is very humble," Nico advised.

"Strip," Liam commanded. "And watch out or I'll gag you."

"How could he say his safe word if you gagged him?" she asked as Nico stripped off.

Holy hell. How was she going to survive this? They weren't even doing anything to her, and she felt like she could go off. She wanted to touch herself. But she wasn't sure it would be enough.

Why don't I own a vibrator?

"I'd give him some other way. A signal. Maybe something to squeeze that made a sound. Although, I've got a good idea of how to gag him effectively."

By now, Nico had his shirt off, revealing his beautiful, tanned skin. He had a tattoo that wound up one side of his chest, over his shoulder and up his neck. It was a gorgeous dragon.

Then he bent over, pulling off his jeans. She got a glimpse of the wing on his back but wasn't able to take much in before he straightened.

And then, whoa, baby, she couldn't see anything or anyone else.

Because Nico was standing naked in front of her, and it was a sight to behold. All that tanned skin. He was built leaner than Liam but every inch of him was strong, muscular. Abs rippled down his stomach toward his long, firm dick.

"He doesn't like underwear," Liam told her. "Which makes it easier to get to him whenever I want. Do you like what you see?"

How could he even ask? Wasn't it obvious? She more than liked what she saw. She wanted to devour him. To lick every inch.

"Have you had any fantasies about Nico?" Liam asked.

"W-what?" she asked, feeling herself turn red. Did he really just ask her that?

Liam moved his hand around the back of Nico's neck.

"Liam, I don't know if this is the best idea."

She expected Liam to bite back at him, instead his expression softened as he cupped Nico's face between his hands. "She needs to see that you trust me. And I have an idea that the thought of the two of us together turns her on."

Of course, it damn well did. Look at them. Individually, they were so gorgeous they muddled her mind and took her breath away, but together . . . was she still breathing?

"Yeah, she likes that idea. Don't you, baby? Have you dreamed about us together? Touching each other? Or were we touching you? Was Nico between your legs, licking your pussy while you took my cock deep into your mouth?"

"Fuck," Nico groaned and her gaze dropped to where Liam had Nico's cock in his hand. Liam still had his jeans on and she nearly whimpered, wanting to see him naked. Both of them. Wanting to watch as Liam jacked Nico off before the other man dropped to his knees and took Liam's dick in his mouth.

"He hasn't shaved in a few days, baby. But he'll shave before he gets between your legs."

She shuddered.

"Unless you don't want him to. Unless you like the idea of his stubble rubbing against you. Of wearing the mark of his possession. Do you like that, Lottie?"

"Is it wrong?"

"Pretty girl, nothing is wrong between us," Nico told her.

"Really?"

"Yes," Nico reassured her. "I promise. I want this so fucking bad. The three of us. I don't want us to do anything that frightens you away."

She saw it then. The hope. The need. The worry. Liam hid it, locked it away. But Nico didn't have those same abilities. It was out there for her to see.

Licking her lips, feeling brave, she stood and walked over, quickly pressing her lips to his before taking a step back, her heart racing. It was a simple kiss. No tongue. Fast and soft.

Yet, it felt momentous. She felt lighter. Free.

"Can I get one of those?" Liam asked.

She blinked at him, shocked he'd actually asked instead of just taking. She placed her hand on Nico's shoulder to use him to steady herself as she went onto her tiptoes and brushed her lips against his. She half-expected him to take over, to push against her. Maybe grab her and press her up against the wall, pressing his tongue inside her.

And to her surprise, part of her wanted that.

But he didn't do any of those things. Like a predator aware that his prey was skittish and easily frightened off, he stood tensed and aware but doing nothing to set off her fear radar.

"I want this. I want the two of you."

"All of us?" Nico asked.

"All of you."

"Good," Liam practically purred. "Tell me what you want, and it'll be yours."

It was like being given her pick of things from the Queen of England's treasure room.

"You'll control what I do to Nico. His pleasure. His release."

Nico groaned.

"That's what you want?" she asked Nico.

While it might seem like Liam was giving her control, she knew that wasn't really the case. He was still firmly in command. Which somehow filled her with more self-confidence. Because if she made a wrong move then she knew he would step in.

"Yes," he groaned. "But fuck, please don't draw it out."

"What would you have us do?" Liam asked.

"No one controls you," she replied. It was the truth. No one could tell this man what to do. He might have gone to her brother to get permission to stay, but that was likely more about making things easier on her, keeping the peace.

"Don't they?" he murmured.

What did he mean by that?

Oh. Lord. She was way out of her league. Hell, she didn't even have a league in comparison to these two. They could run circles around her. Could overwhelm her.

Was this why Liam was doing this? To show her that they had the self-control to hold back? That she had power?

Maybe.

Or perhaps he was just trying to drive her insane. To make her want them so badly that there was no room for doubt in her mind.

To be honest, she wouldn't be surprised if it was both.

Liam moved to stand beside her, both of them looking down at Nico.

"Look at his magnificent cock. Isn't he beautiful?"

She nodded.

"Remember what I said about using your words," Liam warned.

Right. Words. She knew how to speak, didn't she? She needed to try to remember, anyway.

"Yes, he's gorgeous. Sexy. Amazing."

"He certainly fucking is." Crouching down, Liam took hold of Nico's cock, tugging at it with firm, sure strokes. Her mouth watered. Suddenly, the urge to kneel came over her, to put her mouth around the head of Nico's cock.

She had no idea what she was doing, but she wanted to try to pleasure him. To please them both. But she forced herself to sit back down. This time, she'd just watch. Eventually, she'd take him in her mouth. But not today.

"Do you want to see his ass?" Liam asked.

"Yes." She obviously wasn't very good at taking charge.

"Turn around," Liam commanded. "Lottie wants to see your ass."

When he spun, she spotted the most delectable ass in existence. Firm and hard. Liam smacked his hand down on one cheek making Nico groan and her jolt. Nothing more happened and she realized that Liam was studying her. Waiting for her reaction.

She met his gaze, and to her shock, he winked at her. That was a reaction she'd expect from Nico. The playfulness wasn't something she associated with Liam.

"Jesus, Liam."

"Like that?" Liam asked, running his hand over his ass. "Because our girl sure did."

Our girl.

Holy fuck. Did he know what he was doing to her? At this rate, she was going to leave a damn wet patch on the seat. This was just embarrassing.

Nico turned his head, looking back at her. "Did you? You liked seeing Liam smack my ass, pretty girl?"

"I . . . I don't know . . ." She grimaced at herself.

"First rule of this relationship is honesty," Liam told her. "No lying."

"I'm not used to talking about everything."

"Try."

She didn't know why she'd been expecting him to cut her some slack. Her mouth dropped open slightly in shock.

"If you can't tell us something, then just say that," Nico told her, turning back to face them.

Liam grunted, not looking happy at that but he reluctantly nodded. "Fine. For now. But not forever."

"It's not like we don't have our own secrets, Liam," Nico pointed out. "It would be hypocritical to expect her to spill when we haven't done the same."

What secrets? Okay, she was starting to understand why Liam didn't like things left unsaid between them.

"Fine," Liam agreed. "As long as you don't lie, you don't have to tell us everything either."

"All right." She could deal with that. "And, uh, yes, I like seeing Liam smack your ass."

"That's good because I can't wait until the day when he takes you in hand. When I get to see him smack that gorgeous ass of yours." Nico reached down to wrap his hand around his cock. "Fuck, Liam, I need to come."

"Tough," Liam told him. "Lottie? What do you want to see?"

She didn't know. She couldn't decide. "I . . . I'm not sure. Maybe, could you take charge?"

Liam studied her. Then he nodded. "Nico, get down on your knees. You're going to suck me off."

She half-expected Nico to balk. To tell Liam to fuck off. Surprise filled her when he elegantly moved onto his knees and reached up to undo Liam's pants, unzipping them.

"I see you don't believe in underwear either," she whispered without meaning to. Right now, she was starting to see it their way. Her underwear felt constricting, damp, and uncomfortable.

Liam grinned. Damn, he was gorgeous when he smiled. He was sexy all the time, but when he smiled, it sent her free-falling over the edge.

"Don't want to be a hypocrite."

Nico snorted out a laugh as he freed Liam's monster of a cock. Holy shit. Did Nico seriously take that thing in his ass?

"I sure do, pretty girl." Nico turned to grin at her.

She groaned, putting her hands against her cheeks. She'd said that out loud? What was wrong with her?

"Don't worry, we use lube," Nico told her. "I buy in bulk. And we'd get you all nice and ready for his huge dick. All you'd feel is fucking pleasure."

"That only happens when you're ready," Liam told her.

Nico took Liam's cock into his mouth.

Liam groaned, pleasure filling his face as Nico bobbed his mouth back and forth, taking him in deep then releasing him. Then Liam wrapped his hand in Nico's hair and dragged his mouth back.

"Did I tell you to take me into your mouth yet?" he growled.

"No, Liam."

"No, I didn't. You'll pay for that. Later. Now suck me until I come."

And that's what happened. She sat there, watching as Nico moved his mouth up and down that huge dick. Liam moved his gaze to hers and left it there. The weight of that gaze made it difficult for her to breathe. So, she dropped her eyes once more to Nico. And that didn't make things any easier. Any lighter.

It just stirred her in different ways. She wanted to kneel beside Nico, to worship Liam's dick with him. And yet at the same time, she wanted to curl up against Liam, to have him hold her, to kiss him, have him touch her. Taste her.

"That's it. Good boy. Take me deep. Fuck, you feel so good, Nico. So damn good. That's it."

Liam guided Nico's movements, fucking his face and she honestly thought she was moments from coming without even touching herself when Liam drove deep and groaned. He threw his head back, the noise filling the room, the muscles in his neck tightening as he emptied into Nico's mouth.

Finally, panting, he drew Nico back. Then held out his hand to help the other man up before wrapping his hand around the back of his neck and kissing him.

This felt like such an intimate moment. Maybe she should leave them to it.

"Come here."

She glanced over at Liam. Surprised to see his gaze piercing her. Then he crooked a finger and pointed at the floor next to him.

"Here, Charlotte. Now."

Getting to her feet, she walked over to him. He held out an arm but didn't grab her even when she was close enough. Instead, he let her come to him. When she was a few inches away from them, he reached out and gently grasped her chin. Then he tilted her face up.

"I'm going to kiss you, girl."

She kind of liked when he called her girl. It was so far from princess. Yet, she preferred it. He lowered his lips slowly, no doubt giving her time to move away. But she wanted to feel his mouth against hers. He started off slow, light, then the kiss deepened. His tongue ran over her lips as he placed pressure on her chin. Opening her mouth, she let out a small murmur of pleasure as he deepened the kiss. He didn't touch her anywhere else, just her mouth.

She felt Nico move away and let out a protesting noise. Liam drew back as she saw Nico pulling up his jeans. She frowned as he covered up his beautiful body.

"No," she groaned.

He froze. Then stared at her. "I thought it would make you less nervous if I was covered."

"But you're so pretty."

"He is, isn't he?" Liam added.

"Hey, I'm not pretty. I'm manly." Nico crossed his arms over his bare chest, glaring at them both.

She found herself sharing a grin with Liam. Then the other man's smile dropped. He held out a hand to her. "Come, we need to talk about this. About us. About the rules."

12

Nico couldn't sit still.

And it wasn't because of his ass. Truth was, he couldn't even feel his ass. His balls, now they fucking hurt. And he knew there wasn't any relief in sight. But his main problem was her.

He could smell her arousal. He knew her panties had to be soaking wet. She'd watched him suck Liam off. And fuck if that didn't make Nico's dick even harder.

She was perfect for them.

Just like he'd thought she would be.

Now that Liam was fully onboard, Nico knew he wouldn't stop at anything to get her. To claim her.

But he wanted to tell her everything. Liam shot him a look, part-amusement but with an undercurrent of steel.

"You all right there, Nico?" Liam asked as he sat back on the sofa next to Lottie. Liam had his arm over the back of the sofa.

Nico sat on the armchair across from them. "Fine."

"Does he . . . I mean . . . will you . . ." She pointed down at Nico's erection which was pressing uncomfortably against his jeans. Her face was bright red.

"Am I going to do something about his painful erection?" Liam mused.

"Um, yes," she squeaked.

"No, I think I'll let him suffer for a while."

Her eyes went wide. "Okay."

"Okay? Don't you think he's being cruel, pretty girl?" Nico asked, palming his erection and giving her a sad look. "I mean, if you were to ask, I'm sure he'd get down on his knees and suck me off."

Liam shot him a warning look. "Be careful, there, boy."

Fuck. There was definitely something wrong with him. That tone, Liam's words, the look on his face, they were all a warning.

And Nico lapped them up like a dog taking a drink of cool water on a hot day. He was so fucked.

"Let's talk about the rules for our relationship," Liam said, bringing his attention back to the here and now. "They might change over time. Or at least, boundaries might shift as you start to trust us more."

"What things are a hard no right now, pretty girl?" Nico asked leaning forward.

She sucked in a breath, looking back and forth between them. Her hands moved into fists, and Liam stiffened.

Slowly, he moved his hands over hers, pulling them apart and turning them over. It was obvious she'd been pressing her nails into her palms.

"Rule two is no hurting yourself," Liam told her.

"I didn't . . . I wasn't hurting myself."

"Don't bullshit yourself or us," Liam said sharply.

"I didn't mean to. I mean, I wasn't thinking about it. I just . . . this is hard to talk about. What he did to me."

Nico frowned. "You said you talked to a therapist."

"Yes, but after a while she became more interested in Regent than me. She spent more time asking about him than she did speaking to me about how I was doing. I told Regent and she never came back but I couldn't trust anyone else after that."

"What a bitch," Liam spat out. "What was her name?"

"Why?" she asked suspiciously.

"Name."

"Yeah, no, that's not happening."

"Are you refusing to do what I want, girl?" he drawled.

Would she cave to Liam?

Many would, and Nico wouldn't blame her if she did. But instead, she lifted her chin and looked up at Liam. "Yes."

Pride filled Nico and despite Liam's stern countenance, he knew that the other man felt the same way.

She was strong enough to deal with them.

"I don't think I'm happy about that. You should tell me whatever I want to know."

"Like you would do the same? You have secrets you're not telling me, don't you?" she challenged.

Good girl.

"Fine. But anything I need to know for your care, you will tell me."

"Ditto." She looked from Liam then over to Nico. Warmth filled him.

"Everything I've done is yours to know, pretty girl."

"Christ, don't tell her that. There are things you don't want to know about his youth," Liam warned her.

"Eh, I've already told her how I thought I was going to be a rock star, and about my family. Oh, I also told her how we met."

"Did you?" Liam murmured.

"Uh-huh. Told her how you're a marshmallow."

"What?" Liam asked.

"Yeah, you're like a toasted marshmallow, crust on the outside and gooey in the middle."

"Good Lord." Liam shook his head. "Charlotte, look at me." He waited until she looked at him. "It's better that we know about what he did to you, so we don't set off a trigger."

"What if I can't talk about it?"

"You'll be able to. When the time is right," Liam reassured her.

"And nothing you say will make us think about you differently," Nico added. "You're our beautiful strong warrior princess."

She gave him a small, wobbly smile. "I guess I'm scared to try in case I freak out and have flashbacks. But he didn't rape me."

"It doesn't have to be rape for it to be traumatic," Liam growled at her.

She sucked in a breath. "No, it doesn't. My therapist kind of made light of the fact that he . . . that he touched me."

"Jesus, where did Regent find her?" Nico asked. "The back of a crackerjack box?"

"Bet she was angry when he told her not to come back," she said. "She definitely set her sights on becoming Mrs. Regent Malone."

"Then she was an idiot, wasn't she?" Liam drawled. "Because anyone who knows Regent knows that the surefire way to get in his bad books is to slight his sister."

Lottie gave Liam a tentative smile that grew into something stronger. "Yes, I guess that's right."

"No guessing about it," Liam growled at her. "You're the adored fucking princess of the Malone empire. But you're also a warrior, a fighter. No one fucks with you."

"No one fucks with the Malones," she muttered then looked up at them. "It's something my cousins say. They call it the family motto."

"I like it. Although you won't always be a Malone," Liam warned.

Nico sucked in his breath. While Lottie just looked confused. "Why?"

"Because you're ours. You'll be a Carmichael. We'll create our own family motto."

"You don't think you're moving kind of fast?"

"Baby, this is me going slow. Once I'm in, I'm all in."

"This is you going slow? Are you serious?"

Nico knew that he was. "Once Liam makes up his mind about something, that's it. Even if everyone else around him is scrambling to keep up. See, you've been ours for a long time, you just didn't know it."

"She wasn't ready then," Liam said. "She's ready now."

"And how do you judge that?" she asked.

"I just know. In here." Liam patted his chest.

"Just go with it," Nico said to her. "It's easier. So, in Liam's mind you're already his and if he wasn't going slow, well . . . "

"You'd already be under my roof, in my bed," Liam told her.

A glimpse of panic filled her face and they both stiffened.

"But I am going slow, baby," Liam reassured her. "So, you don't have to worry. This goes at your pace. For now."

"For now?" she asked.

"Well, when you're ready we'll move it forward."

"And you'll just know when that's right?"

"Yep." Liam grinned.

"Not arrogant at all, is he?" she said to Nico.

"Who, Liam? No, not at all. Not our lord and master," Nico replied sarcastically.

"Anyone would think you didn't want to come for the next week," Liam drawled.

Nico sat up straight. "Wait, no, what? I didn't mean it, your hotness. You're the epitome of arrogance, so full of ego that it sweats out of your pores."

Lottie started giggling and Nico gave Liam a smart-assed smirk.

Liam just stared back at him darkly, making him shiver. Oh, yeah, he was going to pay for that.

Nico licked his lips in anticipation.

"But even if this craziness does work, I won't actually be a Carmichael, will I?"

"What makes you say that?" Liam looked like a giant, lazy cat, leaning back into the corner of the sofa, but Nico sensed the energy amassing inside him. Wanting a way out.

Yep, his ass was in definite trouble later.

"Well, you're already married."

She looked between them both, chewing at her lip.

"Is it a problem?" Nico asked nervously. She could ask Liam to divorce him and marry her. Nico didn't want her to feel left out. But it might just break his heart.

"A problem? Why would it be a problem?" Lottie asked.

Liam was watching him with a narrowed gaze.

"Are you going to want Liam to marry you?" he blurted out.

Both of them gaped at him.

"What?" Lottie asked.

"Nico, what are you talking about?" Liam asked, leaning forward. "Are you saying you want a divorce?"

Nico jumped to his feet, unable to stay still. His emotions "What? No! I don't want a divorce. But what about Lottie? She would be the smarter one to marry. And she should have your name. She needs your protection more. I'm no one, but Lottie she's—"

"You're no one?" Lottie yelled.

Nico froze, staring down at her.

"I'm sorry for yelling," she said, but then her face filled with ire. "But that's the stupidest thing I've ever heard. Are you serious? You really think that Liam would divorce you to marry me? And then what? We'd live happy ever after? The two of us, with you in the background because you're no one after all."

His mouth opened. Shut.

She turned to Liam. "I think maybe you should let him come, all his brains seem to have diverted from his brain to his cock."

"Lottie!" he finally said, shocked. He'd never heard her say the word cock. It was sexy, but still surprising.

"You be quiet," she told him fiercely. "You're not to talk until you make sense."

"But it's true—"

"You should spank him too," Lottie told Liam. "He spoke badly about himself, and that's a rule, right?"

"Lottie is right, Nico, you're not to put yourself down."

Lottie gave him a triumphant look. He glared back. "You don't top me, brat. If Liam isn't here, then *I* top *you*."

"What? Who decided that?"

"We did," Liam told her. "Nico is a switch, and if I'm not around, he's responsible for your safety. So, you'll obey him if I'm not here."

"Not if he's gonna be an idiot and call himself a no one."

"I didn't call myself a no one," he muttered.

"That's exactly what you did," Liam growled at him. "Come here."

Nico moved over to him as Liam sat up and parted his legs. "Kneel."

He knelt between the other man's thighs, staring up at him. Liam reached down to cup his face between his hands. "You're a fucking idiot."

"But—"

"Quiet," Liam commanded.

He closed his mouth.

"I would never set you aside."

His words filled the part of him that was always uncertain of his place. That needy spot inside of him he wished didn't exist but he seemed unable to eradicate.

"You are mine."

"I didn't mean you'd set me aside—"

"Do I need to gag you?" Liam asked.

Nico shook his head.

"Because it might be good for you to be gagged and bound, dick in a cock cage while I torture you. Would that help you to remember that you are *not* a no one to me?"

Nico shook his head frantically. No, he didn't need that to remember who he was.

Liam ran his thumb over Nico's lower lip, and he parted them, letting the other man press his thumb inside his mouth.

"You are mine Nicolas Carmichael. Do not forget it."

He wouldn't. His breath came in fast pants, his pulse racing. But he couldn't help looking at Lottie, worried she would feel left out. Instead, she was staring at them hungrily. Liam removed his thumb and leaned down, pulling Nico up to meet him halfway. Then he kissed him. He claimed him. Owned him.

When he drew back, Nico let out a pained groan. "You're a good boy, but you're getting punished later for keeping that worry from me."

Liam gave him a knowing look and Nico knew it was pointless to argue.

"Damn, that was hot," Lottie muttered.

They both turned to stare at her, and she blushed. "Sorry, didn't mean to interrupt."

Liam let out a deep sigh. "I know we've got some way to go until we're more comfortable with this sort of relationship, but you both need to stop being so fucking stupid."

"Stupid?" Lottie spluttered.

"Stupid," he repeated. He pointed at Nico. "You are mine. Always. There will be no divorce. You mention it again, and you won't sit for a week or come for a month. And you," he turned to Lottie, his face softening slightly, "you are not interrupting, you're not a bother, and you're not more trouble than you're fucking worth, got it?"

Her eyes widened. Nico knew she wasn't used to being talked to that way. But Liam would always be like this, especially when he thought someone he cared about was being an idiot.

"I understand," she whispered.

"Good."

"But how will we do this then?" Nico asked.

"Don't worry, I'll figure it all out. And I don't fucking care if it's legal or not, it's about our commitment to each other."

That knot in his stomach eased and he went to pull away, to sit back on his armchair.

"Stay where you are," Liam commanded.

Shit.

This was a small punishment for being an idiot, he knew. Kneeling here. But it wasn't necessarily a bad thing, being close to Liam never was. He wasn't the most demonstrative man in public, but in private he became more so. Liam ran his fingers through Nico's hair, making him shiver.

"Back to the rules," Liam said quietly. "No talking badly about yourselves." He tugged Nico's hair lightly.

"Yes, Liam," Nico replied.

"Yes, Liam," Lottie repeated.

"The two of you please me," Liam told them. "Nico knows his rules and they won't necessarily be the same as yours. But safety is a common one. Neither of you is to put yourself in a dangerous situation. And if you do find yourself in one, you're to call me as soon as you possibly can. Understand?"

"Yes, Liam," they said together.

"Lottie, if you're with Nico and I'm not around, then he's in charge. I trust him to take care of you. Understand me?"

"Yes, Liam."

"Good girl," he praised her. "We're going to spend this time we have together working on trust, on getting to know one another."

"But how long can you stay? What if you have to go and I can't . . . I can't go with you." Worry filled her face.

"I've bought us enough time, I think," Liam replied. "We need to find you a new therapist."

"If you're willing to speak to one," Nico added hastily.

She licked her lips. "Actually, there's someone one of my cousins mentioned, she lives in their town, Haven. I was thinking that maybe I could call her and see if she'll do some sessions over the phone."

"I'm proud of you for seeking out help," Liam told her.

Happiness flooded her face. Nico knew how amazing it felt to have Liam's praise.

"But what did you tell my brother you'd do for him to let you stay?" she asked.

"I told him I was going to help him find the rat in his ranks."

"There's a rat?" she asked.

"Regent thinks so. And with everything that's happened, I agree."

"Will that be dangerous?" Lottie chewed her lip.

"I'll be fine, baby. I know how to protect myself. That's why Victor had to leave, he's dealing with a supplier in Mexico. Last shipment nearly got intercepted by the cops. Now the supplier is antsy."

"We could just tell him about us. I don't like lying to my brother."

Nico and Liam shared a glance. "How do you think he'll react?"

She bit her lip. "He'll throw you out. But this is my house too."

They just stared at her. "Yeah, you'd be dead meat. Darn it."

"Baby, he wants to protect you. You're his baby sister and you were hurt. You're vulnerable. And he's right to feel that way, even if he doesn't need to protect you from us. Telling him would make things a lot harder. It's not forever."

"He wants me to be happy."

"Of course, he does," Nico said. "But he'll think we've taken advantage of you."

She sat. "This is my fault, if I was stronger, if I didn't have a panic attack whenever I try to leave the house, then we could see each other like normal people."

"It's not your fault," Nico told her fiercely, moving to her. Liam didn't try to hold him back as he knelt in front of her. "It's his fault. That bastard who took you."

She nodded shakily. "I know. I just wish I could move past it. I want a life again."

"We'll help you," Liam told her. "But for the moment, it will be easier to keep things between us."

"Yes, you're right."

He tilted up her chin, studying her face. "You're exhausted. You need a nap."

"I just got up."

"Your health worries me. Do you sleep much?"

She glanced away. "Not much, no."

"Nightmares?" Nico asked.

"Yes."

"You'll call us when you have one," Liam decreed.

"What? But I'll wake you up."

"So? If you're awake and in need, do you really think we'd want to be sleeping peacefully?"

"Liam doesn't sleep well either," Nico told her. "You won't disturb us."

"And you need to stop skipping meals as well," Liam told her firmly.

"I just forget."

They both stared at her.

"Okay . . . okay . . . eating hasn't been a priority."

"Self-care is important," Liam lectured. "And until you remember to do things like rest and eat, we'll be helping you. Understand?"

"Yes, Liam."

He smiled. "Good girl."

13

Liam watched as the two guys in the ring pummeled each other. They were at one of the underground fighting rings Regent operated. He had several business interests all over New Orleans. Some of them were legitimate, like clubs and restaurants. Others, less legitimate like where they were now.

Then there were the drugs and guns. But they didn't talk about that part. Liam might have made cash in his younger days doing less than legal things, but he'd shifted all of his cash into legitimate businesses now.

Sometimes he missed being in the ring. But he was too old for this shit now. He stared around at the people in the room, yelling out encouragement or insults at the two fighters. The scent of blood, sweat and desperation was heavy on the air.

He wished he was back at the house with Nico and Lottie. He had barely seen her these last two days. Even when he was at the house, other people always seemed to be around. Today, Jardin had brought Thea and her brothers over. That littlest kid, Ace, was very possessive of Lottie.

Moving away into a quiet corridor, he drew his phone out and sent a text to Nico.

Liam: *How's it going?*

Nico: *It's not going to be long before we're caught. We need to speed things up.*

Liam: *I know.*

Nico: *She needs to spend time with you as well.*

Liam: *I'll figure it out.*

Nico: *We need to tell her the full truth.*

His first instinct was to say no. She didn't need to know. But that wasn't fair to her. She had questions he could answer. And the only reason he'd never come clean was to protect his asshole of a brother, who didn't deserve his protection.

Liam: *You're right. We'll do it. Soon.*

Once she trusted them more. He was about to put his phone away when it started to ring. He groaned when he saw who was calling. He wished he could ignore him.

But that wasn't happening.

"Grandfather," he said, moving into an empty room.

"Always so formal, boyo," came the deep voice down the phone.

"What would you have me call you? Granddaddy?"

"Now, that just sounds wrong."

He snorted. "What do you want?"

"Never got any time for an old man. I could be callin' to tell you I'm dyin'."

"You'll outlive all of us and you know it."

"Well, maybe I'm not destined for hell just yet."

"Hell doesn't want you. The devil would be worried that you'd give him a run for his money."

The old man laughed. "That I would, boyo. That I would."

"What do you want, old man?" Liam asked tiredly. He wouldn't call unless he had something to say. And whatever it was, Liam wasn't sure he wanted to know.

"Heard some rumors. Thought I'd check with my boy that they weren't true."

"And what's that?"

What the fuck was he hearing from New York?

His grandfather had a wide reach so it shouldn't surprise him. But then he was also known to put guys on Liam, without his permission.

"Do you have people watching me?"

"You told me I couldn't do that anymore."

"Doesn't mean you're not doing it."

"Boyo, I told you. You're family. Got to protect you."

"And you also want me to take over the family business," Liam said tiredly. The family business being the Irish mob.

"There's not a smart one among your cousins," his grandfather complained. "Bunch of fools."

"They're not fools. Any one of them could take over if you'd give them a chance. But whoever you choose, it won't be me. I'm out. I'm legit now."

"Oh, yeah? Then how come I hear you're workin' out a partnership with Regent Malone."

"I'm friends with Regent."

"I'm hearin' it's more."

"I've got something going on here, Grandfather. I just need a week or two to sort something out."

His grandfather grunted. "Got somethin' to do with Malone's pretty sister?"

Fuck. It wasn't a good idea for Lottie to be on the radar of the head of the Irish mob.

"Charlotte isn't any of your business."

"It is if you're plannin' somethin' with her. I always knew you weren't destined to be with that Greek boy."

He sighed. "I'm married to that Greek boy. I love him."

"Then what's goin' on?"

"What's going on is none of your business," he told him firmly. "It's mine."

"If you want the girl, grab her and get back here. Heard some rumors I don't like about what's goin' on down there in New Orleans."

"What do you mean? What rumors?"

"Someone is gunnin' for Regent Malone, and you don't want to be caught in the crosshairs."

Fuck.

The call ended.

He needed to talk to Regent.

~

LIAM WAITED until they got back to the Malone mansion to speak to Regent. The house was quiet, everyone else in bed. He followed Regent into his office.

"I need to talk to you."

"What is it?"

"My grandfather called me."

Regent stared at him. "What did Sean want?"

"To warn me that he's hearing rumors about someone coming after you."

"He's hearing this from New York?"

"Grandfather has ears everywhere."

Regent nodded thoughtfully. "Thanks for the warning. Appreciate it."

Liam didn't like being dismissed, but the fact was he had better places to be.

LOTTIE AWOKE with a scream hovering on her lips.

Her breathing was ragged, her pulse so fast that she felt ill. Sitting up, she glanced around, the nightmare overlapping with reality.

Home. She was home.

Moving to the side of the bed, she stood and walked into the bathroom. The light was on. She couldn't sleep in the dark anymore. She had trouble sleeping at all. Splashing water on her face, she stared at the woman in the mirror.

Pale, too thin, haunted.

She leaned her hands on the counter and bent over, letting out a strangled scream. She was so sick of this.

She was not weak.

He couldn't have this hold over her anymore. She refused to allow him that power. Finally, she pulled off her nightgown, it was plastered to her body with sweat, and threw it in the hamper. Then turning on the shower, she climbed in before it had even started to heat up. She shivered in the cool, trying to remind herself that she was alive.

She'd survived.

She was a survivor.

Getting out, she dried off then moved into her bedroom to pull on some pajamas. Then she sat on the bed, feeling exhausted. There was no point of going back to bed. She wouldn't sleep.

You should call them.

They'd made her promise to call if she had a nightmare. Two nights had passed since she'd watched Nico suck Liam off. She hadn't seen Liam much since then, he'd been busy with her brother.

She sighed and pinched the bridge of her nose. A headache thumped in her temples.

Call them.

She'd had that dream again. The one where Liam was there the night she was rescued. Which was utterly ridiculous because she knew he hadn't been.

You'll disturb them if you call them.

But she'd be in trouble if she didn't. And she wanted to hear their voices. Oddly, in only a few short days they'd come to represent safety to her. It had always been this house. Her brothers.

But now, it was starting to become them.

Without thinking about it anymore, she hit call on her phone for Liam's number. Then she stopped the call after three rings. She wasn't going to wake them.

She'd managed up until now without any help from them.

Then her phone started buzzing in her hand. She had it on silent. Liam's name came up.

Shoot.

"Hello?"

"Baby, what's wrong? You all right?" he asked worriedly.

"I'm fine."

"Why did you call and hang up?" Nico asked. She must be on speaker.

"I'm sorry, I didn't want to wake you up."

"Charlotte," Liam told her firmly. "We told you to call us at any time, didn't we?"

"Yes, but it's four-thirty in the morning," she replied. "That seems above the call of duty."

"There's no duty here, pretty girl," Nico murmured. "This is what we want to do."

"What we need to do," Liam added.

"Did you have a nightmare, pretty girl?" Nico asked gently.

"Yeah."

"Tell us," Liam ordered.

She rolled her eyes at the bossy command.

"No." How would she explain her stupid, crazy dreams. They didn't even make sense.

"Are you sure?" Nico pressed. "Sometimes it takes away their power to talk about them."

"I just . . . I don't understand them. They're confusing. I was drugged most of the time and I don't remember most of it. I think that scares me as much as anything. If I just knew it all, I might feel better. But I don't. And so I have these crazy dreams."

"Oh, pretty girl," Nico crooned.

"I can remember him t-touching me. Holding me down. I can't stand to have my hands pinned. To be in the dark. I was often in the dark. Tied up. There was no evidence I was raped, but I didn't feel clean for a long time."

Liam started swearing. Low, harsh words that made her eyes widen.

"Liam, stop it," Nico said firmly, making her gasp. She wouldn't have thought Nico would take that tone with Liam.

"We're coming down to you," Liam told her.

"What?" She sat up, looking around. "Liam, you can't. Regent might see you. God, this is so ridiculous. I'm a grown woman. If I want to have two men in my room, I can. And yes, I'm well aware of how crazy that sounded."

Nico let out a burst of laughter. "You go, girl."

She groaned and lay back, an arm over her eyes. "I'm a fool."

"Careful," Liam warned. "That felt very much like you were putting yourself down. That's a rule, remember?"

"What happens if I break a rule?" she asked boldly. They hadn't talked about that part yet.

"That depends on your limits," Liam replied.

"What happens if Nico breaks the rules?" she asked.

"I get blue balls," Nico moaned. "Like right now. You wanna help me with that, pretty girl?"

"Nico," Liam warned.

Nico sighed. "So hard to be me."

She had to smile.

"Punishment for Nico is usually to be denied an orgasm. I might use a paddle or belt on his ass, which just gets him hot. Then have him suck me off, which gets him even hotter. Then leave him like that, without permission to touch himself."

"He's cruel," Nico whined.

"Would you do that to me?" she asked.

"I'm not sure that it would be such a good idea for you."

She shuddered out a breath. "I won't have a punishment?"

"Nice try," Liam said dryly. "How am I meant to ensure that you stick to the rules if there's no deterrent?"

"You know, you could work on a reward system."

"Hey, I like that idea," Nico said enthusiastically.

"No," Liam told them both.

"Damn it. I saw a whole lot of blow jobs in my future, Lottie," Nico moaned. "And now they're disappearing."

Liam just snorted. "Dream on. That wasn't happening."

"He's so mean to me, Lottie. Why don't you come up here and be nice to me?"

She sucked in a breath at the idea. Sneaking into their room, they'd be lying in bed, and she'd climb in to find Nico naked. His cock thick and hard.

"Lottie?" Nico asked. "You okay? Shit, sorry. I didn't mean that the way it sounded."

"That's too bad." She slammed her hand over her mouth. Fuck. She hadn't meant to say that.

"Really?" Nico drawled. "So, you'd like to give me a blow job?"

"Nobody is giving you a blow job," Liam said firmly. "If anyone gets any release, it's going to be our baby."

"W-what?" she asked.

"Would you like that?" Liam said in a low voice. "I know Nico's been dreaming of it. Of getting his mouth between those thighs."

"I . . . I . . ." Holy crap. "It's gotten really hot in here suddenly."

Liam let out a low chuckle.

"Fuck, yeah," Nico said. "I'm so hard thinking of eating you out."

That should that make her uncomfortable. Did she want that?

"Remember, nothing happens that you don't want to happen," Liam told her.

She sucked in a deep breath and let it out slowly. This was Liam and Nico. One of them might be bossy and arrogant, the other flirty and a joker, but they were being so careful with her.

"Is he any good?" she asked.

Dear Lord? Did she just ask that?

"Well, I can only speak to his blow jobs, but he's got a mouth like a vacuum," Liam said with a hint of amusement.

"I'll have you know I'm multitalented. I'm just as good at eating pussy as I am cock."

She didn't want to think about where he'd gotten that experience.

"I still think we should come to you. Or you could come to us," Liam said. "I don't like you being by yourself."

That was awfully sweet. Not something she usually associated with Liam.

"We can't risk it. I'm all right. But you should get back to sleep."

"Actually," Liam said. "I might head down to the gym. Join me."

"What?"

"Come with me."

"But I never go to the gym. What if one of my brothers comes in?"

"They were out late. Are they usually up this early?"

"Oh, um, I don't think so. I suppose I could come watch you work out."

"You're not just going to watch. You're going to join in. Do you exercise regularly?" he asked.

"No, and I don't think I need to start."

"Exercise gets endorphins pumping and can clear your mind. Help with your mental health. It will be good for you."

"But I don't want to," she whined.

"Get up, get dressed and meet me downstairs in fifteen minutes," he commanded.

Damn it.

She guessed she was going to work out.

The lord and master had spoken.

14

Liam kept his face impassive, but on the inside, he was grinning as she dragged her feet into the gym.

"You're late."

"It's five in the morning, you can't be late when it's this early."

"That makes no sense."

"Nothing makes any sense at this hour. If Regent comes in here, he's going to know that something is up. There's no way I'd be in here. One of the guards could see us."

"If they do, tell them you've decided to take up exercising. They'd have to come in here to see you." This room was in the basement and only had windows high up on the walls.

Still, he knew she was right to be cautious. They were playing with fire. It was only a matter of time before Regent found out what was going on under his roof. He just hoped to be in a place where she trusted them enough to leave her safety net. To find it with them instead.

She'd contacted the therapist her cousin had talked about last night, so he hoped that would help.

Walking over to her, he grasped her chin, tilting it up. She was getting far better about letting them touch her. And he was grateful for that.

"Leave the worrying to me, all right?"

"Liam, you can't take on all my worries."

"Try me."

"You shouldn't take on all my worries," she amended. "I've got to take care of myself."

"No, you don't need to do it all yourself. You can lean on other people and still be strong."

"Oh, yeah? Do you do that?"

"I lean on Nico when I have to. You can lean on both of us and still be your own person, baby."

"Okay. All right." She nodded. "So, what are you doing here?"

"First, it's what are *we* doing here," he told her. "You're here to work out as well. We'll go slow. Here, I brought you a protein drink. It will help give you some energy."

She gave him a wary look but took the drink. After a sip, she looked pleasantly surprised.

"This actually tastes good."

"Drink it down."

After she'd finished, he took her through a few stretches.

"Here, like this." He carefully took hold of her hips. "Now lean forward. That's it."

Fuck. This was probably a bad idea. She was wearing yoga pants and an oversized T-shirt. Nothing too revealing. Until she bent over. That ass in those pants . . . fucking hell. He already had a hard-on and they'd only just begun.

"That good? Liam? You okay?" She turned to look at him.

He nodded. "Yep." He did his best to keep his mind off that spectacular ass as he took her through some more moves.

"Good. Now we're ready to work out."

"What? You mean that wasn't the workout?"

He had to grin. "You sound like Nico."

"Where is Nico? Why isn't he down here being punished like me?"

"You're not being punished, baby," he said to her, cupping her cheek and tilting her face back. "When you're being punished, you'll know."

"I will?"

"Hm. I've been thinking about that. My preference for punishment would be to put you over my knee and smack that ass of yours until you're squirming and begging to be released."

He studied her for any fear, but all he saw was arousal. Her breath quickened, her cheeks grew flushed.

"Does that idea scare you?"

"Maybe a little."

"Doesn't have to be that. We can take spanking off the table. You can think on it, decide if it's something you want. Now, let's get on the treadmill."

THIS WASN'T A PUNISHMENT, it was damn torture.

Although she wasn't certain if she was talking about the exercise or watching Liam work out. The man was a god. Gorgeous. Strong. Lethal.

Lickable.

Okay, down girl.

"Right. Good girl. Here, you need to do it like this." He moved in behind her, his front pressed to her back as he tried to show her some ridiculous thing to do with a dumbbell. She didn't care about any of that, but having him so close . . .

Yeah, torture.

"Are you paying attention to me?" he suddenly asked.

"What? Yes, of course I am."

"I don't think you are, baby girl," he murmured.

Oh, holy fuck. That turned her on so much. "I think we need to do something to make you more focused. Put the dumbbells down," he ordered.

She placed them on the floor and started to stand.

"Uh-uh, I didn't say stand."

Oh, hell. Her heart started racing. Trepidation mixed with arousal.

"Now, you're going to pay attention and do exactly what I say, without argument. Understand? If you don't listen, then you'll be punished."

Holy crap.

"Stand up."

She stood, feeling a little light-headed and he grabbed her shoulders. "All right?"

"Yes. Just a bit light-headed."

He frowned. "You need to eat more."

"All the blood rushed from my head."

"You're still eating more."

"I remember the rule."

"Have you been doing it?" he asked.

She. Bit her lip. Drat. "You mean you don't know? I'm sure Nico is keeping you up to date."

"I want to hear it from you."

"Okay, well, um, mostly."

"Mostly?"

"I turn up at meals. That's good, right?"

"Only if you eat as well." He gave her a look.

"Right."

"What's your safeword?"

"Oranges," she told him.

"Good girl. Now, bend over. You're getting five for not eating."

He stood there, not touching her, not moving. Just waiting. It was up to her whether she wanted to do this. If she didn't, all she had to do was say her safeword.

Instead, she turned and bent over.

"Good girl. Count of five."

The smacks landed quickly. And they barely stung. He was obviously going easy on her.

"Very good. What a good girl, taking your punishment." He ran his hand over her ass, and she took some deep breaths in.

Holy. Crap. Her panties were soaked with need. Could he feel them?

"Stand up and look at me."

She stood and turned. He cupped her chin in his hand and kissed her lightly. "That was just a small example of what you can expect. Understand?"

"Yes, Liam."

"Good. Now turn back around and try doing those exercises again."

Oh, shit.

She turned and bent over, then pulled the dumbbell up.

"Nope. That's not right."

He ran his hand over her ass then lightly smacked it. She let out a small groan.

Shit. Shit. Shit.

"Someone seemed to like that. Keep going. That's it. No, slower."

Smack! *Smack*!

Holy. Crap. She had to put the dumbbell down before she dropped it.

"Other arm."

"You're going to kill me," she told him, moving onto the other arm. She drew it up and down.

"I hate that I've barely seen you the past two days. Have you thought about hurting yourself?"

That one she could answer.

"No, I haven't."

"Good girl. Stand up."

She stood, her bottom throbbing. Drawing her close, he kissed her. Her heart skipped, her insides warming. She pressed against him and reached up to wrap her arms around his neck. He put an arm under her ass and lifted her.

Putting her legs around his hips, she held on tightly, kissing him back until he drew away.

"Liam," she moaned.

"My baby likes kissing."

His baby liked pretty much everything he did to her. Except for the exercise. That sucked.

"We have to stop," he told her, trying to set her down. But she clung to him. She didn't want to be put down.

"Girl," he warned. "Let go."

"And if I don't? Whatcha gonna do?"

"This." He gave her four sharp smacks on her ass. Then lifted her away from him.

Yeah, if he thought those spanks were a deterrent, then he was sadly mistaken. He sat her on the weight bench then loomed over her. Her heart raced for a different reason.

This is Liam, stupid body. Stop.

As though he sensed her unease with his position, he dropped to a crouch.

"Sorry," she said breathlessly.

"Enough of that," he growled. He took hold of her chin, holding her stare to his. "I'm not putting up with that nonsense, understand me? Any more talk of being a burden or apologies will result in you going over my knee."

He watched her carefully, taking in her reaction.

"Are you waiting for me to say my safeword or be scared?"

"Are you? Scared?"

"I don't think I would've just climbed you like a monkey if I were."

His lips twitched. "You can do that anytime you like, baby."

She grinned then frowned. "I don't like sneaking around. We're going to need to tell Regent eventually."

"We will," he promised. "Nothing stands between me and something I want."

"You really are the most arrogant man."

"Does it turn you on?" he asked.

"There must be something wrong with me because I think the answer is yes."

He grinned then stood and held out his hand to her. "Come on, shower time."

"Oh my God!" she squealed, jumping to her feet. "I stink!"

That grin turned into a laugh.

"And I climbed you while I stunk!"

More laughter. She whacked him on the chest with her hand. "You're an ass."

He turned her to the door with a slap on the ass. "Go clean up, baby. I'll expect you at breakfast in an hour. I'm just going to do some more reps. We need to start some self-defense lessons too."

Stomping along the hallway, she muttered to herself as she reached the stairs. "Arrogant man, thinking he can make me all stinky. Rude."

"Lottie?"

She gasped, her hand going to her chest as she scrambled backward.

"It's me. Vic."

Oh, hell.

Taking a deep breath in, she let it out slowly. "Sorry. I didn't see you."

Victor just studied her.

She smiled at him, trying to push away the last vestiges of panic. Opening her arms, she stepped forward. "You're home."

Wrapping her arms around him, she squeezed tightly then stepped back. He stared down at her in shock.

Uh-oh.

Way to act normal, Lottie.

She couldn't remember the last time she'd hugged her brother. Any of them. Shit. Was this really what her life had become? Where she didn't show the people she loved any affection?

"Sorry." She grimaced. "I'm all sweaty."

He was dressed in shorts and a tank top.

"You're off to the gym?" she asked.

"Why're you sweaty?" he asked.

Victor was the quietest of her brothers, but he was also the most observant. And that quietness hid an intelligence most didn't see. All of her brothers were hellishly smart. Regent was a master manipulator. A natural leader. Jardin was a killer lawyer. Sharp and ruthless. Maxim was the charmer. He'd sidle up to you, sweet talk you until you didn't see him deliver the killing blow. Not literally. Then there was Vic. People just saw him as the muscle.

They were wrong.

"I've been in the gym."

"You? Working out? You hate exercising."

"I know, but . . ." She didn't want to lie. "My new therapist said that exercise is a good way to clear my mind."

That was actually the truth. She'd only spoken to Molly once, but they'd gone through a few things she could do to help her deal with the nightmares and the negative thoughts that plagued her. Exercise had come up. Although Molly had suggested starting off with a walk.

She probably hadn't anticipated Liam trying to kill her. She could barely walk.

"You've started seeing a new therapist? How long have I been gone?"

"I just started. She's someone who lives in Haven. Maddox actually mentioned her to me when he was here a while back. I want . . . I want to try and get better, Vicky. I'm tired of living like this. Of being scared of everything."

He just nodded.

"Oh, Liam's down in the gym too."

Victor scowled. But she knew it would look weird if she didn't tell him.

"With you? Alone?"

"Liam's a friend, isn't he?"

"Well, yeah."

"You trust him, don't you?"

He simply grunted.

"You guys wouldn't let him and Nico stay if you didn't. And they're becoming my friends too. Don't give him a hard time, okay?"

"You seem different."

She shrugged. "I feel different. More determined. More in control. That's a good thing, right?"

"Yeah. Lottie?"

"Yeah."

"You know we love you, right?" Victor looked hugely uncomfortable as he told her that.

"Yeah, Vicky. I love you too."

15

She could do this.

She could totally do this.

Wow, she really couldn't do this.

Take a step, moron. Don't be such a wimp and take a step.

Boy, Liam would be furious if he could hear her thoughts. But they were her thoughts, and he wasn't privy to them. Only what would she do if he asked her in that low, commanding voice? She doubted she'd be able to resist him.

And if she told him, he'd order her to bend over so he could smack her ass or maybe he'd take her over his knee . . .

Okay. Hush.

Concentrate.

She was going to step out of the house. Just a few steps out on her own. There was no danger. One of Regent's men would be patrolling the grounds. There was always a guard at the front gate.

Nobody was out here, about to snatch her.

She took a step out, holding onto the doorframe.

See? Easy.

Now she just had to let go.

"Lottie? What are you doing, honey?"

"Oh!" She turned with a screech, her hand reaching for her necklace as her stomach dropped. Her flight instinct kicked in, and she nearly took off into the gardens until she saw who was standing there.

"Damn it, Maxim," she swore.

"Sorry." He moved forward, looking worried. He was dressed in a white shirt and jeans, looking casual but gorgeous. Maxim was the biggest playboy of her brothers. She never got introduced to any of his girlfriends, but she'd heard rumors about him among some of the staff.

Regent would probably fire them if he knew how they gossiped, so she pretended to ignore it.

"I didn't mean to scare you."

"Do you guys have a high insurance policy on me or something," she muttered.

"What?" He came close and held out his hand to her. She took it, letting him pull her back inside.

"Vicky nearly gave me a heart attack this morning, now you're doing the same. I'm thinking you're trying to do me in."

"Nah, of all my siblings, you'd be the one I'd take out last."

She grinned. "Who'd go first?"

"The dictator, of course."

A giggle escaped her, and Maxim studied her closely. "You okay? You seem different. Almost happier."

"I feel better," she confessed. "I'm trying to move forward rather than just existing."

He squeezed her hand. "Good. I can't tell you how worried we've all been about you."

She leaned her forehead against his chest. Leaning down, he kissed the top of her head.

"I'm sorry for worrying you."

"Don't be. That's a big brother's job, right? Now, what were you trying to do, squirt?"

She rolled her eyes at the nickname. She drew back so she could look up at him. "I was going to go for a walk outside."

His eyebrows shot up and he looked around. "By yourself?"

"Yes."

"But . . . you . . . right." He scrunched his eyebrows together. "Do you want me to go with you?"

"No," she told him firmly. "I'm trying to do this without a crutch."

"Victor said you have a new therapist, is this on her advice?"

"You know for a guy that doesn't say much, he sure does gossip a lot."

Maxim snorted. "I dare you to tell him he gossips."

She gave him a devilish grin. "Challenge accepted. What're you gonna give me if I do it?"

They'd always been competitive in the past. Bets, challenges, contests.

"What do you want?"

"Family lunch," she said promptly. "With everyone. Lots of fun, laughter."

"Squirt, you know we'd give you that anyway."

"I know. But it's still going to be funny when I call Victor an old gossip."

"Why're we calling Victor an old gossip?"

She glanced over with a smile as Nico entered the room.

"Nico!" Maxim greeted him, walking over with an easy smile to share some complicated handshake. "I heard you and Liam were extending your stay at Casa Malone."

"Yeah, Liam's helping Regent out. So, I'm just lazing around here like a bum."

"Dude, if you want some more action, come stay with me."

"You get too much action for me," Nico joked. He swung his gaze over her as though checking she was all right.

It filled her with warmth, the way the two of them always checked in with her.

"I'm guessing Liam is a bit possessive," Maxim joked. "Heard he'll be at the club tonight, so I'll see you there too."

"Oh, is he? I wasn't planning on going."

"Well, now you are. I'll stop you from getting too bored."

"What about Lottie?" Nico asked.

Maxim gave him a confused look. "Lottie? Oh, she doesn't come to the club. You know that."

"Lottie, will you be all right here alone?" Nico asked her.

"She won't be alone. There will be guards."

Who would barely talk to her. Funny, it hadn't struck her exactly how lonely she was until it was pointed out. She'd never considered how many nights she spent in this house on her own.

Too many.

But she couldn't exactly ask them to stay in and watch a movie with her.

"I'll be fine."

Maxim was now studying her. "Would you like us to stay, squirt?"

"You? Stay in on a Saturday night?" she joked. "Have pigs started flying?"

"Hey! I'm not that bad."

They both stared at him.

"Okay, I am. I'm needed at the club. I'm the manager."

Uh-huh. She wasn't buying that either.

"But if you want me to stay here, I will," Maxim added.

"Why would Lottie need you here?" Regent asked. He strode into the room. Victor and Liam were with him. Both Regent and Liam wore suits while Victor had on a black shirt and pants.

"Lottie's going to be all by herself if we all go out," Maxim said.

"But that's not unusual," Regent said with a frown. "Has something changed I need to know about?"

"Of course not—" she started to say.

"She was trying to go for a walk outside," Maxim said.

Suddenly, five pairs of eyes focused on her. She resisted the urge to squirm.

"There's nothing wrong with that, is there?" she challenged, putting her chin up.

Regent's eyebrow lifted, while Liam and Victor's expressions remained unchanged. Nico sent her a discreet wink which filled her with confidence.

"Alone?" Regent asked.

"Yes. It's not like there's any danger. And it's time I started leaving the house without having to rely on you or the others as a crutch."

"Is that what your new therapist suggested?" Regent asked.

"We talked about it." They hadn't spoken at length about when and how. They'd only had one conversation, after all.

"Is she moving too fast for you?" Regent asked. "I don't like it."

"It's been years, Reggie," she said quietly. "I don't think there's been anything fast about my recovery."

Regent studied her then moved his gaze to Nico. There was something in there. Something suspicious. "I think you should be doing those sorts of things with us. I want to talk to your therapist."

"You won't bully her."

Regent just grunted.

"Lottie wants a family lunch, with the whole gang," Maxim suddenly said.

She sent him a thankful glance for changing the subject. He wiggled his eyebrows at her with a grin.

"Vicky, you're a gossip," she blurted out.

"What?" Victor frowned.

"You heard me. That is all. Now, are you all going to the club? Because I'm going to watch some ridiculously romantic comedy movie and go to bed early."

"I don't want you trying to walk outside when we're not here. Next time you want to attempt it, you're to tell one of us," Regent commanded.

"Sir, yes, sir." She saluted him.

He just studied her closely.

She knew what he was thinking.

She'd changed.

And thank God she had.

"I DON'T LIKE LEAVING her here alone," Nico said as soon as they entered their bedroom.

Liam moved into the bathroom and turned on the shower then took off his clothes.

Nico paced back and forth, barely paying attention as his husband stripped.

"I know," Liam said.

The last thing he wanted to do was go to some damn club and have Maxim attempt to ply him with alcohol. He liked Maxim but the guy partied hard. That might have been Nico's scene once, but not anymore.

He'd much rather stay at home with their girl and watch some sappy movie.

"We need to tell them." Nico turned to find Liam standing in the shower. Fuck. He was so gorgeous. He ran his hand over his thick body. "And it'll be worse for us if that happens."

Liam leaned his hands on the side of the shower, bending his head down. "Fuck."

"They'll be even more pissed off when they find we've gone behind their backs."

"Fuck. Shit. So, what you're saying is that I should just straight out tell Regent we want his little sister? The one he guards better than the secret service protects the president."

Nico just stared at him. "This isn't the way you usually do things, Liam. You go for the jugular and damn the consequences."

"She's important. I don't want to fuck this up. Everything else, except you, I could stand to lose. None of it means anything. Only you. And her."

"I get it. But . . ."

"But this isn't the way to do things. Fuck. I get it. I do."

He just didn't know the best move forward. He really wished he did.

FUCK.

Liam should have found some way to leave Nico home with Lottie. He fucking hated this shit. But what he really hated was knowing she was home alone with just the guards.

He wrapped his hands around the rails of the balcony he was standing on. Downstairs, everyone was dancing to some song he didn't know. It was all fucking bullshit. This place was packed, the way it always was. Maxim ran it along with a number of the Malones' other legit businesses. Regent oversaw everything, the legal and illegal parts, while Victor worked as his second.

It worked well for them.

Or it had until someone had started messing with their supply chain.

LIAM: *Everything okay?*

Lottie: *Just sitting here, bawling my eyes out.*

Liam: *Why? What the fuck happened?*

Lottie: *The dog just died.*

Liam: *What dog?*

Lottie: *The one in the movie. It's awful. Why did they have to kill off the dog?*

He slumped in relief. She was talking about a movie.

Liam: *You just gave me a heart attack. I thought you were really upset.*

Lottie: *I am.*

Liam: *It's a movie. I've a mind to punish you for making me panic.*

Lottie: *Doesn't seem fair. How's the club?*

Liam: *Boring. Hot. Crowded.*

Lottie: *Filled with hot girls in short skirts?*

Liam: *It is? I haven't noticed.*

Lottie: *Good answer.*

Liam: *Jealous, baby girl?*

No reply.

Liam: *You don't trust us?*

Lottie: *I trust you. I just feel...*

Liam: *What baby?*

Fuck. He wished he was with her. He wasn't good with this soothing shit, but it was even harder over text. Maybe he should find Nico. Get some help

. . .

Lottie: *Left out, I guess.*

Liam: *We'd rather be with you than anywhere else. Or with anyone else.*

Lottie: *Wow, you're much sweeter over text.*

He shook his head.

Lottie: *I'm sending that message to Nico. We might need to get it framed.*

He chuckled.

Liam: *Only if you want a spanking every time I walk by it.*

Lottie: *Worth it.*

Liam: *I've created a monster.*

Lottie: *Rwr.*

Liam: *What?*

Lottie: *I was trying to make a monster noise. But that was lame.*

He grinned.

Liam: *You really tried to go walking outside today?*

Lottie: *Yeah, I didn't do well, though.*

Liam: *Proud of you for trying, baby. You know all you have to do is ask and we'll help you.*

Lottie: *I know. Miss you.*

Liam: *We'll be home late. Don't wait up. Text me when you go to bed.*

Lottie: *Aren't you gonna say nighty-night, don't let the bed bugs bite?*

Liam: *Brat.*

"YOU'RE TEXTING NICO?" Victor asked as he sidled up next to him. "You know he's just down there."

He stared down at his husband who was at the bar where Maxim had dragged him. He couldn't see his face from here, but he could tell from the slump of his shoulders that he was having as much fun as Liam was.

Which meant none at all.

He just grunted without answering. Nico and Lottie were right. This had to come out. This wasn't the way he did things. If Regent tried to shut them out of her life, then he'd have to come up with another plan.

Because Charlotte Malone was his.

Theirs.

And he never let go of what belonged to him.

"Regent told me the plan. You really think the rat will come out of the woodwork?"

Hopefully.

Probably more likely if he actually did some circulating. He needed to be seen.

"I'm going to let it be known that I'm looking for business partners."

"You want people to think you're acting on your grandfather's behalf? Sean okay with that?"

"He's fine with it." Not really. "All I'm looking for is a better offer than from your brother. Or that's what we want the rat to think. You don't think it will work?"

Victor shrugged, looking out. "Maybe. What I want to know is what's in it for you?"

"There has to be something in it for me? I can't be doing this out of the goodness of my heart?"

"Come on, Liam. Known you a while now. You don't have a heart."

"That's not true. Might be easier if it were."

Victor looked down at where his hands were tight around the balustrade.

"Regent is distracted at the moment."

"Yeah?"

"Yeah. But he's gonna start noticing what I have."

"You've been home a day. What could you have noticed?"

"Play with fire, you'll get burned."

Liam stared at him coolly. "I've played with fire my entire life. I always come out on the other side. Scorched, burned but whole."

Victor stared at him. "Just make sure that no one else gets burned. Or I will destroy you."

Fuck. Victor was back one day and he'd figured out something was going on. He was right, Regent might be distracted but it wouldn't take him long to figure it out.

Liam sent a text to Nico and Lottie.

Liam: *Tomorrow we tell them.*

~

Liam resisted yawning as they walked back into the house. Maxim had stayed at the club. He had his own apartment in the city anyway.

Fuck, he was too old for this.

"I'm too old for this," Nico complained, as though he'd read his mind.

Victor just grunted.

"Anything happen?" Regent snapped at him.

"No, not yet."

"It's not working. We might have to pivot."

"It's only been a few days," he pointed out.

"Still, we can't keep you here forever, helping us."

Liam shrugged. "We're friends, aren't we?"

"Perhaps," Regent said.

Liam raised an eyebrow as Nico stiffened beside him. Then a sudden scream pierced the air.

"Lottie!" Nico said frantically, taking off in the direction of the cry. It hadn't come from upstairs, but from the living area. Liam followed after Nico. Regent and Victor were close behind.

Victor reached around to the small of his back, pulling out a gun. Regent and Liam drew theirs. His heart raced. Fuck. What the fuck was happening?

When they slid into the room, Nico was standing in front of Lottie, his arms out to his side.

"Lottie, it's me, it's Nico. You're safe. You're safe."

There was something frantic in Nico's voice that stabbed him in the gut. They both loved this girl. They'd do anything for her. Sacrifice themselves for her.

He didn't risk a glance at her brothers. Nico's love for her was clear in his voice.

"No! No! Don't touch me! Don't hurt me! No!"

Liam slid his gun away, her brothers doing the same when they realized that she was trapped in a nightmare rather than being threatened.

"Step back from her," Regent said calmly. "She doesn't know

who you are. She might think you're him, and you'll scare her more."

Nico turned his frantic gaze to Liam, and he nodded.

"She's hurting herself though," Nico told them.

Fuck! He glanced down at where she'd scratched her arms with her nails. Fuck. Fuck.

"Lottie, darling. It's me, Regent." Regent moved toward her, his voice calm, hands out to the side.

"No, no, no! I won't let you hurt me!" She stumbled back, nearly tripping over a footstool.

"Don't get closer to her," Liam warned. "She could hurt herself further."

Regent shot him a look.

"Want me to get the Doc?" Victor asked. "She might need a sedative."

"Drugs?" Nico snapped. "How would drugging her help? She hates to even take fucking ibuprofen when she has a headache."

"It's better than her hurting herself," Regent snapped.

"Lottie?" Liam said quietly but using a firm voice.

"Liam?" She stared directly at him.

"That's right. It's me, baby."

"Baby?" Regent snarled.

"Liam, we have to get out of here. He could come back. He could hurt you too."

"He's not here, baby. He can't hurt you."

"But he might have a gun. He might try to shoot you."

"Nothing is going to happen to you or me," he soothed. "You're having a nightmare, baby. He's gone."

"He's gone?"

"Yes."

"Did you kill him?"

"Yes, I killed him," he lied. He wished he had.

"I remember you said that you wouldn't let him hurt me anymore."

She remembered that? "That's right."

"But you left!"

"I didn't leave, baby girl." She was killing him. Her cries, the tears running down her face, the scratches on her arms. All he wanted was to take her into his arms and make everything better.

"You did! You left! The first person I saw when I woke up was Detective Sands."

"Mike said he got a tip-off," Regent said, referring to the NYPD detective.

"He did," Nico confirmed. "From us."

"I watched until they were right there. I promise I didn't leave."

That had killed him more than anything. To stand in the shadows, waiting until the cops were close enough he could practically feel their hot breath on his neck. But if he'd stayed then they would have arrested him. The grandson of Sean Carmichael. They wouldn't have cared that he was innocent. Still, he'd have stayed with her if he had thought she was that coherent. He'd thought her too drugged up to remember.

"You said you'd stay."

"I stayed as long as I could, baby. I promise."

"You never break your promises."

"I don't. I never break my promises."

"Promise you'll always stay with me from now on. Promise."

"I promise," he whispered.

"And Nico. You and Nico. The three of us."

"The three of us, baby girl." She collapsed, and he leaped forward to catch her. He lifted her up into his arms and she clung to him, her front pressed against his. Glancing over at Nico, he saw the fear and horror in the other man's face.

"Come here," he said softly.

"I don't want to scare her."

"You won't. She needs to feel both of us."

"Why?" Regent snapped. "Why the fuck would she need the two of you when she has her brothers?"

"Because she loves us," Liam told him. Victor walked out of the room. That was weird.

"What the fuck? And how would that have happened?" Regent asked coldly. "Just what the hell have you been doing with my sister?"

"Nothing like that," Nico told him.

Regent stepped forward. "If you've been using my sister, then there won't be enough of you to feed all the fish in the ocean once we dump your bodies."

"Nico, here," Liam warned. He wanted his husband close to him where he could protect him. But Nico remained where he was, glaring at Regent.

"I get that you wanted to take care of her. But did you ever think about what she might need? She's been drowning and you've been doing nothing! When we arrived here, she'd lost weight, was barely sleeping, wouldn't step outside without help. Today, she took several steps outside on her own. She's eating three meals a day. And when the nightmares hit, she has someone to talk to rather than lying in your office for half the night."

"You fucking bastards," Regent swore. "I give you hospitality, consider you friends, and this is how you betray me!"

"It's not a betrayal, Regent," Liam told him. "But it was also never about you."

"What?"

"It's always been her," Nico whispered. "Always her."

"Nico, over here. Now," Liam warned in a stern voice.

His husband snapped his gaze up to him then strode over, placing his hand gently on Lottie's back. She turned her head toward him and he cupped her face. She let out a small whimper and he leaned in, kissing her forehead.

"It's all right, pretty girl. We're here. There's nothing to be afraid of."

"Nico?" she whispered, proving she was back in the here and now. Although she hadn't tried to move away from him. Fuck, he'd hold her forever if he had to in order to keep the monsters at bay.

"You back with us, baby?" he asked, before kissing the top of her head.

"I'm so tired," she said in a low voice that ended on a sob. "I'm sorry. I'm so sorry."

"You've got nothing to be sorry for, Lottie," Nico told her fiercely. "Absolutely nothing."

"I hurt myself. I didn't mean to do that. Don't be mad."

"Mad?" Regent repeated. He looked like he was about to explode. Victor walked back in, carrying a first aid kit.

"Hush," Liam told her. "You were stuck in a nightmare. It's okay. Nobody is mad at you."

"Regent sounds mad."

Liam met the other man's glare, raising an eyebrow.

"I'm not mad at you, darling," Regent said in a soft voice. "Never you."

"But I kept my feelings for them from you. I didn't want you to get mad and send them away because then I'd never see them again. I'm too much of a coward to leave the house."

"What have I said about you putting yourself down?" Liam said to her in a low voice.

"Do not speak to my sister like that. Give her to me." Regent stepped forward to take her, but Lottie let out a small noise of distress and clung to Liam.

"Not happening," Liam replied.

"Think of your sister rather than yourself," Nico urged.

"Nico," Liam warned.

"No, it's not fair that all his anger falls on you. This isn't all on you."

"So, the two of you think that what? You're gonna share my sister? Add her as a third wheel to your marriage? You don't think she deserves better than that?"

"Charlotte would never be a third wheel," Nico snapped back. "She's our heart." He ran his hand over her tangled hair. "She's everything. We're just the lucky bastards she chooses to care about."

Lottie grabbed hold of Nico's hand, holding it tightly.

"I'm the lucky one," she whispered.

"No, baby," Liam told her. "Nico has it right. We're the lucky ones. We don't deserve someone as sweet and lovely as you."

"Damn right you don't," Regent said. "And you won't be having her either."

"It's my choice," Lottie said in a quiet voice.

Regent stood up straight, staring at his sister as though he'd been slapped. "You don't know what you're saying, darling. This has been too much. You need to go to bed, rest. Things will look different in the morning. Victor will take you up."

"You don't need to talk to her like that," Nico said hotly. "She's not a child. She doesn't need you to make decisions for her."

"She's been through a traumatic experience, she needs support not the two of you to try and debase her."

"Jesus," Liam muttered. "Just what do you think we've been doing?"

"I wouldn't know, since you've hidden it from me."

"Put me down, Liam. Please."

He set her down reluctantly. Letting her go wasn't something he wanted to do. But she didn't move away from him, just turned around to look at Regent.

"Please don't be mad, Reggie. Please."

Liam stiffened. If that bastard said that he was upset with her . . .

But Regent's face softened in the face of his sister's pleas. "I'm not mad at you. You know I could never be upset with you. I promise."

"Don't be upset with them either, Regent. We didn't set out to . . . to deceive you. It's just we figured you'd make them leave."

Which Liam knew was exactly what Regent wanted to do. Although he'd likely have them leave in a body bag.

"Lottie, why don't you go with Victor," Regent said. "He'll put you to bed."

She leaned against Liam tiredly and he wrapped an arm around her. She held onto Nico's hand.

"Reggie, I love you. But Nico's right. I'm not a child. I needed . . . I needed to be coddled when I first came home. Needed it for longer than was probably healthy. But if I want to have a life then I have to be brave. I have to push the boundaries. I'm drowning. Every day, a bit more, I can feel myself drowning."

"You just need some more therapy, that's all." His face was filled with a plea that Liam felt in his gut.

"I hurt myself again," she whispered.

Regent froze. "What? When? Because of this thing with them?"

"No! Regent, they're not the bad guys in this."

"Are we?" Victor rumbled, watching them all intently.

"What? No! Of course not. I hurt myself because I was getting so frustrated because I couldn't just do things. Things that are normal like going to West's wedding! Like managing to take my nephew to the hospital without having a freaking panic attack."

"You hurt yourself after that?" Regent's eyes widened and he looked her over. "Where? How?"

"I didn't that night because . . . because Nico and Liam found me. They helped me."

"You should have come to me," Regent said to Liam.

"You're right," Liam agreed. "I should have. Lottie and Nico wanted me to. But I didn't think you'd be reasonable. And I'm not giving her up. No matter what you threaten."

"You'll have to give her up if you're dead."

"Regent, no! Don't you get it? You can't hurt them."

"Why? Because you care about them? You'll forget them."

"Because I love them."

Liam froze. He stared down at her head.

"You love us, pretty girl?" Nico asked, breaking the silence.

"I love you. Sorry about telling you like this."

"No, no, this is . . . wow." Nico moved in front of her, cupping her face between his hands, and ignoring her brothers' noises of displeasure. Liam watched them carefully. He wasn't going to let either of them hurt his husband or their girl.

"I love you too, pretty girl," Nico told her.

"Yeah?" she asked, sounding almost shocked.

"Oh, yeah, I think I've loved you since the first moment I met you. That first time you smiled, everything else faded away for me. I knew you were going to be mine. One day."

She let out a small sob, and Nico leaned in to kiss her.

"Fuck," Regent muttered. "Are you seriously asking me to be okay with this? It sounds like you've wanted her for years!"

"When we first met her, we felt this pull toward her. Then when I realized she'd been kidnapped," Liam let out a breath. "I felt fucking wild. All I knew was that I had to find her. And kill whoever took her."

"Was she right?" Victor asked. "Were you there that night she was rescued?"

"Yes."

LOTTIE WAS FEELING spacey as Liam led her over to the sofa. He settled on the seat with Nico next to him then he pulled her onto his lap. She still held Nico's hand. Her lips tingled from their kiss and her insides danced with warmth.

But it kind of felt like this was happening to someone else. As though she were seeing everything through a long tunnel. She knew it was partly because she'd just come out of a nightmare, and she was exhausted.

God, she was so tired.

"You can sleep soon, baby girl," Liam told her.

"By herself," Regent snapped, sitting across from them.

She stiffened.

"She'll sleep where she wants to sleep," Liam countered.

God. This wasn't what she wanted. She got what Liam was trying to avoid, even though it hadn't felt right. But this . . . the two of them snapping at each other. It was hurting her. She loved them both.

Maybe she should tell them that.

Sitting up, she glanced over at Regent.

"Reggie, you know I love you. You too, Vicky," she said to her big brother, who seemed to be taking this the best of everyone. He walked over with the first aid kit, handing it to Nico, who immediately started cleaning up her arms.

"We know, darling," Regent said.

"Liam." She turned her head to look at him. "I love you too."

Satisfaction filled his face. "I know."

"Liam," Nico growled.

She just glared. She knew Liam wasn't always an overly demonstrative guy, but he had to say it. He surprised her by chuckling. "That look on your face. And I used to think you were so meek and mild."

"Liam," she growled. "What do you have to say to me?"

"Hmm, I'm not sure."

"Are you overly fond of your balls? Because Nico and I were thinking of taking up tennis."

"Great idea, pretty girl," Nico said. "But maybe we should play golf. I don't think his balls would bounce enough for tennis."

"True."

"Neither of you are getting hold of my balls. Brats."

She caught sight of her brothers, both of them were staring at her like they'd never seen her before.

Then Liam grasped her chin and tilted her face back. "I love you too, Charlotte Rosa Malone."

Then he kissed her. It wasn't quick and it wasn't light. She could practically feel the testosterone amassing in the room as he drew back.

"You fucker," Regent spat out.

Liam met his gaze, his face growing cold. "Mine."

"No."

"Yes."

She sighed. "Both of you stop. You're both acting like I can't make up my own mind. I'm not a child, as Nico pointed out."

"Hear, hear," Nico cheered.

"As I was saying. I love everyone in this room. And none of you are going to hurt each other. Not because you think you know what's best for me. I know what's best for me."

"Lottie," Regent said, with doubt in his voice. It hurt, even though she told herself she only had herself to blame.

"I get it," she told him gently. "For so long, you've taken care of me. Made all the decisions. And I've needed that. But I'm growing stronger, Regent. Don't you want that? For me to be stronger?"

"Of course, I do. But you don't have to be with the two of them to do that."

"I'm not with them to feel stronger. But I do feel better with their support. They stand with me, help me."

"You barely know them," Victor pointed out.

"I've known them for years. It's just . . . I didn't realize I felt this way toward them until lately."

"I don't know how you can love them in such a short time. How do you know you do? How do you know it's not just something else, something that you're mistaking for love?" Regent asked.

"Like lust?" she asked.

Regent grimaced.

"All right," she conceded. "So we'll just have to spend more time together to know for sure." There, she had him.

"Fuck," Regent said. "I don't want them here with you."

"Then I'll have to go with them," she told them.

They all gaped at her. Her pulse sped up, her palms growing sweaty at the thought.

"No," Regent said.

"I need to do this, Regent. I need them. If you can't handle this happening, then we'll have to go elsewhere. It's not an ultimatum. I understand it. I'm your little sister. You've protected me for so long. I don't want to upset you."

"Fuck. Fuck." Regent leaned his head back, looking up at the ceiling.

"This is your home," Victor finally said. "You'll stay here. Where you feel safest."

"And Liam and Nico?"

Regent groaned. Lifted his head to look at them all. "They can stay."

"And you won't do anything to them," she pressed.

"Of course not."

"Promise," she pressed.

"I promise." The words were wrested from him, but she knew he meant them.

It wasn't acceptance. And their friendship was likely ruined. But it was enough. For now.

"Now that that's settled," Victor moved his gaze to Liam, "I want to hear about how you ended up with my sister the night she was rescued. And why we've never heard about this until now."

Right. That. She was dying to know about that as well.

"I always thought it was a weird dream," she said before Liam could speak. "That for some reason, I kept planting you into my nightmares. I could never work out why my brain was putting the guy I was attracted to into my nightmare."

"Well, if that's what it was doing, I'd be there too, right?" Nico joked. Or tried to joke because she thought she saw a flash of hurt in his gaze.

He hid it behind a smile and a smart mouth, but she knew she saw it.

"Which is exactly why I couldn't understand it," she said, climbing over into his lap.

Regent grunted. "Two guys. Seriously. What is happening? Is it something in the water? First Jardin, now Lottie. If you tell me you have two women locked up in a dungeon somewhere, I'm going to lose my mind." That last part was directed at Victor who just stared back at him.

"It's the Texas Malones fault," Regent muttered. "They live in that town, with all that polyamory. They've infected us."

She just shook her head at Regent.

"And couldn't it have been a normal guy? Not . . . not him." He waved a hand at Liam.

"What's wrong with Liam?" she challenged.

She glanced up at Liam, wondering if he was feeling insulted. But he was smiling. Men. They never reacted how she thought they would.

"He's a damn criminal."

"Um, Regent," she said slowly.

"Yes, I know," Regent said. "But why couldn't it be someone safe? An accountant or doctor or something. It's not too late. I can find you one."

"We're not talking about finding me a dog."

"Do you want a dog?" he asked desperately. "How about a horse?"

She groaned and pressed her face into Nico's neck, breathing him in and letting him soothe her. "Someone please tell him that I'm not ten. He can't bribe me with a pony."

"It was worth a shot," Regent muttered. He met her gaze as she turned her face and grimaced.

"I want them, Regent."

"Fuck."

She knew that Regent was driven to provide her with whatever she wanted. Maxim had once joked that Regent wasn't the most powerful person in New Orleans, she was. Because there was nothing he wouldn't do for his sister. And Victor, Jardin, and Maxim would back him completely.

"Fine. You'll have them. Now, tell us what happened."

LIAM SUCKED in a breath then looked over to where Lottie was cuddled up on Nico's lap. Fuck. This wasn't the way he'd imagined telling her this. He thought he'd tell her when it was just the three of them.

Nico met his gaze and gave him a small smile. A hint of encouragement.

"My grandfather is the leader of the Irish mob as you all know. My mother tried to get out of that life by marrying my father. The thing I didn't realize until I was older was that my father's money was actually mine."

"What do you mean?" Lottie asked.

"My father was living off the interest from my inheritance from my mother. According to her will, he could do that while I lived at home. Then the money was mine once I turned twenty-five. I didn't know that and I left home at eighteen, without anything. Started boxing to make some cash, while he lived off my money."

"You gave them money, didn't you?" Regent asked. "When you

came into your inheritance. That's how come they can live the way they do."

"Yeah. It was for Michael. He was only fifteen." He shook his head. "Little did I know he'd grow up to be just like her."

"Spineless little bastard. He's never done a thing for himself, just lived off you," Regent said.

"Yeah, well, that's not all. He also got himself into a shitload of debt gambling."

"He owed money?" Regent asked.

"How did we not know that?" Victor asked.

"How much?" Regent asked.

"Half a mil."

She sucked in a breath. "What? Michael owed half a million dollars?"

"And the asshole who took you is the guy he owed it too," Liam told her gently.

"Are you saying that my sister was kidnapped and terrorized because your brother owed money for gambling?" Regent asked the question in a quiet voice, and it was all the deadlier because of it.

"I feel ill," she said.

Liam took her into his lap, holding her close. "I'm sorry I didn't tell you this before." He turned to Regent. "I was using my resources to search for her. I told you I would do whatever it took to find her."

Regent nodded.

"I overheard Michael receiving a ransom demand for her the day after she was kidnapped. He was hysterical. Said he'd received a ransom for her of a million dollars. I asked him why the ransom would go to him and not to her brothers. His reasoning was that the person had likely been following them for a few days, that they probably thought he had money."

Her kidnapper had been waiting in her hotel room. He'd

drugged her, stuck her in a laundry basket then pretended to be an employee, pushing her down to a van waiting in the back alley. No plates. Nothing on the cameras to be able to recognize the guy who'd kept his head down or the vehicle

"I told him I was going to tell you. That's when he panicked, and it all came tumbling out. He owed money and he figured the loan shark he owed it to was the one behind her kidnapping and ransom. Which made more fucking sense."

"That fucking asshole," Regent spat out. "The loan shark probably had someone on him, they saw him with her and decided she was the key to getting his money back."

"Yeah, that's what I figured," Liam said.

"You still should have come to me."

"I know." He let out a deep breath. "But he's blood. And you would have killed him."

"Fucker deserves to die."

"I told him I'd take care of it. But that he had to leave. Get out of my sight and never return."

"That's why I never heard from him again?" she asked.

Liam grimaced. "Yeah, baby."

"So, what happened?" Regent asked.

"I pretended to be Michael and I got instructions on where to leave the money the next day. I put a GPS chip in to one of the stacks of cash. Nico and I followed the fucker back to where he was keeping her. I pulled up outside, assessed the situation. Nico made a tip-off call to the detective in charge of her case. I always have a burner phone in my vehicles.

"As I entered the building, I saw the bastard running out the back door. Got a pretty good look at him. I was going to give chase but then I saw Lottie. She was . . . lying on this filthy mattress, face battered, bruised, and beaten. I rushed over to her. I, fuck, if there had been someone else in that house, they could have shot me before I even saw them because all I saw was her.

"I had just reached her when Nico rang me. The cops were pulling up, they must have been close by. I wanted to snatch her up, take her with me. But I also wanted to chase down the bastard who'd taken off. So, I ran out the back of the house. Nico followed her to the hospital, and I went on the hunt." Liam looked over at her. "I have few regrets in life, baby girl, but leaving you . . ." He shook his head.

"Oh, Liam." She wrapped her arms around his neck. "If you'd stayed, the police probably would have arrested you."

"And with his past arrests, it wouldn't have been good," Nico added, resting his head on Liam's shoulder.

He wrapped his free arm around Nico, drawing him close. He kissed them both, breathing them in, not caring about his audience.

"I should have told you sooner, but I didn't want you to hate me."

Liam could feel the walls inside him crumbling. They were the only ones with this ability. Nico and Charlotte.

"No," she whispered. "I could never hate you."

He kissed her gently.

"You two saved me." She turned to Nico and kissed him as well.

"I tried to get in to see you at the hospital," Nico told her. "But they wouldn't let me in."

Regent cleared his throat, bringing back their attention. "So, you followed that bastard and killed him? You didn't do a good job of getting rid of the body."

Liam frowned. "It wasn't me. He had a head start, but I was tracking the chip. Only the chip had been left on a fucking bus."

"How'd he know the chip was in there?" Victor asked

"I don't know. But he acted quickly, going through the money, finding the GPS, and placing it on a bus. He barely had a fifteen-minute head start on me. My guess is he jumped on a bus, went through the money, and found it. Left it, then jumped off the bus with the money."

"So, we still have no idea who killed him." Regent frowned.

Liam shook his head. "Don't know. I'm guessing he was jumped. The money was never recovered."

"I'm sorry," Lottie said.

"Don't," he told her firmly. "I would've have paid a hundred times that for you to be safe."

"You still should have told us," Regent said.

"And what would you have done differently? I needed to move quickly."

"It gave your brother time to escape my wrath."

"I don't like the little bastard any more than you. But he didn't mean for her to be kidnapped."

"I've change my mind, I think it would be best if you both found a hotel to stay in."

"Regent, no," Lottie said, tightening her hold on him.

"I think some space is needed and I don't want them doing anything under my roof."

"This is my house too, isn't it?" Lottie asked.

Regent's eyes widened. "Of course, it is."

"Then I can have whomever I want stay over. I'm not some young teenager, Reggie." Lottie rose and went to her brother. Liam wanted to pull her back, but he forced himself to let her go. She knelt in front of her brother. "I know you want to protect me, and I love you for it. But when I'm with them, I feel safe. Protected."

"You don't feel that with us?" Regent asked stiffly.

"Of course, I do. But you shouldn't dedicate your life to taking care of me. And the truth is, you're all so busy. I want something more than sitting at home while life happens around me."

"It's late," Victor said. "Be hard to find a hotel now."

Regent turned to look at him. "You support this?"

Victor frowned. "Lottie's right. She's not a child. She's smart.

Although she is naive." He looked to Liam and Nico warningly. "And she will not be pushed into anything she's not ready for."

"We would never do that," Liam replied stiffly.

"You're asking for a lot of trust," Regent said.

"I trust them. Doesn't that say a lot?" she asked.

"If they're here, then you can keep an eye on them better," Victor pointed out.

Liam scowled. "We're not fucking teenagers driven by hormones."

Regent grunted, not looking convinced.

"She's different, changing," Victor said to Regent. "She stepped out of the house on her own today. I think you should give them a chance."

"Lottie is ours," Liam growled. He'd had enough of this. They didn't need fucking permission. But Nico put his hand on his arm warningly, while Victor sent him a glare.

Right. Fuck. He was trying to help.

"I just want to do what's best for you, darling."

"Then you'll let them stay. You raised me to be smart and take what I wanted. I'm who I am because of you. You're more of a parent to me than anyone. I adore you. Please be okay with this."

Because she was going to do it anyway.

The words were unsaid but he saw Regent acknowledge them in his head.

"Fine. You can stay." Regent scowled at them. "But fucking hurt her, either of you and . . ."

"We're fish food, got it," Nico said, but there was a smile dancing on his lips, and he stood, opening his arms. Lottie rose and rushed into them. He spun her in his arms while she giggled.

Liam watched Regent and Victor as she laughed. Their faces displayed their shock and he thought for a moment, he caught a glimpse of tears in Regent's eyes. But he must have imagined that because the other man gave him a stern look as he stood.

"Bed time," Regent ordered. "Separate beds."

Liam just smiled. Oh, Regent could dictate all he liked. But Lottie had just told them all that she loved them and was theirs.

And nobody got between Liam and those that belonged to him.

"Come, baby. We'll walk you to your room." Liam held out a hand to her.

"Actually, I'd like a word," Regent said smoothly.

"I'll come back after I've put Lottie to bed."

Lottie said a quiet good night to both of her brothers before Liam swept her out the room. They moved up the stairs toward her bedroom. Once in her room, Nico quickly wrapped an arm around her waist and drew her to him, kissing her.

"Fuck yes, pretty girl. God, I love you."

Liam loved seeing them together. His dick hardened, his balls tightening. He was gonna need some release once he got Nico back to their room.

"I love you too, Nico. I don't know how I could be without you now. The two of you, you're everything." Then she turned to Liam. "I love you."

"I know."

Both Nico and Lottie rolled their eyes at him. His brats.

"Liam doesn't like to say it much. He thinks actions speak louder than words."

"I can understand that," Lottie said. There was a mix of relief and sadness on her face.

"You okay, baby girl? Upset with me for not telling you? If you are, don't blame Nico. He wanted to tell you earlier."

"Would you have told me? Eventually?"

"Of course. I admit I was waiting until you trusted us more. I know I should have told you all right away, but I didn't see how it could help. And I was still protecting the worm. He's an asshole, but he's also my brother."

"I get it. I do. I just can't believe he was the reason I was taken."

"He's gone. He won't be back." Liam pulled her close, hugging her. He could sense her exhaustion. It called to him, pushing him to take care of her.

"That went better than I thought it would," she said leaning back with a grin.

"Well, we aren't fish bait yet," Nico joked.

"I still have to go down there," Liam reminded them.

Lottie worried at her lip. "They won't hurt you."

"Hey, stop." Liam drew her lip from between her teeth. "You're not to worry about me. I can take care of myself."

"You're not invincible, Liam."

"He thinks he is," Nico said.

"I'm not the one who spent most of his twenties trying to kill himself."

"I didn't try to kill myself. And it wasn't most of my twenties. Just the first few years."

"Until you met me."

"Yeah, and then you stopped all the fun."

"I stopped you from risking yourself. You had a death wish. Do you have that any longer?"

"No, Liam."

"Will you be putting yourself in dangerous situations again?" Liam pressed.

"No, Liam."

Lottie watched them, eyes wide. But he saw the flush of arousal in her face.

"That's my good boy." Liam cupped the side of his face. "I'm going to need you to suck me off when we get back to our room."

"Yes, Liam."

"No fair, I want to see that." She pouted.

"Do you?" Liam grinned at her. "Well, we'll have to see what we can do. Although I don't think here is the best place with your brothers' rooms just down the hall."

"I could come to your bedroom," she said. "Although . . ." A hint of concern entered her gaze, and he knew she was thinking about her brothers and their reaction.

This would be a lot simpler if he had her in his house.

"Tomorrow," he promised her. "You're going to sleep in. We'll meet for breakfast at ten. Come in workout gear."

"What? Nooo."

"Hush," he told her firmly. "Yes. We're going to start self-defense lessons. Nico will be coming too."

"What? Nooo," Nico groaned.

Liam just shook his head at them. "Yes. And if you're both good and do what you're told without complaint, you'll get rewarded. If you're naughty, then it will be punishment. Understand?"

"Yes, Liam," they said together.

"Nico, stay with Lottie until she goes to sleep. I'm going back down to talk to Regent and Victor," Liam ordered. He then drew Lottie close and placed his hand lightly behind her neck. "I want you to try to go to sleep. Nico won't leave until you do. If you have another nightmare, what do you do?"

"Call you," she said.

"Good girl. If you're too tired when you wake up, we'll postpone the self-defense lessons. What's most important is your health." He kissed her gently. "Sure you're not upset with me?"

"I'm just glad to know I wasn't going insane imagining you there. And I know you were protecting Michael."

Liam winced. "I don't know why I did. Little bastard didn't deserve it."

"Because you're a good person, Liam."

"A good person? Baby, I'm anything but . . ."

"No. I know there's things you've done that weren't good. But you can't be bad if you protect those that belong to you. If you love us as fiercely as I know you do."

"Things could have gone wrong. I should have put you first."

"You did."

He shook his head. He wasn't so sure.

"I wasn't yours then," she pointed out. "Michael is your brother. You did the best you could. I'm alive. I'm here. With you and Nico. That's what matters."

Finally, he nodded and turned her toward the bathroom. "Off you go." He smacked her ass, and she gave him a mock-glare over her shoulder.

Liam turned to Nico and crooked a finger at him. Nico walked over with a smug grin.

"Think you know everything, don't you?"

"I told you she wouldn't blame you. Or be upset."

Liam grunted. He pulled him close, pressing his body against his. "It could have backfired."

"It didn't."

"You're to stay with our girl until she's asleep. Keep her safe. Then go up to the bedroom and strip. I want you kneeling by the door, waiting for me. If I get back to the room first, then same thing applies. Soon as you get back to the room. Strip and kneel."

"Whatever you say, Liam. You're the boss."

"I am? Sometimes I wonder."

Liam left and moved downstairs quickly. He wanted to get this part over and done with. Regent was waiting in the office, staring out the window. Victor was on the sofa, his feet on the coffee table, eyes closed. But Liam didn't believe for a moment that he was asleep.

"Where's your brother?" Regent asked, turning to face him.

"I don't know. I don't want to know."

"Because then you'd have to tell us?" Victor asked slowly.

"Because I don't want anything to do with him. When I learned that he was to blame for her being taken, I told him to leave and never return. That we were done."

"He's your brother. She was nothing to you."

"She was an innocent. And . . ."

"And?" Regent pressed.

"There was something there. I tried to deny it for a while, but Nico felt it."

"So, you only became interested in her because your husband wanted to fuck her?" Regent asked.

Liam ground his teeth together. He was on Regent's turf. But that didn't mean he had to fucking take his shit.

Be diplomatic.

Fuck. He should have brought Nico down with him. But he didn't want Nico exposed to any of this.

"No, you asshole. That's not why I wanted her."

"Why do you need her? The two of you love each other, right?" Regent pressed.

"Yes."

"So, why introduce someone else? Is Nico not enough for you in bed? You need another fuck toy?"

He had Regent pressed to the back wall, his arm across his throat. "Ever talk about Lottie or Nico like that again and you're dead, got me?"

"Lottie might not like that," Victor said casually, as though he didn't have his brother pinned, half-choking him.

"She'll get over it. I'll see to that. Lottie will never want for anything, not as long as I'm around."

"Let him go," Victor commanded.

So far, Regent hadn't fought back, he just studied Liam calmly.

"Now, Liam."

Liam stepped back while Regent straightened his clothes, looking unperturbed. Cold bastard.

"Must be that Irish blood that makes you so hotheaded," Regent commented.

"Or maybe it's just that you set me off," he countered. Turning, he saw that Victor had a gun out, resting on his knee. "You were going to shoot me? And here I thought you liked me."

Victor shrugged. "Family first."

"I want your brother," Regent told him.

"I can't help you there."

"I'll pay you back the money you lost."

Liam sighed. "I really don't know where he is. You think I feel any allegiance to him anymore?"

"Family first," Victor repeated.

"Lottie and Nico are my family now. She wasn't mine then. She is now. Michael has gone."

"What's he living off?" Regent asked.

He frowned. "I don't know. Likely my stepmother sends him money."

Regent and Victor shared a look.

Liam sighed. "If you go after her, just make sure it can't come back on you or me."

"You're not going to try to protect her?"

"No. That bitch can protect herself," Liam said bitterly. "If that's all . . ." He moved to the door.

"I'll give you five million dollars to disappear out of my sister's life."

Anger filled him then he stilled and thought it over. "Fuck." Turning, he stared at Regent. "You paid him off, didn't you?"

"What?"

"You paid him to leave her. Didn't you? How much?"

"Two million dollars. He was surprisingly cheap."

"Motherfucker. Why bother? Why not just get rid of him?"

"More hassle that way. This was simpler, cleaner."

"You really are an interfering bastard." He frowned.

"I paid the money to him the day he broke up with her, before I knew she'd been kidnapped. She texted me while he was driving her back to the hotel to tell me. I had the money transferred to an offshore account for him. Later on that night, I realized something was wrong when I couldn't get hold of her. She refused to have a bodyguard, but I had one watching from a distance. However, they were watching the hotel lobby, not the service entrance where the kidnapper left with her. Not that he would have seen her in the laundry trolley anyway. It's a wonder he never spotted a tail if Michael had one though."

"Michael could have used that fucking money to pay his debt," Liam said in a cold voice. He couldn't believe that bastard. He best never show his face again. He was dead to Liam.

"Yes, he could have."

"Fucking hell." He ran his hand over his face. "I really don't know where he is. But if you want to find him, my stepmother would be the place to start."

Regent just nodded. "I think it goes without saying, but you will not tell Lottie we paid off your brother."

"I don't think she'll be upset. But I'll tell you what, I'll give you the chance to tell her yourself."

"Fuck," Regent muttered.

16

Lottie rolled over and looked across to where Nico sat in a chair he'd pulled up by her bed.

"You look tired," she told him.

He opened his eyes and gave her a lazy grin. Love for him filled her. Other people would say it wasn't love, would say it was too soon.

But Lottie knew what this was. For years, they'd rented space in her head. Now they were buying permanent real estate.

And she was fucking ecstatic.

"And you're meant to be asleep, Lottie-bo-bottie."

She rolled her eyes at him.

He pointed a finger at her, giving her a stern look. "Sleep."

"Or what? You gonna spank me?"

He ran a finger over his lips. "I usually leave the Dom stuff to Liam. But since he's not here right now . . ."

"What?" she squeaked.

"The idea of smacking that delicious ass of yours holds a lot of appeal."

Her breath caught in her lungs. Her heart raced. She cleared her throat. "If you were trying to help me get to sleep, you've epically failed."

"Why is that, pretty girl? Did I turn you on with all that talk of dominating you?"

Yes, that's exactly what he'd done. The bastard.

"Too bad you're under orders to sleep, huh?"

She pouted. "I'll fall asleep easier if you're not here."

Rather than get insulted, he just laughed. "And why is that? Do you think that as soon as I leave you'll get to touch yourself?"

"What? Nico! You can't say those things."

"I can't? Too bad. I was going to suggest that you do it right now."

"Now? I can't do that with you here," she squeaked.

"Really? That's too bad. I guess you'll just have to close your eyes and count sheep or something to get to sleep."

She glared at him. "You're so mean."

"I can be. Tell me how you usually get off. Do you have a vibrator?"

"I . . . no."

"No vibrator? That doesn't sound like much fun. We'll need to do some shopping and change that."

"Why would I need a vibrator when I've got . . ." she trailed off before saying it.

Nico's grin widened. "When you've got two men, you mean? Two mouths, two cocks, four hands to please you? But I don't think you're ready for us just yet, are you? However, we could help you prepare. Buy you a few vibrators, a smaller one to begin with then work you up to a nice fat one. With those vibrating ears. And we'll need butt plugs too. Lube. I've got plenty but I think we'll get some of that flavored stuff, yeah and we'll need—"

"Nico!"

"What?"

"Maybe we should just start off small?"

"Small?"

"Yeah, small."

"Pretty girl, there's nothing small about your men."

She groaned. "I walked into that one."

"Yep. But I know what you're saying." He knelt by the bed. "We're not going to rush you."

"I just don't know how I'll react. I don't want to disappoint you both."

Nico rocked back, as though he'd been slapped. "Wait. You're worried about disappointing us?"

"Yes," she whispered.

"Okay, you've got to know that's bullshit."

"What do you mean?"

"There's no fucking way you could ever disappoint us. Only thing that would disappoint us is if you stopped loving us. You gonna do that?"

"No, never." She grabbed hold of his hand, holding it fiercely. "I don't throw away the people I love."

Something moved in Nico's face. And he gave her a fierce look back. "Neither do I, pretty girl." Leaning in, he kissed her. The kiss lingered on, he explored her lips with his tongue before sliding his tongue into her mouth.

"Fuck, I so want to taste you. Christ. I bet you taste delicious."

"You . . . you could," she said shyly.

He groaned. "Don't tempt me. I think we should wait for Liam to be with us, though."

"Then what are we going to do? I'm not going to sleep like this."

"Me either." He sighed. "Sure you can't touch yourself while I'm here? That would be hot as fuck."

She bit her lip. He drew her lip free and kissed it.

"I have an idea. What if I was pleasuring myself at the same time?" he asked.

"Are you allowed to do that without permission?"

He snorted. "No. But neither are you."

"Liam hasn't said that."

"Oh, but he will. And I'm telling you now. No touching yourself without permission."

She raised her eyebrows, feeling confused. "But . . ."

"I give you permission to touch yourself right now."

Okay, this take-charge Nico was totally doing it for her. Not that she didn't love joker Nico or sweet Nico. He was damn sexy and gorgeous no matter what.

Standing, he stripped off his pants and then sat back on the seat with his dick hard and ready to go. She licked her lips.

"You can pull off the covers or touch yourself with them on," he told her as he ran his hand up and down his thick cock.

"Okay," she whispered, watching him. Wow. He was gorgeous.

"I take it you're okay with me having my dick out?"

She snorted. "You know I am. It's so pretty."

"A lesser man might feel insulted by that. Dicks are manly or sexy or handsome. Not pretty."

"I think he's pretty." She sighed, watching as he moved his hand up and down the shaft.

"Wanna touch?" he asked

She glanced at the door. "What if someone comes in?"

"Do people usually just barge in?"

She shook her head.

He sent a quick text. "Just telling Li I'm going to be a while."

"Will he be mad?"

"No, pretty girl. Of course not. And if he was, this is my idea. I'll take the punishment."

"That doesn't seem fair."

"You're not worried about Liam punishing you, are you?" He watched her with concern. "You don't have to agree to any of that, to being our sub."

"No, no, I'm not worried. I just don't want him to ever be truly mad at me."

"The only things that would make Liam or me mad was if you deliberately put yourself in danger or if something was hurting or harming you and you didn't tell us. Okay?"

"Okay."

"Now, are you going to touch yourself or just watch me jack off?" he asked with amusement.

Heat filled her cheeks. "I don't know, I think I might be able to come just watching you."

He gave her a satisfied smile. "Touch yourself, pretty girl. Reach down and cup your breast. Play with your nipple."

Taking in a deep breath, she reached down and ran her thumb over her nipple. It felt a bit odd, doing this with him watching her. But she was so turned on that she needed the release. So, she played with her nipple, feeling electric shocks move through her body. She pressed her thighs together.

Nico moved his hand faster with a groan. "That's it, pretty girl. Let me hear all the noises you make as you play with yourself."

Shit. He was killing her.

"Reach down and cup your mound. Tell me, are your panties wet?"

She moved her hand down to touch herself, even though she already knew the answer to his question.

"Well?" he said in a low, demanding voice.

"Yes," she told him. "They're wet."

"Take them off. You don't need them. Hand them to me."

"Nico," she whispered, feeling weird about doing that. Why would he want her damp panties?

"Don't think about it, pretty girl. Just do it. When Liam takes charge, I can let go and just do what he says because he'll catch me. But it takes trust, being that vulnerable. So, if you can't do it, I get it."

She was nervous, yeah. But she also wanted to try. Nico didn't have Liam's natural dominance. But there was a subtler strength to him. And she felt safe with him. So, she pulled off her panties and handed them to him, knowing she was bright red.

"Thank you," he told her sincerely, reaching down to put them in the pocket of his jeans.

"Nico! You can't take them."

"Spoils of war." There was that devilish grin she knew too well.

"There's no war."

"Pleasure then," he joked.

Oh. Lord.

"Now, part your lips and run your finger up and down. Nice and slow."

Her heart raced, she grew hotter as she ran her finger along her lips. Her gaze remained on his hand, fascinated as he took a firm grip of his shaft. She wondered what it would be like to kneel in front of him and take him into her mouth, as he'd done with Liam. She wanted to try that.

"Fuck, pretty girl. That look on your face. You're going to have me coming before you."

"What's wrong with that?"

"Nuh-uh, orgasm etiquette demands that you come first."

"What? There's an orgasm etiquette?"

"Course there is."

"And I have to come first?"

"Yeah, you have to come first."

She didn't believe a word coming from his mouth. But since she desperately wanted to come, she was willing to go along with it.

"Flick your clit. Yeah, that feels good, doesn't it?"

So good. So very good.

She could hear herself panting, small whines escaping her mouth as she moved her finger faster.

"That's it. You're going to come for me, aren't you, pretty girl? You're going to come all over your fingers. And you're not going to make a sound."

What? Nooo.

She begged him with her gaze.

"No," he said in a low voice. "No noise. We don't want your brothers to hear, do we?"

"Do you have to talk about my brothers right now?"

He grinned. "Sorry. Fair point. Push two fingers of your other hand deep inside you. In and out. That's it. Good girl. You're going to come, aren't you?"

"Y-yes!" And she had no idea how not to make a noise. And then she was coming, her eyes closed as she clenched down around her fingers. A low whimper escaped, but otherwise she managed to somehow keep her cries locked inside.

"Fuck. Fuck!"

She opened her eyes just in time to see Nico come. She watched in fascination as he closed his eyes, his head leaning back, his hand slowing on his cum-slickened cock.

It was beautiful and she wanted more.

But exhaustion washed over her in a sickening wave. She desperately needed sleep. Turning his head to her, he smiled lazily. "That was so good, pretty girl. Now give me your fingers. The ones that you had buried deep in your pussy."

With a blush, she drew her hands out of the covers and held them out to him. He grabbed hold of her hand and dragged those fingers close, licking them.

Holy. Heck. That was so hot.

"Just what I thought," he said, as he tucked her hand back under the covers then drew on his jeans, tucking himself away. "Delicious."

"Really?"

"Really. It's time for sleep." Kneeling next to the bed, he ran his fingers through her hair as he started singing.

"Your voice is amazing. You should have your own band. Why don't you?"

"I don't know. Maybe I'm scared of trying and failing."

She opened her eyes. "You're amazing, Nico. Never forget that."

"Thanks, pretty girl. Now, go to sleep."

17

Nico walked into their bedroom on the third floor.

He wished he could have carried Lottie up with him. It was getting increasingly difficult to let her sleep on her own. If she had another nightmare, he wanted to be there for her.

When he shut the door, he turned to see that Liam was sitting on the bed with just his pants on, although they were unbuttoned. He had his phone in his hand.

"You know what to do," he said.

Stripping, Nico got into position on his knees. Liam didn't usually require any formality to their play, but he loved having Nico on his knees.

Nico put his hands behind his back.

"Did you touch her?" Liam asked, standing and taking off his pants.

"No, Liam."

Liam froze. Which looked kind of funny as he was in the middle of pulling his pants off one foot. He quickly recovered, placing his pants on a chair before moving toward Nico, naked. His erect cock called to Nico, who stared at it hungrily.

"You didn't?"

"No, Liam."

"You didn't finger her pussy? Lick it? I know you're dying to."

"I am, but I'm . . ."

"You're what?"

"I'm scared of overwhelming her. Doing something to scare her. And it doesn't feel right to do that for the first time without you."

A pleased look filled Liam's face and Nico knew he'd done the right thing. Liam ran his fingers through Nico's hair then tugged at it. A delicious pain filled him, and he shuddered with pleasure.

"What happened?"

"She was . . . she couldn't sleep. I could tell she was turned-on, but she wouldn't do anything in front of me. So, I offered to touch myself while she did the same."

"What a hardship for you," Liam said dryly.

"You know me. I'm a giving sort of guy." He grinned as Liam snorted.

"She got herself off."

"Yes, and she was so beautiful while she came." He worried Liam might be upset, jealous and he was prepared to take his punishment for moving forward without permission.

But the other man just smiled. "Good."

"You're not upset?"

"Upset that you got her to relax enough to make herself come with you in the room? Not at all. But there is the fact that you came without permission. That should probably be addressed."

"I'm sorry."

"No, you're not. You loved every minute of it."

"I did."

"Now, it's your turn to pleasure me. You're going to suck my cock, aren't you, boy?"

"Yes, Liam."

"And swallow everything I give you."

"Yes, Liam."

"And thank me afterward."

"Oh, yes."

"Then open."

Nico opened wide as Liam thrust his dick into his mouth.

Fuck. Fuck.

He was starting to get hard again. Liam held the back of his head, driving back and forth. Nico reveled in not having control, in giving everything over to his husband. He gave. Liam took. But Liam also gave back.

It was a circle. Not a one-way street.

And now their girl was going to be a part of that.

And Nico would have the two people he loved most. And Liam would have the family he deserved.

Lottie would be their queen.

"Fuck. You don't know how good it feels. So hot. So wet. You're going to suck me all down, Nico. Good boy. That's it."

Liam came with a groan and Nico swallowed hastily, determined not to miss a drop. As Liam drew back, he licked his dick.

"That's it. Fuck. Yes. Good boy."

Suddenly, Liam dropped in front of him. Then he used his hand at the back of Nico's head to draw him close and kissed him.

"We have our girl, Nico."

Happiness filled him. "We do."

"And I'm never letting either of you go."

"We wouldn't let you go either, Li."

"A fucking family, Nico. We're going to be a family."

Lottie was the last piece, the missing bit, and now they could be complete.

18

Lottie felt a hand grab her arm from behind. She froze.

No, don't freeze.

With a cry, she kicked back, trying to slam her foot down on her attacker's before she turned and brought up her knee toward her attacker's cock.

She stopped before she could make contact, though. After all, she didn't want to actually hurt him.

"Good girl," Liam called out. "That was much better."

It didn't feel better. This was her third day of self-defense lessons, and she was still freezing up.

"I still froze."

"But only for a few seconds," Nico said to her.

She didn't want to freeze at all. And she knew it was Nico reaching for her. What would happen if it wasn't Nico? If it was someone intent on hurting her? That moment where she froze could spell disaster for her.

She had to get this right if she was going to move on.

Each morning they'd been working on self-defense and in the afternoons, she'd spend time with them in the solarium or her sitting room. She'd paint in the solarium while Nico read, and Liam was often on the laptop working. He had managers for all his business dealings back in New York, but there were still things he had to do. She wondered how much of a nuisance it was to be here.

But what was the alternative? For her to go with them to New York? She couldn't manage that, could she?

Although she could walk all over the gardens now when one of them was with her and she'd stopped panicking when she couldn't see the house, she still felt stressed at the idea of going off the grounds.

"I need to be doing better." Frustration filled her. "It's not good enough."

"Come here," Liam commanded from where he stood at the side of the mats. He looked so good in his workout clothes. So did Nico.

"I want to go again." She turned her back on Nico. She was determined not to freeze this time.

"No. No more."

She glared over at Liam. "Yes, more."

He raised his eyebrows. To her surprise, her brothers had been remarkably good about giving them time to themselves. Then again, they had a lot going on. Apparently, more shit had gone down. A business deal had fallen through, the other party having gone elsewhere. She didn't know the details. That was something she was never privy to. Maxim had once told her that Regent kept a hold on the underbelly on the city because leaving would create too much of a vacuum and put them all at risk. But she figured there was as much risk in staying.

At least she didn't have to worry about that with Liam and Nico. Liam told her that all his businesses now were legitimate. Although there was Liam's family to be considered.

"I said no. Come here, Lottie."

"Damn it, Liam." She stomped over to him. "I'm not going to get better unless I push."

"Better? You think there's something wrong with you?"

"Well, obviously! Even though I know it's Nico grabbing me, I still freeze. I can't go off the grounds without freaking out. Can't even have you touch me because we don't know if I'll panic."

Liam watched her thoughtfully. "You can't expect everything to instantly change."

"I'm not. I just . . . all right, maybe I wish it would instantly change. I know it's not going to. Molly said I have to have patience, it's just hard. I want . . . I want to be perfect for you."

With a sigh, Liam grabbed her hand and led her to the weight bench. He sat then lifted her onto his knee. Nico came and sat next to him.

"That's what you don't get, you are perfect for us," Liam told her.

"But what about when you get sick of staying here? You need to get back to New York eventually, right? I . . . I'm scared to go there." She looked down at her hands. "It's not even about my fear of leaving the safety of his house. It's about New York itself."

"Because that's where you were hurt," Liam said quietly.

"Yes."

"Would it help if I sold everything and we moved here?" Liam asked.

She raised her head. "You're not serious?"

"Of course, I am."

"You know Liam doesn't say something unless he means it," Nico pointed out.

"But I . . . you can't do that."

"Why not?"

"Your home is in New York."

'My home is with the two of you," Liam told her.

"Same," Nico added.

"But your families—"

"You know I don't care about my family," Liam said.

"And I can go back to visit mine," Nico added. "It's no different than asking you to move away from yours."

She guessed so. Still . . .

"Can I think about it?"

"Of course. But just know that if that's an added stressor, I will take it away," Liam told her firmly. "I won't have that causing you anxiety when I can easily fix it."

Not such an easy fix as he was making it out to be, but she did feel a sense of lightness.

"We're taking a break from self-defense lessons and from everything else that's pushing your limits."

"I don't need a break," she protested.

"You do. And we have the whole day together."

"Whatever will we do with the rest of the day," Nico mused, wriggling his eyebrows up and down.

She couldn't help but giggle.

"Is there another reason for your frustration, baby?" Liam asked her. "It's not like you to get so upset as you did just now."

"I'm sorry about that," she said, wincing as she recalled her behavior.

"I'm not sure sorry is enough. You did stomp your foot at me."

Shoot. She did. She didn't think she'd stomped her foot since she was a child.

"And she refused to come to you when you told her to," Nico added.

"Hey, you're not supposed to give him ammunition!" she protested.

"Why not?"

"I don't know, you're just not supposed to."

"But maybe I want to see you get your butt spanked."

She sucked in a breath.

"Do you think that's what you need, Lottie?" Liam asked. "Do you need me to spank you?"

"I . . . I . . ."

"Or do you need something else? Maybe you need to get rid of some of this frustration in another way?"

Was he suggesting . . .

"The vibrator and anal plugs I ordered arrived this morning," Nico said. "And some lube. We could start by playing with them."

"What? You got sexy toys sent here?" she said.

"Yeah, where else would I get them sent to," Nico replied. "Won't do us any good if I got them sent somewhere else."

"What if my brothers saw them?"

"I'd just tell them they were for me."

Her eyes nearly bugged out of her head. Nico broke into laughter. "Don't worry, they were all wrapped up. Even if they'd seen them they would have had no idea what they were."

He was killing her.

"Now, baby, this is what's going to happen. You're going to go take a shower. Drink some water. Then you'll put on a skirt or dress but no underwear and meet us in your sitting room."

Her heart started racing. "Are we . . . are we . . ."

"We're just going to play," he reassured her. "Nothing happens that you don't want to."

"But I'll bring the vibrator, just in case you want to try it out."

She groaned.

"Your brothers are out for the day. No interruptions. But you always have your safeword and if you're not comfortable with anything, then you're to say it. Understand?"

"Yes, Liam."

"Good girl. You have half an hour."

She shot up with a squeal and raced out of the gym, ignoring their laughter.

Half an hour!

EXACTLY THIRTY MINUTES LATER, Lottie walked into her sitting room. The sight that greeted her made her freeze. Her mouth went dry. Her body heated until she was sweating.

Dear. Lord.

"Shut the door, baby," Liam told her as he drove a finger in and out of Nico's ass. "We don't want someone walking by and seeing something they shouldn't."

Oh, shit!

Turning, she hastily shut and locked the door then leaned her back against it. Her legs weren't really up to holding her weight and it had nothing to do with her workout earlier and everything to do with the two men in front of her.

Nico was naked and bent over, his chest resting on a foot stool. His arms were behind his back and bound with leather handcuffs. His legs were apart, and Liam knelt behind him, driving his fingers in and out of his ass.

"Fuck," Nico groaned.

"I need some help, Lottie," Liam said to her, drawing her out of her stupor.

"What? Oh, yes. What do you need?"

"Get that plug for me and put some lube on it."

"I bought those plugs to use on her," Nico complained.

"She's not ready to be plugged," Liam replied almost cheerfully.

Not ready? That implied that at some stage he'd want to plug her.

Holy. Heck.

"And it seems a waste not to use them. Baby, put some lube on the plug. Not too much. You don't have to drown it. That's it. Good girl. Now bring it here."

She walked over slowly with the glistening plug, watching in fascination as Liam removed his fingers from Nico's ass. She'd never seen an anal plug before let alone held one. It was smaller at the tip and the other end she held was flat and wider.

Should this turn her on as much as it did? She had no idea, all she knew was that she couldn't tear her eyes away from them.

Liam held his hand out for the plug. "Thank you, baby. Stand right there and watch, okay?"

Oh, yeah. She could do that.

She could watch the shit out of this.

Liam slowly pressed the plug into Nico's ass. The other man let out a low groan.

"Is it hurting?" she whispered, worried.

"How would you say this plug compares to me in size?" Liam asked instead of answering the question.

"Way smaller."

"Jeez, pretty girl, way to boost his ego."

"Thank you, baby. You're right, of course. It's way smaller than me. And he can take me just fine, can't you, Nico?"

"Yes, Li," Nico moaned as Liam situated the plug inside his ass, the end sticking out slightly between his cheeks. "Answer our girl, does it hurt?"

"No. No, it doesn't hurt."

"These plugs are small. I really should punish him for buying such tiny plugs."

Nico moaned again, but it wasn't a moan of trepidation. Nope, he sounded like he wouldn't mind being punished one bit.

"What do you think, baby girl?" Liam turned to look at her. "You think we should punish our boy for buying such small plugs?"

She glanced down at Nico. That didn't seem fair since he'd bought them for her. But then he turned his head and winked at her. Yeah, he wanted that punishment.

"Yes, I think so."

"Good choice. I want you to go sit on the sofa, Lottie," Liam commanded.

She moved to the sofa, grateful to sit. Her legs felt like jelly.

"Did you drink any water, baby?" Liam asked.

Oh, shit.

"Um, no, sorry. I forgot."

"You were given an order, weren't you?"

"Yes, Liam."

"What do you think, Nico? Does our girl deserve a punishment as well?"

"Hell, yeah. Can I give it to her?" Nico begged.

Liam raised his eyebrows, looking surprised. "You want to spank her?"

"Uh-huh." He rose up onto his knees and grinned at her. "Nothing I'd love more than to spank her ass."

Her mouth dropped open. So mean. And after she'd helped him get what he wanted.

"Nobody said you could get up, boy." Liam grasped Nico around the back of the neck and pressed him back into position. Then holding him there, he smacked his ass several times. The noise jolted her, and for a moment she didn't think she would handle it, but then Nico turned to grin at her.

This was Liam and Nico.

This was all consensual.

She let out a deep breath.

Liam rose and picked up a bottle of water sitting on the coffee table. He handed it to her. "I want you to drink all of that while I punish Nico." He crouched and cupped her chin in his hand. "You okay?"

"Yes, Liam." She should have noticed he'd see her momentary brush of panic.

"Your safeword is something you can use at any time, understand? This is just a bit of fun, and even if it weren't, remember that Nico also has a safeword."

"I also like the pain," Nico called out.

"Hush, boy," Liam said affectionately. "Sure, you're fine with this?"

"Yeah, I'm sure."

Leaning in, he lightly kissed her. "Good girl. Now, drink all that water by the time I finish, and we might go easy on you."

"Or not." Nico winked at her.

"Nobody asked for your input, boy," Liam said in that stern voice.

Her hard nipples rubbed against her silk top. Shoot. She drank down some water, more to try and cool herself down than because she felt thirsty. Liam crouched behind Nico, running his hand down his back. Then he tested the handcuffs. "They okay, boy? No pins and needles? Not hurting?"

"They're fine, Liam."

"You tell me immediately if that changes."

"I'm fine, sugar tits. Let's get onto the good stuff." Nico wriggled his ass. "Come on, you know you want to smack that."

She found herself giggling as Liam sighed, rolling his eyes. "Jesus, help me."

"He says that a lot," Nico said to her.

"Do I need to gag you?" Liam asked.

"No, Li. Unless it's with your cock? That makes a good gag, pretty girl. It's so thick, it stuffs me up good."

She giggled again then smacked her hand down on her mouth. "Sorry."

"Why are you sorry, baby girl?" Liam asked.

"It's not supposed to be funny, right? I'm not supposed to laugh."

"Why can't it be fun?" Nico asked.

"Well, I, uh, I don't know."

"It can be whatever we want," Liam told her gently. "And unless I gag him, Nico will continue to run his mouth. Giggle as much as you want."

That made her relax and she sipped at some more water.

"Actually, let's take these off," Liam said, removing the handcuffs then rubbing out Nico's arms for him. "Stand on your feet but lean over with your hands on the footstool."

Nico got into position. Heat flooded her. Then Liam moved up behind him and smacked his hand down on his ass once more. This time, she didn't jump. However, her eyes widened as Liam continued to spank Nico. After a while, Nico groaned. She watched him worriedly, concerned it might be too much. But when she managed to get a glimpse of his face, he looked so content. So satisfied.

It kind of blew her away.

He really liked this.

Liam stopped and rubbed his ass. His now pink ass.

"How are you doing?"

"Great, Liam. More."

"Ten more." Liam glanced over at her. "Drink your water, baby girl."

What? Oh, her water. Shoot. She'd forgotten about that.

Liam applied the next ten spanks to Nico's ass, and honestly, the guy looked like he was in heaven. It was fascinating and amazing to her.

"How are you doing, boy?" Liam asked.

"More," Nico demanded.

"No more."

Nico let out a noise of complaint.

"Any more grumbling and you won't get spanked for a week."

"What? No complaints from me, you must be mistaken. I never complain," Nico said hastily.

Liam winked at her, and she felt herself smiling.

"Is that water all gone, baby girl?"

Oh, shoot.

There was about an inch left in the bottle.

Liam shook his head as though disappointed in her. "What did I say?"

"That I had to drink the water while you spanked Nico. I nearly did it."

"I'm afraid nearly isn't going to cut it."

Liam walked over to her and held out his hand. She took it and let him pull her up. Then he sat, settling her on his lap. Then he took the near-empty bottle and held it to her lips, holding it up until she drank all of it.

She blushed. It felt surprisingly intimate.

"Now, how should we punish you," Liam mused.

"A spanking!" Nico suggested.

"No surprises there," Liam said dryly. He moved her hair to one side then kissed down her neck. "Have you got underwear on?"

"No," she replied.

"Good girl. This is what I want from you. I want you to sit on my lap while Nico eats you out."

"Th-that's my punishment?"

"No, your punishment is that you don't come until I say you can."

Oh, God.

"I'm going to cuff Nico's hands behind his back again. He'll only touch you with his mouth. I'll keep my hands off you. You don't have to sit on my lap if you'd rather not. But I promise, I won't touch you. Are you ready for that?"

Was she? This was moving forward. It was what she wanted. For them to touch her more intimately. Maybe she hadn't expected them to jump straight to this, but damn, she really would like to feel Nico's tongue in her pussy.

"I want to try."

"My brave, beautiful girl. Nico, get the cuffs."

"Yes, Sir!" Nico jumped to his feet with a salute.

"Lord," Liam muttered.

She found herself giggling.

After Nico was cuffed, he moved between her legs then knelt there, looking up at her. Liam put his arms along the back of the couch.

"Put your legs on the outside of mine, baby girl," Liam urged. "Then move your skirt up."

She rested her legs over his and he widened his, spreading her. Holy crap. With nervous movements, she tugged up her skirt, revealing her pussy.

"Damn, that's the prettiest thing I've ever seen." Nico stared at her hungrily and she blushed. "Fuck, I just know you're going to taste so good."

Her breathing grew faster as he leaned in and kissed up her thigh.

"Remember, at any time you can say your safeword," Liam told her. "No judgment. You start to panic, you don't like what he's doing, you say it."

"Not like what I'm doing?" Nico queried. "I admit, it's a while since I've done this. But it's like riding a bicycle, right?"

Then he took a long lick along her slick lips.

"Did he just compare my pussy to a bicycle?" she asked on a groan.

"I believe he did. And to think I let him have the first taste of you." Liam shook his head. "What was I thinking?"

"I won't do it again," Nico said quickly. "I'm not going to say anything else. Quiet as a mouse."

He returned his mouth to her pussy, flicking his tongue over her clit. Again and again. Then he pushed his tongue lower into her passage. She cried out, writhing on Liam's lap.

She needed something more. Something she couldn't put her finger on.

Then it hit her.

"Liam!"

"Yeah, baby girl?" he said in a husky voice.

"Please touch me!"

She sensed rather than felt him tense. "Are you sure?"

"Yes. Yes. Please. I need something more. I need you to touch me." She felt a bit out of control. Like she couldn't find her center. And she worried she was about to float away without something to anchor her.

"Okay, it's okay, my baby girl. I'm going to touch you. Just calm down a little for me."

He ran his hands over her arms as Nico drove his tongue in and out of her.

"Not there," she moaned.

"No?" Liam asked. "Where would you like to be touched?"

"My breasts. Please, touch my breasts."

He moved his hands over her breasts, touching her through her silky blouse. But it wasn't enough. She wriggled around on Liam's lap.

"Stay still," Liam commanded. "Remember, you're to stay still and let Nico eat you. Is he doing a good job? Do you feel like you're going to explode? What's he doing?"

"He . . . he . . ."

"What's he doing, baby girl?"

"He's driving his tongue in and out of me!" she blurted out.

"Is he? So, your poor clit isn't being touched?"

"Nooo," she moaned. "I need him to touch my clit. I need you to touch my breasts."

"I am touching them."

"My blouse, take it off."

Liam stilled. "I'll compromise. I'll undo a couple of buttons. Is that all right?"

"Yes, yes," she said frantically. "Just touch me, please."

Using his hands, he undid three buttons then drew her shirt apart to reveal her breasts.

Oh, hell. Oh, hell. She was so close.

"Remember, you're not to come until I give permission," Liam told her as he ran a finger lightly over her nipple.

She cried out. She couldn't do it. She couldn't stop herself. It was impossible.

Nico sat back on his heels, staring up at them. His lips were glistening with her dew, but she didn't have it in her to feel embarrassed.

"Did I tell you to stop?" Liam growled at Nico.

"No, I just thought I'd have a look at the most spectacular breasts I've ever seen."

"Oh, and giving our girl a chance to gain control back had nothing to do with it, I suppose," Liam said dryly.

Nico's eyes widened. "Now there's a thought."

"Get back to what you were doing," Liam commanded.

Nico sent her a wink that made her grin, thankful for the help.

"I saw that," Liam said but didn't make any more complaints as Nico returned to flicking her clit with his tongue.

Liam lightly twisted her nipples with his fingers, sending flicks of intense pleasure through her blood. She writhed, pressing up, needing more.

"Easy, baby girl. Easy."

"I can't, Liam. I can't stop it."

"You can. Just calm your breaths. Good girl. You're so responsive, so beautiful in your pleasure. What do you need?"

"More. More."

"More what?"

"Nico. Fingers. Please."

"Are you sure?"

"Yes, yes. Please!" she cried.

Liam released the other man from the handcuffs. "Nico, use your fingers to pleasure our girl."

"Fuck. Yes," Nico replied, removing his mouth for a moment. "God, you have no idea how good she tastes."

Then he returned to torturing her, his fingers pressing deep into her pussy. In and out.

"Oh. Ohhh."

"Ask for what you need," Liam commanded.

"I need to come. Please," she begged.

"Come, baby girl. Come all over Nico's fingers. Come for us."

She threw her head back, her entire body shuddering. Nico drove her up, higher and higher. Lord, what that man could do with his tongue. Then he gave her clit a final flick, and she shattered.

It was like nothing she'd experienced before. Not even with Nico when she'd pleasured herself. Nothing came close to it. Eventually, she floated back down to earth to find that Liam had moved them onto the floor. She was still on his lap but both men were petting her, talking to her in soft voices, giving her praises.

"Such a beautiful girl. So proud of you," Nico said.

"Our good girl," Liam added.

Opening her eyes, she gave them a shy smile. Glancing down, she saw that someone had done up her blouse and her skirt covered her. She leaned her face against Liam's chest.

"Back with us, huh, pretty girl?" Nico asked. "Thought I might have pleasured you into a coma."

"Nearly," she joked.

"Give me your fingers," Liam commanded. "I want to taste her."

Her heart raced as Liam took hold of Nico's hand and sucked

his fingers into his mouth. He made a murmuring noise of pleasure then pulled his mouth back. “Fucking delicious.”

She could feel herself blushing and shifted around on Liam’s lap as pleasure flooded her again.

“Easy, baby girl.” Liam grasped hold of her hips with a grimace.

“Oh, no, did I hurt you? Am I too heavy?”

They both gave her looks of disbelief.

“Too heavy?” Liam asked. “You could gain ten pounds and a stiff wind would still bowl you over.”

Nico groaned, hiding his face behind his hands. “I can’t believe you said that.”

“What? It’s the truth.”

“Yeah, but you basically just told her that she’s too skinny.”

“You don’t like my body,” she asked, putting a sad pout on her lips. Truth is, she knew she was too thin. And she got that Liam wasn’t saying that to hurt her feelings. It was just his way.

But teasing him was way too much fun.

“What? Why? How?” He let out a growling noise. “Are you serious? Not find you attractive? I turned into a fucking schoolboy the first time I saw you because you’re so beautiful.”

“That’s so sweet,” she said.

“It is. Are you feeling all right, Liam?” Nico held up his hand to Liam’s forehead as though taking his temperature.

“Quit it,” Liam commanded.

“So, if I’m not too heavy, what’s wrong? Does your back hurt?”

Liam gave her a look then nodded to Nico. “See his cock?”

Fact was, she couldn’t see much else but Nico. All that bare skin, gorgeous tattoos, and his thick cock.

“Yep?”

“Now think about what would happen if your cute little ass was pressed against it.”

Huh? What . . . Oh. He meant that he . . . She turned to look at Liam and he nodded.

"Oh, sorry. Are you . . . do you need some help, um, oh . . ."

"She's so cute when she's flustered," Nico said.

Liam grunted then lifted her off him. "I don't think you're quite ready to help me with that."

"I could though," Nico said eagerly.

"I have an online video call in ten," Liam said. Then reaching over, he cupped Nico's chin. "But later."

"Well, then maybe Lottie can help me." Nico stared over at her suggestively.

"Nice try, not happening. Both of you tidy yourselves up. Nico, you can get dressed but you're to leave the plug in for another hour. I'll meet you both downstairs."

Getting up, Liam adjusted himself then drew her in for a quick kiss. "My turn to taste you next."

She swayed on her feet as he left.

"Damn, he's being so much more dominant lately," Nico complained.

"He is?"

"Yeah. Which means I get to come much less."

"Sorry?"

"You're not sorry, brat," Nico growled at her. "Just remember, I get you all to myself tonight. While the master is away, his subs are gonna play."

"Better to ask for forgiveness than permission, huh?"

"You're starting to get this brat thing down."

"So, Liam has to go out again tonight." As soon as she said the words she wished them back. She dropped her gaze to her feet. Crap.

"Hey, look at me."

"I really need to go get into some painting clothes." The urge to paint was overwhelming. It was her saving grace.

"Charlotte, look at me."

A shiver raced over her, and she readied her gaze. Didn't matter that he was standing there naked, he had completely commanded her attention with that voice.

"That's better." He narrowed his gaze, studying her. "You don't want Liam to go out?"

"I don't . . . I just . . . it's nothing. Forget I said it."

"Stay still," he ordered.

Damn it. She sighed.

"It's not nothing if it's upsetting you."

"It's not upsetting me. I just thought it might be nice to spend the night with the two of you. But I understand. He's got to help my brother, and I'm grateful. I'm worried about Regent. I have no right to complain."

"You weren't complaining. You were just asking a question and expressing a need."

"I don't want to sound too needy."

Nico snorted. "Oh, pretty girl, you have a lot to learn. You tell Liam you need something, and that man will move heaven and earth to get it for you. Don't you get it? He thrives on being needed. Even when his scum-sucking brother needed him, he was there for him. If it's you doing the asking . . . Lottie, Liam wants to know that you need him."

"He does?"

"Just because he's a Dom doesn't make him a mind reader. And Doms have feelings too you know." He winked at her, and she rolled her eyes at his silliness. "Tell him. Trust me."

"But you're both already doing so much for me . . ."

"None of that matters. It's our choice. Because you are ours and there is nothing we wouldn't do for you."

"ARE you ever going to let us see what you paint?"

Lottie glanced over at Liam, who looked up from his laptop. He'd pulled a desk in from one of the other rooms so he could work in the solarium while she painted. Nico often worked with him, although he'd just left to go get them a snack.

"Oh, um, I guess maybe one day."

Liam frowned slightly and she felt like she'd let him down.

Ask him.

"Nico said you have to go out again tonight."

"Yes, unfortunately, we're no closer to figuring out who this rat is."

"Are my brothers in danger?"

"This sort of business isn't a safe world, baby," he said softly.

"Right. I know, I just . . ." she put her hand over her tummy.

"Hey, your brothers know what they're doing."

"I just wish they'd go completely clean. But I know that it would likely create more issues than it would solve."

"Likely. Everything okay?"

She bit her lip.

"Uh-uh, come here." He crooked a finger at her, and she moved over slowly. He turned, then lifted her onto his lap. Reaching up, he pulled her lip from her teeth. "None of that. What's wrong? Are you upset because of what happened earlier?"

"What? No! Of course not. I, uh, wouldn't mind some more of that."

"I think we could arrange that. What's wrong?"

"I'm already asking so much from you," she told him. "It feels wrong to ask for more."

"Asking so much from me? I wish that you were. What exactly do you ask from me?"

"Well, you have to stay here to be with me. Your life would be easier if you were back in New York."

"But then I wouldn't have you," he replied. "How would that

make my life easier? When all I'd want is to be back here with you? When I'd be worrying about you?"

"Really? You don't mind?"

"Fuck, no, I don't mind. What else?"

"Well, I can't . . . I mean, you have to go slow when it comes to sex because . . ."

"You think I'm going to become upset because I need to be careful with you because you were terrorized? You think that little of me?"

"What? No, of course not, I mean, I don't . . . Liam, I think you're one of the best people I know."

"You don't know many people."

"Hey, if I'm not allowed to put myself down, then neither are you," she complained.

"Is that so?" he said with amusement. "All right. You still haven't asked me for what you need."

"I wasn't going to say anything, but Nico said I should. I just wondered if one night you could stay home. With us."

"You want me to stay home with you?"

"Well, yes, of course. I mean, we spend lots of time together and everything, it's just, at night, sometimes I miss you."

"Then I'll arrange to spend more nights with you."

"I don't want to be a nuisance."

"Little girl, are you asking for a spanking?" he growled.

"What? No!" She scrambled off his lap, her hands going behind her butt. "Not me. No way. Uh-uh."

"What's going on? Ooh, is someone getting a spanking?" Nico asked as he walked into the room.

"Nope, I'm not!"

"She just keeps trying to make out like she's a nuisance."

"Ah, yeah, she does that." Nico shook his head. "I mean, I think there's only one way to get her to stop."

"What's that?" Liam asked.

"Fill her mouth."

He did not just say that!

"Nico!"

He grinned and brought the fruit platter he'd made over to the table. Leaning down, he lightly kissed her.

"Next time you say anything like that about yourself, you're getting punished," Liam warned.

Oh, no.

"I've been very patient and lenient, but that stops now."

He'd been patient and lenient? Really?

"Yep, he's serious," Nico told her. "I wouldn't get away with half the shit you have been."

"That's probably been a mistake," Liam said.

"Yep," Nico said. "You've been spoiling her."

"So, I have. I see that someone won't be sitting much in her future." Liam watched her carefully, as though trying to see if that would freak her out.

"That's so not fair! You haven't been spoiling me."

"He totally has. If she does it when you're not around, does that mean I get to spank her?" Nico asked. "I haven't gotten to do that yet and I really want to."

Liam raised an eyebrow at her. She just blushed, looking between them both.

"Yes."

"Liam!"

"Yes?" he said calmly.

"This isn't fair. You can't both punish me."

"Sure, we can," Nico grinned. "It's easy. We just tip you over our laps and smack your bottom."

"You'll always have your safeword," Liam said quietly. "And at any time, you can change your limit. Spanking can be taken off the table."

"Hmm, we could always tease her without letting her come. It's only fair since that's the punishment I keep getting."

"Poor Nico. Are you feeling frustrated?" Liam said with false sympathy.

"Yes, I'm dying."

"Then we'll just have to take care of that tonight, won't we? If you're a good boy and take care of our girl while I'm out."

"I will," Nico said eagerly.

"Glad that's settled. Come here, baby. Eat your snack."

A FEW HOURS LATER, Lottie stepped back from her painting, looking over at where they were working.

She froze, heart racing as she took them in. Liam was working on his laptop, looking every inch the successful businessman while under the table, Nico sucked him off.

She realized that she wanted to be under the table with Nico, worshipping Liam. To be totally part of their relationship. To give herself fully.

"Okay, baby?" Liam asked.

She met his bright blue gaze and smiled ruefully. "Epiphany."

"Yeah, good one?"

"Yes, I think so. I want it all, Liam. Everything."

His eyes flared wide. "As in . . ."

"Your dominance. And Nico's. To be loved by both of you. I want to be completely part of your relationship."

"You are."

She shook her head. "I'm still holding back." She moved closer and stared down at Nico who peered up at her from between Liam's legs. "I need to trust. To be vulnerable."

"There's no rush."

"I know. But it's what I want." Liam wrapped an arm around

her middle. "I trust you both not to hurt me physically. I mean, I wouldn't consent to being your sub and discipline if I didn't. But I need to trust you not to hurt me emotionally as well."

"That's something we all need to work on," Liam replied.

"I know. Can I watch?"

"Baby girl, whatever I have to give, it's yours. Forever."

Forever.

19

"Old man," Liam growled into the phone in irritation. "This better be good."

He'd walked outside into the cool air. Tonight, they were at another underground boxing fight, and it was a fucking trying night. So many people came up to him, trying to ascertain whether he was planning on getting back into the ring. His patience was short. It didn't help that he'd rather be back at the house with Nico and Lottie.

They'd looked so comfortable, curled up together on the sofa under a blanket. He wouldn't be surprised if they got hot and heavy with each other. Nico had been given orders not to come until Liam allowed it, but that didn't mean he wouldn't play.

And fuck it, Liam wanted to be there with them.

"Well, I'm startin' to regret doin' the Malones a good deed by warnin' them."

"Warning them of what? Have you heard who the rat is?"

"No, but I have heard that there's an FBI raid about to be conducted on the Malone mansion," his grandfather said slyly.

"What? Fuck! Nico and Lottie are there alone."

"I suggest you get them out of there. Quick. And get Malone to clean house. This fucking rat isn't going to go down easily."

His grandfather hung up and he called Nico quickly as he rushed back to Regent.

"Come on, pick up," he urged.

~

NICO RAN his fingers up the inside of his girl's thigh. She was wearing a pair of silky shortie pajamas and it left a lot of skin for him to play with. He was wearing a T-shirt and sweatpants.

Fuck, he was still hard as nails. He had been all day. It felt like he'd been hard since they arrived there. Liam wasn't in a much better position. Oh, except he was getting some release several times a day.

Not that Nico was complaining about that. But he was starting to think that his dick might fall off soon if this kept on.

Sure, okay, Liam had jacked him off in the shower this morning, but that was freaking ages ago. He was a growing boy who needed lots of stimulation.

"Nico," Lottie turned to him.

"Hmm?"

"Are you even watching the movie?"

"No."

"Oh, okay. Are you just going to stare at me all night?"

"You're so pretty," he sighed.

She grinned at him. "You're crazy."

"You wanna be my wife?"

She stiffened. "You know that's not possible."

"But if it was, would you marry me? Marry us?"

"Well, I'd expect a proper proposal."

He straightened, excitement filling him. "All right. I can do that." He slid down on one knee. "Charlotte Rosa Malone, will you marry me?"

"Nico! Stop playing around." She gave him an embarrassed look, but there was a hint of hurt in her face.

Oh, no, he couldn't have that.

He threw the blanket off her and moved between her legs, taking her hands in his. "Pretty girl, I'm not joking. I want you to be mine. Ours. Our wife."

"But . . ."

"And if you think the fact that a ménage marriage isn't possible will stop that from happening, then you need to think again. Liam will make it happen."

"You'd really want to marry me?"

His eyes narrowed. "And why wouldn't I want to marry you?"

"Um, well, I . . ."

His phone rang. "Fuck. I have to answer that, it's Liam's ringtone. But afterward, you're going to tell me why you think I wouldn't want to marry you."

"I don't want to," she wailed.

"Why? Because you were going to say something naughty that would get your butt spanked?"

"No! Who me?"

He snorted. "Can't kid a kidder, pretty girl."

Shoot.

She was an idiot.

And now she was an idiot, in trouble because she had no doubt that Nico would follow through on any sort of threat.

Drat. Drat. Drat.

"What?" Nico asked, growing tense. She studied him. He crooked his finger at her. She jumped up and raced to him.

"What is it? Is Liam okay? My brothers?"

Nico shook his head at her. "Okay, yeah. Where do I go? Got it. Yeah, I will. Right."

He ended the call and looked at her, eyes wide.

"What is it?" she asked, feeling herself starting to crumble. "What is it?"

"Calm down."

"I can't calm down until you tell me what's going on."

Calm down? Was he serious? Did he want her to remove his balls from his body?

"We need to leave."

"Leave? What do you mean, leave?"

She couldn't leave. Her breath grew faster.

"Okay, pretty girl. Listen."

"I can't leave."

"Lottie—"

"I can't."

"Charlotte," he said sternly, making her jump. She'd only heard that tone from him a few times, but it quickly got her attention. "We are leaving. There is about to be a raid on this house. And neither you nor I can be here. I want you to go and pull on some clothes. Grab anything that is small and irreplaceable. Leave everything else. I have to rush and do a couple of things for your brother."

"Nico," she said.

"No. You are not going to think. You are just going to do what you are told. No thinking. Just obey. Understand?"

"I . . . I . . ."

"Understand?" he said sternly.

"Yes."

"Yes, Nico."

"Yes, Nico," she repeated.

"Good. Go." He turned her, giving her a smack to the ass.

She raced upstairs. When the panic started to hit her, she held onto his words.

Don't think. Just obey.

Don't think. Just obey.

She changed, pulling on dark clothes and tying back her hair. She grabbed a bag and rapidly picked up her jewelry box, her phone and charger and Hero, her teddy bear that she'd had since she was a baby.

She had to leave. Panic clawed at her.

Don't think. Just obey.

Her phone buzzed and she looked down at it. Regent.

"Reggie?" she asked.

"Are you ready to leave?"

"Y-yes."

"You're going to be fine. Understand me? But I need you to do something."

"What?"

"Go into the safe and grab everything in it. There's not much, but I need you to take it."

"Yes, okay. I can do that. Regent," she cried.

"It's okay, darling. It will all be all right."

Her breath sobbed out of her as she raced downstairs. She found Nico already in the office, grabbing a laptop and putting it in a backpack. He had dark clothes on too.

With a shaky hand, she opened the hidden safe and grabbed everything out, dumping it in her bag. It wouldn't all fit and she let out a sob.

"It's all right, darling," Regent said in her ear. "You only need to leave for a short time. I promise."

"Here, I'll help." Nico took the rest of the stuff. "Tell him we have everything."

"I heard," Regent said. "Lock it back up and then you and Nico need to use the tunnels."

"Regent," she cried.

"You can do this, darling. You can't take a car out. They're at the gate. Okay? Go to the tunnels."

"What is it?" Nico asked her. "What's wrong?"

"We have to go through the tunnels." She grabbed his hand and dragged him toward the back of the house where the kitchen was. None of the staff were around, most of them lived off-site except for Gerald, who waited in the kitchen with the trap door open.

"I'll close it off when you go in," he explained to them both. "You need to go now."

"I can't!" she cried.

"You have to," Regent implored.

"Give the phone to me," Liam said in the background.

"Fuck!" Regent swore.

"Baby girl, can you hear me?"

"Y-yes. Liam, I don't want to. I'll stay. Nico can go."

"No," Liam said firmly. "You're going with him. Take his hand."

"I have it."

"Let him lead you in. You trust him, don't you?"

"Yes."

"And you trust me?"

"Yes."

"Then you're going to do as you are told. Follow Nico into the tunnel."

"Yes, Liam."

"Let me talk to Nico." She handed the phone over and Nico spoke quickly before ending the call. Then he gave her a determined look. "Let's go, pretty girl."

Nico led her down the stairs. She'd always hated the tunnels. When she was a small child, she and Maxim would play in them. They weren't supposed to, but that just made it more exciting. But then she'd gotten lost in them, and it had been hours until she'd been found.

Her breath came in harsh pants as they made it to the bottom of the stairs. And then the door above them closed, sending them into darkness.

A sob escaped her. She couldn't do this. She had to get out. The darkness. She was going to suffocate.

"Lottie, Lottie, you're fine. I'm here. You're not going to die. I have you. Hush, pretty girl. You're killing me here."

The worry in Nico's voice broke through her panic. "Sorry. Sorry."

He turned on the flashlight Gerald had handed him.

"Listen to me. I need you to breathe with me. That's it. Slow it down. Big breaths. Good girl. I'm sorry, but we have to move. Okay? I need you to walk with me. We can't risk staying here."

"I know. I know."

"Just hold my hand, close your eyes if you need to. I'll walk you out."

"But you don't know where you're going."

"I'll figure it out."

"No, I have to . . . I have to show you. I can do this. I can."

I can't. I can't.

He cupped her face between his hands. "You can do this. I believe in you. I'm right here. I'm going nowhere."

He was here. He wasn't going anywhere. He wouldn't leave her. She could do this.

NICO COULD FEEL her shaking and it killed him.

He wished he could just pick her up and carry her out of here. But he couldn't. He needed her to keep it together, so the best thing he could do for her was to be strong.

She led him through the underground tunnels that must have been here for years. It was cold and damp and he had to admit, he fucking hated being in here as well.

Every so often, red eyes glanced out at him, and he heard the scurrying of rats along the ground.

Lottie would let out a small whimper, but she would keep going, her hand wrapped around his. It was a double whammy for her. Leaving the house as well as walking through these fucking awful tunnels.

"You're doing so good, pretty girl," he murmured when he heard her breathing speed up. She dug her nails into him, but he didn't care. Better him than have her hurt herself.

"I hate it down here. I want to go home."

"I know. I know you do. Not much longer."

He had no idea how much longer it was. Fact was, she was doing far better than he'd thought. He figured she would have frozen up. And he'd been prepared for that. Liam told him to get her as far as he could and that they would find them. No matter what.

He had complete faith in Liam. All he had to do was keep their girl safe until their Dom could get to them.

"Nico," she whispered on a soft cry. She stopped, her hand pressing to her chest. "I . . . I . . ."

"You got this, pretty girl. You're doing so well. Come here." He drew her close, hugging her tightly.

"I . . . I can't go any further."

"You don't have to. You got us far enough away. We can wait here."

"But . . . but . . ."

"We can stay here. Liam will come for us."

"He'll come for us?"

"Do you doubt that anyone would stop Liam from finding us?"

"Right. Right. Liam will find us. Can you . . . can you . . ."

"Can I what?"

"Can you t-tell me n-not to think? In that c-commanding voice. W-when you say it l-like that. It's e-easier. I can b-breathe."

Got it. Maybe now wasn't the time for gentle. He grasped her cheeks in his hands and raised her face. The light tilted up at the ceiling but that didn't matter right now. There was still enough illumination to see her.

"You are going to listen to me," he commanded. "You are going to keep walking. You will get us out of here. Because it's what I want. Understand? You're going to do as I say, aren't you, Charlotte?"

Her breathing started to calm.

"Yes."

"Yes, what?" he asked sternly.

"Yes, Nico."

"You're not going to think about anything else but what I want. What Liam wants. We both want you to lead us out of here. Understand?"

"Yes, Nico."

"Good girl." He longed to kiss her, but she was growing calmer, and he didn't want to do anything to ruin that.

Fuck, she was so brave. So beautiful.

A miracle.

~

LIAM FELT like he was going to crawl out of his skin.

"What if they're not there? What if they can't get through the tunnels?"

Regent glanced at Victor. Their driver was taking them to where Lottie and Nico were supposed to end up. What if something fucking happened to them?

"I should never have left them alone," he said.

"If they're not there, then we'll have to go in. Lottie won't be coping," Victor said.

Regent's phone rang and he answered it.

"Lottie's stronger than you give her credit for," Liam told them. But he didn't see how she could managing this. Leaving the house, going through the tunnels, the FBI raiding her house.

"The lawyer is at the house," Regent said, hanging up.

"Jardin?"

"No. Jardin needs to be kept separate from all this. Maxim and my trusted lieutenants have gone to each legitimate business in case the FBI turn up there."

"Feels like plugging holes in a sinking ship," Victor muttered.

Regent grunted. "The plane is ready to take Lottie to our place in Mexico. I assume you'll want to accompany her."

He shook his head.

"You're not going with her?"

"No. She's not going to Mexico. She needs to be far away from you and your family."

"No one will get to her there. No one knows about the house in Mexico."

"Someone knows a lot about your family."

Regent ran his hand over his face. "Fuck."

"I'll take her somewhere else."

"How do we know she'll be safe?" Victor asked.

"Because I'd die before I let anything happen to her."

"She won't cope with going to New York," Regent pointed out.

"I'm not taking her to New York, I'll take her somewhere else."

"Fuck." Regent was silent for a long moment. "Fine, but you'll be in contact constantly. I want to hear from her three times a day. And it's only until this mess is sorted. Then she'll be coming home."

"If she wants to come home after this mess is sorted, including finding the rat, then I will bring her. But it's not safe for her until you clean house."

"Agreed," Regent said between clenched teeth. "Here we are."

"The exit comes out here?" They looked to be in suburbia. A

normal neighborhood with average houses. Their driver pulled into a driveway and then a garage door went up.

"We own the house. The tunnel comes up inside it. A friend lives here."

The door opened. Regent got out. Then Victor and Liam.

They entered the house and a woman appeared in front of them. She was curvy and beautiful, but Liam didn't have any attention to spare for her. "Where are they? Are they here?"

The woman looked over at him as Regent moved to her side.

"No, they're not here yet. I've got the tunnel open. I haven't heard anything."

Liam stalked behind her into a back bedroom. A closet door was open, and a trapdoor was pulled back.

"I'm going in to find them," he said.

"You don't know where to go," Regent pointed out.

"I'll go," Victor said.

"Hush," the woman said, kneeling. "I hear something."

There was the sound of something. Voices and then a light.

"Nico? Lottie?" he called out.

"Li?" Nico yelled. He nearly collapsed in relief. And then Nico appeared in the hole. He glanced around then disappeared. And Lottie came up the stairs. She was pale, shaky, and her breathing was too fast.

But she was there.

Before she'd even managed to climb out, he had her in his arms, lifting her and holding her against him.

"It's all right, gorgeous girl. You're okay."

Nico came up next and he reached for him, hugging him tightly. But he pulled away quickly as the others shut the trap door.

"We need to calm her down," Nico said. "She's been so brave. So fucking brave. She showed me how to get here even though she was panicking and terrified."

"That's my girl. My amazing girl." He didn't care that the others were there, watching. He'd do whatever Lottie needed him to do. Sitting on the bed, he arranged her on his lap while Nico knelt on the floor next to him.

"You did it, pretty girl. You got us here. But you need to slow your breathing. Follow me," Nico coached. "In. Out. In. Out."

But she was struggling. He could feel it. Feel her panic.

"Get out of the way, I'll help her," Regent said. "Come here, darling."

"Charlotte, listen to me," Liam said firmly. "You need to breathe, baby girl. Or you're going to pass out. You're safe. I'm here. Nico is here. So are your brothers. So, take a breath. Come on, baby girl. Breathe."

SHE COULD HEAR Liam's words.

But they were coming from a distance. And then a warm hand was placed around the base of her neck. Warm breath moved against her ear.

"Listen to me," Liam said firmly. "Relax. Breathe. One. Two. Three. Out. Good girl. Again."

His words flowed through her. And she gasped in a breath. Nico held her hands, squeezing them tightly. She squeezed back.

"You're safe. Just breathe," Nico told her.

She was safe. She just had to breathe.

When the panic attack faded, and she came back to herself, she realized she was in the bedroom at Jilly's place. Where the tunnel came out. She'd only been here once. She didn't know Jilly well. And was embarrassed to have panicked in front of her.

But she also wasn't moving off Liam's lap.

As the panic faded, she realized there was an argument going on around her. Jilly had left the room and Victor stood at the door while Regent stood by the closet, which was now closed.

"How is she supposed to cope with leaving?" Regent demanded.

"She's stronger than you think," Liam argued back.

"She just had a panic attack."

"After she had to leave her house in a hurry, running from the FBI through dark, damp tunnels," Nico argued. "Most people would have a panic attack after that."

"She isn't weak. She has demons, but so do a lot of people. Lottie is a fighter," Liam added.

Their words filled her with strength and even though she was exhausted, she straightened up. "Wh-what's this about leaving?"

Regent looked down at her for a moment before his phone started ringing. "Fuck."

Shit. He must have a lot to take care of.

"Regent, you need to go. I'm all right."

He shook his head. "Nothing matters as much as you. I need to take care of you first."

"No." She stood, and Liam held her hips as she wobbled. "I'm fine." She walked over to him and wrapped him up in a hug. "I know you've sacrificed so much for me. Spent so much time worrying about me. But right now, you need to take care of you. I'm all right, Reggie."

Regent looked to Liam then back to her. "I want you to go to our place in Mexico."

"What about you guys?" she asked him and Victor.

"Victor and I need to stay here," Regent told her. "But I want you well away from New Orleans."

Liam ran his hand over his face. "You're going to come with us. We'll take you to Mexico if you want, but I don't think it's a good idea right now. I'd rather take you somewhere else."

"Where?"

"We'll figure it out."

She knew what she should suggest. But could she do it? Go back there? Panic welled again.

"See?" Regent said. "She's not ready. She can barely leave the damn house."

"Lottie, baby girl," Liam crooned, coming up behind her and placing a hand on her shoulder. "It's all right. Just breathe. You're safe."

"I really have to leave?" she asked. She glanced around, and everyone gave her a sad look.

"It will be safer if you're not here," Regent admitted. "Whoever this rat is, they've really fucked shit up for us."

"Will you be all right staying here?"

"We'll be fine," Regent told her firmly. "Nothing is happening to us. I'm just concerned about you."

And if he didn't have her to worry about, he could concentrate on everything else.

She stared back at Liam then Nico. She could do this. She could do anything as long as she was with them.

"I love you both. Make sure that you take care of yourselves and everyone else. But you don't need to worry about me. I'll be with Liam and Nico."

"You're sure?" Regent asked her.

"I'm sure. I have this, Regent. Look at me. Out of the house and only one panic attack." She crossed her fingers behind her back, where she knew Nico could see them. She just hoped he knew not to talk about the panic attacks she'd had in the tunnel.

"Okay, darling, if you're sure. But I want you to check in often. And you can come back as soon as this is done with, all right?"

She nodded.

"We better go," Liam said. "My plane is ready and waiting."

"Where are you going?" Victor asked.

"New York," she blurted out.

Everyone froze then stared at her.

"Lottie, no," Liam said gently. "No one expects that."

"You need to go back. You have work to do. You have a place there. That's where we should go."

"You're not going back there," Regent said.

"I have to," she whispered. "I think it will help me move forward. Even if it's just for a few days."

"You sure?" Liam asked her.

She straightened her shoulders. "Yes."

"So brave," he told her. "We'll go. But if you can't deal with being there, we'll leave. No arguments."

"No arguments."

"I don't like it. But fuck, okay," Regent groaned. "Do you need to be sedated?"

"I . . ." Shit. She wished she could say no, but the idea of getting on a plane and flying off . . . but then, she would be asleep, helpless. "I don't know."

"Jilly might have some. Take them with you. You can always take them on the plane. I love you, sister."

"Love you too." Regent hugged her then disappeared to talk to Jilly.

Victor came up to her and lifted her up. "You'll call."

"I will. Take care of him."

"Of course."

20

Nico brushed Lottie's hair back from her face as he stared down at her.

It had been a brutal night for her. Fuck. For all of them. Going through the tunnels, the plane trip then car ride here. But she was finally in their penthouse apartment. In the end, she'd asked for the sedatives once on the plane. She'd been worried about getting hysterical and causing issues.

Fuck. They didn't care what issues she had. All they wanted was her with them.

Didn't matter anymore. She was here. She wasn't going anywhere. Leaning down, he kissed her forehead. He'd gotten her undressed and into one of his T-shirts. He should let her sleep.

And go and deal with their lord and master.

Hell, his work was never done.

He strode into the living room and slumped back on the sofa, watching as Liam paced back and forth. The tension coming off him was palatable.

No way would he get to sleep like this. Nico would have to help him calm down first.

Liam stilled and turned to him. The anger and anguish on his face floored Nico. "She's safe, Liam."

"She nearly wasn't. You nearly weren't."

"We weren't in any danger. It was the FBI, they wouldn't have hurt us."

"They could have taken you both from me."

"We would have been okay."

"You had to walk through damp, dangerous tunnels to get to safety. Without me. That's not fucking acceptable." Liam turned, slamming a fist into the wall.

Aw, hell.

"Liam, stop it!" he said sharply.

"What?" He was so shocked by Nico's commanding voice that he stopped and turned. "What did you say?"

"I said stop it, you're acting like an ass."

"An ass?" Liam took a step toward him.

That's right, come to me. Take it all out on me.

Nico knew he'd never hurt him. And he needed to get it out.

"That's right. An ass. Lottie and I were the ones who had to run. She's the one who's been through multiple panic attacks because of her anxiety and fears. Now, she's sleeping peacefully while you're taking your aggression out on that poor wall."

"Nico," he said warningly. "Go to bed."

"Can't do that."

"Yes, you can. Go to bed."

"And what are you going to do?"

"Hit the gym."

"Or we could go to the playroom."

"I'm not in a good place to play."

"But—"

"No, Nico. I won't risk you. I won't ever risk you."

"Then let me help you. Please, Liam. I need you to."

Something came over Liam. Then he ran his hand over his face. "Fuck, I'm being a selfish ass."

"I get it," Nico told him, standing and moving over to him.

"I can't be gentle right now," Liam warned.

"Not asking you to."

When he was close, Liam reached out and grabbed him. Spinning him, he pressed him to the wall. Then he placed his hand around Nico's neck. He arched his head back, offering his submission, needing Liam to take everything he had to offer.

"Fuck, I don't deserve you."

"Don't be a fucking idiot, Liam."

"You've forgotten how to talk to your Dom, boy."

"I always talk to you like that," Nico countered with a grin.

"And it always gets you into trouble," Liam murmured.

Yes. But the most delicious kind.

Liam tightened his hold on Nico's neck, and he let out a low moan of pleasure. Then he kissed him. It was hard. Brutal. He bit his lip while his free hand grabbed at Nico's T-shirt, tugging at it.

"Let me strip for you, Liam," Nico told him. "Let me help you."

"Fuck!" Liam took a step back. "Strip."

Nico hastily got rid of his clothes, throwing them in a pile, then he reached for Liam, pulling off his clothes. Once the other man was naked, Nico started kissing his way down his chest, his stomach. Then he kneeled, taking the head of his dick into his mouth. Liam stayed still, silent, but he could feel the tension in him. He took his cock deep.

"Fuck," Liam muttered. "You better have fucking lube on you."

"When don't I?" Nico asked, drawing back. He cupped Liam's balls, playing with them as he licked his way back up his dick.

"Get it out. Then bend over, hands on the wall."

Nico scrambled for his sweatpants, grabbing out the lube. Yep, he kept packets everywhere. He handed it to Liam who had his belt in one hand.

Oh, fuck yes.

Nico rose and turned, leaning over and bracing his hands on the wall. The belt landed without warning, and he hissed at the sting. But it filled his body with warmth, pleasure. The first few licks were the worst, then he managed to relax into the pain. Christ, he wished he could reach down and play with his cock.

"Liam!"

"Yes?"

"Can I touch myself?"

"No."

He groaned. God, he could be such a motherfucking bastard sometimes.

The belt landed again. And again. Until Nico was floating. Fuck. He felt so good.

Then the belt dropped on the floor and his ass cheeks were parted. A slippery finger prodded at his entrance, and he let out a low moan as Liam pushed two fingers deep. He relaxed as Liam thrust his fingers in and out, stretching him.

"I can't wait, Nico. Fuck."

"Don't wait. Take me, fuck, take me, sugar plum."

Liam removed his fingers, replacing them with his cock. Nico let out a low moan.

"Fuck, Nico. Fuck, you feel so good."

"Take what you need from me, Liam. I'm yours to use."

It was as if Liam was waiting for permission to let go of the reins. He became almost wild. His thrusts were deep and fast. Rough. He grasped hold of Nico's hips, drove himself deep.

Christ. Christ.

Nico groaned. He needed to come so badly. Liam kept him on the edge. He filled him, driving him insane. Then Liam moaned behind him, coming deep inside him. Nico was breathing deeply, sweat coating his skin as he leaned against the wall. Liam slid out of him, and Nico tried to catch his breath.

Suddenly, he was pulled up then spun around and pressed to the wall. Liam kissed him. There was such ferocity and passion in that kiss that Nico melted against him. But Liam wasn't finished with him, he started kissing his way down his body.

"Liam?" Nico queried.

It wasn't often the other man sucked him off. And he never got on his knees for him. However, Liam was now kneeling, looking up at him. "I fucking love you."

"I love you too. You don't have to do this."

"No. But I want to."

Then he took Nico's cock deep into his mouth. Nico groaned, his eyes practically rolling back in his head at the sensation.

This was fucking heaven. It wasn't long until Nico was on the edge. Liam had a fucking talented mouth

"Liam, please, I need to come."

Liam drew back, running his hand up and down Nico's dick. "Then come."

He took him deep once more. Up and down, sucking him in. Pleasure rose inside him, and he cried out as he came, releasing into Liam's mouth. His husband sucked him down, licking his dick clean before he rose and drew Nico close.

"Thank you for keeping both of you safe."

"Always, Liam. You never have to thank me for that."

They were pulling apart as a scream ripped through the penthouse. Liam turned and ran into the spare bedroom where they'd put their girl. Much as they wanted her in their bed, neither had been sure how she'd take waking up between them.

By the time Nico entered the bedroom, Liam was already talking calmly to Lottie. She shied away from him with a cry.

"Lottie, baby. It's me. It's Liam."

"We're here, Lottie," Nico said, walking slowly closer. "You're safe. You're with us. You're safe."

A shuddering sob ripped through her, and she slumped back on the bed. "Liam? Nico?"

"That's right," Nico told her. "You're safe."

"Where am I? I don't know where I am!"

Her fear-filled voice ripped through him.

"You're at our penthouse," Liam told her. "I know it's somewhere new, and it's scary but you're with us. And we're not going to let anything happen to you."

"Your penthouse. With you. And Nico." She glanced around as though looking for him. Satisfaction filled him. He knew now that he'd never be a second-fiddle to her. To either of them. They needed him.

"I'm here."

"Nico," she moaned. "We went through the tunnels. He helped me. Helped me stop thinking."

"Good, I'm glad. I'm sorry I wasn't with you."

"You . . . you were with Regent. Don't be sorry. Don't. I'm thirsty."

Liam helped her sit while Nico poured her a glass of water from the carafe he'd put by her bed earlier.

Nico helped her drink while Liam sat next to her, supporting her with his arm.

"I'm in New York," she said quietly as Nico drew the glass back.

"You are," Liam agreed.

Nico watched her fingers curl into one another and shared a look of concern with Liam. They'd need to watch her closely. If anything was going to make her feel out of control, it was coming back here.

"Was this too much? We can go somewhere else," Liam told her.

"No, no, of course not."

"Charlotte," Nico said warningly.

He was aware of Liam's raised eyebrow at his tone. He was also very aware that they were both naked. But she hadn't seemed to notice.

"Don't push aside your feelings just for us," Nico said to her. "Talk to us."

"I-I'm scared. I've barely been able to leave our property and now I'm back in the city where I was kidnapped."

"Right, we'll make arrangements to leave tomorrow," Liam said firmly.

"No. No." She shook her head.

"Lottie, staying here isn't worth risking your mental health," Liam told her.

"You're worried I'll hurt myself?"

They shared another look.

"I . . . I'm not going to do that anymore. I hope. Or at least . . . I have ways to cope. I have both of you and Molly. If I feel like that then I'll talk to one of you."

"That's right, you do," Nico said to her. "You're so fucking brave."

"Home was always my safe place, but now, it's the two of you. You're my safe haven." She looked at Nico then up to Liam.

"Fuck, baby girl, you don't know how happy that makes me," Liam told her. "But I also want your promise that if that changes, if you feel unsure, or like you're going to hurt yourself, that you'll tell us."

"Why don't we stay in here until you fall asleep?" Nico suggested, seeing how exhausted she was.

"Actually, would you both sleep with me? I don't want to be alone."

"Of course, baby," Liam said. "Let's go to our bedroom, the bed is bigger. It's where you belong anyway."

He picked her up after she nodded and carried her into the room.

"So, um, I'm guessing I interrupted something," she said with a blush as Liam set her down.

"Interrupted, no," Nico replied with a grin. "You timed it just right." He winked at her, and she giggled.

It was the sweetest sound he'd ever heard. And once he'd had a shower, he was going to cuddle the shit out of their girl. They had her all to themselves.

Everything was going to be perfect from now on.

21

Fuck.

Things were a mess. Lottie pressed her forehead to the glass window of the penthouse, looking out at the New York skyline. Outside this penthouse, people moved around, going on with their business while she was stuck here. The princess in the tower. She'd exchanged one prison for another.

Not that either of them were keeping her there. The only person holding her captive was herself.

A week had passed since they'd come here. The first few days had been a mess. She'd had so many nightmares. Liam had threatened to stick them all on a plane to somewhere else so many times. Nico had been the one stuck holding them all together.

Why won't my damn brain work properly?

She was so sick of this. She kicked the window then let out a cry, hopping around, holding her foot.

"What is it? What happened?" Liam ran into the room from his office. Both men had been sticking close by and honestly, those first few days she'd needed it. She couldn't have done this without them. She hadn't been lying when she said they were her safe place.

So why can't you leave this apartment?

Just step outside. No one is going to grab you. Hurt you.

Molly had been cautioning her about pushing herself too fast. About being too hard on herself. But she just wanted to be better.

Molly claimed this was actually a good thing. Lottie wasn't so sure.

The second day here, Nico had gone out and bought out half of an art store for her. But she couldn't paint. She didn't know why. And she checked in with her brothers constantly. The FBI hadn't found anything thanks to what she and Nico had squirreled out.

Somehow, Liam had managed to get the plane's manifest changed so that it looked like she and Nico had flown out earlier that day. She didn't know how, she guessed a lot of money crossed palms. The FBI had sent requests to talk to her, but since they had nothing on her or her family, they couldn't force her to talk to them.

"Banged my toe."

"Poor baby. Let me see." Liam picked her up and carried her to the sofa.

The guys were being so sweet with her, treating her so gently. But that was starting to frustrate her too. Sure, she'd needed it to begin with. And she wasn't saying that she wanted it to stop, necessarily. Just she knew that they were holding back.

There had been hardly anything sexual between them.

She wanted to be more than someone they took care of.

She wanted to be the sexual goddess they couldn't take her hands off.

"What happened? Is she all right?"

"Bumped her toe," Liam replied to Nico. "Get an ice pack."

"It's fine," she told them. "It barely hurts."

But Nico had already returning soon with an ice pack. He sat on the sofa next to them and applied it gently to her toes.

"There, is that better?" Nico asked. "Poor toes. What did you hit them on?"

"The glass."

"The glass?" Liam asked.

"I kicked it."

"You kicked the window?" Nico asked.

"Yes."

"Why?" Liam asked.

"Because I'm frustrated. I want . . . I want . . ."

"Yes, baby?" Liam asked.

"I want to give you a blow job," she blurted out.

There. She'd said it. There was no taking it back. What she wanted was to give him a blow job.

"And you," she said to Nico. "And I want you both to fuck me. That's what I want."

She folded her arms across her chest and gave them a nod.

They gaped at her then each other.

"That's what you want, huh?" Liam asked.

"Yes. I just . . . I don't want to be on the outside anymore, looking in."

Liam gave her a shocked look. "You don't feel like you're part of this relationship?"

"No, that's not it . . . " She let out a frustrated groan. "I know you both love me."

"Good," Nico said. "Because we do."

She climbed off Liam's lap to look down at them both. "I needed you to be careful with me, in the beginning. Probably will still need that sometimes. But I'm tired of being the weirdo that worries about leaving the house because she thinks she'll have a panic attack. Or has to be closely watched to make sure she doesn't hurt herself. Or can't be fucked for fear she'll break."

They were silent for a long moment.

Great, did I break them?

"Did she just call herself a weirdo?" Liam asked Nico.

"Yep. She sure did," Nico replied.

"Is that acceptable?" Liam asked.

Is he talking to me?

"Oh, no, it's definitely not." Nico gave her a sharp look. "That's breaking the rules."

Her breath caught. Were they going to . . . oh, holy crap. She may have bitten off more than she could chew. But she knew they wouldn't harm her. This was what she wanted.

"You have two choices, girl," Liam told her.

Her heart raced at his firm tone.

"What?"

"You can go snuggle on the couch with Nico and watch a movie."

Good choice. But not exactly what she wanted.

"Or you can strip and put yourself across my knee for a punishment."

Holy. Fuck.

LIAM WAS PRETTY sure he knew what she would choose. But he wanted to give her that choice. He waited, expecting her to say she chose the movie. Then he was going to give her a good scolding.

Instead, he was shocked when she reached for the bottom of her top. Reaching out, he grabbed her hand. "You sure?"

"I'm sure. I want this."

He stared up at her.

"You've got to trust me too, Liam. Trust that I know my limits. That I know what I want."

Fuck.

She was right. He nodded. "Okay, then continue stripping."

Both of them sat on the sofa, watching, enraptured as she slowly took off her clothes. He found himself swallowing heavily, his mouth growing dry as she took off her bra, revealing those perfect breasts.

"Jesus, pretty girl. You're gorgeous," Nico told her. "I'm so fucking hard right now."

"Nico, you strip as well," Liam ordered.

"Fuck, you don't need to ask me twice."

Nico whipped off his top, revealing that smooth dark-toned skin.

Lottie grabbed the top of her yoga pants as Nico stood to take off his jeans. She whipped them down, revealing everything.

"Shit, she's not wearing underwear," Nico said in an amazed voice.

"I thought I'd join you both," she said with a tiny grin. It was clear she was nervous, but she wasn't trying to hide. She wasn't panicking or shaking with fear.

She stood there, beautiful and strong.

"So proud of you, baby," Liam told her.

Nico had stripped as well by now.

"Nico, sit back down next to me. Lottie, over my knee." He held out his hand and she slipped her hand into his.

Her hand was slightly cool, but he knew it was normal for her to be a bit anxious; this was new territory. He held her over his lap, her face was practically in Nico's lap.

"Hallelujah," Nico said. "I've died and gone to heaven."

Lottie giggled.

"Quiet, both of you," he mock-growled. "This is serious business."

"Sorry, Master," Lottie told him.

"That's lord and master," Nico said to her.

Another giggle escaped her. He shook his head. Then he got back to the task at hand. He rubbed his hand over her ass.

"Why did you kick the window, baby?" he asked in a gentle voice.

She sighed. "I don't want to say."

"Well, I want you to tell me."

"Fuck, she has the most beautiful ass," Nico said on a sigh.

"Doesn't she? Too bad I'm going to have to turn it red. Especially since someone isn't answering my questions." He smacked his hand down several times on her ass. Not very hard. He didn't want to really hurt her. Nico could take pain. He enjoyed it. Lottie was far softer. Delicate. Gentle.

But she was still going to get her butt spanked.

She let out a low moan.

"Fuck, I can feel her breath on my cock, Liam."

"Look how hard he is, Lottie. Just from having your mouth so close to him. Imagine what he's going to be like once your mouth is on his dick."

"Yes, please," Nico breathed. "Tell her to take me into her mouth."

"Soon," Liam told him. "But first, her punishment." Several more smacks to her ass later, he stopped to rub her lower back. Her bottom was pink, and she'd started shifting around on his lap. But he wasn't entirely sure if that was due to the pain from the spanking or because she was enjoying it.

"Why did you kick the window?"

"I was frustrated," she admitted.

"Why?"

"Because I . . . I'm here and yet I'm stuck again. I move forward one step and back two. I'm just . . . I want everything to move quicker."

"And what does your therapist say?"

"That I've already taken a huge leap, before I was ready to and that I have to give myself a break. Time to come to terms with moving from my home, from my brothers back to the place which held so many nightmares for me."

"Does she think it was a bad idea to come here?" Liam asked.

"She wasn't too enthused, no. She said she would rather have worked me up to where I was comfortable going out in public back home first. I think she saw this as several months down the track, maybe longer."

"Fuck," he muttered. He'd made the wrong move. Instead of listening to her, he should have taken her somewhere else.

He shared a look with Nico who appeared equally worried.

"I should talk to this therapist," Liam suggested.

She turned her head to look at him. "Actually, she suggested that might be a good idea."

"Did she? When?"

Lottie bit her lip on a wince. "Um, well, oh . . ."

"Charlotte," he said in a low, warning voice.

"When we first got here."

He stilled his hand where he'd been rubbing her lower back. "Really? And why didn't you tell us that?"

"Um. I . . . I don't know exactly. You guys were busy . . ."

"We're never too busy for you," Liam told her sternly.

Nico frowned. "Add on some extras for that."

"Oh, you read my mind."

His hand landed five more times. She started wiggling around on his lap and he placed a heavy hand on the small of her back. "Not telling us something like that is unacceptable, Charlotte. I get that this has been hard. It was possibly the wrong move. But you should have told us what your therapist said. You should have told us that she wanted to speak to us. That sort of thing is not something that you keep to yourself. Do you understand?"

"Yes, yes," she sobbed, between spanks. "I understand."

"What if we'd done something that damaged you irreparably?

Something that we could have prevented? How do you think we could live with ourselves if we did that?"

"I'm sorry, Liam. I'm sorry, Nico."

He stopped. That was enough. Especially for her first real punishment. She was crying. Big tears that didn't show any sign of letting up. Worry flooded him as she didn't quieten.

"Lottie? Are you all right, pretty girl?" Nico asked her.

Fuck!

Liam managed to turn her, arranging her on his lap with her bottom off one side.

"Charlotte? Did I hurt you? I mean, really hurt you? Scare you? Charlotte, talk to me!"

"I'm fine," she finally managed to get out. "Sorry. You didn't hurt me. I'm all right."

"You don't seem all right," Liam grumbled.

Nico moved so he could rub her back. "She's just releasing all those emotions she had pent up. That right, Lottie?"

Lottie nodded.

Relief filled Liam. He'd never forgive himself if he'd hurt her.

"That's okay, pretty girl. You just cry as much as you need. We have you."

"Fuck. She scared me," he muttered.

"Big bad Dom all frightened by a few tears," Nico teased.

"Shall this big bad Dom put you over his knee?" Liam growled.

"Oh, yes, please, Sir."

Liam snorted. Gradually, Lottie's tears faded, and she sighed, leaning against him heavily.

"Baby girl?" Liam asked.

She tilted her head back to look up at him. "I really am okay. Actually, no, I'm better than that. Lighter. Freer."

"Good." Liam kissed her nose. "Don't do that again."

She smiled. "I can't guarantee that."

Liam let out an irritated breath.

"Poor Li," Nico said with false sympathy. "Think how hard it is for him. Loves nothing more than punishing poor, innocent subs but he can't handle a few tears. Hard to be him."

"Oh, I've got no problem bringing you to tears," Liam warned.

"Hey, double standards. My feelings are hurt." Nico put his hand on his chest with a dramatic sigh.

Brat.

"Poor Nico. Such a smart mouth," Liam said. "Always getting him into trouble."

"But the best kind." Nico winked at Lottie. "How about we go snuggle on the couch now?"

"What? Why?" she asked.

Nico looked up at Liam, then back at her. "You've just been spanked and cried your little heart out. Time for some aftercare."

"I thought that was what this was." She waved her hand at where they had her sandwiched between them.

"Well, yeah, but don't you want more?" Nico asked.

"You know what I really want?" she said.

"What's that?" Liam asked.

"For Nico to teach me how to give you a blow job."

~

HOLY. Crap.

So, Nico never thought he'd be kneeling naked on the floor, while teaching the woman he loved how to suck off the man he loved.

Someone should make a movie out of this shit. They'd make a mint.

After she'd told them what she wanted, he could tell Liam was reluctant, not wanting to push her. But that was what she'd just told them she wanted. To be pushed and to have the kid gloves come off.

Nico had quickly convinced him to let her. She was right. They had to trust her to know what she needed.

And fuck, he was glad that he had because this was pretty much the hottest thing he'd ever seen.

"That's it, sweet girl. Lick along his shaft. Yeah, now take the head into your mouth. He likes when you suck on him with just the tip in your mouth. Listen to his groan."

Nico glanced up at Liam who was breathing heavily, sweat coating his forehead. He guessed this was the sweetest kind of torture. Having her practice on his dick, trying to hold back the urge to fuck her mouth, to take what he needed.

Better Liam than him.

"Bet her mouth feels really good, doesn't it?" he asked Liam.

"Fuck, you have no idea."

But he intended to.

"That's it, good girl," Nico praised her. "Take as much of him into your mouth as you can. Just hold him there. Uh-huh. Now, go back nice and slow, sucking on him."

"Fucking hell, Nico. I'm going to kill you."

"Why?" Nico asked with fake innocence. "For showing her how to take care of you?"

"For torturing me," he moaned.

"Am I doing something wrong?" she asked worriedly.

"No, baby," Liam told her. "It's just you feel so fucking amazing, it's hard to stay in control."

"Oh, that's good then, isn't it?"

"Hmm. Now take me deep again. That's it," Liam told her, gently reaching out to place his hand on the back of her head. He turned to look at Nico. "Next time you need to be punished, I'm going to tie you to the bed, put a cock ring on you then have her do this to you."

Oh, fuck.

So, this might have backfired on him.

Shit.

"I don't think we have to be that nasty," Nico said. Liam just gave him a dark look. Well, fuck. Might as well get his kicks in while he could because he could foresee that happening fairly soon. "That's it, pretty girl. Now reach up and grab his balls. No, don't worry. You won't hurt him. Just lightly. Good girl. He loves when you play with them. Just like that."

"Fuck it. That's enough," Liam said sharply. "I can't take it anymore. Lottie, pull back."

She drew away from him. "Are you all right?"

"No, I'm not." Liam cupped her chin in his hand. "You're ready for us? You're sure?"

"I'm sure," she said breathlessly.

"Then both of you get into the bedroom. Lottie, sit back against the headboard. Nico, get between her legs and eat her out. Neither of you are allowed to come without permission."

Nico jumped up then reached down to pull Lottie up. He led her into the bedroom, then helped her get into position

"Is Liam okay?" she asked as Nico moved between her legs.

"He's fine. Just taking a moment to calm down."

"Oh." She smiled. "I did that?"

"You sure fucking did, you little minx. Now, hush. I'm about to feast."

And damned if she wasn't his favorite meal.

~

LIAM WALKED in a few minutes later to find Lottie had her fingers in Nico's hair as he lay between her legs, driving her insane.

Her eyes opened and she stared at Liam pleadingly. "Please! Please!"

He stood at the end of the bed, arms folded over his chest.

"Please what?" he asked.

"I have to come."

"Oh, baby girl. You're going to have to wait a bit longer for that." He moved around the bed and reached out to tilt up her face, bending down to kiss her.

Hot. Hard. Delicious.

He dropped his hand to her breast, running his thumb over her nipple. Having her mouth around him had driven him to the brink of insanity. It was only fair the two of them felt that.

He moved his hand down, over her tummy, then over to Nico. He brushed it down his back, over his ass which he gave several hard smacks, reveling in Nico's pleasure-filled groans.

"I can't . . . I can't . . ."

"Nico, sit up. On your knees."

Nico rose even as Lottie let out a distressed cry at the loss of his mouth on her pussy.

"Look how hard he is, baby," Liam said to her, reaching out to run his hand up and down Nico's dick.

Nico gave a deep grunt as Liam jacked him. "Would you like Lottie's mouth on your cock, Nico?"

"Yes. God, yes."

"Shuffle back to the end of the bed."

Once Nico was kneeling at the end of the mattress, Liam crooked a finger at Lottie. "Hands and knees, suck him off. Nico, remember, no coming without permission."

Liam watched on with satisfaction as Lottie took Nico's dick into her mouth.

Fuck. Yes.

This is what they'd all been waiting for. The three of them. Perfect together.

Liam grabbed a condom from the drawers, knowing that Lottie wasn't on birth control. Moving in behind her, he couldn't resist rolling onto his back between her legs and drawing her hips down until her pussy met his mouth.

She let out a cry as he licked her. From her entrance up to her clit. Then he pressed his tongue into her passage. Her muffled moans were music to his ears, as were the curses coming from Nico.

Finally, unable to hold back any longer, he moved onto his knees behind her. Opening the condom, he rolled it onto his dick. He stared down at her pink ass then cupped one cheek, squeezing it.

"I'm going to take you, Lottie. If at any time you start to feel sore or uncomfortable or just want a break, you say your safeword or lift your hand into the air. Understand?"

She drew her mouth from Nico's dick.

"Yes, Liam."

"You'll both wait until you are given permission before coming."

"Fuck, you're killing me, Liam."

Bastard deserved some torture.

LOTTIE COULDN'T BELIEVE she was doing this. She was sucking off Nico while Liam fucked her from behind.

It felt like a dream. A really sexy dream.

Liam pressed his way inside her and she had to pull off Nico's dick to take a deep breath and relax.

Fuck. He was huge.

"That's it. Good girl," Nico praised her. "I know he's big, but you were made to take him. Good girl."

She let out a small moan as he pushed inside her. She'd hadn't had sex in more than three years, but they'd prepared her well. It wasn't painful. But she felt stretched. So full. When he was fully seated, they both took a moment. Liam rubbed his hand up and down her back.

"All right, baby?"

"Yes, Liam."

He moved his hand around to her clit and rubbed his finger back and forth until she was moaning, shaking. She clenched down around his cock.

Oh. That felt so damn good.

"That's my girl. Just relax. There you are. Now, take Nico's dick back into your mouth. That's it."

Liam's murmured words gave her direction, spurred her on. She took Nico as deep as she could, while Liam remained still behind her. Nico moaned as she swallowed around his dick.

"Fuck. She learned how to do that far too quickly," he moaned.

"Her mouth is heaven and so is her fucking pussy," Liam agreed, moving his finger away from her clit.

She moaned out a protest, but then he started moving.

Holy. Hell.

So good. Back and forth. She could barely concentrate on sucking off Nico, Liam was driving her insane. Then Liam pushed deep and remained still.

"Suck Nico off. Make him come."

She put all her attention into making Nico come. She grabbed him around the base of his dick with one hand, while sucking on the head then drawing more of him into her mouth. Suck. Pull back. Take him deep. Repeat.

"Fuck. Fuck, yes. Lottie, I'm going to come. Pull back if you don't want to swallow."

"She'll swallow," Liam said darkly.

Hell. Yes. She would.

When Nico came, a feeling of elation filled her as he let out a huge shout. His taste filled her mouth. Slightly salty. She licked her way up his cock then across the head before he fell back, lying on the bed and panting.

"Fuck. Killed me. She's killed me."

"Your job isn't done," Liam told him. "Get under her and lick her clit. You're going to make her come while I fuck her."

Nico scrambled underneath her, so his spent cock was just below her face, teasing her. Then she felt his tongue against her clit. Arousal burst through her.

Liam started fucking her again.

It was too much. She couldn't think. Couldn't catch her breath. It was insane. Pleasure ripped through her with the ferocity of a tornado.

"Liam! Nico!" she yelled out, needing an anchor. Needing them.

"Come for us, baby," Liam told her. "Come. We'll catch you. You don't have to be afraid."

No, she never had to be afraid when she was with them. That thought seemed to be the trigger she needed as she screamed, falling over the edge into bliss. Liam slammed into her, rocking her forward as Nico moved away from her clit. Liam's shout of satisfaction filled the room.

She collapsed forward. Spent. Barely able to breathe. They sandwiched her between them, hands moving over her, soft words filling the room. When she came back to herself, she looked up into Liam's face. Nico was wrapped behind her.

"Okay, baby?" Liam asked tenderly.

"Any better and I think I'd die," she told him.

Nico moved his mouth along her shoulder. "Well, don't die before I get to fuck you, okay?"

"Nico!" Liam said.

She burst into giggles.

"I'll try not to."

"Good," he said, lying on his back. "Since necrophilia just isn't my jam."

"Is having your ass plugged and your cock caged your thing?" Liam asked in a low, soft voice.

Nico just grinned. "Funnily enough, no." He put his arm over his eyes. "Wake me for round two."

Leaning over him, she started to tickle him. His peals of laughter filled the room and he tried fighting her off.

"Mercy! Mercy!" he cried.

"Never!"

Liam's phone interrupted their play and he sighed, climbing off the bed.

"Poor Liam, a boss's job is never done," Nico sang. Then he picked her up, placing her on top of his chest. His hands moved down to her ass, massaging. "How's this bottom? Sore?"

"Yes, ow. Ouch." She pouted down at him.

"What? What happened?" Liam asked sharply, making them both freeze.

Nico sat up and arranged her on his lap, holding her tightly.

"Is he all right? Fuck. Yep. We'll come back. What? Sure? She won't like that. Yeah. Absolutely. Fuck. Yes, I'll tell her."

By the time he ended the call, she was so tense she felt like she was going to shatter.

"What happened? What is it?"

"Baby girl, it's Regent."

"What?" she screeched. She could feel it boiling up inside her. "What happened to him?"

"Baby, he's been poisoned."

22

She couldn't breathe.

She clawed at her neck, trying to force a breath of air through her constrained throat and into her lungs.

"Charlotte. Breathe. You breathe right the fuck now," Liam demanded.

A trickle of air made its way into her lungs right as the world spun around her.

"Listen to me. Look at me. Right now."

The world started to right itself as she stared into Liam's eyes.

Regent. Poisoned.

"He's all right. Charlotte, Regent is all right. He's alive."

"A-alive?"

"Yes, baby girl. He's alive. Fucked up. But alive. Victor got him help quickly, but he's going to be fine."

"Oh, God. Oh, God." She burst into tears. Nico held her close, rubbing her back until she managed to calm down.

Someone had poisoned her brother.

"We need to go. I need to see him." She tried to scramble off Nico's lap.

"We can't do that, baby," Liam said to her.

"What? Why?" she asked. "I want to see him. Is he in the hospital?"

"He's already discharged himself," Liam told her. "But he doesn't want you there."

It was like a blow to her heart.

"For your own safety," Liam told her quickly. "They know who did it, but they don't know who she's working with yet."

"Sh-she?"

"Alice, the maid. She gave Regent the tea. Prepared it herself."

"Oh my God. I can't believe she'd do that."

"She was always weird," Nico said.

"I'm going to call Peter," Liam said. "Get him to give me updates."

"Why would you call Peter?" she asked, confused and unsure why they'd want to speak to one of Regent's guards.

Then she noticed that both of them had strange looks on their faces.

"What?"

"Peter actually works for me," Liam confessed.

"He what?"

"Yeah, I paid him to keep watch over you."

"You what?" Her mind spun.

"How mad are you?" Nico asked. "He didn't give us day-by-day updates or anything. Just kept watch over you for us and told us if anything major happened."

It was an invasion of privacy. But it wasn't like there had ever been much to report.

"You should have told me."

"It just slipped our minds," Liam told her, watching her closely.

"Regent is going to kill you."

"Which is why I vote that we don't tell him. Who's with me?" Nico held up his hand and they both stared at him.

"Actually, that's probably for the best," she added. "Is he going to stay working for Regent?"

"I told him that he no longer has to stay now that you're here with us, but he likes working for your brother."

"Are you sure I can't see him?" she cried. It didn't feel right to be so far away from him.

"Once it's safe, I'll take you back to see him. I promise."

"He's really all right?" she asked.

"Really. I promise."

She shuddered, leaning back against Nico. "I think I'd like that snuggle and movie now."

"Coming right up, pretty girl."

"Whatever you need."

"Hey, you're painting?" Nico asked as he walked into the room that she'd taken over as her studio.

After two weeks of not being able to paint, she'd suddenly had the urge to start painting again that morning. It might have been something to do with the fact that they'd finally moved forward in their relationship yesterday. It was cleansing in a way. A new start. A push forward.

She was still worried about Regent, but she'd spoken to him briefly last night and he'd told her that it was a good thing Alice had made a move. They finally had the rat, and they'd discovered who she worked for. Patrick. His rival. He'd wanted Regent's territory and had been using Alice's intel to work against him.

Regent was pissed. She just hoped that there wasn't too much blood shed. Regent had assured her time and again that he could look after himself.

She didn't want to think too closely about how they would do that.

She put the paintbrush down. "Would you like to see?"

His eyebrows rose. "Really?"

"Yeah. But remember, I'm not trained or anything."

"I don't care. Yeah, I want to see." Nico practically ran forward then came to a stop, breathing in sharply.

"Well?"

"Lottie, it's amazing."

"Do you think so?" she asked.

This painting was of Liam. He had his arms crossed, a stern look on his face, but there was something in his eyes that said he was amused.

"Fuck. I fucking love it. Oh my God. We have to hang it up. We have to show him."

"Not until it's finished. Please?"

Nico just nodded. "Okay, but fuck, Lottie. With talent like yours, you should be sharing it."

"You really think it's that good?"

"I do." He came over and wrapped his arms around her from behind. "I think it's amazing, just like you." He kissed up her neck. She shivered and turned in his arms, tilting her head back for a kiss.

"You know, I think you're amazing too. You write your own songs, don't you?"

He gave her a quizzical look.

"I've heard you in the shower," she confessed.

"Lots of people can sing."

"Not like you do."

"Damn, pretty girl," he groaned before kissing her. "Fuck me."

"All right," she agreed with a grin.

He moaned. "We've created a monster. I want to fuck you so bad."

"So why don't you?"

"Because Liam told me that if I fucked you while he was gone then I wouldn't get to touch your pussy for a whole month."

She pouted. Liam had gone into work. She'd been hoping for some fun one-on-one time with Nico.

"No fair."

"Tell me about it." He stepped back with a groan. "Best we don't even touch. I don't trust myself."

She had to grin, liking that she pushed his control.

"I'm going to make coffee. Want some?"

"We're out of hazelnut creamer."

"No problem, I'll go grab you some."

"I don't want to be a bother."

"Pretty girl, you're never a bother. I've got to grab a couple of things. I'll be twenty minutes. You'll be okay here?"

"I'll be fine." Although she hadn't actually been alone in the penthouse before. But it was only twenty minutes, and it wasn't like she wasn't used to being alone.

"Sure?"

"Sure."

"I have my phone. Evan is right outside if you need anything, okay?"

"I'll be fine." Evan was one of the guards that Liam had hired to stand outside the apartment door and be bored all day long. Three guards worked in rotation. But you couldn't even get up to his level without a key card. Plus, there was a doorman on the building. She thought he was overreacting, but Liam wouldn't be budged.

"Love you, pretty girl."

"Love you too!"

Instead of going back to painting right away, she decided to go put the coffee on and get a glass of water. Grabbing her phone, she sent off a text to Victor, checking in. As she started the coffee her phone started ringing. She smiled as she saw Ace's name.

She put him on speaker and set the phone on the counter as she grabbed a bottle of water from the fridge and poured some into a glass.

"Hey, buddy, how are you?" she asked as she heard the door to the apartment shut. Had Nico forgotten something? Or maybe Liam was back early. That would be fun.

"Lottie, when are you coming home?"

Aw. Poor Ace.

"I'm not sure, buddy. Are you all right?"

"I miss you. I don't like that those guys stole you away. It's Keir's birthday soon."

"I'll come back to visit as soon as I can, I promise," she said, turning as she heard someone approach. The glass slipped from her hand, shattering. "How did you get in here?"

"End the call."

"Lottie? Lottie?" Ace called through the phone.

"End the call. And don't do anything stupid."

"Um, Ace, buddy. I have to go, all right?"

"What's wrong?" Ace asked.

"Nothing, honey. Say hi to Maxim for me. I'm sorry I can't get home for his birthday." She winced as she said that. What was she doing? Leaving a clue for a seven-year-old?

Fuck. She ended the call.

"Slide it along the floor."

Crouching, she pushed the phone along the floor.

"What are you doing here, Eleanor? How did you get up here? And why the fuck are you holding a gun on me?"

A gun with a silencer on it.

Eleanor James, Liam's stepmother, clicked her tongue. "Such atrocious manners. You were such a sweet girl before. That must be Liam's influence. He always was uncouth. It's his Irish blood. He even uses *their* last name, rather than his father's."

"Maybe he'd rather be as removed as possible from that man and you."

Oh, God, what was she going to do? Necklace. She needed to hit the panic button on her necklace.

Please let it work from this far away.

"Liam will be home soon," Lottie lied. "You should go."

"Oh, I am going. You're coming with me, though."

"Why? Why do you want me?"

"You mean you don't know? Charlotte Malone, beloved younger sister of the New Orleans Malones. The very rich and powerful New Orleans Malones. Lover to one of the richest men in the country. And you really have no idea?"

"Money? This is about money? Seriously?"

"Actually, it's about love. Now, we're going to leave and you're not saying a word to anyone. Or I'm going to have the man who I have following Nico shoot him in the head."

Fuck. Fuck.

Was she serious? Lottie had no idea. But she knew that she couldn't risk Nico. Her hand twitched, wanting to use her necklace now. However, she didn't want to draw attention to it.

Feeling numb with fear, she made her way out of the apartment. A gasp left her lips as she saw Evan lying on the floor in a pool of blood.

"We have to help him. Call the paramedics."

"Don't be stupid. He's dead. Come on." Eleanor dragged her to the elevator.

The walls aren't closing in on me. I'm fine.

They rode down to the ground floor without anyone climbing in. Eleanor had hidden the gun in her huge handbag. Lottie wondered about the doorman. Worry for him filled her. But Eleanor had her arm in a hold.

As they got toward the door, panic started to fill her. She couldn't do this again. Couldn't let herself get taken. Her breath started coming in sharp pants.

"Stop it. What's wrong with you? Get outside. I told you if you make a scene I'll kill Nico."

Lottie managed to step outside. But the whole world spun dizzyingly. She was barely coherent as Eleanor practically dragged her toward a town car with tinted windows. She was shoved inside and landed against someone. As she managed to right herself, she stared up into a familiar-looking face.

"M-Michael?" She gasped for breath. Panic had her in its tight grasp and wasn't letting go.

Michael smiled down at her, his eyes cold and calculating. Then something pricked her neck, and the world went black.

Liam answered his phone without paying much attention to who it was.

"Yeah?"

"Liam?"

He frowned, recognizing the voice but unable to place it.

"Yeah? Who is this?"

"It's Jardin, Lottie's brother."

"Everything okay?"

"That's what I hope you can tell me. Are you with Lottie?" he asked.

"No, but Nico is."

"Well, Ace was just talking to Lottie, and he said some lady came in and interrupted their call."

"What? Who?"

"I don't know. Lottie ended the call. But before she did, she told him that she'd come home for Maxim's birthday. They'd just been talking about Keir's birthday."

"Maybe she got confused."

"Maybe."

A strange feeling filled him.

Who could the woman be?

"But you need to check on her. And Liam? She better be fucking all right or it's on your head."

"Fuck." He ended the call and was about to call Nico, when his phone vibrated.

Fuck.

"Grandfather, I don't have time to chat—"

"There some reason why your girl would get into a car with your stepmother?"

He stilled.

A woman's voice.

Fuck!

"What the hell? How would you know . . . I told you not to put guys on me."

"I didn't put anyone on *you*. I have someone watching the apartment. They just called me to tell me that your girl got into a town car with some old, well-dressed, pinched-looking bitch. I instantly knew that it was Eleanor. Your girl was pale, barely standing."

"Fuck. She must have threatened her. She wouldn't leave the apartment otherwise. Was Nico there?"

"No."

"Is your guy following them?" he asked.

Don't panic. You have to help her. You cannot panic.

"Yep."

"Tell me where they end up."

"Already on top of it, boyo."

As he ended the call, another call came through.

"Nico? Are you all right?"

"Evan's dead, and she's gone! She's not here! Liam, she's not here!"

"Easy, calm down," Liam reassured him, rushing toward his car. He kept an eye on his surroundings. No one was around. Although he didn't quite trust the old man not to have someone on him.

"How can I calm down? Lottie's gone and Evan is fucking dead. He was shot."

"I know."

"You know? How do you know?"

"Eleanor has her. Lottie was seen getting into a car with her. She must have shot Evan and threatened Lottie. She was talking to Ace at the time. I have to call them back. Also, the old man has a guy following them. I'm going to swing by and get you. Wait in the foyer of the building, I'll call you when I'm close."

"Okay. What about Evan?"

"I'll call my grandfather. He'll take care of it."

Ending the call, he climbed in his car and sped toward his building. He called his grandfather first. He told him he'd send a clean-up crew. Then he called Jardin back.

"My stepmother has her," he said. "We're tracking her."

"Through her necklace?" Jardin asked.

"What?"

"Her necklace has a GPS tracker. I checked with Regent, and she hasn't hit the panic button in the locket. But the tracker will work."

"Fuck." Of course, it did. "Can you track her from there?"

"Yeah, well, Regent can."

"Do it. I have someone following her. But just in case."

"Find her, Liam."

"I will. Don't worry. And then I'm never letting her out of my sight again."

23

Lottie woke up with the urge to vomit.

Rolling over, she purged everything in her stomach.

"Oh, God! That's disgusting. Couldn't you make it to the toilet? This is what you get from poor breeding."

Confused, ill, and groggy, she stared around. It was so cold and dark. Fear filled her as the room spun.

"Wakey, wakey, Lottie," a sing-song voice urged. "It's time to chat."

A heavy foot prodded her back and she groaned.

"Sit up, bitch," the voice changed, growing nastier, more demanding.

She turned her head, gasping as she saw Michael looming over her.

What the fuck? What is he doing here?

"Why are we even bothering with her?" the feminine voice whined. "We should just get rid of Liam and voila, the money will be all ours."

"Mother, how many times do I have to explain this? We can't

get rid of Liam. He's got ties to the Irish mafia. His grandfather and uncles will come after us."

She let out a huff of breath. "So? We'll be long gone."

"And how do we get Liam's money if we're not here?"

"It will all go to your father. He can send it to us."

Wow. She was really dumb.

"Liam wouldn't leave his money to his father," Lottie said. "Stupid bitch."

Slap!

Pain burst across her face, making her gasp.

"Mother, stop!" Michael complained as Lottie pulled herself up. She felt weak and out of it, Michael had obviously drugged her. But she didn't want to be lying down with these people. She needed to be ready to run at any opportunity. Once she was sitting, she glanced around. They appeared to be in some concrete room. There were no windows and only one door.

Awesome.

"She's right. Liam would have left his money to the little asshole he's married to," Michael said.

"Then we kill him too."

"Which would likely leave the money tied up in court, with us fighting his family. No, this is simpler."

"What is? Kidnapping her again?"

"What? Again? You . . . you kidnapped me the first time?" she asked.

"Michael did," Eleanor said. "But instead of telling me what he did, he got involved with that whiny little rat, Campbell."

Campbell, the man who had held her for those ten days. Who'd touched her. She shuddered.

"Do you know what he did to me?" she whispered to Michael.

He smiled. "Of course. He recorded it for me."

Her stomach rolled again, and she vomited until nothing was left inside her to come up.

"So why didn't the ransom demand go to Regent?"

"I knew he wanted you. Liam. I saw the way he looked at you at that dinner. And I overheard him and Nico talking about you. His money should be mine. He lorded it over me, never giving me what I was due. Always lecturing me on what I should be doing, on how to be better. Then he heard me on the phone to Campbell saying the word ransom. Campbell was getting cold feet about the whole ransom thing. So I spun Liam a story and he bought it. I mean, it was poetic justice, right? That he gave me money I was already owed. With the money your brother had already given me, it made for a nice nest egg."

"What? What do you mean?"

"Oh, he didn't tell you? Regent paid me to break up with you."

What? He had?

"Seems Regent had better instincts than me when it came to you," she said.

"Bitch!" He sneered down at her. "What's happened to you? You were never like this before."

"Apparently, being kidnapped changes you."

"I was going to leave town anyway. I couldn't stick around with all that money and especially not after killing Campbell."

She gasped, putting it all together. "You killed him and took the money?"

"Of course. Who knew Liam would pay all that money to get you back? I took his money and your brother's and I left."

"So why are you back? Why risk it?"

"Because your brother sent people after me," Michael said, pacing. "They nearly found me. I need to go deeper undercover."

"And this time, he's taking me with him," Eleanor said. "Your brother thought he could threaten me and that I'd tell him where Michael was. I would never betray my son. But to leave, we need more money. I bribed the doorman of Liam's building a long time ago to let me know when anything interesting happened. Thought

I might one day need some blackmail material. Imagine how happy I was to learn that he'd come back from New Orleans with you. Course I had to kill the doorman so he wouldn't tell any tales."

"What about your husband?" Lottie asked. What had Michael done with all the money he'd already gotten?

"What about him? Weak and cowardly. I'll be glad to see the back of him."

"So, your plan is to ransom me again? You really think that will work?"

"You don't think Liam will pay up? I'm sure your brothers will," Michael said. "I'm thinking ten million."

"Wow, that's pretty pathetic. And lazy. You could have put more thought into it and kidnapped someone else." She knew that she shouldn't rile them, but she couldn't help it.

That bastard had her kidnapped twice. He deserved to rot in hell. Which is what would happen when Liam got hold of him.

"When Liam gets here, you're dead, you know that, right?"

"Shut up!" Michael roared. "Liam's not going to come here!"

Did the door open slightly? She tried not to look that way, not wanting to draw any attention to it. Diversion, she needed something to distract them.

"Oh, he is. Then you're dead, you pathetic little worm!"

Michael stormed over to her. "Shut up!

"Don't you understand?" Eleanor said evilly. "That money should be ours. Not his. We're only taking what we're owed."

"The money is Liam's. Not yours."

"If your brothers had left me alone, it wouldn't have come to this, Lottie," Michael said.

"And what makes you think you can outrun them after I'm released?"

"Who said anything about releasing you?" Eleanor replied

nastily. "We're going to set up the drop-off, but tragically, you'll die before anyone can get to you."

"Well, now, that's a mighty fine plan," a voice said. Suddenly, an older man stepped into the large room. Lottie's eyes widened. It was like she was looking at Liam in forty-odd years' time.

"Who the fuck are you?" Eleanor screeched, reaching into her bag.

"She's armed," Lottie said quickly.

"Don't be worryin' about that, young Charlotte," the man she assumed was Liam's grandfather said, stepping forward as several more men entered the room. Armed men.

As they surrounded Eleanor and Michael, the older woman let out a loud screech of anger.

"Jesus, that's annoyin'," the older man said. "Think she might have pierced my eardrum."

"What are you doing here? Who are you?" Michael demanded.

"Name's Sean Carmichael," the older man said. "You might know me as Liam's grandfather."

"We'll split the money with you," Eleanor said. "You can have a third."

Sean let out a loud laugh. "A whole third? And you think that would be worth betrayin' my grandson? Me flesh and blood. No, lady. I won't be doin' that. Come here, Charlotte."

He held out a hand and helped her up. For an older man, he was surprisingly strong. He wrapped an arm around her to hold her up as she faltered.

"Liam?" she whispered. "Nico? She said she had someone following him?"

"Someone following him? I doubt that. Nobody would work with these two. And he's with Liam. My boy would have spotted a tail."

Oh, thank God.

"They'll be here soon."

And then she heard a noise from outside, and Liam and Nico rushed in, their faces filled with fear that quickly returned to relief. With a cry, she threw herself into their arms.

Safe. She was safe.

24

Liam walked back into the room where his grandfather stood, staring down at the two people who had dared to take what was his.

Twice.

Lottie had told him everything.

Fuck.

It was going to take him a long time to get over this. He knew that there was no real love between himself and his brother, but he'd never thought he would do all of this.

"Ah, there you are," Sean said cheerfully. "How's our girl?"

"I've sent her home." With an armed escort thanks to his grandfather. The first thing he was going to do tomorrow was hire several more bodyguards for both her and Nico. She hadn't wanted to leave him, had clung to him, crying. It had nearly broken him, having to push her into Nico's arms.

After calling Jardin to update him, he'd come back in here.

"She told you everything about what these two had planned?"

"Oh yeah, she told me everything."

"You can't believe a word from her, Liam," Eleanor said. Her hair was messed up and there was dirt on her face. She'd be horrified if she could see herself right now. "She's obviously got problems. Delusions. We were trying to help her."

"Stop. Just stop." Liam strode over and crouched down by his stepmother. Reaching out, he gently brushed back her hair. "You made my life hell for so many years. Everything was about your son. My father allowed it. Turned his back on your abuse. But I will never forget. This, I can believe of you. But you," he turned to his brother, "we could have had a relationship. Could have been real brothers. But you let her corrupt you. And now, you'll both pay for touching what belongs to me. For terrifying her. For leaving her with that abusive asshole."

He turned to the old man. "You might want to leave."

"I was just goin' to say the same thing to you, boyo."

"This is my problem to take care of."

"There's no need for you to bloody your hands when mine are already drippin', boy."

Liam raised his eyebrows. "Thought you'd want that? Be a way for you to try and force me into the family."

His grandfather shook his head. "Learned a few things in my old age. One of your cousins can take over the family business. All idiots, but I'm hopin' to train one of them up. What none of them can do is replace you. My only daughter's son. To have you in my life, I'd do whatever I had to. Including backin' off from convincin' you to inherit my job."

Liam let out a sigh. Whether he'd do it or not, he didn't know. But those words meant more than his grandfather realized.

"So let me do this for you, boyo. Keep those hands clean for when you go home to your boy and girl." He shook his head. "Ménage relationships, not somethin' I'd ever thought would happen out in the open. Mind you, in my day, plenty of that went on behind closed doors. The stories I could tell you."

"Save them for another day." He looked back at Michael and Eleanor. "If you're sure."

"I am." A cold look entered Sean's gaze as he stared down at them.

"Wait! Liam, you can't let him do this! Liam!" Michael screamed.

Liam left without looking back.

He had somewhere better to be.

WHEN HE ARRIVED HOME, he took a deep breath. He was shaking. He held out his hands, looking down at them as they trembled.

Fuck. Fuck.

He'd nearly lost her. Again.

Walking down the hallway, he paused at the door to see his girl curled up in Nico's lap. She was crying softly.

"I need him to come home, Nico."

"He will. He'll be here soon, pretty girl."

"I want him here now. I'm scared."

"Nobody will get to you. I'll kill anyone who comes through that door."

His fierce husband.

"Not for me. For Liam. If he kills them . . ."

"Hush, if anyone deserves killing it's the two of them."

"It is," Liam said firmly, making Lottie gasp. Nico, who had likely already seen him, didn't react.

Lottie jumped from Nico's lap and threw herself at Liam. "You're all right. You're all right."

"Of course, I am." Liam picked her up, holding her in his arms. He reached out an arm for Nico, drawing him in.

"Sh. Everything's all right, baby. You're all right. I have you."

"Don't leave. Don't leave."

"I'm not going anywhere."

Nico stared up at him, looking concerned.

"I didn't kill them," Liam said.

"You didn't?" Lottie looked up at him too. "What happened to them?"

"I left them with grandfather."

He waited for their reaction.

"Good," Lottie said fiercely.

"Good?"

"I don't want them to live. But I also didn't want you to have to kill them. This is what they deserve. Evil bastards."

Liam, ridiculously, found himself smiling.

"They found the doorman," Nico said. "She must have got him into the backroom and shot him."

Liam winced. "Fuck."

"She'd bribed him to tell her when you did something interesting," Lottie told Liam.

"Guess he got what was coming then," Liam replied coldly.

"But what about poor Evan."

"That wasn't your fault," Liam told her. "None of this is."

She nodded, but he wasn't sure she believed him. Fuck. She was starting to do so well, he hated to think how many more nightmares she'd have now.

Of course, now he had more of his own. And a whole slew of anxiety.

"Why didn't they take me?" Nico asked.

"Probably thought that they'd get money from Regent too. Or maybe it was that they thought it would be easier to get to Lottie. Sounds like they only got desperate enough to do this because Regent was trying to find Michael. Fuck, I need to call him."

"He's going to lose his mind. He'll want me to come home."

"Do you want to go back?" Liam asked her. "Because we can do that. We can do whatever you need to do."

"All I need to do is be with the two of you. That's where my home is."

"That's good," he told her. "Because the two of you are my home. My heart. My two loves."

He held them both tight, never intending to let them go.

25

She knew it was him before he even approached her.

He was always careful to make noise before coming up behind her, not wanting to frighten her. Two months had passed since her second kidnapping and while things hadn't been easy, she at least had the two of them to lean on, to help her through the added nightmares and anxiety.

And she'd been there to help them both with theirs. With Liam's need to keep them safe. With Nico's need to always have her in his sights. They were helping each other.

"Painting me again?" he asked before brushing his lips along her neck. A shudder of desire ran through her. She didn't think there would ever be a day when she didn't want him. Her nipples pebbled as she carefully set the brush down then turned to stare up into those blue eyes that she'd once thought of as cold.

They weren't cold now. No, they were filled with warmth as they stared down at her with hunger.

"My favorite subject."

He raised an eyebrow. "Oh, yeah?"

"You and Nico," she replied.

Liam ran his thumb over her cheek gently. "You need a nap, baby girl. You're paler than I'd like."

She'd had a nightmare last night. They'd become more frequent again after her kidnapping, but this was her first one all week, which she was taking as a win.

"I'm all right." She knew he'd fuss at her until she went to bed unless she distracted him. Liam could be a total mother hen when it came to her health. "Where's Nico?"

He gave her a knowing look. "He'll be in soon. He got mouthy so he's walking a bit funny."

She dropped her lower lip into a pout. "You spanked him and I missed it?"

"Actually, I spanked him then I plugged him, then I played with his cock and denied him permission to come."

"Oh. Ouch."

"But if you're sad about missing out, I can always do a re-enactment."

"As pleasant as that sounds, I don't want to torture him too much."

"Why not? That's my favorite thing to do."

"You're so evil." She grinned up at him.

"You love me the way I am."

"I do," she sighed.

"Good, remember that feeling when I tell you this."

"Tell me what?" she asked, feeling confused and worried as he took a step back.

"You might want to sit down."

"Liam, you're scaring me."

"There's no reason to be scared."

"What's going on?" Nico asked, shuffling into the room. She winced. Liam must have used a very large butt plug on him.

"I have something to tell Lottie. And you. Actually, several things. Both of you sit."

Liam waited until they'd both sat before standing in front of them, his hands behind his back.

"Uh oh, that's his lord and master pose," Nico said, drawing her under his arm and leaning back with a hiss. "Fuck, how big is this plug?"

She settled in against him with a happy sigh. She loved nothing more than being close to her men. They settled her, grounded her, made her feel safe and loved.

"Bigger than me."

Nico swore under his breath as she rubbed his thigh soothingly. "Maybe Liam will let me suck you off."

"And maybe Liam won't," the other man said firmly. "He's being punished for being a mouthy brat."

"But you love my mouth," Nico replied.

"I do. And if you don't stop complaining, I'll put that mouth to good use. I have several things to tell you both so hush. Charlotte."

"Yes?"

"I stole a few of your paintings and took them to an old friend of my mother who owns an art gallery. She would like to have a showing featuring your paintings."

"She . . . you . . . you did what?" she screeched, jumping up. "Liam, you can't do that!"

"Already did. Sit down, please."

"But you . . . I . . . this is insane. Nico, tell him this is insane. He can't do this, can he?"

Nico tugged her down against him again. "Pretty girl, he already did. And didn't you hear him? She wants to do a showing with your paintings! That's awesome! And well deserved. Because you are amazing."

She shook her head. "I . . . I can't do it. I'll have to go to the gallery. I can't . . . I don't . . . Liam!"

Liam knelt in front of her, taking her hands in his. "You can do this. Because we will be with you. All the way, baby girl."

Her breathing was rapid but she wasn't panicking. "You'll both help me?"

"Of course we will," Nico told her.

She could do this. With them. She could.

"We have months to prepare," Liam soothed. "Her gallery is very popular and booked out well in advance."

"Wait! She doesn't just want them because she's your friend?" She would hate that.

"What? No, baby. Of course not."

"She wants them because they're amazing," Nico told her. "I'm so happy for you."

"Glad you feel that way," Liam said, turning to his husband. "Because I have a surprise for you."

"You do?"

She turned to look up at Nico, who appeared shocked. Liam stood once more, affecting his lord and master pose. "Yes, I've bought you some time in a studio to record your music. And I have a music producer lined up to listen to it."

Somehow, Nico managed to jump to his feet, even with a massive plug in his ass. "No!"

"Yes!"

"Liam, no!"

"Nico, yes. It's time you realized how talented and amazing you are. And that you need to share it."

She stood and wrapped her arms around Nico. "He's right."

"Fuck," Nico groaned. "I can't believe this."

"You'll be awesome and you should share your talent," she told him.

"Lord help me," Nico whispered.

"There's more," Liam told them.

"Do you not think you could do one bombshell a week," Nico groaned. "My heart may not take it."

Liam drew him close and whispered to him. Nico's gaze lit up then he turned to look at her. Then he shuffled away.

"What's going on?" she asked.

"Just wait."

When Nico returned, he handed something to Liam, who put it in his pocket. She stared at them both in confusion as they dropped to one knee in front of her. Then both of them held out their hands. Moving on instinct, she raised her hands and slid each hand into one of theirs.

"Charlotte," Liam begun. "I think I loved you almost from the moment I saw you. Without a doubt, you are beautiful, kind, and strong. I want to love you, protect and take care of you for the rest of your days. Will you marry me?"

He drew a ring out of his pocket with his free hand and held it up. It was a gorgeous, clear solitaire diamond. Before she could reply, Nico stole her attention.

"Lottie-bo-bottie," he said with a grin. "You're damn sexy, but you know that. You're always shaking your ass in front of me, tempting me to be naughty and get into trouble."

She gasped, and his smile grew.

"You're also the heart in this relationship. You were the piece that was always missing. And now we want the world to know that you're ours. Become ours, Lottie. Marry us?"

He held up a ring as well. A large pink diamond twinkled up at her.

With a sob, she nodded. "Yes, please. Yes."

They slid their rings onto her left and right ring fingers. Then they stood and Liam drew her close and kissed her. Hard. Hot. Heavy.

When he pulled back, Nico tugged her forward, kissing her like his life depended on it. After he pulled away, Liam drew her up into his arms.

"How will we get married, though?" she whispered.

"I've been talking to your cousins. They know someone who will marry us in that crazy town they live in," Liam told her. "Now this calls for a celebration."

Liam carried her into their bedroom and set her carefully down on her feet.

"Nico, strip our fiancée then take off your clothes," he ordered. "We're going to show her how much she means to us. How she completes us."

"You show me that every day," she told them. There wasn't a moment where she ever doubted their love for her.

"Good," Liam said satisfaction. "But that doesn't mean we're ever going to stop."

"Fuck no," Nico said as he stripped her in record time before pulling off his own clothes. "I wonder if it will be different, now that you're our fiancée?"

"Better. It can only be better," Liam said as he took off his clothes as well.

Her heart raced in anticipation.

"I don't see how that's possible," she whispered. "I might have a heart attack if it gets any better."

Liam grinned. "Nico, get down on your knees in front of our girl and lick her pussy."

She let out a gasp as Nico knelt before her. He wasn't really going to do it, was he?

"Spread your legs, pretty girl."

"Nico," she moaned.

"Spread your legs, Lottie," Liam said in his Dom voice. The one that warned you to disobey at your peril. And since she didn't want to be denied an orgasm, she did as she was told.

She was a good girl, after all.

Nico grinned, as though sensing her thoughts. Then, as soon as she parted her legs, he spread her lips and dove in, his tongue sliding along her slick lips before he concentrated on her clit.

She swayed, feeling off-balance. And then Liam was behind her, wrapping an arm around her to support her. She should have known he'd never let her fall.

"That's my good girl. He's worshipping your pussy, isn't he?"

Her breath grew faster, her body shaking.

"Isn't he?" he said in a low voice.

"Yes, Liam. Yes. Please, let me come," she begged.

"Not yet. Nico, grab her hips to help support her for a moment while I get a chair."

A chair?

Liam disappeared, but Nico kept her steady as he lashed her clit with his tongue. Keeping herself from falling over the edge into bliss was so hard. Impossible. She couldn't do it.

"Draw back, Nico."

She let out a deep breath she hadn't realized she'd been holding as Liam returned, giving Nico that command. Then a chair from the dining room appeared beside her.

"Put your foot up on the chair and hold on to the back, Lottie," Liam told her.

She was aware of how exposed she was as she raised her leg, setting her foot down. But the back of the chair gave her some much-needed support.

"Nico, continue. Lottie, push your ass back slightly. That's it, good girl. No coming without permission."

Crap. Damn it.

"Nico, I'm taking the plug out. Don't you stop licking her pussy," Liam told her. "Good boy."

Liam disappeared into the bathroom with the plug. She heard the water running before he returned and disappeared behind her. He kissed his way down her back. "I have something for you, pretty girl."

She felt something press against her pussy. Something firm and cool.

"Relax," Liam told her. "It's just a vibrator. That's it. Take it. Good girl."

He pushed the vibrator deep inside her, before drawing it back. He fucked her with short, fast thrusts. Combined with Nico flicking her clit with his tongue, it was killing her.

"Please. Please," she begged as Liam situated the vibrator inside her, then turned it on. She needed more. She had to come. Desperately.

"Please, Liam. I need to come."

"Soon," he promised, kissing his way across the back of her shoulders. "You are so beautiful. Fuck, baby girl. How were we ever lucky enough to find you?"

"Liam, please."

"Nico, draw back," Liam commanded as he pulled the vibrator out of her.

No! She'd been so close.

Her breath came in sharp pants, and she was whimpering.

"Sh, it's all right, baby," Liam soothed. "Nico, grab the chair and sit in it."

"Fuck yes," Nico said, moving the chair in front of her and sitting. He looked like a tattooed god sitting there, his cock firm and tempting. She licked her lips.

"Nico, is lucky. I'm going to let you suck him off while I fuck you, girl," Liam told her in a rough voice. "But no one comes until I give permission."

He was definitely trying to kill her.

"Kneel on the floor between his legs and take his dick into your mouth," Liam commanded as he moved to the bedside table and grabbed a condom, putting it on.

She knelt, then took Nico's dick into her mouth, licking the head before taking him deep into her mouth. Liam grasped hold of her hips and pushed his dick into her mouth.

"Christ, yes, that feels so good," Nico told her. "Suck me, pretty girl."

She moved her mouth up and down his cock, sucking on him strongly. Liam drove himself in and out of her, holding onto her, keeping her steady.

Love swelled inside her. She was theirs. Totally.

"I'm not going to last, please, Liam," Nico begged. "You know how good she is at this."

"Fuck, you should feel her fucking pussy clenching down on me."

What they didn't know was that she was close to the edge, needing to come.

"Come! Both of you," Liam ordered. "Come now."

He fucked her with hard thrusts as he reached around to flick at her clit. She exploded just as Nico came in her mouth. Quickly, she swallowed him down as Liam shuddered behind her, his groan of completion filling the room.

She slumped forward as Liam drew himself from her, letting Nico's cock slide out of her mouth. She was lifted into the air and placed on the bed. Her legs were parted, a warm cloth slid between them.

Then she felt them sandwich her between them, surrounding her.

Nothing had ever felt this right.

~

NICO STARED down at their gorgeous sleeping girl. The center of their world. How had they ever lived without her? He had no idea, but he was so grateful to have her in their lives. He looked over at Liam and found him staring down at her, too. The look on Liam's face was a mix of fear, satisfaction and ownership. Nico got it.

They'd nearly lost her for a second time. That couldn't happen again.

"She's ours, Liam."

"She is," Liam replied. "The two of you are mine. And I'm not ever letting you go."

EPILOGUE

E*ight months later*

"You know, I never did understand art. Especially that modern stuff. Looks like something a two-year-old could do. But this stuff, this stuff, I like."

Lottie turned toward Liam's grandfather with a smile. "Grandpa Sean, you made it!"

"Well, of course I did. Wouldn't miss my only granddaughter's first art show, would I?"

She reached out and hugged him. Over the last eight months she'd grown rather fond of the old asshole. Oh, she never forgot who he was, or that not everyone saw the side of him that she did. But he'd helped her, saved her, and since then, Liam had grudgingly let him more into his life. She enjoyed having him around, even if Liam still liked to grumble about it.

He'd stopped putting guys on Liam, which helped. But that

was mostly because Liam had hired a full security crew and moved them out to the country, out of Sean's jurisdiction. Not that that ever stopped the old coot. And she wouldn't be surprised if he had a spy in their midst. But she never said that to Liam.

"Did you come on your own?" she asked.

"No, I brought one of the other grandsons. Useless, the bunch of them."

Liam's cousins were anything but useless. They were all ruthless, savage men. And she wondered how they were fitting in with this crowd. At least it was only a small showing. The art gallery owner had agreed to only allow a restricted number of people to her showings, to help with her anxiety. Surprisingly, there had been a waiting list of people wanting to attend.

"Grandfather, you made it," Liam said, coming up beside her. He wrapped an arm around her. Immediately, she felt more at ease. That tight knot in her stomach disappeared. She'd come a long way, but it hadn't been without its challenges. After everything, Liam had gone into overprotective caveman mode. Neither she nor Nico were allowed anywhere without him. Not that she'd even wanted to for the longest time.

But look at her now.

"Of course, I did. Now, what time should you expect me for Christmas? I'll be comin' up a few days early."

Liam's eyes widened and he glanced down at her. "You're coming for Christmas?"

"I'm family. My granddaughter invited me. I'll be there."

"Come any time you like," she told him.

"Thought I might as well just stay until the New Year."

"What?" Liam snapped, causing a number of people to turn and look at them.

Sean sent her a wink, making her giggle.

"Now, how do I buy up this whole lot?" he asked.

"Right. I'm sure you really want the whole lot," she said teasingly.

"Course I do. I'll go figure it out myself, shall I?" He wandered off, whistling.

"He's not really going to do that, is he?" she asked.

"Oh, yeah, he is. I'll go talk to him."

As Liam walked away, Regent strode up to her. "Hello, darling." Leaning in, he kissed her cheek gently.

"Reggie, thanks for coming." The rest of the family wouldn't be here until closer to Christmas, but Regent and Victor came. Victor was currently standing next to a wall, trying to blend in while everyone stared at him.

Regent had wanted her to move back home after Michael and Eleanor kidnapped her. But she'd worried she'd be taking a step backward. He'd been furious with himself for pushing them into it. It wasn't his fault they were evil bastards though.

"This is amazing," Regent told her, taking hold of her hand. He looked down at her engagement rings, both of them glistening under the lights. They were enormous. Liam and Nico wanted everyone to know she was taken. "All the arrangements are made to get married in Haven?"

"Yep, we're all set."

Regent cupped her face between his hands. "I wasn't sure about them. Didn't think they were good enough for you. And after Michael got to you again, I wanted to kill them."

"I know."

"But I can see now that they're good for you. And, darling girl?"

"Yes?"

"I'm so fucking proud of you."

"WHY DID WE DO THIS AGAIN?" Nico flopped back on the bed.

"I'm pretty sure it was your idea," Lottie said with a groan, lying on her back next to them.

"Both of you came up with the idea." Liam stood at the end of the bed, giving them both a stern look. "I ought to spank both of your asses. Especially for inviting Sean."

It was Christmas. Nearly nine months since she'd been taken by Eleanor and Michael.

They'd bought this huge house about three hours away from the city. Liam still had to make occasional trips in, but he'd bought himself a helicopter so he could get there and back quickly. He'd also hired a number of guards to keep watch over the place.

It was the day before Christmas eve. She and Nico had this brilliant plan to have their families come here. Well, she wanted her family here. Nico wasn't too impressed with the idea of his family coming. They were all due to arrive tomorrow.

Her family had been here for the last few days. As well as Liam's grandfather.

"I'm not ready for my family. Can't we call them and tell them not to come," Nico whined.

As it had grown closer and closer to Christmas Eve, Nico had become more uptight and worried. She shared a look with Liam. Time to distract their boy.

He should be proud of all the things he'd accomplished in these past few weeks. The music producer that Liam had organized had loved his music and his single was nearly ready for release. But he was nervous and that was only adding to his worries.

"Both of you strip. I wanted a nice quiet Christmas and look what you've subjected me to. It's ten for each of you."

"A whole ten?" Nico asked sarcastically.

"That's twenty for you. I want you kneeling, asses in the air, arms out in front of you. Go."

As they stripped, so did Liam then they ended up side by side on the end of the bed, their bottoms up high, waiting for his lord and master to spank them.

Nico turned to face her as Liam started in on his ass. She saw the tension ease from his face. Liam had known precisely what he needed. What they both needed.

She gave a happy sigh as he heated her ass. He was always much more careful with her. Only giving her a light spanking. Unless she really earned herself a punishment. She'd gotten a taste of the belt the other day when she'd spent the majority of the day painting and had forgotten to eat. He'd been in the city and Nico had been sleeping off a terrible headache.

Smack! Smack! Smack!

By the time he'd finished giving her ten, her body had heated with pleasure, her lips slick with need. "On your back, Lottie. Get her ready to take your cock, Nico."

Ooh. She knew what that meant. Nico pounced on her as soon as she'd rolled over, his face between her legs, licking her pussy like his life depended on it. His hands moved to her breasts, playing with her nipples. She moaned, writhing on the bed as he tortured her. Behind him, Liam was putting lube on his fingers.

Fuck. Fuck.

"Nico!"

"Don't you come, baby girl," Liam warned her.

Nico groaned as Liam obviously parted his ass cheeks and slid his fingers inside.

"That's it, boy. Take my fingers. Very nice. Christ, Nico. Fuck. Lottie, you ready?"

"Yes! Yes!" When wasn't she ready for them?

"Nico, fuck her."

Nico rose up and slowly started to enter her. She'd gone on the pill months ago, so no more condoms.

When she was filled up with Nico's cock, Liam moved in beside him. Nico grunted then moaned as Liam filled him.

She looked at them both, love filling her as they moved together, Nico driving into her while Liam took his ass.

This was love.

This was home.

This was her new beginning.

I HOPE YOU LIKED LOTTIE, Liam and Nico's story! Want a bonus scene featuring Lottie's brothers. Grab it here: https://BookHip.-com/DGFSNSR

Printed in Great Britain
by Amazon

44928945R00199